3/15

Y0-CCK-032

MERCY KILL

A MYSTERY

LORI ARMSTRONG

A Touchstone Book
Published by Simon & Schuster
New York   London   Toronto   Sydney

Touchstone
A Division of Simon & Schuster, Inc.
1230 Avenue of the Americas
New York, NY 10020

First Touchstone hardcover edition January 2011

TOUCHSTONE and colophon are registered trademarks of Simon & Schuster, Inc.

Manufactured in the United States of America

ISBN 978-1-61129-247-3

For my family . . .

One day an old Lakota Indian told his grandson about a battle that goes on inside people.

He said, "My son, the battle is between two wolves. One wolf is evil. It is anger, envy, sorrow, greed, arrogance, self-pity, lies, guilt, and ego.

The other wolf is good.
It is joy, peace, love, hope, humility,
mercy, benevolence, empathy, truth, and faith."

The grandson thought about it for a minute and asked the grandfather: "Which wolf wins?"

The old Lakota man simply replied: "The one you feed."

MERCY KILL

ONE

Spring had sprung into full splendor on the western high plains of the Gunderson Ranch.

New baby calves frolicked in the lush pastures under the watchful eyes of mama cows. A cavalcade of colorful flowers bloomed from the fields to the forest. Delicate pale pink heads of primrose, stalwart stems of golden yarrow, the emerald green bushes of sumac grew alongside the caramel-colored stalks of autumn's dried grasses. Birdsong and insect chatter abounded on the ground and in the sky. Spring was a fleeting season at best, and I appreciated the metamorphosis after a long winter.

Sunshine burned the chill from the early-morning air. As much as I benefited from solitary communion with nature, I wasn't out picking posies. I was out picking my first target.

Old habits died hard; hunting was in my blood. Plus, I had nothing better to do until my shift started at Clementine's. And the thought of another night dealing with drunks and bar fights always put me in a killing mood.

I'd hiked to a prairie dog town on what used to be Newsome land, but now belonged to the Gunderson Ranch. The section was remote, a flat area surrounded by craggy rock formations that prevented the persistent buggers from digging tunnels unimpeded across grazing land. But the topography created a bowl effect that I likened to shooting fish in a barrel. Since cover was minimal, I'd crawled under scraggly bushes as my "hide" and with luck I'd stay down wind.

Dressed in camo, lying on my belly, propped on my elbows, I peered through the scope of my dad's varmint rifle. Despite the age of the Remington 722, its accuracy was unparalleled. Out of habit, I used my right eye. The black shadows from the retinal detachment weren't too bad during the day.

A few clicks and the fuzzy brown spots in my sights became clear. Furry heads popped up and disappeared into the mounds of chalky dirt as I scanned the networked holes spread across the rugged plateau.

Bingo. My first target was two hundred yards out. Before I pulled the trigger, a red-tailed hawk swooped down, snatching my kill right out from under me. The prairie dog's surprised screech echoed across the plains. A flurry of panic ensued among the critters as they retreated to hidey-holes.

Their collective caution lasted roughly two minutes. Sleek heads popped up like jack-in-the-boxes. Several brave animals stretched tall, aiming twitching noses to the sky, letting the sun tan their hides.

Suckers.

I zeroed in on one fat rat and fired. The body exploded into hunks of pinkish-red parts. I inserted another bullet, engaged the bolt, and nailed a slow mover; chunks of fur-covered meat rained down. After a quick reload, I picked off another one, ignoring me, on the opposite ridge. *Bad choice, Alvin.* I chambered another round and *bang. Bye-bye, Theodore.* Never turn your backs when danger lurks, boys.

My last target—dubbed Simon—decided to run. I clipped it from the back. The headless body went rolling in a ball of bloody fur and dust. Five for five. Not bad.

I reloaded while I waited for the scavengers to come.

Contrary to popular belief, gunshots don't scare away larger predatory animals. In most cases the sound of gunshots is like ringing a dinner bell—bringing them in for easy pickin's. Nature's version of fast food. A meal without the work of hunting it down.

Damn coyotes were thick around the herd this time of year, preying on new calves. Any time I could put a bullet in a coyote, I'd take it. They weren't funny, misunderstood cartoon creatures but a threat to our livelihood. Worse, scabies thrived in the coyote dens, and it passed like wildfire. An infected mother birthed an infected litter. A mangy, scabies-ravaged coyote was just plain gross—matted fur and oozing sores clinging to a bag of bones. Nasty shit. Shooting them was doing them a favor.

With the cartridge chambered, I re-sited my scope and waited for a flash of reddish-orange fur to dart into view. *Come on, Wile E. Coyote; give me something challenging to shoot.*

Nothing.

No big deal. I could wait. Inhaling the vegetative scents of sun-warmed mud, decomposing leaves, and the sharpness of fresh leaf growth, contentment and a wave of sleepiness flowed over me.

My contentment lasted a mere minute or so. The hair on the back of my neck stood up. A communal silence surrounded me—no birds, no buzzing insects, even the air had gone still.

Something was out there, behind me.

My mind flashed to a predator that commanded that type of respect.

A mountain lion.

Even though I couldn't see it, I knew it was there. I'd bet money it was female. A very hungry female, if she'd ventured out in the wide-open spaces of prairie rangeland in broad daylight.

Fear tightened my skin.

I leveled my breathing, trying not to envision myself getting pounced on and becoming catnip.

How does it feel when the predator becomes prey?

Not good. Seriously not good.

I'd heard talk among the bar regulars who hunted. The mountain lion population in the Black Hills had quadrupled in recent years due to an abundance of game that were their dietary staples: deer, rabbit, and turkey. Several reports of mountain lion sightings in the wooded areas within Rapid City, Sturgis, and Spearfish city limits. Occasionally, local TV stations ran stories where pet owners had witnessed their small domestic dogs carried off by a lion. Chained dogs were an easy target, as were cats. Some ranchers in the Northern Hills reported missing sheep. A few larger hunting dogs had been mauled and left to die.

Nothing to eat over here, Ms. Lion, move along.

I'd spent my life dodging bullets, returning fire, living the "kill-or-be-killed" motto, seeing danger in every shadow. I'd lost track of the times I believed I wouldn't make it out of a situation alive. But somehow, I always did. Somehow, that fear had almost become . . . comfortable. Expected. Routine.

This fear? Anything but comfortable.

A blur of a tan fur entered the sights of my scope. In all the years I'd lived on the ranch, I'd never actually seen a mountain lion. I'd seen tracks. One night I'd heard the distinctive, jarringly human scream so close to the cabin I swore the cat had been lurking below my bedroom window. But I'd never been close enough to one to count its whiskers.

She was about six feet from nose to tail. Her enormous paws could've ripped my face off with one powerful swipe.

But all was not well with the lioness. She panted with exertion. The bones of her rib cage were prominent due to near starvation. Her fur was patchy, worn away in spots on her hind legs and upper haunches. Most of her left ear was missing; the fresh wound had barely scabbed over. No heavy teats swayed from her matted white underbelly. Was she too old to have cubs? Too sick? A freak of nature that couldn't reproduce? Had she been forced out of her natural habitat and was on the run?

My pulse quickened but not from fear. From something far scarier: empathy.

Crouched low, she nosed at the closest prairie dog carcass, the one somewhat intact after my shooting spree. Those mighty jaws opened lightning fast, and the fresh meat disappeared in two violent chomps.

Holy shit.

Leaves rattled above me in the breeze. Her head swiveled in my direction, her muzzle slick with blood. But proof of her extreme hunger wasn't what caught my attention. I noticed the white film clouding her left eye.

She was half blind.

Bone-deep pity replaced my panic. This majestic creature, once a predator of the highest order, was reduced to scrounging for scraps just to survive.

Coyotes howled a warning beyond the ridge.

She opened her mouth and hissed. The sharp teeth I expected

were nothing but broken nubs. No wonder she'd swallowed her food whole. No wonder she was famished. She limped to the next pile of meat, gorging herself before the coyotes chased her away or attacked her en masse.

How much longer could she survive? A week? A month?

End her misery. You have a clear shot. Take it.

I followed her erratic movements through the scope, a lioness beyond her prime, a former predator out of synch with the natural order, a wanderer lost in a place she didn't belong.

Kill her. A quick death will be painless compared to the way she's been living.

I knew I should. I struggled to find that calm center where nothing existed but the target. Where muscle memory and training took over and I didn't have to think. I just had to act.

Do it. She's in your crosshairs.

But I couldn't fire. I slowly removed my finger from the trigger and closed my eyes. Sweat trickled from my hairline down my face. My hand shook. Hollowness expanded in my belly.

Angry at myself for my weakness, for my pity, I pointed the scope at her last position.

She was gone.

Dammit. Only a handful of times in my life had I failed to take a shot. Why now, when there was no moral dilemma?

Guilt gnawed at me as I loaded up. I didn't want to rehash why I'd frozen, but as usual, my brain had other plans for me during the long walk home.

I just hoped this misstep wouldn't come back to haunt me.

TWO

My day went downhill from there.

I broke up two bar fights.

I chased off two punks for trying to buy booze without an ID.

I ran out of Jack Daniel's.

And I used to bitch about my duties as a soldier? I preferred dodging bullets to dumping ashtrays and slinging drinks. But job opportunities are limited for a former army sniper, especially in the backwoods of South Dakota.

After my military discharge, I'd anchored a bar stool at Clementine's damn near every night. Then John-John Pretty Horses—Clementine's owner and my longtime friend—offered me a temporary job. But John-John's stipulation: no drinking on duty. His way of staging an intervention, without formally intervening.

Months later I was still pulling taps five nights a week, waiting for my life to start.

"Hey, Mercy."

I didn't look up at the customer as I was trying to catch the foam spewing out of the Keystone Light tap. Damn keg needed to be changed out again.

"The toilet in the men's can is plugged."

"Fan-fucking-tastic." I locked the register, clipping the key to my lanyard for safekeeping—I didn't trust Clementine's patrons any further than I could throw them. I'd gotten proficient at swapping out kegs; however, my plumbing skills were subpar. I gave up and returned to the main bar to see "Tiny" Tim Waddell filling a pitcher.

He flashed me a moronic smile. "Now, don't go getting that

look on your face, Miz Mercy. I knew you was back there changing the keg, and I thought I'd help you out."

"By pouring yourself a free pitcher?"

"I was clearing the line of foam," he huffed. "Thought you'd be grateful."

The balding, fiftysomething midget could barely reach the beer taps. "Get out from behind my bar, Tiny, before I squash you like a bug."

He focused sulky eyes on me. "I was just helpin'."

"You wanna help? Figure out what the fuck is wrong with the toilet in the men's bathroom."

Tiny flinched. "Ain't no need to use that kinda language."

"Chauvinistic much? Men can say *fuck* whenever the fuck they want, but I can't because it's unladylike?" I crowded him. "Do I look like a lady who gives a shit what anyone thinks of the fucking language I use?"

"Ah. No."

"Good answer. Now, can you fix the toilet or not?"

His shoulders slumped. "Prolly."

I handed him the plunger. "Get it working and I'll pick up your tab tonight."

"Now I wish I woulda been drinking whiskey instead of beer," he grumbled, and headed toward the bathroom.

The door banged open. A barrel-chested biker named Vinnie waved at his buddies, then ambled toward me. "Hey, pretty lady. How about a pitcher of Coors?"

"Coming up." I glanced at the clock after I shoved a plastic pitcher under the tap. Two hours until closing time.

"Where's your boyfriend tonight?"

I squinted at Vinnie. "What boyfriend?"

"That slicked-up dude from the oil company hanging around when you're working."

Damn Jason. I wished he'd find another bar to antagonize the locals and not drag me into it. "Haven't seen him. Besides, he isn't my boyfriend."

"I ain't surprised. A gal like you don't need a boy—you need a man. A real man." Vinnie rested his elbows on the bar top, gifting me with a smoldering stare.

Vinnie might've been attractive—oh, two decades ago. He clung to the biker look: long hair; an unkempt, graying beard; a faded POW-MIA T-shirt; oil-stained jeans draped with chains, and a knife sheathed in a leather case.

Yeah, I was having a devil of a time resisting his charm. I reclined against the bar with equal provocation. "Know what I really need, Vinnie?"

"What's that, sugar? Name it."

"Five bucks for the pitcher and a night off."

Vinnie dug in his front pocket and tossed me a balled-up five-dollar bill. "You're a cool one."

"Stone cold . . . or so I've been told."

His lame attempt at picking me up foiled, he joined his fellow ZZ Top clones beneath the big-screen TV and watched whatever passed for entertainment on the Speed Channel.

Time dragged on like a preacher's sermon. I started closing duties early, and when I returned from the storeroom, he was sitting at the bar. I ducked under the partition and stopped in front of him.

He said, "Hey, South Dakota."

"Hey, North Dakota."

"Heard any good jokes lately?"

I shoved the box of straws beneath the counter. "Did you hear about the two seagulls flying upside down over North Dakota?"

"No. Why were they flying upside down?"

I mock-whispered, "Because they couldn't find anything worth shitting on."

He laughed. "Where do you come up with those, Gunny?"

"Are you serious? Making fun of North Dakotans is our state pastime." I couldn't help staring at him. It was just so . . . uncanny he was here.

Uncanny? Or intentional?

"Once again you're looking at me like you've seen a ghost."

"You'd have to look the same for the comparison to work." The first time Major Jason Hawley had wandered into Clementine's, I'd barely stopped myself from blurting out, "What the hell *happened* to you?"

"Just wait until you've been out more than a few months." He gave me a critical once-over. "You still practicing? Keeping your skill set current? Running five to ten miles a day? Or have you finally figured out it doesn't matter?"

So what if I'd kept up with my PT and marksmanship training? At least I wouldn't look like hell and act touchy about it like him. "What can I get for you tonight, Jason?"

"Jim Beam and Coke. Make it a double."

"Want two cherries in it?"

"You're a fucking riot."

"I try." I mixed the drink and plopped it in front of him.

"Thanks."

Given Vinnie's earlier speculation, I bailed to the back room, where I stacked chairs and picked up trash. But the mindless work funneled my thoughts back to the man out front, the soldier I'd served with off and on for a decade.

Major Jason "J-Hawk" Hawley was a shadow of the man he'd been, but my criticism wasn't just about his appearance. I'd gotten used to returning from deployment and running into people at Fort Bragg I'd served with in the sandboxes, and not recognizing them stateside. Months of desert heat dropped pounds off even the chubbiest soldier. Months of access to real food and no real danger put those missing pounds back on in a helluva hurry.

The major was an exception. He'd lost a solid thirty, all of it muscle. His hair was longer, thinner, worn mullet-style. His skin was a pasty yellowish-white tone I secretly called a North Dakota tan. The physical changes were inevitable, but the personality change bothered me on a whole different level.

War transformed soldiers. Some become destructive outside of their military working hours. Some constantly spoiled for a fight as a reason to show off their training. Some became withdrawn, refusing to fraternize with fellow team members in their off-duty time.

But I'd always noticed the biggest change was in the deployed family men. Balls-to-the-wall aggression was lauded when you were in charge of a platoon or a brigade, but not so much when you were in the States running kids to soccer practice in the minivan. Male soldiers called newly deployed female soldiers "Queen for a Year," but they never applied a like-minded derogatory moniker to themselves. So my all-female team and I referred to them as "Masturbators of the Universe"—henpecked guys, used to their wives calling the shots, who suddenly didn't have a female to answer to. They became over-the-top bulging bags of testosterone, determined to prove to every woman in the compound that they'd brought their manhood with them, and their precious big balls weren't at home with their wives . . . for a change.

J-Hawk hadn't been that type of guy. As a Ranger team leader, he'd commanded respect without demanding it because he'd earned it. Something he definitely wasn't doing in Eagle River County working as a representative for Titan Oil. Now he was a smooth-talking company guy, wearing a three-piece suit, Ray-Bans, and tasseled loafers. No one around here liked him. Plenty of guys were genuinely hostile. I'd tried to remain neutral, but several regulars noticed I wasn't my usual caustic self around J-Hawk, and some people saw my friendliness as cavorting with the enemy. So I was screwed either way.

As I passed J-Hawk on my way back behind the bar, I tripped on the folded corner of the rubber mat.

Bix, the dumb-as-a-brick, but-strong-as-an-ox bricklayer caught me, his thick fingers circled my biceps. "Steady there, Mercy. You all right?"

"Just lost my footing. I'm fine. Thanks."

He glanced over my shoulder, and his pale blue eyes frosted into chips of ice. "I can see why you stumbled. Mighty big pile of shit next to you. You'll probably wanna avoid it next time."

J-Hawk ignored Bix's attempt to bait him and hunkered over his drink.

When Rose Corwin stopped in for her nightly fifth of cheap gin and cheap talk, I indulged her on the latter for a change. I chanced a look at the clock. The bar closed in an hour, and I still needed to change the register tape before I rang the till out for the night. I rummaged in the beer-soaked box beneath the counter for a new package.

The manufacturer had shrink-wrapped six rolls together. I poked my finger in the small hole, trying to rip it open. The plastic had no give, and I lifted the package to my mouth to tear it open with my teeth.

"Here. Save those pearly whites and pretty smile. Use this."

Thud. J-Hawk had tossed his knife on the counter. The knife I'd helped my army buddy and former teammate Anna Rodriguez pick out for him. The knife with the engraving that read: *1001 Nights—4-Ever.*

I met his gaze. "You still have this?"

"I'll always have it. I'm never without it."

"Never?"

"Never. It's the only tangible thing I've got from . . ."

Anna.

"That time," he said.

It was a sweet knife, a stainless-steel Kershaw. I flicked the blade open with the thumb catch. Three and a half inches of steel sliced through the plastic like hot butter, then through the paper roll, leaving a precise starting point to thread through the cash register's feeding mechanism. Hell, I could've cut through skin, bone, and the shellacked countertop with it. I clicked the blade shut into the knifewell and slid it back to him. "Thanks."

"You're welcome." J-Hawk stirred his still nearly full drink. "Look, Mercy, I'd really like to talk to you."

"Sure. If it's about you telling those fuckers at Titan Oil to take their pipeline and jam it up their ass, I'm all ears."

"Regardless of how you view them, I'm asking to talk to you strictly as your friend. I'd like to catch up with what you've been doing."

Right. Most likely J-Hawk wanted to catch up on news about Anna, his former star-crossed lover.

He tugged his sleeve back to look at his watch.

I barely withheld a disgusted gasp. His watchband dug into the flesh of his wrist so deeply I couldn't discern the thickness of the strap. The bloated skin surrounding it reminded me of an overcooked chicken sausage about to burst its casing.

"Can I get a twelve-pack of Keystone Light to go?" he asked, interrupting my gawking at his grotesque arm.

"Sure. Seems a little low-end for you."

He shrugged. "Don't you remember, back in the day? When you were looking for a cheap drunk? What'd you drink?"

"Pabst Blue Ribbon."

"Good old PBR. Brings back memories."

I yanked a twelve-pack from the cooler. Seemed odd Jason wanting a cheap drunk. Odd and sort of lonely. Sitting in his motel or vehicle, drinking alone.

Like you have any room to talk about solo drinking habits.

"What're the damages?"

"Total is twenty-one bucks."

As J-Hawk riffled through his wallet, I noticed another peculiar thing. He didn't carry pictures of his kids. He'd never carried photos of his family in the field. Back then I hadn't thought anything of it; I never carried pictures either. The lack of personal effects was a hallmark of Special Forces rather than personal preferences.

So it struck me as strange that Jason the civilian wouldn't have a few snapshots of his offspring.

"Here." He handed me twenty and rooted in his jacket pocket for a handful of wadded-up ones. "Keep the change. See you around."

As I watched him leave, I felt other bar patrons eyeing me suspiciously. I'd had enough fun for one day. I announced, "Last call, people."

Fourteen minutes after I barred the front door, I'd counted out the till and locked the money in the office safe. A record shutdown for me.

Sad, that my life was still measured in clicks. Not clicks of my scope as I adjusted my sights on a target, but clicks of the second hand on a time clock.

Late spring meant chilly nights, especially at the zero hour, and I shivered in my jean jacket. I set the alarm and started across the pitch-black parking area behind the building. My night vision sucked, but I was too proud to carry a flashlight, so I stumbled around and cursed the darkness.

Amid my silent internal grumbling, a squishing noise sounded off to the left. My eyesight might be for shit, but my hearing wasn't.

The Kahr Arms P380 was out of my back pocket and in my hand instantly. I swung my arms in the direction of the noise, keeping the barrel at my eye level. "Show yourself or I start shooting."

"Jesus, Mercy, are you seriously pointing a gun at me?"

"Dawson?"

"Lower your weapon. Now."

I did.

He sauntered into view. When my stomach dipped, I assured myself it was a delayed adrenaline reaction—not a reaction of pleasure at seeing him.

"What're you doing here, Sheriff? Chasing after bad guys?"

"No. Chasing after you."

"Such a sweet-talkin' cowboy." Dawson and I had been making mattress angels since I'd started working at the bar. We'd kept our relationship—for lack of a better term—on the QT.

"FYI: I'd gone my entire shift without anyone aiming a gun at me."

"So it was a boring day, huh?"

He laughed lightly. "Only you would think that, Sergeant Major."

Then his imposing maleness loomed over me, invading my personal space as only a lover can. He wore his Eagle River County uniform, although he'd ditched the ugly hat. Like me, he carried a sidearm. Unlike me, he hadn't even unsnapped the strap on the holster.

"I can't help it if I'm of the shoot-first mind-set."

"Acting like a soldier when you're a civilian is liable to get you into hot water with the law."

"Bring on the hot water, lawman. I need a shower anyway."

"Feeling a little dirty tonight?"

"You're in a mood," I murmured.

Dawson curled his hand around my hip, letting his thumb sweep the bared section of skin between my jeans and my shirt. "Wanna guess what kind of mood I'm in?"

Damn distracting man. "Depends."

"On?"

"Whether you plan on talking about your mood or acting on it."

Dawson lowered his face to mine until our lips were a breath apart. "Talking is the dead-last thing on my mind tonight, Mercy."

"Good. Meet me at the cabin. You can park—"

"In the carport so no one sees my vehicle from a half mile up the road. Yeah, I'm familiar with the damn drill by now."

Huh. Dawson almost sounded . . . resentful.

But I knew that wouldn't stop him from following me home.

I woke alone in tangled sheets. Sun blazed through the bedroom window. Tending bar until the wee hours made it hard to haul my ass out of bed at the crack of nothing.

Not that I had a reason to get up.

I heard Shoonga whining and scratching at the door. I let him in, resisting his attempt to herd me back outside.

"Not before my first cup of coffee, dog." I yawned and shuffled to the tiny kitchen. I saw the note taped to the coffeepot:

You're out of coffee again—MD

Mason Dawson. In the months we'd been together I'd never called him Mason, just Dawson. Did that bother him?

Probably not as much as the fact you won't acknowledge you're knocking boots with him.

I didn't want to drive into town for a cup of joe, and coffee was always on at the house. Plus, Sophie would be making lunch soon. I could run over, make nice with the fam, fill my belly, fuel my caffeine fix, and get my aerobic exercise in one fell swoop.

Shoonga barked happy circles around me as I laced up my running shoes. Damn dog made me smile. Although Shoonga spent half his time with Jake at the ranch, I considered him my dog, and I'd gotten used to his company in the nine months since my nephew Levi's murder. Shoonga had adjusted to life without Levi much better than the rest of us.

I slipped on my shades and we set off. With the excessive spring rain, the shortcut through the pasture to the main house was a mud bog, so I ran on the road. The gravel made a sodden *squish, squish* with my every pounding footfall.

My mind blanked to everything but the sounds of my huffing

breath, the feel of sweat coating my skin, and the endorphin rush that was almost as good as sex.

Almost. But not quite.

Once the familiar jagged tree line of the Gunderson Ranch solidified, I slowed to a jog. Home sweet home. Not that I was hanging my hat here full time these days.

After Levi's murder, I asked my grieving, pregnant sister, Hope, and Jake Red Leaf, her baby daddy and the ranch foreman, to move into the house we'd inherited from our father. I'd lived in group housing during my military service, so I was accustomed to being surrounded by people almost 24/7. I even believed it might be fun.

Wrong.

The first month of our communal living arrangement, Hope started to miscarry the twins. With the miracle of modern medicine, they managed to save one baby. Upon her release from the hospital, the doctor confined her to complete bed rest for the duration of her pregnancy.

Asking Sophie Red Leaf, our elderly housekeeper, also Jake's grandmother, to play fetch and carry for Hope was ridiculous when I was underfoot and unemployed. Besides, I'd barely dipped a toe into the responsibilities of running a ranch; Jake was essential to the Gunderson ranching operation, not me. So I temporarily shelved my aspiration of becoming a hands-on owner and helped Sophie tend my fragile sister. I nagged Hope to eat, to take her vitamins and stay in bed. I held her hand during the bouts of false labor. Wiped her tears when our conversations shifted to Levi, which they always did.

Growing a new life-form tuckered Hope out, leaving me at loose ends. Overwhelmed with boredom—and probably slightly drunk—I decided to repaint the living room, dining room, and main-floor bathroom. I bought new furniture. Installed new carpet. I paid for everything out of my pocket, not out of the ranch-operating fund.

No one liked the changes in the house. I hadn't cared.

Although Hope appreciated my spending time with her, she preferred Sophie's company to mine. Any need Hope had for me evaporated after Jake finished his daily ranch duties. So every afternoon, as soon as Jake's boots hit the welcome mat, I hit the bar.

No one liked the changes in me. I hadn't cared about that either.

Two months into the living arrangement, I started crashing at the foreman's cabin. I got tired of apologizing for my guns. I got tired of apologizing for my late nights. I got tired of the looks passing between them whenever I cracked open a beer. Contrary to their silent accusations, I craved some semblance of normalcy, not just booze. My life was nothing more than marking time: waiting for the baby, waiting for my retirement checks, waiting for the bank to approve our loan, waiting for calving. I drank to blur the slow passage of time. But I ended up with gaps in my memory and too much pride to ask anyone what I'd said and what I'd done. No one came forward to fill me in.

Except Rollie Rondeaux. Rollie was a full-blooded Sioux Indian with a sketchy past that included a love affair with my mother before she'd married my father. He relished playing the part of the wise old Indian and maintained an arsenal of secrets that he wasn't opposed to sharing—or keeping a lid on—for a few bucks or for a favor. Since my return to the ranch, Rollie had become a serious pain in my butt, determined to fill a father-figure role in my life. But other times, I knew he was the only person who understood me, who saw the real me, and didn't judge me for it.

Rollie had shown up the morning after my drunken middle-of-the-night phone call—a call I hadn't remembered making. He hadn't cared that I suffered from the mother of all hangovers. He'd dragged my ass out of bed and into the kitchen of the cabin. Through bleary eyes, I'd noticed he'd centered a .45 cal Smith and Wesson on the table.

"What the hell is that, Rollie?"

"If you're gonna kill yourself, be a man and do it quick. Put the gun to your head and pull the trigger." He gestured to the empty bottles of Wild Turkey, lined on the counter like good little soldiers. "Save us who care about you the misery of watchin' you kill yourself slowly with that shit."

My reaction left a lot to be desired. I hadn't burst into tears and thanked him for his concern. Instead, I got in his face and pushed back. "Maybe I will just end it. It's not like anyone cares. Oh, right. Unless it comes to the cash I'm kicking into the Gunderson Ranch coffers every month."

"You're wrong, Mercy girl. Lots of people care, but you're keeping them out. Let me take you to the VA. They can help you."

"No. Way. So I can be labeled another PTSD freak and become medicated until I die of boredom? No thanks."

"Then let me help you."

"What can you do? Give me back my eyesight? My purpose? The life I had?"

No response.

"See? You can't help me. And this little 'come to Jesus' talk is just pissing me off, old man, so leave."

"Sorry. I ain't giving up on you because I know where you're coming from. Seeing your face is like lookin' in a mirror."

"Why? 'Cause I'm just another drunk Indian?"

His eyes hardened. "No, you're just another drunk soldier trying to find your way back. You think you're special? Guess what? You aren't the only one to deal with this shit. We all went through it. Coming back from Vietnam wasn't no picnic either. We all seen bad things, *kola*."

"You don't know fuck all about what I saw or what I did, Rollie."

"Yeah? How are the nightmares? Having flashbacks during the day?"

I glared at him.

Rollie's gaze swept the counter. "At least you ain't takin' a mountain of pills." He paused and looked at me challengingly. "Yet."

I glowered even more.

"You think dousing them bad dreams with booze will make 'em go away?"

"Yep. Now why don't *you* go away and leave me alone." I turned around, and his next words froze me to the spot.

"If it were up to me, I would. But John-John wants to talk to you."

"About what? He have a vision or something?"

"You'll have to ask him."

Fucking Sioux woo-woo shit drove me crazy. Problem was, as a *winkte*, the Lakota word for two spirits residing in one body, John-John's visions were usually dead-on. "Why didn't he come here and talk to me about it himself?"

"He tried. Don't you remember?"

An uneasy feeling flitted through me. "No."

"You scared him. And he don't spook easy."

I vaguely remembered a crying jag, throwing empty bottles at the door and screaming. I wasn't sure if the screams had been mine. Maybe I hadn't thrown the bottles at the door. Maybe I'd thrown the bottles at John-John.

Rollie heaved a weary sigh. His gentle hands landed on my shoulders. Even with my super-duper stealthy military training I hadn't heard him move. Yeah, I was pretty much a train wreck.

"I'm not your daddy, Mercy girl. But I do know what it's like to come home to a place that ain't the same as it was when you left. People ain't the same. But mostly . . . you ain't the same. Go talk to John-John. Please. For all our sakes. But mostly for yours."

A day later I clocked in at Clementine's for my first shift. John-John had shared his vision, something about fire and pain, watching my loved ones hurting, while I stood by and did nothing. I'd sort of tuned out the mystical gloom-and-doom forecast, because John-John always added a disclaimer about visions being subject to interpretation. But I knew it bothered him that this particular vision hadn't materialized into reality. The only reality I cared about was that months after my niece's arrival, I was still working as a bartender, unsure how to address my resentment over the situation at the ranch—or whether I even had a right to it.

Shoonga whined, bringing me back to the present. Sophie hated the "dog mess" so Shoonga's meals were served on the porch. I dumped food in his dish, and my stomach rumbled. I kicked off my muddy shoes on the porch and entered the kitchen.

Jake, Sophie, and Hope stared at me like I should've knocked. Not exactly a friendly welcome. In my own damn house.

"Ah. Hi, guys."

"Hello, yourself. You hungry?" Sophie asked.

"I could eat."

"I'll fix you a plate."

"No, finish your lunch. I can do it." After I washed up, I uncovered the pans on the stove. Steamy scents of chicken-fried steak, mashed potatoes, and country gravy wafted out.

Sophie gave my heaped plate a wry look. "Save room for dessert, hey."

Joy fussed. Hope murmured to her while trying to eat one-handed, which was ridiculous when a perfectly good high chair sat right next to her. But Joy rarely left her mama's arms.

I didn't blame my sister for her overprotective instincts. She'd lost her son to a murderer. She'd lost a baby in utero. But her "my baby" attitude and near-agoraphobia were wearing thin for everyone. I'd never even held my niece, though, granted, that was partially my own fault.

Jake pushed his plate aside. "I'll hold her so you can eat."

"I don't mind," Hope said crossly.

"I do." Then Jake did a very un-Jake-like thing. He plucked the baby from Hope's lap and said, "Now eat up so we can go."

Hope watched father and daughter, chewing her lip instead of her food.

"Go where?" Sophie asked her grandson.

"It's a slow day. Thought I'd take my girls for a drive. Get Hope out of the house into the fresh air. Tempt her with a sundae from the Custard Cupboard."

Sophie and I exchanged an "oh crap" look.

"Joy has finally settled into a regular naptime," Hope snapped. "I won't screw that up to go driving around the countryside with you."

"She'll sleep just fine in the car seat."

Wasn't Jake's way to push, especially not with an audience. The fact he was doing both indicated he'd reached the end of his rope with my little sister.

A feeling I was familiar with.

"Jake, you don't know—"

"One afternoon, Hope. The three of us acting like a normal family."

Jake's voice was calm, but pure steel.

Impressive.

Hope continued to gape at him with a mix of confusion and alarm. I half expected she'd snatch Joy and stomp upstairs, and that'd be the end of it.

But Jake reached out, gently touching Hope's cheek with a soft plea. "Please."

She smiled, almost shyly. "Okay. Right after I feed her and get myself ready. I'm kind of a mess."

"I'll feed her. And you always look great," Jake added.

Hope flounced upstairs, her step lighter than I'd seen in months.

Kudos to Jake for his well-played moves.

Sophie's foot nudged mine under the table. Twice.

"What? You need help with the dishes?"

"*Shee*, I think aliens done abducted the real Mercy and left this imposter who volunteers for chores." Her strong, wrinkled hand briefly covered mine. "Ain't it good to see things are getting back to normal around here?"

"Define normal."

She harrumphed. "Such a smarty-pants. What are your plans for the day?"

I glanced at the clock. "Working. My shift starts in two hours." I focused on Jake, murmuring to Joy, waiting for the bottle to heat. "I wanted to tell you that I saw a mountain lion yesterday."

"Where?"

"Over by the prairie dog town in the northwest corner of the Newsome's old place."

"What time did you see it?"

"Morning. She didn't look good. She was mangy. Starved. A bit too long in the tooth to have cubs."

"She attack you or anything?"

As far as I knew, we'd never had a mountain lion attack our cattle, to say nothing of attacking a human. "Nope. Have you seen her around? Or any kind of tracks?"

"I haven't been up in that section for a while. But I ain't surprised. Lots of people are reporting seeing mountain lions where they ain't supposed to be."

In the last few years, the South Dakota Game, Fish and Parks started a mountain lion season to deal with the growing problem. Some folks were appalled, calling it a barbaric practice. But I figured they'd change their tune right quick when the lions started snacking on little kids.

Jake tucked Joy in the crook of his arm and popped a baby bottle in her mouth. Greedy sucking noises sounded. "Did you kill her?"

"No."

He frowned. "You *didn't* shoot her?"

No. "I . . . ah, missed." *Liar.*

"*You* missed? That's a bad sign."

Automatically, I assumed he meant I'd lost the weapons skills I'd spent years honing. I bristled. "Why?"

Jake and Sophie exchanged a look.

"What?"

Sophie pinch pleated the ruffles on the place mat. "You know about spirit animals, right?"

I nodded.

"They're a reflection of ourselves. Sometimes they lead us to something; sometimes they lead us away. You must've seen a part of yourself in her. Destroying her meant you'd destroy that part of yourself, so you didn't."

Of all the . . . "I call bullshit on that, Sophie. I also saw two squirrels going at it for like twenty minutes, up and down a pine tree, bark flying everywhere, and I didn't shoot them. So if what you're saying is true about the lioness, I should also consider the mating squirrels . . . my spirit animals? I should read their intensive mating practices as a sign I'm dying to have wild squirrel sex, hanging upside down in a tree?"

A funny smile tilted the crinkled corners of Sophie's mouth. "That's exactly what it means."

Jake and Sophie looked at each other again and busted a gut laughing.

I wasn't sure if I'd been had. But I was happy to hear laughter in the house again, even if it was at my expense. I got up to leave.

"Seriously, Mercy," Jake called out, "if you see that lioness again? Shoot her."

"I guarantee it. But I'm still undecided on the squirrels."

THREE

John-John was already hauling ice when I strolled into Clementine's. "Hey, Mercy. Vivi's got a sick kid, so you're on mop duty."

"Great." For the next hour I scrubbed the floor and sang along to the tunes on the jukebox. I poked my head into the men's bathroom. Nasty-ass place could stay dirty another night.

Cleanup duties complete, I poured a glass of Coke and studied my boss. It hadn't been an easy transition, going from lifelong friends to an employee/employer relationship.

But some things didn't change regardless if our roles did. John-John had always been more comfortable with himself— body size, skin color, spirituality, sexuality—than any person I'd ever known. We'd always joked he'd never outgrown that horny teen state, nor the husky/chubby stage boys do around age sixteen. So his weight loss concerned me. I knew he hadn't been dieting. "Are you working tonight?"

"Why else would I be here?" he snapped.

I waited, biting back my bitchy retort.

"Sorry, doll. Just a little stressed and touchy about it."

"Have I done something to piss you off, boss?"

"God, no, and stop calling me that." He smoothed his hand over the top of his head and impatiently flicked his braids over his shoulder. "There's some other stuff going on, stuff you wouldn't be interested in."

I lifted a brow. "If it has something to do with you, I'm interested. I remember when you used to tell me everything."

"That was a long time ago."

"Some things might've changed, *kola*, but my ears still work the same as they did twenty years ago." Would he recognize the words he'd thrown back at me when I'd retreated after Levi's murder?

John-John hip-checked me. "Smart-ass."

"So spill it."

"I haven't been sleeping well."

The dark circles under his eyes supported that statement. "You having disturbing visions?"

He sighed. "That's the thing. I don't know. I dream, but I can't make sense of it. I've always remembered the relevant points, allowing me to decipher *Wakan Tanka* symbols when I wake. Not lately. It's frustrating. I've been stuck in that cycle for a couple months. Ever since . . ."

The vision he'd had about me. As far as I knew, it was one of the few times John-John's visions hadn't followed a path to becoming some form of reality. "What about Muskrat? Isn't he your anchor? Can't he help you figure it out?" My knowledge of Sioux rituals was sorely lacking, but I didn't want to lose the conversational momentum since this was the first time he'd opened up to me for months. We'd been working opposite shifts, and I saw him less now than when I'd been on the stool side of the bar.

"Yes. But he's part of the problem."

"Trouble in paradise?"

"No, after fifteen years together we're both too stubborn to teach a younger pup our old tricks, so he's stuck with me. But I ain't happy with him neither. His back problems aren't getting better, and he refuses to go to the doctor for treatment. I've suggested alternatives: a sweat, a chiropractor, a spiritual massage. He's stalling; he's in pain, and he won't talk to me about it. It's driving me crazy."

"Why is he dragging his feet?"

"Because he's scared it's something serious."

I couldn't fathom Muskrat, a solid six-foot-eight-inch ape of a man, with the disposition of a surly bear, fearing anything. But people thought the same thing about me. "You want me to talk to him? Knock some sense into his thick skull?"

John-John sent me a stern look. "Absolutely not, and don't you dare breathe a word of this to him."

"I'll point out I'm awful good at keeping secrets."

"Too good." He chucked me under the chin. "Speaking of secrets, what's up with you and our delectable sheriff?"

I refilled my soda, considering my answer and his evasion. "Who knows?"

"He hasn't been sniffing around lately?" he asked skeptically.

"I saw him last night." I crunched a piece of ice. "Actually, I pulled a gun on him outside the bar after closing, and he still followed me home."

His gaze narrowed. "Were you armed on shift?"

"Yep."

"For Christsake, Mercy—"

"Relax. It was just a small handgun. It wouldn't have made a very big hole in anyone."

John-John mumbled something, probably a prayer. The office phone jangled, and he raced to catch the call.

His inquiry about my relationship with Dawson brought my own questions to the surface.

When the sheriff was off duty, hanging out in the bar, we ignored each other. People expected our animosity because he'd arrested me last summer. The unexpected bonus for us? Our secret sexual encounters after our public sniping were hotter than a blowtorch.

But a good chunk of our hostility wasn't faked. We had differing philosophies, especially recently on the proposed Titan Oil pipeline that would literally cut our county in two. Dawson pointed out that building the pipeline would mean new jobs in Eagle River County for several months at least.

The short-term gain for a select group of specialized construction workers didn't outweigh the cons: lowered property values for every landowner. Environmental concerns, including the landowner's liability if a catastrophic event occurred, hadn't been addressed. None of us liked that the powers that be in state government were willing to bend over for a Canadian oil company and turn a blind eye to the taxpayers' concerns.

The facts were distorted on both sides. From what I'd heard, county residents were divided on the issue. As sheriff, Dawson's opinion held weight. His opponent in the upcoming election, Bill O'Neil, was adamantly against the pipeline.

I wondered where my dad would've stood on the issue. He'd be opposed to the pipeline because of the deep gouge it'd cut across Gunderson land. But I also suspected Wyatt Gunderson, the politician, not the rancher, would've won out. He'd gauge which way the political wind blew on the issue before making a decision.

I stood firmly on the side of the landowners, no matter who tried to sweet-talk me or guilt me into changing my stance.

The door blew open, cutting off my brooding thoughts. Time to get to work.

Once again I was left to lock up Clementine's all by my little self. I took a second to breathe in a lungful of clean air. My least favorite part about working at the bar was reeking of cigarette smoke at the end of my shift.

So quit.

And do what?

Four vehicles remained in the parking area. Not an unusual occurrence since most folks were smart enough not to drink and drive. I'd nearly reached my truck when the back of my neck prickled. Déjà vu rolled through me until I realized I *had* been in this exact same position just last night. And like last night, immediately my gun was in my hand.

"Show yourself."

"It's me, Gunny."

"J-Hawk?"

"Yeah." He materialized beside me, seemingly out of nowhere, which sent a shiver down my spine. I had no idea he'd been so close.

So much for my lightning-fast reflexes. "What're you doing here?"

"I just wanna talk to you."

I kept the gun leveled on him. "If you're here to try and win me over about the pipeline, save your goddamn breath."

"Fuck that and fuck you. Jesus. That's not why I'm here. You know I'd never . . ." He swore. "Can you put the gun down? Please?" He waved a six-pack like a white flag. "Near as I can tell, none of your regular bar rats are around to give you dirty looks for sharing a brew with me."

I ignored the bitterness in his tone, knowing he'd understood the downside of taking on such an unpopular job when he'd signed on for it. "A beer sounds good." I jammed my gun in my pocket and dropped the tailgate. My ass absorbed the metal's coldness, causing another shiver.

The truck bounced as he plopped down. He handed me a Pabst Blue Ribbon. I laughed. "Where'd you find this?"

"At Stillwell's. I figured it'd be appropriate."

After we each cracked one open, I chinked my can to his. "To cheap beer."

"And priceless memories."

"Man, I forgot what a sappy dork you are."

Jason fake-coughed "bitch" in his fist.

I laughed again and sipped my beer. "You know, this stuff ain't half bad."

"Ssh. I'm trying to discern the origins of the different flavors of hops."

This was the J-Hawk I remembered. Not the bloated blowhard who'd been blathering bullshit across my home turf.

We'd met in Afghanistan. As the only two Dakotans in our little slice of hell, we ribbed each other endlessly about the rivalry between our sister states, tossing jokes and insults, but look out if anyone else made a derogatory comment about "The Dakotas."

Major Hawley was an Army Ranger with the 3rd Battalion, 75th Ranger Group, and one of the few clued in to our all-female Black Ops section of the 82nd Airborne Division. Being stationed together across Europe and the Middle East made us uncommonly close—some of us closer than others.

The military discourages fraternizing, a rule I've adhered to for the most part. We all got lonely. We all missed the intimacy that only comes from sharing a bed with a lover. We all dealt with it in our own unique ways. But some chose to disregard the rules completely—like J-Hawk and my teammate Anna "A-Rod" Rodriguez.

I figured out they were sneaking around long before anyone else. Not because A-Rod spilled her guts to me, but because they'd gone out of their way to avoid eye or body contact when in mixed company. Making goo-goo eyes at each other in the chow line would've been less obvious.

Jealousy that A-Rod was getting laid on a regular basis while the rest of us weren't wasn't my issue. They were adults. They understood the repercussions if the brass caught wind of their hookups. But it bugged the crap out of me that J-Hawk had a wife and kids at home in North Dakota.

Anna, who was the biggest skeptic I've ever met, actually believed the line of bullshit cheating men used: J-Hawk's wife didn't understand him. So Anna felt no guilt whatsoever about being with a married man. She fell helmet over combat boots in love with him.

I dreaded the day it'd turn ugly between them, because it was inevitable. When that day came, I was the one who watched helplessly as two lives crumbled. Right then I swore no man would ever wield that much power over me.

"Mercy?"

My focus snapped back to him. "Yeah?"

"I see you're still throwing off those leave-me-the-fuck-alone vibes."

"When something works, I go with it."

He laughed. "I take it Sheriff Dawson isn't cowed by that attitude?"

"What makes you say that?"

"I waited out here to talk to you last night. Shouldn't be sexy as hell when a woman pulls a gun on you, but for some reason it is. Then he was in your face, but arresting you was the last thing on his mind." J-Hawk waggled his eyebrows. "So how long have you two been dancing the horizontal mambo?"

I sidestepped his question. "You didn't think it was so sexy when Anna held a gun on you that last time."

J-Hawk's good humor vanished. He crumpled the beer can and tossed it into my truck bed before reaching for another. "No. It wasn't sexy. Half the time I wish she would've pulled the trigger."

I nearly gave myself whiplash my head whipped around so fast. "Why?"

"Look at me. My life sucks, and it ain't looking to get better any time soon. My wife ain't ever gonna leave Minot. 'Army

Ranger' on a résumé doesn't mean squat. Titan Oil was the only company that'd hire me." He paused and drank. "What about you? How'd you end up tending bar?"

As I debated telling the truth or sticking with my standard noncommittal answer, I drained my beer and reached for another.

"I won't say everything was hunky-dory after I returned from outprocessing. I tagged along with Jake, learning what it took to run a ranch this size. When Hope lost one of the babies, I ended up on nursing duty. Long story short, I resented feeling like the odd woman out and moved into the foreman's cabin. By then the bad dreams started, and the only way to stop them was drinking until I passed out."

"Every night?"

"Pretty much."

He whistled again.

"We're all warned about the adjustment time after retirement, especially just coming back from combat, I just didn't think it'd be so hard to swallow that I'd gone from being a trained—"

Why don't you just blurt it out for the whole damn world to hear, Sergeant Major?

J-Hawk placed his hand on my knee. "I know what you are."

Took a second to gather my thoughts. Seemed pathetic to admit to a superior officer that I needed a crutch to handle my demons. "It got to the point I ended up drunk-dialing an old family friend. He knows what it's like."

"He's been in the war machine?"

"Not ours. Vietnam. Rollie put the screws to me, and I listened. John-John had an opening at the bar, which sounds like putting a fat kid in a candy store. But most nights I'm so sick of dealing with booze I don't bother with it when I get home." I swallowed another drink. "But I'm also too tired to figure out what the hell I want to do now. Bartending ain't it, that's for damn sure."

The silence between us stretched into night sounds of crickets. Rustling grass reeds. The occasional yip of a coyote.

Finally J-Hawk spoke. "Could you ever see yourself doing what Anna does?"

"Hiring myself out as a merc?" I shook my head. "To be honest, I'd rather bartend."

"Do you talk to Anna often?"

"Jason—"

"I know, I ended it like a total asshole."

"No argument from me."

"What Anna never understood was it wasn't my choice."

"It was your choice to get involved with her when you were already married."

J-Hawk flicked the metal tab on the top of the can. "True. Look, you don't know the whole story, no one does, but if it wasn't for . . ."

I waited for him to finish his train of thought. When he didn't, I prompted, "If it wasn't for . . . what?"

"Never mind."

"You wouldn't have brought it up if you didn't want to talk about it."

He struggled.

I let him.

"I do want to talk about it, but swear this won't go any further than us. Ever. No one can know."

"Not Anna?"

"Especially not Anna."

A feeling of trepidation crept in, but I ignored it and said, "Fine."

"About the same time our unit got new orders, my wife found out I'd been involved with another woman."

"How she'd find out?"

"At first I suspected Anna told her to force my hand into choosing between them." He met my gaze. "But it didn't matter after that, because once the wheels were set in motion, everything careened out of control."

I stared at him, totally confused. "You wanna drop the clichés and get beyond the truth-is-out-there bullshit?"

"I see you still prefer taking the easiest shot," he said wryly. "So yeah, it's totally clichéd, the whole 'my wife doesn't understand me' bit, but it's the God's honest truth. Melinda and I had one drunken weekend at a friend's wedding when I was home on leave, and she ended up pregnant. We got married, because that's what people in our neck of the woods do, right? I was headed overseas, so I understood why she wanted to stay in Minot by her family until after the baby was born. But when I returned from deployment twelve months later, she refused to move to where I was stationed. By then, she'd gotten knocked up again."

"She'd gotten knocked up again?" I asked tightly. "All by her little herself?"

He scowled. "No. I'd gone twelve months without sex. And she was on me the instant we were alone. Took me three pregnancies before I realized she wasn't a nympho and didn't like sex as much as she liked having babies. So yeah, we have 'deployment' kids. Between kids two and three, I grew a set and demanded she get her ass to Fort Benning because I was sick of living like a single guy in the goddamn barracks."

"So she moved to Georgia and made your life hell?"

"No. She threatened to kill herself if I forced her away from family. When I basically laughed and called her a drama queen, she attempted it."

I shuddered. "Shit. Jason, I'm sorry."

"Yeah, welcome to my life. From there on out, any time I brought up our problems, she whipped out the suicide card, and I knew she'd play it."

"What did you do?"

"What could I do? I focused on being a soldier. I kept my name on the top of the volunteer list for overseas instruction ops and deployment. I made a point of being on missions or training eleven months out of twelve. Combat? I understood. My passive-aggressive psychopathic wife? She freaked me the fuck out."

"So you started screwing around?"

"Not at first, but when I realized even my own family believed Melinda's lies? I said fuck it. What did I have to lose?"

"Anna knew you'd cheated on your wife before her?"

"Anna knew she wasn't the first one, but she's always been the only one who mattered."

Pretty words. Didn't excuse ugly behavior.

"Here's the kicker. That night after you . . . the night in Bali changed me, Mercy. It finally hit me that life is too short not to be with who you want. For the first time I decided to be proactive in my personal life, rather than reactive.

"I was ready to give up everything, any chance of a relationship with my kids, just to get the hell out of the marriage. When Melinda confronted me, I admitted to the affair and told her I wanted a divorce."

"I take it that didn't go over very well?"

"Might say that. She took it a step further than threatening to kill herself." He chugged his remaining beer. "She threatened to kill our children."

My stomach churned the beer into foam, and it threatened to come back up. "Jesus."

"And if I needed convincing she wasn't bluffing? Melinda called me the next day when our three-year-old daughter fell down a flight of stairs and broke her arm. She said it was too bad Lindsey was so clumsy. She hoped next time our little girl wouldn't fall on a kitchen knife or something horrible. I knew then she'd pushed Lindsey. Melinda has always had an . . . unnatural need for attention. She loved that I was constantly gone, because everyone in her circle of friends worried about how she was holding up. And if one of her children died . . . she could milk the sympathy and attention for years." His voice dropped. "Christ. Even now, years later, I know it sounds far-fetched. It's why I've never told anyone. Who would believe me?"

I didn't respond. I couldn't make my damn mouth work. Because I did believe him. I'd met people like Melinda. Too many people. Any glimmer of sympathy I'd ever felt for Melinda Hawley over the years had vanished.

"That's when I knew I could never be with Anna. That's why I had to be so damn cruel when I broke it off with her."

I'd walked into our tent to see Anna's military issue 9 mm Beretta at the base of J-Hawk's skull. Tears flowed down both their faces; hers were from pure rage. At the time I'd attributed his tears to fear. Now I suspected they'd been born of resignation. He'd expected Anna to kill him. Wanted it. I'd managed to get the gun before she pulled the trigger. Jason had run out without looking back; Anna dropped to a fetal position on the ground and stayed that way for twelve hours.

Now, I almost wished I still thought of him as an unfeeling asshole, rather than knowing what he'd gone through and what he'd given up. "Why're you telling me this, J-Hawk?"

"Because it's been weighing on me for years, and I wanted someone to know the truth before . . ."

"Before what?"

No response, then he chuckled. "It don't matter. I'm getting sappy. I appreciate that you are good at keeping secrets, Gunny."

I'd walked into this secret-keeping mission with my eyes wide open. Still, I didn't understand why J-Hawk unburdened himself on me. Unless . . . He'd always been an excellent tactician. Would this "big reveal" lead to another strategic maneuver? Involving changing my mind about Titan Oil's plans?

J-Hawk passed out the last two beers. We drank, stared at the stars, swinging our legs off the tailgate. "Thanks for not judging me too harshly."

"I'm the last person to pass judgment on anyone."

He snorted. "Always do the right thing, never deviate from the truth, Sergeant Major Gunderson? Right."

If he only knew how far I'd fallen from the ideals beat into my head by Dad and Uncle Sam. "Yeah, I'm a regular poster girl for guts and glory."

From the moment J-Hawk appeared in the area, I'd been suspicious of his motives. Here was my chance, in the spirit of "sharing," to find out if he considered me an easy mark as well as a supreme secret keeper. "Did you ask for this Titan Oil assignment? Or is it just coincidence you're here?"

"Not a coincidence. I switched out sections with another guy when I saw the list of landowners and your last name."

"Why?"

"I wanted to set the record straight with you about Anna. About my fucked-up life." He nudged me with his shoulder. "And, South Dakota, I wanted to rib you personally about how significantly you'd downplayed the size of your ranch."

I shrugged.

"Seventy-five thousand acres ain't nothin' to sneeze at."

"We're at eighty-five thousand now. I bought the adjoining ranch a few months ago." Without an heir, Iris Newsome's death left the Newsome estate in limbo. The state's attorney had to dredge through legal documents dating back to Merle Newsome's will. The will contained a stipulation that the entire property had to be offered to Gunderson descendants first, for fair market value, before it went on sale to the general market. Jake and I debated on whether we could afford it. But ultimately we knew we couldn't afford not to snap it up. We struggled to make the down payment, and I didn't feel a damn bit guilty about buying it.

"So when you switched sections with your coworker, did you hint around to your employers that I might be an easier mark because I owed you for saving my life?"

He faced me, his eyes shining with anger. "You believed I was here . . . Jesus Christ, Gunny, you're the one who said you owed me. I saved you because it was the right thing to do. It's the one decent thing I've done in my life, so don't you dare taint it. Don't. You. Dare."

"I'm sorry. I thought—"

"Well, you thought wrong."

Silence.

"Besides, this job is just a damn job. A shitty-paying one at that."

I gazed at the filmy white clouds drifting across the stars. "So you're not gung-ho about this pipeline project?"

"You ain't gonna want to hear this, but it's pointless to resist. The pipeline will go through, whether the landowners cry foul or not." He pinned me with a look. "And no, I don't have insider knowledge beyond what I've seen happen everywhere else."

"I think you're wrong. With the new administration in power and the focus on alternative energy sources, oil is the evil empire. And since one of the stipulations for getting the pipeline passed is that all-important presidential seal of approval . . . we might actually win this one for a change."

"For a change? This is the first time a pipeline has been proposed."

"But it's not the first time the state has run over us, just like they do when it comes to the railroads."

Eminent domain issues were the bane of landowners'

existence. Some folks mistakenly believe the greed and power of the railroad companies were history in the Wild West. Not so. Railroad companies still had a huge lobbyist presence in Congress. If a railroad conglomerate had permission to bisect your land with tracks, there wasn't a lot ranchers could do. Except pray that the steel wheels screaming across the steel railroad track didn't send sparks flying across the dry grass and start a raging prairie fire.

J-Hawk nudged me. "And you call North Dakotans pig-headed? You people are adverse to change of any kind, aren't you?"

"Not if it's good change." I steered the conversation another direction. "How long have you been working for the evil empire?"

"A year."

I frowned. "Wait. You've been out of the service . . . how long?"

"Three years." Jason laughed. "I see you doing the math. Yep. I was blissfully unemployed for two solid years after I retired from active duty. Man, did that piss Melinda off. I did nothing but lay around the house. And when I started to put on weight? I thought she'd have a stroke, but I'd never be that lucky."

"Looks to me like you've dropped a few pounds since the last time I saw you."

"After I went back to work I began to lose weight. But before that? I'd porked out and hit the three-hundred-pound mark."

"Holy shit. That was your way to retaliate? For her threatening to kill your kids? By becoming a fat bum?"

"That is the worst sort of punishment for her. People in her hometown knew I was unemployed. I sometimes filled out job applications, just so people were aware I needed work. Just so I could embarrass her into explaining why her husband, a college graduate, an Army Ranger and a twenty-year military veteran, applied for a job as a stock boy at the feed store." He swigged his beer. "She was upset I retired from the military. She wondered if I'd be denying future Rangers my expertise by quitting while I still had lots of good years left to teach in the field."

My mouth dropped open. "Are you kidding me?"

"Nope. My retirement pay isn't near what my tax-free deployment pay was. The poor woman had less money to burn and me to deal with every damn day." J-Hawk tipped his head back and studied the night sky. "But know the best part? From the moment I got home she was a cat in heat. She was desperate to have another baby to lord over me. So desperate that she'd even screw her fatty husband all the freakin' time. Of course, she thought I was a pussy-whipped idiot. When two years passed and my seed hadn't taken in her always-fertile womb, she confronted me about taking fertility tests. That's when I told her the truth."

This wouldn't be pleasant.

"On my last mission, during a stopover at Ramstein, I paid a doctor five grand cash to give me a vasectomy off the books. You should've seen the look on her face, Mercy. I told her since she threatened to kill my existing kids, I went ahead and eliminated any future offspring to save her the trouble of taking them out, too."

The swig of beer stuck in my throat and spewed out my nose. J-Hawk slapped me on the back during the coughing fit. When I'd settled down, I looked at him. "I didn't mean to laugh, because none of this is funny, but you really did even the score with her, didn't you?"

His eyes took on a wicked gleam I recognized when dealing with the enemy. "You have no idea. I'm still not done screwing with her. A few months back I had a buddy in the insurance biz bring her papers to sign. Little did she know she'd just taken out half-million-dollar life insurance policies for each one of our kids, naming her as the sole beneficiary. So if an 'accident' befell one of them . . ."

"She'd immediately be under suspicion." I smiled at him. Grinned, actually. "Clever. There's the military strategy I admired."

"It was the only way I could protect my kids by doing what I do best."

"Good for you." I yawned. "Sorry. This conversation has been anything but boring."

"You've had a long day, and I've bent your ear long enough." He hopped off the tailgate. "Thanks for talking to me, Mercy."

"I'm really sorry for all the shit you've gone through."

"You've gone through plenty yourself."

"Somehow I thought being back here would be . . . easier."

"War isn't hell for some of us, Mercy. For some of us, the real hell is going home."

I let that sink in. I heard J-Hawk's vehicle start up. Saw the red flash of his taillights as he drove off toward town. I remained in the frosty air, looking at the twinkling stars, trying to process what I thought I'd known, with the truth I'd just learned. When my teeth started to chatter, I crawled in the truck cab and headed home.

FOUR

Full moon fever wasn't a myth. Folks in the bar business kept close tabs on that, but we weren't due for a full moon for over a week.

So why had all the freaks come out? Clementine's customers were an eclectic bunch. But tonight, even our oddball regulars were looking around guardedly, with one foot pointed toward the closest exit.

The shenanigans might've amused me if I'd been partaking of the craziness. Two couples were playing musical make-out chairs. When the jukebox stopped, they'd switch partners. The guys from the dart league enjoyed watching the wife-on-wife portion of the swap.

Unluckily for us, members of the Use It or Lose It bunco club made good on their motto to play bunco from "every church hall to every pool hall" in our fair county. When Winona explained we didn't serve daiquiris, the ladies ordered gin and tonics by the pitcher—and that was worse. A game of strip bunco ensued with Vinnie and his gang. I no more wanted to see the bunco ladies' saggy boobs flapping in the wind than I wanted to see hairy biker asses sliding on bar stools that I had to wipe down.

I almost said screw it to John-John's no-drinking-on-shift rule right then and there.

Several college kids instigated a beer-pong tournament. Lefty, a crusty rancher who'd last spoken to me when I was a sixteen-year-old with a wild streak and a fast truck, joined the fun. Happy as it made the old coot to be winning, color me glad the vomit-inducing game was held close to the bathrooms.

A cluster of young cowboys wearing big buckles and big

attitudes sauntered in. They loaded up on cheap beer, eventually wandering to the back room, where the construction workers shot pool. The single women immediately followed—not that I blamed them. Before too long I was inundated with orders for blow jobs.

John-John and I managed to keep straight faces for thirty seconds. And I thought I could be crude? John-John let loose a barrage of lewd comments that'd make a porn star blush. Even a gay porn star.

By nine o'clock I'd changed out the kegs seven times.

A group of Indian bikers wearing matching club jackets snagged a table in the corner, where they could monitor the entire bar. Talk about an air of entitlement. Winona rolled her eyes at their impatient finger snaps. Maybe in their normal hangout, bar staff afforded them reverence, jumping at their classy finger-popping attention getters. Not in Clementine's. The governor could grace us with his presence and the wait-your-fucking-turn attitude wouldn't change a lick.

When Kit McIntyre ambled in, the phrase "cowboys and bikers and dickheads, oh my" flitted into my head. Ol' White Hair stopped to schmooze with the drunken bunco ladies before bellying up to the bar. "Hey, Mercy. Where's Muskrat?"

It stuck in my craw, making nice with Kit, but he dropped a pile of cash in Clementine's, so my personal issues went the way of the dinosaur while I was on duty. "He has the night off."

"So you're the bouncer?"

"Me 'n' John-John. Why? You planning on causing problems?"

"With you on duty? Hell no." His greasy smile didn't reach his snake eyes. "We both know you got no problem kicking ass—mine especially."

"Did you come in specifically to flatter me? Or is there something else you need?"

"I'll take a pitcher of Miller Lite and a half-dozen cups."

I shoved a pitcher under the tap. "You guys having another pipeline meeting?"

"No. It's a strategy meeting for Bill O'Neil's campaign committee."

"And you're meeting here?" Clementine's was a rough bar.

Most respectable folks with money, influence, or both steered clear.

"A last-minute change. Had no idea you'd be so busy tonight."

Leon Tasker, a rancher with a low tolerance for bullshit and a high tolerance for bourbon, scowled at Kit. "Don't know why in the devil Bill threw his hat in the ring in the first place. He's too damn old to be sheriff."

"Says the man who asked me for a senior citizen's discount last week," I said dryly.

Kit chuckled.

"I'm surprised you're backing a losing candidate, McIntyre," Leon said.

"Maybe Bill ain't ideal, but he's got a better grasp on what's best for people in this county than Dawson does."

"Think that's enough to win votes?"

"Mebbe. I guess we'll see soon enough." Kit snagged the pitcher. "Any other guys come in here looking for the meeting, send 'em back, will ya?"

"How will I know who they are?"

"Easy. They'll be wearing the hangdog look of defeat."

The door opened again, disgorging another cluster of partiers, and I groaned. Seemed everybody in the damn county had shown up tonight.

Lost in thought, I glanced up at the new customer who'd taken Kit's spot at the bar next to Leon.

Hello, Gorgeous. Talk about being a credit to his Native American ancestry—this guy was Hollywood hot. Built, too. His face was stunning, all sharply chiseled features plus full, pouty lips that should've looked ridiculous on a man, but were sexy as sin. His eyes weren't dark, like the blackstrap molasses color of his hair, but the honeyed hue of cognac.

Mr. Tall, Dark, and Indian earned a genuine smile from me. "What can I get you?"

"A double shot of Crown and a glass of water."

"Coming right up."

I felt his gaze on me as I poured the whiskey. He hadn't been in before; I definitely would've remembered him. "You want to start a tab or settle up now?"

"A tab."

"No problem." I busied myself at the other end of the bar. Chatting up customers wasn't my thing. Luckily, the majority of our clientele were loners who came in to knock back a drink or ten without the social niceties.

Winona did a double take seeing the brooding male sexpot classing up the joint. She turned her head, mouthing "Oh my God," and fanned herself with the tray.

I muttered, "Tell me about it. So whatcha need?"

"A pitcher of Coors Light and three double shots of Chivas. Pronto." She scowled. "What kind of asshole says *pronto*? I wish they'd stop coming in here."

"Who? Those matching-jacket guys?"

She nodded.

"First time I've seen them."

"Consider yourself lucky."

Winona didn't flirt with our good-looking stranger while I filled her order—another reason I liked her. She wasn't working as a cocktail waitress to pick up guys.

I kept an eye on the door to see what respectable citizens deigned to cross our dirty threshold in support of Bill. A few of my neighbors ducked in. The bar filled with people I didn't know. Twenty years can change the makeup of a community entirely.

John-John scooted next to me. "How's the meeting going?"

"The guest of honor hasn't shown up yet."

"It's probably past old Bill's bedtime." He frowned. "Don't know how I feel about Clementine's becoming a meeting place. Don't any of those people know that Dawson is a regular customer?"

"I guess not."

"Be funny as hell if he walked in and saw exactly who was plotting his downfall, eh?"

I bumped him with my shoulder. "Hey, don't be wishing for trouble, since I'm the bouncer tonight."

John-John gave me a sly look. "Neither of us would mind bouncing on the hot dude at the end of the bar, who is trying very hard not to listen to our conversation."

"And you know that . . . how?"

"Years of experience, doll."

"Wanna start touting your blow-job expertise again?"

He smoothed his hands down his leather vest. "I've never been one to brag. Besides, he'd rather have a blow job from you than from me."

I laughed. Hard. I shot Mr. Indian Hottie a sideways glance. He was not so amused.

Bill O'Neil came in, bolting into the back room without so much as a friendly wave.

And the night was just getting weirder and weirder.

With the sundry mix of clientele, Trey's appearance shouldn't have surprised me, but it did piss me off. I said, "Kit's in the back room."

"So? I'm off duty." He parked his ass on the stool in front of me. Threw his keys and his can of Skoal on the bar. "Bottle of Bud Light."

I rooted in the cooler, snapped the cap off with the opener, and slid it in front of him. "Three bucks."

"I'll start a tab." He took a drink. "You know I'm good for it."

"'Bout the only goddamn thing you're good for," I muttered, moving away before I said something I'd regret. Or he said something that'd make me punch him in the face.

When I had to return to his section, he said, "Busy night."

I ignored him.

"Ain't talking to me?"

"I'll serve you, but I don't have to talk to you."

Cowboy Trey lifted his head, peering at me from beneath the brim of his hat. "Afraid you might have to defend yourself?"

"Against what?"

"This and that. Mostly about who's keeping you company some nights."

Trey knew nothing. But his smug attitude burned my ass. "Wanna know what I think?"

"You ain't paid to think."

Ooh. This was gonna be fun.

Trey eased his lanky frame back. "Look how the mighty have fallen. Got no other options besides servicing drunks in this dive? Sad commentary on your skills after your years of military service."

Don't rise to the bait. Don't smack his head into the bar. And for Christsake, don't shoot him.

"Don't got nothin' to say?" A mean smile distorted his mouth. "You're just pissy I got the jump on you last year."

Maybe just one small bullet. Right between the eyes.

"You know I could've killed you in your sleep."

I leaned over the bar and pressed the tip of my index finger into the hollow of his throat. "And you know I could still kill you in yours."

Cowboy Trey froze.

"Don't got nothin' to say?" I mimicked.

"Mercy?" John-John said, "Is there a problem here?"

Pressure-point training, what a beautiful thing. If I moved my finger an inch higher, I could put Trey on the floor, screaming in agony. Tempted, I pushed a littler harder. When he whimpered, I whispered, "*Is* there a problem?"

"Trey?" John-John asked.

"Ah. Nope. No problem. It's all good."

I backed off. Smiled. "Excuse me."

Things slowed down. I restocked my station without fear it'd be overrun with thirsty customers. I was on my knees restacking napkins when I heard, "What's it take to get a damn drink around here?"

I hoisted myself to my feet.

J-Hawk crouched over the bar, impatiently tapping his fingers on the counter. The man didn't look good. If his glassy eyes and sallow complexion were an indication, the last thing he needed was another drink.

"You *are* working. Jim Beam and Coke. A double."

"Jason, you okay?"

"I'm fine, why?"

"You seem . . . I dunno. Off."

"If I'm 'off,' it's because I'm sick of being stuck in buttfuck South Dakota."

Was it my imagination or had he yelled that?

"Hey, buddy, watch your mouth," Vinnie snapped, plunking an empty pitcher on the counter.

"Or what?" Jason sneered. "You gonna kick my ass?"

"Yep. And as soon as I'm done busting you up, there'll be a

line of guys waiting to get their shot in. No one wants you here, so maybe you oughta just leave."

"Make me."

Five guys crowded Jason. Three scrappy construction workers and one of Vinnie's buddies.

Not good.

Jason laughed. "Am I supposed to feel threatened? You're all a bunch of hillbilly douche bags."

The surrounding area didn't go silent, but he definitely got everyone's attention.

"If you don't like it here, go the fuck home," Vinnie's friend suggested.

"Better yet, why don't you go back and tell the oil company greasing your dick and your hand that we ain't like the pansy asses in North Dakota. We can say no. We don't bend over for no one," Vinnie said.

"You're all so stupid. You think anything you do or say is gonna mean jack shit? This is big money. Your state will lay down and spread its legs like a money-grubbing whore, just like mine did. The pipeline is coming, whether or not you like it." Jason grinned and invaded Vinnie's space. "But I bet you like being bent over, doncha?"

Vinnie shoved Jason, and he flew backward.

Jason stumbled but righted himself, flashing the knife in his hand. "Gonna have to do better than that, cocksucker."

For Christsake. A knife fight? Before I could jump in, Vinnie's buddy dragged Vinnie from the fray, muttering about parole.

"That's what I thought." Jason closed the knife and clipped it to his belt. "Anyone else?"

Then two of the construction guys—Rocky and Mike—rushed him, getting him on the ground. Encouraging shouts from other patrons muted the sounds of flesh hitting flesh.

Enough.

I vaulted the bar and dragged their stupid, drunken asses away. Jason just lay there with his eyes closed, letting their punches land without fighting back.

When I turned, I was right in Rocky's line of fire. His wild swing caught me in the face. My head snapped back. The vertebrae in my neck popped like someone had stomped on Bubble Wrap.

Goddammit, that hurt. I squinted through my dimmed vision, slamming my boot heel into Rocky's knee, knocking him on his ass, and leveling a blow to Mike's stomach so hard he doubled over.

"We done?" I asked, watching them both wheeze.

Mike nodded and backed off from me immediately, helping his limping friend to his feet.

"You're throwing *them* out?" someone in the crowd yelled. "That's bullshit!"

"Yeah."

I heard a crash and whirled around to see beer cans and bottles flying at J-Hawk's head. The dumbass lay there. Like he deserved it. God. And I thought I had self-loathing issues? At least mine were private.

John-John materialized beside me with a wooden Louisville Slugger baseball bat. He shouted to be heard above the din. "No more of that shit in here, or me 'n' Louis will start busting heads."

"But he started it," Rocky complained, pointing to Jason.

"Jesus, Rocky. What are you? In third grade?" I demanded.

"I'm finishing it," John-John said. "Any more questions?"

Muttering, background rumbles, but no one piped up to contradict John-John. No more bottles sailed through the smoke-clogged air.

"Mercy, doll, you okay?"

I touched my cheekbone and winced. "I'm fine."

John-John loomed over Jason and spoke succinctly. "If I ever see you in here again, I'll beat you bloody."

Sometimes I forgot John-John wasn't a pushover; he'd split his fair share of lips and heads. Any gay man who participated in the Sun Dance every year was truck tough. He'd forged this bar against all odds, building a place where past misdeeds didn't matter as much as current cash.

"I'll get him out of here."

"No. He'll either walk out or crawl out on his own, but either way he chooses to go, you ain't helping him."

That made no sense.

John-John met my confused gaze head on. "I can't have you

talking to him anymore, Mercy. Look around. My customers are pissed you didn't let Mike and Rocky beat him to a pulp. Your job is to cater to the local folks who spend money in here week after week. You don't owe this flight-by-night troublemaker nothin'."

I owe him my life, danced on the tip of my tongue.

I ducked beneath the bar partition so John-John wouldn't think I was helping J-Hawk to his feet.

He picked himself up off the floor and rested against the counter. "Looks like I'll be drinking alone from here on out." He slid me a twenty-dollar bill. "Can I get a bottle of Jim Beam to go?"

I brown-bagged the bottle and set it next to him. "What the hell were you thinking, spewing that shit? Were you looking for a fight?"

"Didn't get much of one, did I?" he sneered.

I rolled my eyes at the former Army Ranger. "You against an entire bar? Did you whack your head on the concrete in your fall from grace?"

"I wish." Jason grabbed the bottle, acting hesitant.

I didn't want him to leave either, but I had no choice. "Where will you go?" I asked softly.

He shrugged. "Not far. But it'll still feel like I'm light-years away from where I want to be."

"Jason—"

"Go help your loyal local customers, Mercy. Forget about me."

Although everyone stared at him, no one spoke to Jason as he walked out the door.

A bar fight put people in a drinking mood. John-John and I barely kept up. If he wasn't out on the floor helping Winona take orders, he was behind the bar mixing drinks. I handled bottled and draft beer and poured straight shots. Even the traffic for off-sale booze stayed steady. At one point I had five customers in line.

Frazzled, I demanded, "IDs?" to a pair of underage punks.

"We're buying beer for our dad. He's out in the parking lot waitin' for us."

"Really?"

"Uh-huh. He wants a suitcase of Keystone Light."

"Got an ID?"

"No. But—"

"No ID, no beer." I peered around him and shouted, "Next."

"Come on," the short blond argued, getting up in my face. "He's right outside."

The snot-nosed punk was high as a kite and spoiling for a fight. Not a good combo. After the night I'd had, not a smart move on his part to push me. "Then send him in."

"He's handicapped, and you ain't got no wheelchair access," the red-haired one sniveled. He rubbed the back of his hand beneath his nose. "It ain't his fault he can't come in and buy it himself. That's why he sent us. So sell us the god-damn beer."

I hated meth heads. These little lying sacks had thought of everything—except fake IDs. "Nice try. Let me repeat. No ID, no beer."

One last glare at me and they spun away. But they stupidly approached the last guy in line.

I yelled, "I catch any of you buying booze for those two minors, and I will permanently blackball you, got it?"

No response, but they all looked to the real boss.

John-John didn't miss a beat. "Any names she passes on to me, I'll pass along to Muskrat. I guarantee you won't step foot in here again."

Muskrat's name invoked way more fear than mine.

Pissed off, the boys tried to cause a scene but were old news by the time the door hit them in the ass.

People started to clear out. John-John restocked the liquor and ran the industrial dishwasher, hauling clean glasses and stacking them behind the bar. When we were down to only a few customers, John-John made a halfhearted offer to stay and help me close up, but in all honesty, I didn't want him around. After being surrounded by people for the last ten hours, I craved some semblance of solitude.

Being alone allowed me too much time to think. How had this part-time bartending gig morphed into a full-time job? I might've needed direction in my life at one point, but tonight I realized I was tired of breaking up fights, pulling drafts, cleaning up vomit, and working until two in the morning.

It also hit me that my working hours were becoming as much of a blur as the nights when I'd passed out from drinking. And I didn't know which one was worse.

FIVE

Long-assed night behind me, I couldn't wait to get home.

As I crossed the parking area, the universe made a point it could screw with me at any moment; the toe of my boot caught in a gopher hole. Thanks to military martial arts training, I managed to make a safe fall, avoiding landing on my left side and dislocating my shoulder.

Glad no one was around to see that humiliating face-plant.

I pushed to my knees, cursing my lack of depth perception, when a flash of white in the darkness caught my attention. What the hell? I squinted, determining it was a pair of shoes. Namely, athletic shoes with white soles. Shoes still on the feet on the person lying between the two vehicles.

Jesus. Just what I needed, to deal with a passed-out drunk. Then again, it wouldn't be the first time.

I yelled, "Hey, you. Get up."

No twitch of the feet. Big feet. Had to be a guy.

I brushed the dirt off my jeans and stood, but didn't move closer. Maybe I ought to leave the man be. If I woke him up, I'd have to determine whether he was fit to drive. Considering his prone state, chances were slim he'd be coherent, and I wasn't a damn taxi service.

But nights were still cold, and I didn't need a case of hypothermia on my conscience. I headed toward him. "Look, you can't sleep it off here."

Then I smelled blood.

Walk away. Run away. Get in your truck and drive away. Just go go go, and don't look back.

My feet moved of their own volition, and the next thing I knew, I was standing over the body.

He wasn't sleeping; he was dead.

The coat. The shirt. The jeans. All items of clothing I recognized, even in the darkness, even covered in dark splotches of blood and mud. It was the shoes that'd thrown me. J-Hawk had never worn white athletic shoes. Neither of us did. It was a covert-ops thing. Even now, every pair of my running shoes were a shade of black.

Would you quit obsessing over shoes? J-Hawk is lying out here, in the middle of an old pasture, dead. Do something.

I dug out my cell phone and dialed 911. "This is Mercy Gunderson. There's been a fatal shooting at Clementine's. No, the bar is closed. Yes, I'll stay."

Rather than stand around wringing my hands until the cops arrived, I took stock of the situation. What I knew of forensics could fit on the head of a pin. But I knew better than to wander around the crime scene or to move the body.

I forced myself to focus on the visible body trauma and squatted next to him. Shot from close range, at least once. A hole gaped beneath his sternum. Had to be at least a .45 cal to do that much damage. My gaze moved down. His shirt had been cut, revealing a strip of his belly skin that glowed neon white. Dark blood seeped from the long, jagged knife wound—a deep slash in his gut resembling a grotesque smile. I swallowed the bile forcing its way up my throat when I realized whoever had done this had sawed through his midsection. This hadn't been a quick stab and slice. I forced my eyes away only to notice another gunshot wound on his upper right thigh.

His arms were akimbo. His head was at an unnatural angle, tilted to the side. Because of the excess blood on his neck, I couldn't tell if the wound was from a bullet or a knife. I couldn't see his face, thank God.

Or his vacant, accusing eyes.

I saved you. Why didn't you save me?

Startled by the wraithlike words, I stumbled back.

Night became day. The flattened grass became chalky sand. The clothing turned into desert camo. The vehicle became a smoking, overturned Humvee. And I knelt next to the young marine as I tried to keep his guts from spilling out of his belly.

He's dead. Get up and move on. They're coming to get the body.

I blinked, and I was back in South Dakota. Sitting next to J-Hawk's body, my past intruding on my present.

Despite feeling light-headed, I wobbled to my feet.

In the last few years I'd been unfortunate to discover more than my fair share of dead bodies. Even during my time in the army. I found Private Madison in his bunk with his belt wrapped around his throat. I discovered an Iraqi interpreter bludgeoned to death directly outside our "safe" zone. Coming home hadn't changed my bad luck. I'd found my nephew and his girlfriend.

And now this. J-Hawk. Dead.

My gut clenched as a horrifying thought occurred: Had J-Hawk been waiting for me? Like he'd been the last few nights?

Surely someone would've noticed him lying out here? The kind of gun that left a hole that size made a pretty goddamn big bang, too. Surely someone would've heard gunshots?

The whys raced through my head until the sounds of sirens broke the stillness and my communal with the dead. An Eagle River County patrol car pulled in first, kicking dust into ghost clouds against the inky sky. An ambulance, a fire truck, and other vehicles blocked off the parking area. Who were these people? Why were they here?

Fucking voyeuristic bastards.

Car doors opened and closed. I didn't move.

"Mercy?"

I faced Dawson. No surprise he'd responded to the call—homicides were rare in Eagle River County, but it made me highly curious about where he'd been at two in the morning that he was first on the scene. "Sheriff."

"You all right?"

"Besides discovering another dead body?"

"You do have a knack." He realized our banter was a little too easy, and I saw the shift in him immediately. "I appreciate you sticking around. Do you know the victim?"

Admitting my past relationship with J-Hawk now, while we

were standing over his bullet-riddled and carved-up body, might cause problems I wasn't prepared to deal with. I kept my response simple. "Yeah. It's Jason Hawley. The guy from Titan Oil."

"Has anything been moved?"

His question was far less accusatory than the last time we'd had this conversation. "No. Everything is exactly as I found it."

"Good. Now I'm gonna ask you to head on over to the ambulance and wait."

"I can't go home?"

Dawson frowned. "We've done this enough times that you know the drill by now."

"Stay close but stay out of the way," I said to his retreating back.

I tugged my jacket more securely around me and joined the people clustered between the patrol cars and the ambulance. Kiki nodded to me before she joined Dawson at the scene.

Three firemen were talking in a closed group. All guys I didn't know. There'd been a time I knew everyone, their brothers, sisters, aunts, uncles and even the names of their dogs in our small community.

Rome Hall, my friend Geneva's younger brother, sauntered up. "Hey, Mercy."

"Rome." I pointed to his coffee. "Got any more of that?"

"Huh-uh. But I'll share this one with you."

"No way. You'll give me cooties."

He snorted at our long-standing joke. "Maybe you should reopen the bar and brew a pot for everyone. We'll probably be here awhile."

"If I open the bar I can guarantee you the last thing I'll be drinking is coffee."

"I hear ya there." He sipped. "So who's the stiff?"

"Jason Hawley."

"Name isn't ringing a bell."

"He works for Titan Oil, and he's here drumming up support for the pipeline."

"How's that going for him?"

"Doesn't appear to be so good." I looked at Rome. "Thought you had seniority and didn't have to pull third shift?"

"I'm filling in for Cutty. He had a hot date." His gaze drifted over my cheek. "That's not a dirt smudge I'm seeing, is it?"

"Can't get nothin' past you EMTs."

"What happened?"

I shrugged. "My reflexes were a little slow breaking up a bar fight. It's sore, but I'm fine."

"So in addition to doing double duty as the bartender and the bouncer, John-John is slaving you on the close-down crew?"

"There'd have to be more than me for it to be a 'crew.'"

Rome's thumb scraped the plastic cover of the coffee cup, in a *click-click-click* sound. "Maybe it's none of my business, but how long you gonna keep slinging drinks?"

"Why? Is there a job opening on the county ambulance crew?"

"No. It's just . . . you working at Clementine's seems a waste. I've known you since we were kids, Mercy, and you're not one to settle for the easiest option."

I bit back a smile at the brutal honesty that was a hallmark of the Hall clan. "True. But options around here are limited."

"Also true."

We fell into silence. Law enforcement scurried about while the rest of us stood around. Rome was called over, leaving me alone.

Talking to people kept a lid on my unease, and I could handle my growing anger. Standing alone, not knowing what was unfolding beyond the flashing lights, sent my anxiety off the charts.

My annoyance quadrupled when Kit McIntyre sidled up beside me.

What the hell was he doing here?

"Bet you didn't mean to say that out loud, Mercy," he remarked gruffly.

"You're cruising by Clementine's at two o'clock in the damn morning just because?"

"No. I heard about this on the police scanner. I figured I'd drive out and have a look-see."

Seemed fortuitous, Kit tuning in to the scanner in the middle of the night. Almost as if he'd been expecting something bad to happen.

Or he'd made something bad happen.

An icy finger of suspicion slithered down my spine.

Kit's opinion about Titan Oil was identical to mine. But how far would he go to ensure his interests were served?

As far as he could. He'd employed plenty of dirty tricks to convince me to sell the ranch last summer. And both Kit and his lackey, Cowboy Trey, had been in the bar tonight. As I racked my brain trying to remember what time Trey had left, Kit spoke.

"The real reason I'm here is to see if Dawson is doin' his job. Some folks are questioning his abilities."

"Some folks meaning . . . who? Bill O'Neil?"

"For starters."

"Is Bill questioning Dawson's methodology, too?"

"Shouldn't we all?"

Dawson whistled loudly, and the ambulance backed up. He barked at the firemen. Then his deputies.

"He sure ain't your daddy, is he?" Kit commented.

With that, I walked away.

Two firemen hustled over to help the EMTs load the body. Jason wasn't a giant, but moving deadweight was harder than it looked.

Just another fun fact I knew firsthand.

Dawson conferred with his deputies and started toward me. But with each footstep, it became apparent his focus wasn't actually on me.

His furious gaze remained on the person behind me. "Who called you?"

I turned around. Whoa. Mr. Indian Hottie from the bar had propped himself against a parked car. His position afforded him a bird's-eye view of everything that'd gone down.

The man shrugged. "Police scanners are public domain, Sheriff. I was in the neighborhood and thought I'd check it out."

His inflection held the cadence of a reservation, but he didn't say more than he had to, so I couldn't quite place it.

"As you can see, I have it under control," Dawson said.

"Good to know. See you." He uncrossed his arms and walked toward the road, vanishing into the darkness.

"Who was that?"

Dawson glared after him, scowling, before he refocused on me. "No one you need to concern yourself with."

That smart retort got my back up.

"Was Clementine's busy tonight?"

"Packed to the rafters. Why?"

"I'll need you to make a list of everyone you remember being in the bar, as well as customers who bought from the package store. Arrival and departure times."

"No can do."

"Run that by me again?"

"No." Before he started his spiel about a crime being committed on the property and my responsibility to grease the wheels of justice, I held up my hand. "For that confidential information, Sheriff Dawson, you'll have to get a court order."

He blinked at me as if I were joking.

I wasn't. "Besides, I'm the lowly bartender. I don't have the authorization to share that information even if I wanted to. You'll have to ask John-John and Muskrat the company policy on clientele disclosure."

Dawson loomed over me, which was never a good move on his part unless we were in bed. "I've got a dead guy. As you're the person who discovered his body, I'd think you'd be eager to cooperate. If not for yourself, for the safety of the patrons who frequent this bar."

"Right. A murder victim won't keep customers away, Sheriff, it'll bring 'em in droves. So try again."

The ambulance bumped past us, but no other vehicles followed suit. As much as I hated the sound of sirens and the strobe-like effect from the flashing lights, a slow-moving ambulance was worse.

"Full cooperation and full disclosure will clear you from suspicion much faster."

After the ambulance taillights disappeared behind the rolling hills, I faced him. "You suspect me?"

"You found him. You admitted there were no other witnesses. I'm just following standard procedure, Mercy."

"Bullshit."

His shrewd eyes dropped to my right hand, jammed in my jacket pocket. "You carrying?"

Always. Which he knew. "Yes. I have a permit to carry concealed. You want to see it?"

"The permit? No. The gun? Yes." Dawson turned his head and yelled, "Deputy Moore?"

Kiki bounded over. "Yes, Sheriff?"

"Grab an evidence bag. Then I'll need you to glove up and remove the firearm from Miz Gunderson's right jacket pocket."

"For Christsake. I can just take it out—"

"No. You will hold still and let the deputy do her job relieving you of your weapon."

"Fine." Jerk wad.

"Slowly raise your hands and put them straight out in a *T* formation."

"Is this because I refused to tattle on my customers?"

Dawson's face was pure stone. "You need me to remind you that you are armed, in an area where a crime was committed using a firearm?"

"I'm not the only one who carries a gun."

"This is standard procedure. And if you continue to resist, I will cuff you and haul you to the station. Now, put your arms out, palms facing me."

Breathe. Stay in control.

I complied.

"Proceed, Deputy Moore," he said, hands resting on his hips, close to his gun.

I felt a hand in my pocket, and my jacket become lighter.

"The firearm is bagged and tagged, Sheriff," Kiki said.

"Thank you." He gave me a critical and slow once-over. "Are you carrying concealed elsewhere on your person, Miz Gunderson?"

"No," I snapped. I could not believe he'd taken my gun. He knew how I felt about my guns.

"Deputy Moore, if you'll verify that by patting her down?"

"Yes, sir."

Impersonal hands swept over my body as I seethed.

Dawson, the pompous prick, could've done this differently.

You could have, too.

"No other weapons, sir," Kiki said tightly.

"Good. Miz Gunderson, please hold out your hands so Deputy Moore can test them for gun powder residue."

My gaze snared his. "Are you fucking kidding me?"

"Do I look like I'm kidding?"

No, you look like an asshole who decided to make an example out of me at three o'clock in the goddamned morning.

I thrust my hands out and didn't bother to hide my fury.

When Kiki finished, she passed me an alcohol-soaked cleanup cloth and murmured something to Dawson.

I methodically wiped my hands, my blood pressure veering toward stroke level. Dawson's treatment of me rankled because he'd made it personal. But what really pissed me off? This show of his supposed power was a big waste of time. We both knew I hadn't killed Jason Hawley.

"Now, Miz Gunderson, you'll need to come with me to the sheriff's department to answer a few questions."

Like hell. "No."

"No?"

I canted my head. "I've been more than cooperative. I've stuck around the crime scene after a ten-hour shift, outside, in the cold. You've confiscated my gun. You've determined I haven't fired that gun—or any other gun—recently. You've got no reasonable cause to keep me here."

Dawson lifted both eyebrows. "Don't test me on that."

"If you want to arrest me and take me to the station, fine. Do it. But be aware: My attorney won't allow you to question me unless she's present. Since she's out of town for the next two days . . . you'll have locked up an innocent person, while whoever killed Jason Hawley is still out there, a danger to the entire community. I can't imagine that would look good for you while you're campaigning."

His body language betrayed nothing.

"Or you can let me go home, and I'll come to the station tomorrow voluntarily. Your choice, Sheriff Dawson." I'd backed him into a corner, but no tighter than the one he'd backed me into.

Curtly, Dawson said, "I expect to see you in my office by noon. Are we clear on that?"

"Yes, sir."

"And since you've had such a long day, I'll follow you to make certain you don't fall asleep at the wheel."

He had no idea how dangerous it was to be around me right now. "Not necessary. I'm sure Deputy Moore would be happy to ensure I get home all right."

"No problem, Mercy," Kiki said.

I stepped back and headed toward my truck, ignoring the stares of the people who'd stuck around to watch the show. Word of this humiliation would spread like wildfire.

And the worst of it wasn't over yet.

SIX

Kiki flashed her lights once after I turned down the driveway leading to the cabin. She spun a U-turn on the gravel road and headed back to town.

A hot shower did nothing to induce sleepiness. I slipped on my flannel pajamas, grabbed the bottle of Wild Turkey, and climbed into bed.

With my back to the headboard and bundled beneath a goose down comforter, I wasn't feeling warm. A coldness had permeated me since the moment I'd seen J-Hawk's body.

I swigged straight from the bottle, swallowing slowly, savoring the mellow burn. I repeated the process until my head was muzzy and my thoughts could bounce around freely, instead of obsessively returning to the brutal way J-Hawk's life had ended.

In the past few days, I'd tried to reconcile J-Hawk the soldier with Jason the civilian. I thought the lines were too rigidly set for me to see him as anything but the Army Ranger with nerves and balls of steel.

Now, I feared I'd forevermore see him covered in blood.

I let my head fall back into the pillows. Another slug of whiskey, and drunkenness overtook me.

I dreamed of the night I died.

Booze flowed freely. Crappy techno music vibrated the table and my teeth. A rainbow of laser lights cut through the clouds of smoke. Scantily clad, sweat-slicked bodies gyrated to the beats on the elevated dance floor.

Definitely not in Kansas anymore, Toto.

I preferred the barbed-wire compound to this.

I knocked back my seventh—or was it my eighth?—slug of

whiskey. As I slid forward on the plastic-coated bar stool—and eww, I didn't want to consider why everything in this nightclub was encased in plastic—a large male hand squeezed my upper thigh.

I was buzzed, but not nearly drunk enough to let some wet-behind-the-ears junior officer cop a feel. "Remove your hand, flyboy, or I'll cut it off at the wrist."

The hand dropped like a stone. But the British airman—full of machismo and rum—wouldn't let up. "Come on, luv. Relax. We're here on R and R."

"Don't remind me."

"You'd rather be back at the hotel?"

"Absolutely."

He snorted, and it wasn't nearly as charming as when Hugh Grant did it in the movies.

Besides, it hadn't been my idea to slink into a crowded nightclub in Bali. I'd succumbed to peer pressure from A-Rod and J-Hawk, lured by the chance to get shitfaced.

"Would you like to dance?" Lieutenant Happy Hands asked in his British lilt.

"To this techno shit?" I shuddered. "Hell no."

J-Hawk laughed. "Gunny prefers two-stepping to hip-hopping. It's a South Dakota thang. You wouldn't understand."

"That's rich, coming from a North Dakota plowboy," I shot back. "Tell me, J-Hawk, did you hear about the North Dakotan who stepped in a pile of cow shit and thought he was melting?"

Anna nearly fell off J-Hawk's lap, laughing. "She's got your number."

"And you've got it, too, baby."

A-Rod smooched him on the nose. Then the mouth. The smooch turned into a full-on make-out session.

Jesus Christ. They were adults. We were in public. Not to mention J-Hawk was married—and higher-ranking than either A-Rod or me.

J-Hawk was in select company as far as knowing about our team. Not even J-Hawk's trainee Lieutenant Happy Hands was aware of our designation in the murky military soup known as the "division of special troops." He believed we were attached to the Pentagon, since we were stationed in Indonesia with JCET, training the

Indonesian Special Forces, Kopassus. We had a little more freedom to roam around the country than those stuck in the world's sandboxes, but we were supposed to be discreet.

J-Hawk and A-Rod weren't being discreet at all. Lieutenant Happy Hands and I had both been dragged into this situation so the amorous couple could knock combat boots in a real bed in our hotel, instead of sneaking trysts on cots or in the back of a helicopter.

A-Rod scooted off J-Hawk's lap and tugged him to his feet. "Time for a little dirty dancing." Her eyes flashed me a warning. "Don't leave."

Damn woman knew me too well. I'd purposely chosen a table closest to the exit so I could make a quick getaway. I hated being exposed from all sides—I preferred my back to the wall. I hated the crush of people surrounding me. Mostly I hated that I was unarmed. "Fine. But you've got thirty minutes, and then I'm outta here."

She nodded, and they headed to the dance floor.

"You sure you don't want to dance?" he asked again.

"No. But I'd take another shot."

He ordered two more. After we chinked our glasses together, and knocked it back, he gave me a curiously disdainful look.

"What?"

"Are you a lesbian?"

The question might've bothered me if I hadn't been asked it a billion times before. "You think I'm a dyke because I'm career military? Or because I'm not ripping off my clothes and yelling—'Whoo-ee, take me right fucking now, you hot English flyboy!'"

"If the strap-on fits . . ."

"I like men. I like sex. I just don't like you."

His smirk faded. "Why the bloody hell not?"

"Because you're too pretty. Too young."

Indignant, he demanded, "So if I was old and ugly?"

I lifted my shot glass. "I'd do you in a heartbeat."

Lieutenant Happy Hands scowled.

I sipped the whiskey and wondered how long the lieutenant would stick around now that there wasn't a chance he'd get lucky with me.

He pushed to his feet and jammed his hands in his pockets. "Think I'll stroll and—"

The rest of his words were lost in the explosion that shook the rafters.

I hit the ground and reached for my gun, only to come up empty-handed. Before I had a chance to process the screams competing with the blaring music, another explosion rippled through the building, louder and more intense than the first. Light fixtures crashed, becoming bombs of glass and gas. From my position curled on the floor, I saw the lieutenant's polished dress shoes, which meant he was still standing.

Why wasn't he ducking for cover? I screamed at him, but the sound was lost in another explosion.

The table wobbled. I managed to roll out of the way before it crashed and the marble top decapitated me, but the heavy iron pedestal table base pinned my lower torso to the floor. I tried to pull myself out of the path of people racing for the exit. My hair was stepped on, entire chunks ripped out by the roots. Several hard kicks to the head made me woozy. My ears rang. Blood trickled down my face and neck. People fell on me. No one helped me up, rather they used my body as support to scramble back to their feet and get the hell away.

The real horror of the situation hit me; I'd lived through countless battles and mortar attacks, I'd dodged sniper rounds, only to be trampled to death in a sleazy nightclub.

Through the pain and panic, I glanced up when Lieutenant Happy Hands attempted to shove the table off me.

Before I could mouth "thank you," another blast rocked the building. Our eyes met and the words dirty bomb *flitted through my mind as I watched nails imbed in him, turning him into a human pincushion.*

The young flyboy dropped to his knees, blood gurgling from his mouth as he tried to speak. He fell forward, his big, heavy body landing on my legs. I reached for him, digging my fingers into the fabric of his shirt, intending to yank him away so I could finally free myself. Immediately, another bloody body riddled with shrapnel fell on top of me with enough force I felt my rib crack beneath the deadweight. Panic like I'd never experienced set in. My arms were pinned to the front of my torso as my fingers gripped a dead man's shirt.

I couldn't move at all.

I screamed until my lungs were devoid of air. I thrashed, but when I moved my head, a jagged chunk of fluorescent tubing dug into my neck, dangerously close to my jugular. Trapped like an animal. An ominous screeching followed a deafening groaning sound above me. I looked up through the haze of smoke as a steel girder splintered. Shards of metal whizzed through the air like flying razors as the remnants of the ceiling plummeted to the earth. The bodies piled on top of me took the brunt of the impact, as the roof joists bounced around me like pieces of a life-sized Erector Set.

My relief that I hadn't ended up a shish kebab was short lived. Weirdly colored flames licked across the gaping hole above me. Debris floated down. Paper of all sizes and colors swirled in an industrial blizzard. At first the flaming pieces burned to ash before they hit, dusting my face with gritty powder. But the pieces got progressively bigger and were strangely warm when they landed on my skin. I squinted through the dusty air and realized the paper had been replaced by plastic.

Chunks of plastic backing that'd been attached to insulation floated down.

The pieces were getting bigger.

And I couldn't move my head.

One piece of warm plastic landed on my lips, and I puffed out a breath. It floated away.

Okay. If I could just keep blowing away the plastic pieces, not allowing anything to cover my face, eventually somebody had to notice me. Eventually someone had to come by and rescue me, right? Firemen, police, ambulance crews, militia?

Where were A-Rod and J-Hawk?

They'd been on the dance floor when it blew up. What if they were dead, burned beyond recognition, wrapped in an eternal lover's embrace?

I couldn't think about worst-case scenarios because I was in one.

Warmth dripped down my cheek. For a second I thought I was bleeding. Maybe crying. But it wasn't tears. It was water. I squinted at the ceiling. The flames above me were now tendrils of sooty black smoke.

Oh God. They were spraying something on the fire, and it was weighting down the plastic. Now the pieces were splatting like raindrops. Sticking like glue.

No! I screamed. Stop! Turn off the goddamn water!

But no one heard me above the pandemonium.

A wet chunk splatted onto my right eye. I pursed out my bottom lip and attempted to blow upward, like I had as a girl whenever my bangs hung in my eyes. I puffed out breath after breath until I was dizzy from lack of air, but the warm plastic had molded to my forehead.

Dread and panic created a lethal cocktail, and I debated the fastest way to die. Crank my head to the side and let the glass sever my jugular? Bleeding out wasn't painful.

Was it?

Yes. I remembered the guard in Afghanistan. I sliced his throat, watching gurgling foamy blood dripping from his lips as he struggled.

Payback is a bitch, ain't it?

With half my vision compromised by the plastic molding to my forehead and eye, I didn't notice the larger chunk of plastic until the sheet covered my entire face. I gasped, allowing the warm plastic to line my mouth. The immediate suction pulled the plastic into my nostrils, too. I couldn't breathe. At all. My heart raced so fast it nearly burst.

I was suffocating.

I pushed at the plastic with my tongue. Closed my jaw and tried to grind my front teeth through it or even bite a little hole that'd allow the tiniest bit of air in.

No such luck.

I used my last breath to try to force the plastic back out, but it'd formed to my mouth like shrink-wrap.

My lungs were devoid of air. My chest felt full, yet it was empty.

My life didn't flash before my eyes, nor did a montage of my favorite memories, or a vision of unrealized hopes and dreams. No, my last thought was regret that I hadn't died in combat, in uniform, as a soldier.

My body twitched. The throbbing in my head abated. Consciousness faded. Then nothing.

I sputtered awake now, like I had then, with big gasping breaths and no freakin' clue where I was or what'd happened.

Fuck. I pushed back in the darkness of my room, heart jackhammering, blood pumping hot and fast; clammy sweat coated my brow, my neck, my chest, my belly. Even my toes were damp from pure fear.

As much as I hated combat nightmares, this one was worse.

It was a memory, not a fucked-up collection of faraway places, random body parts, death, destruction, and the graphic vileness of war. This had really happened.

I'd died.

Jason Hawley had brought me back to life. He'd dug me out from beneath the pile of bodies and debris, peeled the plastic off my face, and given me mouth-to-mouth. He returned me to the land of the living almost by sheer will.

Of course, I hadn't known any of it until days later.

For a while I'd considered calling him Jesus, secretly hoping he'd rechristen me Lazarus, but J-Hawk hadn't found any humor in it.

During my stay in the military hospital, I had plenty of time to relive that night. The term "reliving" something that'd killed me made me crazy. The army sent in shrinks to evaluate my mental state. I'd sent them away after answering the minimum number of questions. The army sent in a clergyman. I'd sent him away, too.

But he was persistent. He kept coming back until I informed him I no longer believed in God because there was no afterlife, no heaven, no hell, no nothing. In the minutes I'd been dead, I hadn't been shrouded in white mist. I hadn't felt a sense of ultimate peace. I hadn't seen the faces of my dearly departed loved ones. I hadn't heard angelic voices warning me it wasn't my time. Neither had I heard the devil's gleeful cackling. Or felt the heat from the fiery pits of hell. None of the near-death experiences I'd seen on TV or heard about was true.

Everything about the afterlife was a big, fat fucking lie.

The clergyman never returned.

I'd mostly blocked the Bali incident from my mind in my day-to-day life. But I was indebted to Jason Hawley in a way no one who'd never lived through a death experience could possibly understand. The only time we'd talked about that night, he said he saved me because he couldn't have my death on his conscience.

But now his was on mine.

SEVEN

My night had too little sleep and my morning wasn't starting out better. No coffee. I dressed in my favorite Johnny Cash T-shirt, jeans, turquoise ropers, and my ARMY OF ONE ball cap. I didn't wear a sidearm, but I brought one along.

Once I hit town, I bypassed the Q-Mart for my morning cup of coffee. Margene, a sweet-natured cashier with a mouth the size of the Grand Canyon, would grill me about finding Jason's body. I wasn't in the mood to feed her gossip hunger just to fuel my caffeine addiction.

Shocking, to see John-John's El Dorado in the parking lot of the sheriff's department. After I parked, he motioned me over, and I climbed in his passenger seat. The scent of patchouli nearly choked me. "What are you doing here?"

"You didn't get my text messages?"

I shook my head. He wouldn't find the humor in my remembering to bring a gun but not my cell phone.

His piercing gaze wasn't as unsettling as his clipped tone. "Why didn't you call me last night?"

As Clementine's owner, John-John should've been notified immediately, probably before I called 911. Chalk it up to another instance of handling things myself. "Believe it or not, I was pretty damn frazzled. I waited for the cops to arrive, and it went downhill from there."

"Downhill?" he repeated. "Tell me everything that happened after I left."

I laid it out exactly as I remembered it.

A lull filled the air. John-John's fingers tapped out the passing seconds on the steering wheel. When he finally looked at me, he was far calmer than I'd expected. "Let's go in and get this over with."

"You're coming with me?"

"Of course." His gaze dropped to my chest, and he rolled his eyes. "Really, Mercy? A FOLSOM PRISON BLUES T-shirt?"

I smiled. "Just be happy I didn't wear my I SHOT THE SHERIFF T-shirt."

Inside the reception area, a young chickie, who'd look more comfortable in a cheerleading uniform than in a county uniform, manned the receptionist's desk. Blue eyes appraised us coolly. "The entrance to the jail is around back and down the stairs. But visiting hours don't start until three o'clock."

This blond bimbo saw an Indian guy and automatically referred him to the jail? I braced my hands on her desk blotter and got right in her face. "I'm here to see Sheriff Dawson."

"And you are?"

"Mercy Gunderson. He's expecting me."

Her smooth brow wrinkled as if she should recognize the name. "Have a seat. I'll buzz the sheriff."

But I was feeling ornery and stayed put during her brief phone call. Poor little twig. Made her nervous to have me looming over her.

"Like I said, if you'll take a seat—"

"I'm fine right here."

Her berry-colored lips pursed, and she buzzed the sheriff again.

Worked like a charm. She shooed us down the hallway to Dawson's office. I wouldn't have put it past her to spray the reception area with Lysol after we left.

As acting sheriff, Dawson had taken over my father's office. I'd been in here before; heck, I'd been arrested in here before. But it was still disquieting not to see the mounted antlers for the nine-point buck my dad had shot. Or the row of family pictures. Or the expert marksmanship award certificates adorning the south wall. Certificates that'd all been mine.

Dawson stood and held his hand across the desk to John-John. "Thanks for coming, John-John."

"No problem, Sheriff."

He didn't offer me his hand, just a curt, "Miz Gunderson."

I managed not to roll my eyes at his formality. But he wasn't aware John-John knew about our playing slap and tickle; I felt a little smug in the secret.

We settled in the chairs opposite the desk. John-John spoke first. "I know it's been less than twelve hours since Mercy discovered the body, but do you have any new information?"

"Just our suspicions from last night, which haven't changed."

"What suspicions?" I asked.

"We suspect it was a robbery gone wrong."

My mouth dropped open. "Are you fucking serious?"

John-John kicked my foot to shush me.

"Yes. His wallet was gone, and preliminary tests indicate the fatal injuries were consistent with a robbery."

"A robbery. Out in the middle of nowhere? Jesus. Why didn't the would-be robbers try to rob Clementine's? There's a helluva lot more cash inside the bar than trying to roll customers in the parking lot for a few bucks. And I usually close up by myself, which isn't exactly a secret either. I can't believe—"

"Mercy," John-John cautioned. "Listen."

Dawson looked at me. "The point is, a list of who was in the bar last night, from all Clementine's employees, would help us narrow down the possible suspects."

I started to speak, but John-John beat me to the punch. "Absolutely, Sheriff. I was there for a good portion of the night, so I'll compile a list. Winona's and Mercy's lists will be more complete since they both worked a full shift."

Again Dawson's gaze pinned me. "Are you willing to cooperate, Miz Gunderson?"

I flashed my teeth at him. "Absolutely, Sheriff."

That shocked him; he'd expected me to resist. My only reason for insubordination last night? It was John-John's call whether we violated our customers' privacy, not mine. I, probably more than anyone, wanted to see that whoever killed J-Hawk was caught.

"Good to hear." He unearthed a small notebook and flipped to a clean page. "Can you tell me what happened last night? From the start of your shift up until you came across Jason Hawley's body?"

"Sure." I have an eye for detail, which Dawson had counted on. As I rambled, I figured he might get a hand cramp. Served him right. If he wanted no stones left unturned, I'd give him a rockslide of information.

But I wouldn't offer up details about my previous relationship with the victim, unless he specifically asked me.

Dawson kept writing long after I answered his last question. He paged back through his notes before tucking the notebook in his desk drawer. He addressed John-John. "I appreciate your cooperation. Let me know as soon as you've completed your lists."

"You've got it, Sheriff."

I asked, "Has the victim's family been notified?"

"Yes. They've requested immediate transport back to North Dakota."

"Is Titan Oil taking care of the costs of transporting the body? Or is the family?"

Dawson gave me an odd look. "Why does it matter?"

"It just does."

"That's a crap answer, Mercy."

Oh, so *now* he was addressing me by my first name? "Fine. You know how I feel about Titan Oil and what they're trying to do in this county. It'd reflect even more poorly on them, after they've claimed to be such a family-friendly company, if word got out that they balked at paying to send their field operative back home after he was brutally murdered while in their employ."

"How would 'word get out'?"

I shrugged. "People talk. Maybe locals will think twice about going to work for Titan Oil when it's obvious the company doesn't give a damn what happens to their employees. Maybe then they'll shitcan their plans to destroy our county and move on."

"Mercy," John-John warned.

"As far as I know, the coroner is doing the exam at Clausen's Funeral Home today, and Clausen's is transporting the body. Don't know who's paying for it."

The lighting tubes above us buzzed in the silence.

"If that's all?" John-John said.

When the sheriff nodded at John-John, we both stood.

But I had one more question. Before I could speak, my boss grabbed my elbow and hustled me out.

In the parking lot, I jerked out of his hold. "Since when do you manhandle me?"

"Since you were gearing up to spar with Dawson even though our business with him was done," he retorted.

"Maybe I just wanted to ask when it became county policy to hire a racist receptionist."

"Doll, I get treated worse than that in my own bar. Let it go." He kissed my forehead. "But, thank you, *kola.*"

"You're welcome. I'll come to the bar and get the other lists in a few hours so Dawson can get going on this case."

I stopped at Besler's grocery store and loaded up on single-girl supplies. Coffee. Soda. Peanut butter. Apples. Crackers. Batteries. On an end cap I noticed a display of Memorial Day remembrances, including a red, white, and blue stuffed frog. What the hell a puffy patriotic frog had to do with Memorial Day, I didn't know. But the bug-eyed critter was cute, and Joy might like it, so I tossed it in the cart.

My self-congratulation on avoiding eye contact with anyone was premature. Effie Markham bumped her cart into mine to get my attention.

"Why, Mercy Gunderson, I didn't expect to see you out and about after you found a man bludgeoned to death last night."

I started to correct her that J-Hawk had been shot and sliced up, not bludgeoned, but she kept talking.

"And you poor thing, finding another body. What's that? The fourth one since you've been home?"

"The third," I said tightly.

"You seem to have the worst luck." Effie leaned closer and confided, "Pity that man was murdered, but I'm not surprised. His presence was . . . unwanted, and I hope Titan Oil takes notice."

The he-got-what-he-deserved attitude wasn't new, or surprising, but it set me on edge. "Your concern is noted, Effie."

I raced to the checkout line and hoped my back-off vibe would keep other nosy busybodies at bay.

While I deposited the bags in the truck bed, my cart made

a break for freedom. A man stepped out from between two parked cars and snagged the runaway before it smashed into a Gran Torino.

The cart savior was none other than the Indian hottie who'd been drinking at Clementine's last night.

The same man Dawson snarled at for lurking around the crime scene in the wee hours.

A weird vibe rippled through me. "Who are you? And why do you seem to be everywhere?"

He shrugged. "Eagle River County is a small area."

My gaze took in his long hair, fringed leather coat, plain black T-shirt, khakis, and steel-toed boots. "Are you from the rez?"

"In a manner of speaking."

"Who are you?" I repeated.

He cocked his head. The move might've looked flirtatious, but it wasn't. His assessing eyes weren't quite threatening, but not friendly either.

My fingers curled into the metal bars of the shopping cart as I awaited his response.

Finally, he said, "My name is Shay Turnbull."

"Should I know you?"

"No." He passed me the bag from my runaway cart, quirking an eyebrow at the stuffed frog.

I didn't explain the toy was for my niece. Let him think I planned to kiss the damn thing, hoping it'd turn into a prince. "Thank you."

"You're welcome."

"I guess I'll see you around."

"Count on it." He took about ten steps and stopped, turning to look at me. "The lady in the store was right."

Jesus. Had this dude been stalking me in the store, too? "About what?"

"About your bad luck in finding dead bodies. Major Hawley won't be the last one."

"What's that supposed to mean?"

"You died, and your spirit is still drawn to death. Especially the newly dead. It's the price you pay for your life." Shay Turnbull climbed into a black Ford Explorer and drove away.

How could he know about that? And if I had the "I see dead people" vibe, why hadn't the people around me, like John-John, Sophie, and Rollie, who believed in all that cosmic mumbo jumbo, warned me?

Because you haven't told them what happened in Bali.

Halfway home it hit me: he'd called J-Hawk by his military rank.

Son of a bitch.

Groceries put away, dog fed, laundry sorted, I knew I had to quit stalling and make the damn list.

As I doodled in the margins of the notebook paper, I understood Dawson's push for detailing the information ASAP. Even twelve hours later the faces weren't as crystal clear as I expected.

I counted eight construction workers, all of whom I knew. Ditto for the pack of cowboys. Maybe a half-dozen women hung around those groups of guys. Four college kids. Lefty. Kit. Trey. Bill. Shay Turnbull. The fifteen or so campaign supporters. The two couples playing wife swap. Four two-person dart teams. Eight league pool players. With my quick calculation I'd already written down sixty possibilities.

Up front were at least ten bunco ladies. Vinnie and his six buddies. The Indian bikers, five strong, and their female companion, who'd darted in and out so I'd never gotten a good look at her. Several couples danced in front of the jukebox, but I wasn't positive they weren't part of other groups.

Plus the usual bar rats. Most of our regulars had vanished after one drink last night because "their" bar had been overrun. We'd also done a steady stream of sales with the package side. If I had to venture a guess? I'd say over 120 people partied in a building that'd been rated for a maximum occupancy of 80.

Lots of suspects.

Lots of suspects I didn't know.

Hopefully Dawson had more to go on than I did, because looking at this incomplete list, I couldn't fathom who hated Jason Hawley enough to kill him.

• • •

At Clementine's I photocopied all three lists. The originals went into a Gunderson Ranch envelope, which I sealed. I shoved the extra copies in my messenger bag.

When I turned around, John-John was in the doorway. "You're still here? Get those lists to the sheriff before he arrests us for obstruction of justice."

"You're probably safe. Although we both know he has no problem arresting me."

John-John pierced me with his schoolmarm look. "Does volunteering to take those to Dawson mean you're mending fences with him?"

"Not hardly after he took my damn gun."

He sighed dramatically. "Mercy. Doll. Dawson's not the type of guy to put up with this much longer."

"Put up with what?"

"The shot to his ego. The fact you won't publicly acknowledge there's something going on between you two. Even when the two of you fight like the dickens all the time."

"Dawson doesn't give a damn what the public knows, just as long as we keep spending private time together between the sheets," I retorted.

"Don't be so sure. He's not just the sheriff. Why do you insist on seeing him only in that role?"

"Because when it comes right down to it, especially stuff like this?"—I flapped the envelope at him—"I can't separate the man he is from the job he does."

John-John floated a deliberate pause. "Think about what you just said, Mercy."

I think I should've kept my big mouth shut.

"Dawson looks beyond what you did for a living in the army and what you do for a living now. Maybe you should do the same for him."

He turned abruptly, his braids swinging haughtily.

Petty, but I flipped him off.

While waiting for my audience with the sheriff, I asked Deputy Moore if the coroner had finished her exam, half expecting that snoopy question would get eagle-eared Dawson out of his office. But it didn't. However, she informed me that when the medical examiner from Rapid City was done, the body was being transported.

After five minutes of watching me pace in front of her desk, Kiki let me into Dawson's office. His argument on the phone escalated, but he gestured for me to stay until he finished the call. I shook my head and handed him the envelope, my mind elsewhere.

I parked down the street from Clausen's Funeral Home, where I had an unobstructed view of the back. One of Clausen's hearses was parked by the fence, which meant the other one was inside the closed doors. I sat in my truck for an hour, waiting, brooding, feeling ridiculous, when the garage door finally scrolled up.

Do it. He'd do it for you.

Scrambling out of my truck, I silently bemoaned my lack of proper attire. Major Jason Hawley deserved full military dress. As the hearse passed by me, I stood at full attention, offering my salute. I held that final salute until the hearse was a black dot on the horizon, and he was really gone.

I owed him. Finding out who'd killed him was a piss-poor way to pay him back for saving my life. But it was all I had.

Three shots later I was as ready to make the call as I'd ever be.

The stone path around the foreman's cabin was ringed with logs of varying heights and widths. Perching on two logs that formed a natural chair, I flipped open my cell phone and dialed, watching the watery beams of light contort shade and shadow.

One ring. Two rings. Three. Four. Five. I was prepared to wait until twelve, but she answered on ring nine.

"Why is it you always interrupt when I'm watching porn online?"

"You're always watching porn online, A-Rod."

She laughed. "You know me too damn well."

"Does your porn watching mean you've got home-field advantage?" Anna never liked talking about where she was. Home-field advantage meant she was in the States. Playing for the other team—our private joke since we'd fielded the are-you-a-lesbian question numerous times—meant she was somewhere else in the world.

"Yep. So why're you calling me, Gunny?"

"I need a reason to call you?"

"No. But you always do. You aren't asking about updates on the soccer team. As far as I know, the roster hasn't changed since the last time we talked."

We'd christened our elite army squad the soccer team. "Good to know. Have you talked to the coach lately?"

"No, but I checked in with the team captain last month. She said the rainy season was brutal this year."

That meant the team had been grounded, stuck at some base without new orders. "That's a shame. Hopefully they'll get to travel to an away game soon and utilize their new talent."

"As nice as it is to know that you can make idle chitchat, Gunny, cut to the chase."

My stomach twisted. And I thought I was ready for this conversation? I blew out a slow breath. "Okay. Remember the last time we talked, and I bitched about the Canadian oil company that'd been looking to put a freakin' pipeline right across my land?"

"Vaguely."

"Well, they passed the first hurdle. They sent a rep to try to convince us that millions of gallons of oil traveling underground to some refinery in Louisiana would be a great benefit to our county."

"Get to the point," A-Rod grumbled. "I don't give a damn about your land issues, because, dude, city girl here. I hate nature and shit."

"The point is . . . the rep they sent to Eagle River County? None other than Jason Hawley."

Dead silence.

"You're fucking kidding me, right?"

"Nope. Titan Oil has a base of operations in North Dakota, near Minot, and they hired him."

"When?"

"Last year. He's been making his way down the proposed pipeline route."

"Jesus. I know you and J-Hawk joked about your states being incestuous, and the normal six degrees of separation was about two degrees of separation, but that's beyond bizarre. Of all the places you guys could cross paths again . . . What are the odds?"

I swallowed a mouthful of whiskey. "J-Hawk stacked the odds, Anna; he requested to be sent here."

Her bout of silence scared me to the bone. Anna could morph from personable to stone cold in the blink of an eye.

So can you.

"And?" Anna said quietly. "Why did J-Hawk ask to be sent there?"

Like a total chickenshit, I hedged. "I think he came to collect on his debt for saving my life."

"Bullshit. He flat-out said that to you?"

"No."

"See? That's not Jason's way, and we both know it."

I bristled. "It's been what? Five years since you've seen him? Are you positive he hadn't changed?"

"Yes, because I know him down to the core. You don't have a fucking clue why he saved you in Bali, do you? I guarantee it wasn't so you'd owe him an unnamed favor that he'd have to track you down to repay."

"What are you talking about?"

"Jason saved you because he'd lost two Ranger team members in a bomb attack the year before. Why do you think he never wanted to talk about it? Why do you think he didn't strut around acting like a hero? That night in the club when he saw both you and Nigel in the rubble? It was déjà vu for him. He flipped out, Mercy. He swore you weren't dead, just playing possum—whatever the hell that meant. As soon as he had you breathing again, he wanted to work on Nigel. The rescue team had to tranq Jason to get him to stop."

"Why didn't I know any of this?"

"Because the files were sealed, remember? Any military personnel records associated with the training ops with JCET in Indonesia became classified, because we weren't supposed to be in Bali, let alone pretending to be civilians when those bombs went off in the nightclub district and at the U.S. Consulate."

Stunned by her disclosure, I was even more guilt ridden.

"So you and J-Hawk get into a pissing match or something?"

"No."

"Then why'd you call me?"

"Because he's dead." I repeated it so Anna didn't have to ask me to repeat it. "Jason is dead, Anna. That's what I called to tell you."

Soul-sucking silence descended.

With luck, I'd be drunk when Anna found her voice. I drained the bottle and tossed it aside, hearing the glass chink against the rocks.

A cough. Then her customary brusqueness. "How'd he die?"

"Anna—"

"Tell me all of it."

I spoke, stumbling over the words like I was picking my way through a minefield.

Finally, when she'd had enough, she whispered, "Stop."

Her snuffling sobs burned my ear. The tears dampening my face felt like acid rain. For several long moments, our grief tethered us.

I shivered. My vision dimmed. What I wouldn't give to pass the fuck out right about now.

Then Anna severed that bond, and she was done with sorrow. "Has he been sent home yet?"

"He went back to North Dakota today."

"Any idea on the memorial service arrangements?"

"No."

I could almost see her, phone jammed between her shoulder and her ear. Her dark brown hair obscuring her face as she loaded clips or cleaned her gun—tasks Anna could do without thinking.

So can you.

"Tell me, Gunny. What's up with you? First you skip out on fulfilling your ranching destiny, then you pick something easy like bartending?"

I understood her need to turn the tables; I'd do the same if I teetered on the verge of a breakdown. Like me, she preferred to fall apart alone—and the world outside wouldn't know.

Wouldn't ever see the gouge in her soul even when it was big enough and black enough to swallow her whole.

"I didn't skip out on ranching duties. I was forced out."

"You? Forced out? Bullshit. No one can take advantage of you without your permission. Unless you're drunk."

Heat flared in my cheeks because that was partially true. "You don't understand. Jake doesn't want me there."

"Sounds like whining to me."

I froze. "What?"

"Snap out of it. Be a rancher. Don't be a rancher. But don't sit on the fence about it. Ha-ha. Fence. Get it?"

"And how am I supposed to do that? Beg Jake to show me how to run the place I *own*?"

"That's what eats at you, doesn't it? You can't order him to fall in line. So instead of accepting that you're not in control, you slink away like a whipped pup. Put up or shut up, Gunny. Besides, why would you want to bust your ass outside every day anyway when you have someone to do it for you? Especially when you've got a sweet and easy gig like tending bar?"

"Bartending is far from easy. It's a ton of work for slave wages."

"Sounds like a government job." She laughed, and I heard her swallow. "Shit hours at a shit job that don't pay shit? When'd you turn into a martyr? Oh right, you've always been one to suffer for the cause."

"Fuck off, A-Rod."

"Think about a change of venue, Gunny. Slaughtering is slaughtering, whether it's in an abandoned oil field or out on the range. My company would hire you in a heartbeat."

"I know. But that's not the life I want."

"Don't knock it until you've tried it."

Neither of us pushed our point. I'd never sign on to be a paid killer; she didn't see a difference between working for a private "protection" company or for Uncle Sam.

"Look, two hot porn stars are waiting to get it on for me, so I'm signing off."

"You gonna be okay?"

No answer, which was my answer.

The phone went dead.

I stared ahead, tried to process the conversation. Not the parts about J-Hawk, but what Anna had said about how I'd handled the situation with Jake.

Had I misread it?

Had I become what I hated? A quitter? A . . . whiner?

Only one way to find out.

I staggered into the cabin and set the alarm for four a.m. before I let drunken sorrow drop-kick me to la-la land.

EIGHT

The sky was full-on black the next morning. No moon glow or sherbet blush of sunrise.

My brow was damp as I scaled the porch steps. Shoonga greeted me, tail wagging, tongue lolling, rubbing against me like he'd gone feline.

After I started the coffee, I fed Shoonga—outside. I gulped a glass of water, feeling like a stranger in my own house. The floorboards creaked above my head. Since the noise hadn't been preceded by a baby's cry, I bet Jake was up. I poured two cups and stifled a yawn.

Jake looked groggy as he entered the kitchen, but not particularly surprised to see me. "Mornin', Mercy."

"How'd you know it was me?"

"*Unci* ain't about to haul her carcass out of bed this early, so it was either you or a break-in. I doubted a thief would've started coffee." Jake took a big gulp of the steaming liquid and curled his hands around the mug. "What brings you by at o'dark thirty?"

"We need to talk."

"I figured."

No need to beat around the bush with Jake. "Was it all bullshit? The speech you gave me last summer about embracing my heritage and us finding a way to work together since we were both tied to the ranch? Or were you feeding me lines so I wouldn't sell?"

"No."

"What happened?"

Jake stared into his coffee cup, avoiding looking me in the eye, so I knew what he had to say wouldn't be easy for either of us to hear.

"A combination of things. I remembered something Wyatt had said to me right before he died. He warned me not to push you too hard and too fast if you returned. Said you'd burn out quickly and be full of resentment that you'd made the wrong decision."

Not the answer I'd expected, and I couldn't contain my skepticism. "Really? You just conveniently remembered that while I was gone?"

His cheeks flushed with color. "Actually, *unci* brought it up right after we'd sent the cattle to market."

I frowned. "The ones that tested negative for pregnancy, right?"

"Yep. You mentioned to her that the burdens of being barren were the same in bovines and human females—shipped off for slaughter or forced out to pasture to die alone."

Man. I did not remember saying that. "Had I been drinking?"

He nodded. "A couple days later you went off on a tangent about how you'd lost everything that'd ever mattered to you. You said you'd sunk so low as to look for life answers in manure."

"To which you responded I wasn't gonna find answers in the bottom of a whiskey bottle neither," I murmured. Some of the conversation was coming back to me. The ugly parts. Hell, knowing me, it'd probably all been ugly.

Jake drained his coffee and refreshed both our cups. He sat down and looked me in the eye. "I understand your loss. First your dad, then Levi . . ." He cleared his throat. "But then I realized you weren't only talking about human loss. You were talking about losing your career, your livelihood, losing who you were. None of us knew that side of you, Mercy, although soldiering played a big part in who you've become. I don't know what that's like. Going from being highly trained with specialized skills. Ranch work is all I've ever known. Ridin' the range. Fixin' fences. Birthing, feeding, and selling cattle. Military work is all you've ever known. And I imagine you'd be pissy if someone said your life had been a big waste of time and the skills you honed were useless. You said a trained monkey—"

"Could do your job." That jab I remembered. Guilt vibrated through me. What a drunken self-righteous jackass I'd been. In voicing my frustration, I'd leveled the biggest insult on Jake and how he'd chosen to live his life. No wonder he hadn't wanted anything to do with me. At this point I wanted nothing to do with me either.

"I ain't proud of it, but I stopped trying with you right away. I expected you'd get in my face and accuse me of bein' set in my ways, cutting you out, but you didn't. Not once."

"So you backed off completely."

"To be blunt, when you came back from the war, nothing changed for me. Stuff around here still needed done, no matter who did it. So yeah, I resented you and the luxury you had of tuning everything and everyone out."

The truth of my selfishness, meanness, and stubbornness sucked the air from my lungs.

I don't know how long I sat there, mired in flashbacks of my self-indulgent and self-delusional behavior.

Jake repeating my name brought me out of my stupor.

Embarrassed on so many levels, I don't know how I mustered the guts to look him in the eye. "Jake. I'm sorry. So damn sorry."

He studied me for several long seconds that felt like minutes. Then he said, "'Bout time," and finished his coffee. "Chores ain't gonna get done with us sitting here yakking about the past. Come on, let's get a move on."

That was that. I never appreciated Jake being a man of few words until right then.

The salmon rays of sunrise reflected off patches of dew like pink pearls. With the wet spring, the pastures were laden with newly sprouted grass. But it also meant the cow/calf pairs were relocated frequently to prevent overgrazing.

We'd taken the four-wheelers and managed to move part of the herd. One calf got tangled in the barbed-wire fence. He bleated in fear while mama kept trying to bump us out of the way so she could get to him. Be hard for her to untangle him without opposable thumbs.

Exasperated, Jake said, "Keep her away, or we're gonna lose this calf."

"How do I do that? Got a red cape handy?"

"No, and I ain't got a cattle prod either. Block her line of sight, and nudge her when she gets too close."

Nudge a fifteen-hundred-pound agitated animal? Right. I'd definitely be buying my own cattle prod. I gritted my teeth and pushed. "Come on, Bessie."

She huffed a weird noise at her baby.

I blocked her view of the calf with my body. She put her head down and butted me in the stomach. I lost my balance and almost fell into the damn fence.

"Watch it," Jake said.

I patted Bessie on the neck, slyly attempting to turn her head to the right. "Hey, look! They are some hot bulls in the next field. Man are they hung. Check it out."

That actually got a laugh out of Jake.

But Bessie? Not so amused. She flicked her tail at me with the precision of a cattle driver wielding a bullwhip. The sting could've been worse, had I been closer. I shoved her fat ass. "Knock it off, you old sow."

Finally, Jake freed the little guy. The young steer trotted after Mama into the herd. Mama, who'd been willing to take on both Jake and me mere minutes ago, now ignored her precious baby.

"Let's break for lunch," Jake said.

Back at the house, I eyed the freshly dug flower beds running the length of the porch. Sophie hadn't yet planted petunias, zinnias, snapdragons, and geraniums, but the promise of the bare dark earth bursting with blooms buoyed my mood. I wiped my feet on the welcome mat, the scents of coffee and laundry detergent teasing me through the screen door as I stepped into the kitchen.

Sophie had braced one hand on the counter and one on her hip. "I didn't know you were here."

"I've been out with Jake. He said to tell you he'll be along shortly." I chugged a glass of tap water and poured another. "How are you today?"

She shuffled to me, placing her hands on my forehead, checking for goose eggs or skull fractures. "Did you slam your head in the pickup door again?"

"You are such a riot, Sophie."

"I'm happy to see you." She patted my cheeks affectionately. "I miss you hanging around, brooding, snapping at me. You hungry?"

"Starved."

"Lucky for you I was gonna fry up some egg sandwiches."

"Sounds good." I sipped the water, noticing the quiet in the house—highly unusual with a fussy five-month-old baby. My gaze hooked Sophie's, and I lifted a brow.

"Sleeping. Both of them. Finally."

"Rough morning?"

"A rough night, according to Hope. You didn't stay here?"

And things had been going so well. "I work late nights, Sophie. Rather than get my ass chewed by my sleep-Nazi sister for waking up Joy, I crashed at the cabin."

Sophie muttered, "It ain't right."

"What?"

"You not being able to come and go in your own house."

"It's Hope's house, too," I reminded her. "As long as she's happy here, I don't mind."

"What makes you think she's happy?"

That stopped me. "She's not?"

"Ain't my place to say."

I snorted. "Since when have you ever let that stop you?"

Hope came into the kitchen with Joy cocked on her hip. As always, the pleasure at seeing my niece was laced with wariness. Ironically, the same feelings Hope brought out in me.

"Mercy. I didn't know you were here," Hope said.

"Seems to be a theme today."

Sophie said, "That nap didn't last long, eh?"

"No." Hope turned to talk to Sophie, and Joy faced me.

The one-two punch of her sweet baby face settled low in my belly. Joy's anime eyes were the same golden brown as Levi's. Her dark hair stood straight up in a funky baby Mohawk. With her chubby cheeks and perfect rosebud mouth, she epitomized adorable. Then she blinked those haunting eyes at me and gave me a drooly grin.

Damn kid was wearing me down.

"Hey, Poopy. Nice threads." Joy was dressed in the bright purple onesie I'd bought for her; it was dotted with golden crowns, the word *Princess* in fancy lettering above each tiny tiara.

She immediately screwed up her face and wailed.

Shit.

Mama Hope whirled on me. "What did you do to her?"

"Me? I just poked her in the eye a little." When my sister's mouth widened in horror, I backtracked. "Hope, I'm kidding. I did nothing. I didn't even move. Hell, I didn't really even look at her."

"Like that's something new," Hope sniffed.

I forced a smile. "You know, Sophie, thanks for the lunch offer, but I'm gonna head out. See you."

"But—" The rest of her protest was lost when the screen door slammed behind me.

I'd had my fill of overprotective mamas—bovine and human—for one day.

Seemed I was the one who needed a damn nap.

On the rare nights Dawson and I both had off, he'd show up, ply me with food, challenge me to a game of cards before we fell on each other and into bed.

Last night he'd been a no-show. On one level it bothered me; on another level I admitted Dawson had a right to his anger as much as I did. We'd always butted heads when it came to his job, or maybe my issues with the way he did his job. Since we were both stubborn, we'd need a few days apart to cool off. Not that I missed him or anything.

I'd spent the morning helping Jake and the afternoon finishing ranch paperwork. Following a supper of peanut butter crackers and an apple, I'd crawled into bed. I counted the chinks in the log walls, the ceiling, and the floor, instead of counting sheep. Damned insomnia. But I was determined not to drink myself into a coma. I'd drifted off, dreaming of a fifty-two-inch big-screen TV, when my cell phone buzzed on the pillow. "Hello?"

"Mercy? Thank God you're still up. I don't know what to do. He won't even let me see her—"

"Whoa. Slow down, Geneva. What's going on?"

"Dawson arrested Molly!"

"Where are you?"

"At the jail."

"Hold tight. I'll be right there." After three decades of rock-solid friendship, Geneva and I had hit the skids upon my permanent return to South Dakota last summer. It'd taken effort on both our parts to repair the rift, and we were almost back to normal.

Twenty minutes later, a loud argument involving a half-dozen people greeted me as I entered the sheriff's department.

"—absolutely ridiculous! This has been going on for years!" a plump redhead insisted.

I recognized her as Brenda Simmons. She'd graduated two years before me.

"Which is why it's past time it was stopped, Brenda," Dawson calmly replied.

"So rather than giving them a warning, you're throwing them in jail?"

"They're all eighteen."

Some wormy-looking guy with sandy-brown hair stepped forward. "It was sneaky as hell, how you and your deputy just waited out there in the field for them to show up."

"And when they did show up, they broke the law."

"Where's the harm?" Brenda demanded. "It's just a prank. Otis always gets his damn ugly statue back."

"That's hardly the point," Dawson said.

Geneva waved me over.

I muttered, "Who are all these people?"

"The other parents. In addition to Molly, Sheriff Dawson arrested Jaci Carr, Robby Brinkhouse, and Lyle Evans for attempted robbery and trespassing."

I whistled. "Heavy charges. What'd they do?"

"Snuck into Otis Brandhier's pasture to borrow his prairie chicken statue for graduation."

That was still an Eagle River High School tradition? I'd heeded Dad's wishes not to participate in the annual event, but he'd never taken it as a serious crime.

"Don't you think jail is excessive punishment?" BeeBee Carr

asked me. "God knows your dad never would've done anything so harsh."

I avoided meeting Dawson's eyes.

"Wyatt Gunderson isn't sheriff, and I don't give a good goddamn how you all think he'd react. If he'd nipped this 'prank' in the bud years ago, we wouldn't be standing here right now."

That shut them up.

"Look, it ain't gonna hurt any of them to spend the night in jail. Maybe next time they're tempted to instigate a dumb prank, they'll remember their stint behind bars and make a better decision."

Everyone talked at once. The verbal sparring was pointless: Dawson wouldn't budge.

Then Geneva leveled the final blow. "This is grandstanding, Sheriff. Maybe you think these pissant arrests will convince voters you're finally doing your job, but there are plenty of us in this county who know better. And guess what? We vote, too."

"And guess what else, Missus Illingsworth? You've wasted enough of the taxpayers' time by harassing me into changing my mind." His hard gaze encompassed the group. "We're done. You can bail your sons and daughters out tomorrow morning at nine a.m. Deputy Jazinski will escort you out of the building."

The beanpole deputy started herding angry parents. But Dawson said, "Miz Gunderson? A word, please?"

The parents waited, even Geneva had a hopeful look, like I could magically change Dawson's mind.

Wrong. I shook my head at her.

As soon as they were gone, Dawson said, "What are you doing here?"

"Geneva called me for moral support, you know, since I've spent time in the county slammer. She's afraid Molly will become a hard-core criminal after a single night behind bars."

No smirk. No biting remark. Were we beyond a smile or a snarky comment easing the tension between us?

"I won't apologize for doing my job, Mercy."

"You made that clear."

His focus shifted to my right cheekbone. "Jesus. Is that another bruise?"

Under normal circumstances I'd tell him about the stupid sow knocking me into the stock tank. We'd laugh. He'd tease me about being blind as a bat. But I kept the tale to myself. "Yeah. I seem to be collecting them."

"I wish you wouldn't."

We stared at each other uneasily.

I brought the conversation back around to business. "Did you get the lists?"

"Yes. I haven't had much of a chance to look at them."

"Been too busy staking out teenage pranksters?" Right after it tumbled from my mouth I knew it'd been the wrong thing to say.

His lips compressed into a thin white line. "Like I said, I won't apologize for doing my job."

"But *are* you doing it?"

Flared nostrils, clenched jaw, eyes hard as granite. I'd struck another nerve, this time intentional. "What's that supposed to mean?"

"If you've got time to waste in Otis's pasture, does that mean you've made progress on finding out who killed Jason Hawley?"

No answer. No change in his demeanor. He offered a flip "Why do you care?"

I had my answer.

"Maybe the question should be why you don't." I turned on my heel and walked out.

The parents grilled me the instant I cleared the doorjamb. I suggested that if they were worried the incident would show up on their kids' permanent record, they should head out to Otis Brandhier's place and convince him to drop the charges.

Evidently that hadn't occurred to them; they took off en masse.

I meandered through town, dwelling on what Dawson wasn't doing. It was frustrating. Dawson hadn't changed or learned from his mistakes from last year. Talk about a case of déjà vu— I'd had these exact same issues with his investigative technique last summer. It appeared that after he left the crime scene and finished interviewing the witnesses at said crime scene, he rarely followed up.

You don't know that. Maybe he's changed.

Doubtful, from what I'd seen. He hadn't even checked the lists yet. It bugged me he wasn't more concerned with a murderer running loose in Eagle River County. But not as much as my suspicion he'd dismissed J-Hawk's murder as an unfortunate accident, affecting a no-account out-of-towner that no one liked anyway. I'd expected that attitude from locals—not local law enforcement.

NINE

anch work used different muscles than running or yoga. Despite three days off from bartending, my entire body was sore. I couldn't continue closing the bar after midnight and then hauling my butt out of bed at six a.m. to start chores. So I gave notice, effective immediately after my scheduled shift. John-John took it in stride, given Clementine's increased popularity in the last month. Then again, he might've seen my resignation in a vision and already hired a replacement.

As soon as I stepped behind the bar, Winona was on me. "Did you hear? Bill O'Neil had a heart attack."

"Really? I had no idea." Bill and my dad might've had their differences, but he'd been my dad's deputy for ten years, and I was surprised no one had called us. "That's too bad. When?"

"They medevaced him to Rapid's cardiac care unit late last night."

"Any word on how he's doing?"

"Nope, but I'm sure someone who comes in tonight will know more."

Clementine's was hopping with new customers. Old customers. Package sales customers. Being busy meant time sped past, although I was glad the place emptied out at eleven-thirty.

I groaned when the door opened again at eleven forty-five as I finished closing duties. But my "We're closed" response dried up when Geneva strolled in.

"Hey. I never thought I'd see you in here."

Her wide-eyed gaze lingered on the bar's back shelves, which were lined with liquor bottles. Most bar's back shelves were mirrored, but John-John had learned the hard way that mirrors, glass, and volatile tempers were a dangerous combination in a joint like this.

"Can I getcha something to drink?"

"Diet Coke."

As I waited for her to explain why she'd shown up at Clementine's, the door opened again. Kit McIntyre headed toward us, followed by Rollie Rondeaux. Deputy Kiki Moore brought up the rear. A motley group. None of them were friends with one another, and chances were slim they'd become drinking buddies.

My heart damn near stopped. Was Kiki here on official business? Had she called Geneva and Rollie because I'd need support from my friends when she delivered bad news? "What happened? Is Hope okay?"

"Everything is fine with your family, Mercy," Kiki assured me. "But we need to talk to you about something else."

"What?"

Once they'd seated themselves on the bar stools next to Geneva, they all looked to Kit.

The white-haired pain-in-my-ass was their leader? Not good.

"As you've probably heard, Bill O'Neil suffered a massive heart attack. He'll recover, but not in the time frame needed to continue his bid for sheriff. According to state and county regulations, if a serious health issue or death prevents a candidate for running for office, the candidate's proxy can choose a substitute to run in his or her place."

"And this concerns me . . . how?"

"As Bill O'Neil's campaign manager, I'm his proxy." He preened a bit. "We're asking you to be Bill's replacement candidate, Mercy, and run for sheriff."

My jaw nearly hit the counter. "You cannot be serious."

"We wouldn't be here if we weren't."

"No."

"But you haven't heard—"

"I've heard enough. My answer is no."

"Here's your chance to help the community, Mercy, on a number of levels."

I whirled on Kiki. "By running for sheriff? Need I remind you that my dad handpicked Dawson as his replacement? So I'd be running against my father's endorsement? No thanks."

Kit leaned in. "The only reason Wyatt endorsed Dawson was because he had no one else. It'd been a different story if Wyatt had known you were coming back to Eagle River County permanently. Everyone knows Wyatt would've wanted you as his replacement."

Behind me, John-John asked, "Anyone want a drink?"

"No booze for these guys, since I'm pretty sure every single one of them is already drunk."

"Four Diet Cokes coming up."

I stared hard at Geneva. "So you're supporting Bill O'Neil for sheriff?"

Geneva wrinkled her nose. "Better him than Dawson. That man . . . Jesus, don't get me started on what's wrong with him."

Masking my response was second nature; still, Geneva's intense dislike for the man I'd been spending time with for the last few months stung a bit. But like me, she questioned Dawson on a professional level, not on a personal one. "Is Dawson doing such a lousy job?"

"He arrested you last summer. He arrested Molly and her friends. And yet he looks the other way at other things going on in this county."

"What other things?"

She waved off my question. "The point is, yes, I was supporting Bill. When Kit approached me today and brought up your name as Bill's potential replacement, I was immediately on board with you running against Dawson."

"Why? I don't have the experience in law enforcement that Dawson has."

"But you've got other qualifications," Geneva argued. "You were in the army for twenty years. That right there says discipline and commitment. Plus you've got the community dedication covered with your generational ties to the area."

Unbelievable. My head spun. How'd they come up with all this so fast?

"Can you just hear us out?" Rollie asked.

They'd hound me until I agreed to at least listen. "Fine. How would your campaign strategy for me differ from what you'd planned for Bill?"

"Besides the fact we might actually have a shot at winning?" Kit said.

Geneva hushed Kit. "The best strategy we have on the fly is playing on the fact that you're a native of this area and Dawson isn't."

"That's it? That's your reasoning behind choosing me?"

"You are your father's daughter, Mercy. That means something in this county. Don't discount it." John-John slid the lowball glasses across the counter and walked away.

Rollie's shrewd gaze watched as John-John retreated.

Kit looked longingly at the bottles of booze behind me.

Geneva reached for a straw and stirred her soda.

I decided to pick them off one by one, choosing Rollie first. "Why are you involved? You and my dad weren't exactly best buddies."

"I ain't best buddies with Dawson either. I don't know him." He offered me a challenging look. "But I do know you, Mercy. I know you have ability, and integrity, and, most important, roots here. You'd do a great job as sheriff. Not only would you try to live up to your father's expectations, you'd live up to the expectations you've always had for yourself."

Uncomfortable with any type of praise, I looked away.

Kiki fiddled with her glass and spoke without my prompting. "From the law enforcement perspective, I can tell you I loved working for Wyatt Gunderson. He taught me how to be a good, honest cop. He taught me pride isn't a bad thing when it's deserved. He was constantly striving to make us all better public servants because he never forgot who paid our salary. He was a tough man, but a fair man. He cared about people in the community. Being sheriff wasn't just his job, it was his life."

Murmurs of assent.

"I see a lot of Wyatt in you, Mercy. We all do."

My hands clenched into fists, a little appalled they were laying it on so thick with the "your father" line of guilt.

"I've embraced Dawson's way of doing things. Some I've

agreed with, some I've disagreed with, though never publicly," Kiki added.

"Why don't you step up to the plate, Deputy Moore? You have the experience and community commitment."

Kiki seemed shocked by my suggestion. "God, no. I'm a better Indian than a chief." She turned to Rollie. "Umm. No offense."

"Speaking of Indian . . . since you finally enrolled in the tribe, you'd get the Indian vote," Rollie pointed out.

"Don't discount all the people who listened to you lay into them oil people at the first town hall meeting," Kit said.

Another situation I'd found myself in that was out of my realm. But the underhanded way Titan Oil set up the meeting with the affected landowners, during calving season, had made me see red.

And why had this call to duty happened now? Despite their claims that I'd be a chip off the Wyatt Gunderson block, Dad had never said he wanted me to follow in his footsteps for law enforcement. He'd wanted me to follow in his footsteps and keep the ranch alive.

He did both, why can't you?

Could I see myself slipping on the uniform and the ugly hat every morning? Strapping on my gun and a set of handcuffs? Hadn't I just left that regimented life?

"You running for sheriff shows the whole county you care, Mercy," Geneva said.

Kiki said, "I know your dad would be behind you."

"You'd be good for the community," Kit added.

"And this would be good for you," Rollie said.

"You've given her enough to think about." John-John's gaze darted between them. "Mercy doesn't have to decide at twelve-thirty after she's worked a full shift. When do you have to have her answer?"

"We've got forty-eight hours to find a replacement."

"Why so fast?" I asked.

"The ballots are scheduled for printing in three days, according to the county regulations for providing absentee ballots."

"Well, then she has some time to think it over." John-John set his hands on my shoulders. "Get your stuff and go on home, doll.

I'll close up and keep your wannabe campaign managers occupied until you're gone."

"That's not necessary."

"It is. You've had enough shitty things happen to you in the parking lot of this bar. You don't need harassment from your *friends* added to the list."

I kissed John-John's cheek and whispered, "Thank you."

As I putted home in the old ranch truck, I wished I'd driven my Viper. I had the overwhelming urge to drive as fast and as far away from Eagle River County as I dared.

My headlights reflected off Dawson's truck parked under the carport, and I wondered if I was hallucinating.

Or maybe I was sacked out in my bed in the middle of a bizarre nightmare. My friends and enemies conspiring to get me to run for sheriff against the man sharing my bed?

Had to be an alcohol-fueled dream.

But after I hopped out of the truck and caught a whiff of Dawson's aftershave, my belly swooped. We hadn't spoken since the night he'd arrested Molly, and I was ridiculously happy he'd made the first move.

Then my happiness dimmed. Had he gotten wind of Bill O'Neil's campaign workers' plans for me? I braced myself, not for his sexy, hey-baby, wanna-get-lucky smile, but for accusations. Anger. Harsh words.

Dawson just said "Hey" from where he'd sprawled in the chaise longue, Shoonga snoozing at his feet.

"Kinda late for a social call, isn't it?"

"Not for us."

"True. You been here long?"

"About fifteen minutes. Shoonga clawed at the door, so I let him out. I stuck around to ensure he didn't run off."

I knocked my knee into his. "So you're my petsitter now?"

Dawson shook his head. "You really should lock your door."

"Worried about my safety, Sheriff?"

"No. I'm worried about someone breaking in and stealing your massive gun collection."

"The guns are locked in the gun case at the ranch."

He squinted at me. "All of them?"

"Should I include the one you confiscated in my official count?"

"Smart-ass. That gun wasn't used in the crime at Clementine's."

He'd known that when he'd taken it, and he'd still taken it. "Is that why you're here? To tell me I've been cleared as a suspect?"

A scowl crossed his face. "No, that's not why I'm here. But you can come by the station and pick it up tomorrow if it'll make you happy."

"Finally. I've been missing that piece something fierce. It's my favorite small cal handgun." The clip on the Kahr Arms P380 wasn't much bigger than a cigarette lighter. It didn't have much stopping power, but it was cute. In a deadly sort of way.

"They're all your favorites," he said dryly. "So are your firearms locked up?"

"All but four."

"You keep four guns . . ." His gaze lingered on some highly improbable hiding spots on my body. "Where?"

"One on my person, one in my truck, and two in the cabin." Sometimes two on my person, but I didn't share that tidbit. I added, "But I did leave my Taurus in the truck when I saw you were here."

"You scare me sometimes."

"It's part of my charm."

His rich, warm laughter loosened the tension. When he tugged me until I sat crossways on his lap, I didn't resist.

Dawson wasn't a snuggler, nor did he give casual affection easily—a trait we shared. So his action left me more unbalanced than if he'd yelled at me. Yelling, I could handle just fine. Snuggling? Not so much.

Maybe he thought it'd be easier to ask about my potential candidacy if he didn't have to look me in the eye. Or maybe he planned to ask about my past with J-Hawk.

Or maybe he just wants to sit outside with you on a starry spring night.

I wasn't sure I bought that argument, but I went with it anyway. I nestled my cheek against his neck and curled my body into his. Absorbing his heat. Sucking up his sweet side like candy.

We stayed locked together for a nice long while, existing in the same space without antagonism, mistrust, or the ulterior motives that sometimes clouded our alone time.

When I squirmed to get more comfortable, he sighed. "I bet you sucked at staying in stealth positions for very long."

"Why?"

"'Cause you're wiggly as a worm."

"I'm not used to sitting on your lap," I retorted.

"And that's a damn crying shame."

I elbowed him lightly in the gut. "Smart-ass. FYI: I once hid in a ghillie suit, flat on my belly, in the freakin' desert, for thirteen hours straight."

"Impressive." His lips brushed the top of my head in a move that was both sweet and seductive. He did it twice more.

Was he building up to the question by softening me up?

I veered the conversation a different direction. "Tell me something about you that I don't know, Dawson."

His body stiffened, and not in a good way. "Why?"

Because tit for tat. If you share something with me, I'll share my oh-so-interesting chat with Bill O'Neil's campaign committee with you.

"Mercy?"

"Because we're either fighting or fucking, and there's a lot I don't know about you."

"There's a lot you haven't *wanted* to know about me," he corrected.

"So here's your chance, Dawson. Talk to me. Tell me something juicy."

Dawson toyed with my hair, a sure sign he was deep in thought. "This is a whopper of a secret. You sure you're ready?"

No. "Yep. Unless it's something kinky, like you're into submission games."

"That'd be an easier confession if it were true."

Maybe this game of secret swap hadn't been such a hot idea.

He inhaled. Exhaled. "I have an eleven-year-old son."

I remained curled into him, listening to the increased tempo of his breathing. Waiting.

"Ain't much to tell, to be honest. His mother was a cocktail waitress at the bar where I moonlighted as a bouncer in Minnesota. She moved away, and I became a cop. End of story, right? Five years later she informed me via legal summons that I'm a father and demanded child support. I called bullshit, but the paternity test confirmed that I am, indeed, this boy's father."

A secret love child *was* a whopper of a secret. "Do you share custody or anything?"

"No. I see him maybe twice a year, for a day at the most. Mona doesn't encourage it, and he's shown little interest in me, no matter how much interest I show in him."

That made my insides ache. "Where does he live?"

"Denver."

"Is that why you moved out here?"

"Yeah. I thought if I was closer, maybe we'd connect or some-thing . . . but it hasn't changed a goddamn thing."

I thought of Jake. Even though Levi hadn't known Jake was his father, Jake had gotten to watch Levi grow up. That's more than Dawson was getting. "What's his name?"

"Lex. Lex Pullman, not Lex Dawson. Seems pointless to talk about him, when there ain't anything to talk about, know what I mean?"

I adjusted my position so I faced him.

His eyes searched mine. "You're taking this well. It doesn't freak you out that I hadn't told you before now?"

"No. If you don't hold it against me that I can't reproduce, then I figure I can't hold it against you that you have." I maneu-vered him closer until we were mouth-to-mouth, wanting to end this conversation.

Wasn't the whole point of this "sharing" exercise so you could come clean about the campaign committee before he heard it from someone else?

Damn conscience. I eased back only far enough to speak. "Dawson, I should tell you—"

"It'll keep." He fed me those drugging soft-lipped kisses I craved. "Now can we go inside before I freeze my ass off?"

I tried one last time. "Don't you want to talk—"

"No talking, because if we talk, we'll fight. And I don't want to fight with you tonight."

"We do get into less trouble when talking isn't on our minds at all," I murmured against his throat.

"See? We can agree on something." Dawson carried me inside and locked the door.

I rolled out of bed three hours after Dawson left. I'd needed the intimacy of connecting with him, a man whose baser instincts matched mine, yet it'd muddied the waters, regarding my choice to let the campaign committee run me as a replacement candidate.

Phrased that way it seemed less my decision.

But my cynical side suspected Dawson had shown up, acting sweet, loving, spouting the "I don't want to fight" line, knowing full well I'd been asked to run against him.

Would that bother me if it were true?

Not as much as it'd bother me if Dawson had shown up, acting sweet and loving, spouting the "I don't want to fight" line because he hadn't known I'd been asked to run against him.

What if Dawson *hadn't* been making a political maneuver by using our sexual relationship to confuse me? What if he'd shown up because he'd . . . missed me? Was it time that I owned up to the fact that we were involved on a deeper level than just casual sex? Probably. I wasn't exactly sure how to go about it.

I ended up at the sheriff's office, telling myself it was only to pick up my gun. Not to look for a sign. Not to go googly-eyed over the man who'd rocked my world and had finally opened up to me.

Jolene manned the front desk, not Robo-Barbie. Dawson had stepped out, but she told me to hang out in his office—a natural reaction after all the years she'd sent me back to wait for my dad.

With time to kill, I examined Dawson's meager personal effects. A framed commendation and a silver star from the president of the United States for bravery, valor, and service in Desert Storm. A diploma from a vo-tech school in Minnesota for his law enforcement degree.

I stopped in front of the last item on the wall; a sizable shadowbox. Inside was a gigantic fancy silver-and-gold championship belt buckle with a hand-tooled brown-and-black leather belt, from the PRCA Midwest Circuit, for first place in bull riding, inscribed to *Mason "Mad Dog" Dawson*. Alongside the buckle was a picture of a much skinnier, much younger cowboy, wearing chaps, a neon-green western shirt with red flames on the sleeves, holding the buckle, almost with a look of surprise on his lean, handsome face.

With my propensity toward picking cowboys, if Mad Dog and I had crossed paths in our younger years, would we've given each other a second look? Was part of the reason we ended up together now because neither of us had a better option?

Such a cynic.

I wandered to the chairs across from his desk. The same desk my dad had used, but neater. The out-box was emptied. Campaign promotional materials were strewn across the surface. Notes scrawled in a spiral-bound notebook sat directly below the phone. I told myself it'd be wrong to snoop so I plopped into the chair on the right side of the desk.

And that's when the in-box caught my eye, seemingly empty, save for one envelope. A familiar envelope. The envelope I'd dropped off at Dawson's request.

A solid minute passed. I don't think I blinked as I stared at that envelope.

Maybe he kept it there for quick reference.

My hand was in the basket before I'd thought it through.

Heart pounding, I flipped over the plain cream-colored envelope with the Gunderson Ranch logo in the upper-left-hand corner. The envelope I'd personally sealed.

Almost a week ago.

The fucking thing hadn't been opened at all.

Oddly, red rage didn't consume me. I was plenty mad, but the feeling that followed on the heels of disbelief was worse than blind fury.

Disappointment.

In him. In myself.

Had I really believed Dawson would do his job? It was obvious he hadn't. Every doubt I'd ever had about him resurfaced.

His heavy tread stopped behind me when he saw the envelope in my hand.

"Mercy?"

I very carefully replaced the letter where I'd found it. My resolve helped me get to my feet and face him.

Something—regret or guilt—flashed in his eyes, and then it vanished. He sidestepped me and skirted his desk. I heard his chair squeak as he sat. I heard him sigh. What I didn't hear? An explanation. An apology.

An excuse?

There was no excuse. I let him stare at the rigid line of my back for another minute before I whirled around.

"Why are you here?"

"To pick up my gun and to tell you that Bill O'Neil's campaign committee asked me to run as his replacement candidate."

No change in his expression. "And what did you say?"

"Yes." My gaze swept his office before my eyes caught his. "Don't get too comfy here, Sheriff."

I spun on my heel and walked out.

TEN

Geneva dragged me to the courthouse to officially verify my candidacy. One of my stipulations for running was working with her for this campaign, not Kit.

An hour later we sat in the Blackbird Diner, poring over preliminary campaign strategy. She counted off the talking points on Bill's election platform.

"How do you feel about the county commissioners slashing the emergency services budget by ten percent?"

"Pissed off."

She rolled her eyes. "Language. Remember, no one likes a gutter mouth."

Stupid double standard. Dawson could say pissed off, and he'd be lauded as a "straight talker," whereas I'd be called a gutter mouth. I slapped on a beauty contestant smile. "I'm upset with the commissioners shortsightedness. Injuries and tragedies don't cease because we don't have the money to properly deal with them."

"That's good, keep going."

"In a rural area, especially in a county our size, we should be increasing the amount of money on a yearly basis, rather than slashing it, forcing us to rely on other counties' emergency services to fill our needs."

"Excellent. Next question. The pipeline."

"Against it."

"Care to elaborate?"

"You want me to go off on a tangent about eminent domain? The company is planning to go to the governor, knowing he'd side with them and grant it. Then there'd be a slew of condemnations in the courts. Titan Oil's using other scare tactics to get ranchers on board. Or should I deliver the even more dire news that as long as Titan Oil complies with every step of the regulatory process, and gets the proper permits from the DOT, the EPA, the PUC, the DENR, and finally that all-important presidential permit from the State Department, there isn't a single thing we can do? And if the pipeline fails and there's a spill, the landowner's on the hook for the cleanup because the state's thrown away everybody's rights for a few tax dollars?"

She tapped her pen on her notebook. "Okay. It's great you're up to speed on this issue. But right now, I'm not sure if the brutal truth is the best option."

"Or I could go with the optimistic idea that we should be looking for alternative energy resources indigenous to our part of the world, like wind and solar power? And we can all hope that the president will refuse to sign the State Department permit, tabling the issue, at least until there's a new bunch in Washington."

"Better. So let's skip to . . . your qualifications."

"Twenty years' military service. Daughter of the sheriff who held the office for almost thirty years. I've had personal experience with violence directed toward my family and me, so community safety is my primary goal. And I'll use all the resources at my disposal to solve the crimes that come across my desk. None are too big or too small."

"Now that sounds like a candidate we can sink our teeth into, eh?" Rollie scooted in the booth next to Geneva. "Whatcha ladies doin'?"

"She's grilling me on my platform."

He peeked at Geneva's notebook from beneath the brim of his dirty, stained, crumpled PI hat. "Don't see nothin' on there about race relations."

"I was getting to it." Geneva looked at me expectantly.

"What?"

"Race relations."

"I don't got no Indian relations I can race, hey. And I'd probably lose because them injuns run fast, *whoo-ee*."

Geneva whapped me on the arm. "Don't joke about stuff like that, Mercy. You're liable to get hung."

"Or scalped, eh?" Rollie winked at me.

She whapped Rollie on the arm, too. "Don't encourage her."

"I'd be a lot more encouraged if I could have my pie now."

"Fine. Stuff your face. I need to call Brent anyway." Geneva slid closer to the wall, cell phone trapped against her ear.

The waitress brought out two pieces of warm rhubarb cream pie. I ate mine like I eat everything—super fast—and watched Rollie savor every bite. He pushed his plate back and squinted at me.

"What?"

"Gonna tell me what's on your mind, Mercy girl?"

I glanced at Geneva, still chattering on the phone. "Besides the fact I'm now a candidate for sheriff?"

"That ain't what's eatin' at you."

The doorbell chimed. When Rollie looked up to see who'd entered the diner, his brown eyes turned flat and cold.

He scooted out of the booth. "Think about it. I'll catch up with you later, hey."

What was up with the hasty retreat? I peeked over my shoulder to see who'd caused Rollie to turn tail and run.

Shay Turnbull sat at the lunch counter.

Geneva clicked her phone off and nudged a stack of papers toward me. "Here's your homework. Go over it thoroughly. We'll powwow tomorrow morning at the conference room in the library, okay?"

"Fine. Sure. Whatever." What the hell was Shay Turnbull doing here?

Geneva leaned across the table to ensure she had my full attention. "You're doing the right thing. You'll make a great sheriff, Mercy. Your dad would be proud." Pep talk over, she sailed out the door.

I picked up my coffee cup and snagged a chair next to Turnbull. "Mitzi, could I get a refill?"

"Sure, sweetie."

Turnbull didn't look up from his newspaper when he said, "Some of us are offended by the use of the term *powwow* in that context."

"And some of us aren't."

"I forget you're Indian." He folded his newspaper and faced me. "So. I hear you're running for sheriff."

"Didn't anyone tell you it's impolite to eavesdrop?"

"Oh, I didn't hear it from listening to your conversation; I heard it at the post office about an hour ago."

"You're quite the man about town."

"Like I said before, Eagle River County isn't exactly a metropolis. So tell me, candidate Gunderson, what will you do differently as sheriff if you're elected?"

"I'll pursue every lead on a case, no matter how insignificant it might seem."

"Even if there are extenuating circumstances?"

Puzzled by his cryptic comment, I looked at him. "If a crime occurs in the county, it's the job of the sheriff's department—specifically, the sheriff—to investigate to the end. Period. Extenuating circumstances have nothing to do with it."

Mitzi appeared, setting a white bakery bag and a Styrofoam cup in front of him. "That'll be three dollars and eighteen cents."

Turnbull passed her a crisp five-dollar bill. "Keep the change."

"Thank you."

He smiled, showing beautiful, straight white teeth. "You're welcome." He slid on his shades, grabbed his food, and stood. "See you around, Mercy."

I don't know what I'd hoped to accomplish with him, but that sure as hell wasn't it.

Hope, Jake, and Sophie ambushed me the second I walked into the kitchen.

"You're running for sheriff in Bill O'Neil's place?" Hope demanded. "And you didn't think to tell your family?"

Jake stared at me coolly, yet I could read him as clearly as if a cartoon bubble bounced above his head: *You lasted less than a week a rancher. I can't count on you.*

Sophie came to my defense. "Leave her be. I'm sure Mercy had a good reason for keepin' it to herself."

I dropped into the closest chair. "The campaign committee only asked me last night. I was almost certain I'd tell them no today."

"What happened to change your mind?"

"I stopped in the sheriff's office, looking for a sign from Dad, or any kind of sign, really." I let my gaze wander to THE BUCK STOPS HERE plaque that'd always hung next to the sink. "When I was in Dawson's office, I saw something that changed my mind. So in some ways it was a spur-of-the-moment decision."

"And in other ways, it was what you were always destined to do," Sophie said.

Was Sophie pleased or appalled by the prospect?

"Let's celebrate." Sophie dished up spice cake with maple frosting. Pie for breakfast. Cake for lunch. If I continued to stuff my face like this, I'd need to add more miles to my PT.

"Well, it's good you're here, because we need to talk," Hope said.

I scraped the last of the cake crumbs onto my fork before I looked at my sister. "About?"

"About me—us—moving out."

Jake froze. Sophie froze. Evidently this was news to them.

"Where would you go? You sold your trailer. The cabin is too small for all three of you to live in."

Hope's chin lifted; her eyes gleamed defiance. "Iris Newsome's house has been sitting empty since we bought their land the first of the year."

I couldn't look at Jake. I knew he wasn't looking at me.

"It's a perfect solution," Hope pointed out. "You can move back in here all by yourself, which is what you want. This place has always been more yours than mine."

"That's not true."

"It is, especially since you redecorated the downstairs. It's like I've been living in a stranger's house."

Ooh. That stung.

"Iris's place is close, and it won't affect Jake's foreman duties."

My gaze collided with Jake's. "Did you know about this?"

"No." Angrily, he pushed his chair back. He shot Sophie a dark look. "Was this your idea?"

Her black eyes snapped fire. "I will caution you to watch your tone, *takoja*."

Jake was beyond upset. With good reason.

Hope had just opened a big ol' can of worms. She had no idea our neighbor Iris Newsome had actually killed Levi, not Hope's dead ex-lover Theo, as I'd sworn in a courtroom.

As much as I dismissed that evil-spirit crap, Iris's house pulsed with malevolence. Hoping to exorcise the demons, I'd hired an auction company to sell every last piece of the Newsome's household belongings. When I had to sign off on the contents, requiring another inspection of the empty house, anger and bitterness still clouded the space.

"Hope," Jake said her name as a weary sigh. "Can we wait and talk about this later in private?"

"No. I'm tired of waiting. I want my own house again. As half owner of this ranch, I'm also half owner of the Newsome place. So I'm moving into that house, whether or not *any* of you like it."

The emphasized *any* was directed at Jake, not me. Had Hope brought up this crazy idea with him before?

Didn't matter. Any negative comment would cement the idea in Hope's head. We all had to tread lightly.

"I don't think you understand that you can't just pack your shit and move in. Especially with a baby."

"Why not?"

My eyes narrowed at her. "How many years has it been since you've been in that house?"

"A long time," she snipped, "but that's not the point. You're just trying to keep me here."

"Hope. Listen to your sister," Sophie cautioned.

As always, Hope listened to Sophie. "Fine. Tell me how stupid I am, Mercy."

I ignored her taunt. "When the auctioneer came by with the appraiser, they said the house needed major updates. Not just cosmetic, but structural."

"Like what?" she asked petulantly.

Jake paced to the sink and rested his backside against it. Arms folded. Legs crossed at the ankles.

I continued to detail the issues. "The porch sags because of water damage to the cellar. Which also means the foundation is cracked from one end of the house to the other. The heating and electrical systems haven't been updated since the Newsomes moved in forty years ago. Some of the windows are painted shut. The ones that aren't painted shut won't open because of the foundation settling."

"So? This house isn't perfect either, Mercy."

"If it's so bad here, why haven't you left it more than ten times in the last four months?"

"That's not fair."

"But it's true. You've been so protective of Joy that you rarely take her out in public. Yet you'd drag her to a drafty old farmhouse with all sorts of serious problems and health risks to both of you . . . just to get away from me? Or to prove a point to me?"

Hope pressed her cheek to the top of Joy's head, and a tear slid free. "I knew you wouldn't understand."

How many times had I heard that accusation? How many times had I fallen for the tears and the woe-is-me routine? Too many. But this time, I would not succumb.

"I knew you'd be like this," she said with a bitter edge.

"Like what?"

"Pretending we're all one big happy family when we're not. How long did you last with all of us living together? Two months. Then you lit out for the cabin and haven't looked back. You lasted barely a month working with Jake. But you've had no problem working at Clementine's for several months. What is the draw? Free booze? Oh right, we all know how much you drink, but God forbid we ever say anything to piss off Mercy the almighty."

"Hope. That's enough," Sophie snapped.

But Hope didn't listen to Sophie for a change. "No. It's time to get it out there instead of letting it fester. Are you running for sheriff because of Daddy? How do you think he'd feel that you were blowing off your responsibilities to the ranch *again*?"

Hope knew right where to strike. I took the hits like a soldier. Bleeding and howling inside, but outwardly, standing strong, tall, proud, and bulletproof. Because no matter how hard she cried, no matter how many foul words about my character fell from her mouth, no matter how many accusations she lobbed at me, there was no way in hell I'd ever let my sister or my innocent niece live in that hate-haunted house. Ever. I'd die first.

In order to protect her, I had to go into full retreat. Appear contrite, appear to be giving in to her. In short, lie my ass off while I reconfigured my strategy. I softened my tone. "Look, Hope. I want you to be happy. But rushing into this isn't the answer either."

"But I'm not rushing into it. I've been thinking about this ever since the day we signed the papers buying the Newsome place."

Jake and Sophie exchanged a look.

"Tell you what, sis. I know a couple of guys, Clementine's regulars, who run their own construction business. Maybe they can look at the property and give us an idea on what it'd take, dollar-wise, to make the structure habitable."

Hope's head came up. She stared at me, eyes liquid, lower lip quivering. "Seriously? You'll do that?"

Fuck no. "Sure. But it'll be preliminary. There is no guarantee what they find will change anything."

"I understand that. But if it's about money, I have some left over from selling the trailer, and I'm sure Jake is willing to pitch in."

Not a question for Jake, but a statement.

"If we get the go-ahead, and the repairs are affordable, can we start fixing it up right away?"

"Absolutely," I lied.

"Oh, this is the best news!" Petulant Hope vanished. Hope the conqueror beamed sunshine at Jake. "I know we didn't talk about this, but it'll be a good thing for all of us. A fresh start."

Jake couldn't muster a smile. Not even when he reached out and played with Joy's tiny sock-clad foot.

"I'll get her ready for her bath," Hope announced, and flounced upstairs, jabbering away to her baby.

"Ah. I'll help her," Sophie said, and scurried out.

Neither Jake nor I spoke.

Jake's hands tightened on the back of the chair. His voice was barely a whisper. "I can't do it. I can't live there. I just . . . can't."

"I know, Jake." I had half a mind to squeeze his shoulder. Offer him reassurance. But actions spoke louder than a pansy-assed gesture. "Don't worry, I'll take care of it."

"How?"

"Do you really want to know?"

Took about ten seconds, but Jake shook his head and walked off.

Hope would get suspicious if a tragedy befell the Newsome house the very day she'd announced her intention to inhabit it. I'd give it another day.

Looked like John-John's vision was about to come true after all.

In the meantime, I hit the ground running investigating J-Hawk's murder. I locked myself in the office and took out the three lists I'd photocopied. Winona's was the most detailed. I cross-checked the customers' descriptions I'd jotted down. When an hour passed and I hadn't made progress, I realized I'd have to ask for help deciphering the names. Hopefully Winona wouldn't ask how I'd gotten ahold of a list that was supposed to be confidential.

The parking area at Clementine's was deserted, except for Winona's rusted-out Toyota Camry and John-John's El Dorado.

But John-John wasn't behind the bar; Muskrat was.

His eyes lit up. "Have mercy."

Before I braced myself, Muskrat picked me up in a bone-crushing hug. When he set me down, I wheezed, "That couldn't have been good for your back."

Muskrat scowled. "John-John oughten been telling you stuff like that about me."

"He was worried." I straightened the collar on his plaid shirt. "And he didn't tell me anything you wouldn't have told me if you'd been around."

He grunted.

"Where's Winona?"

"Taking a smoke break. Why?"

"I need to talk to her."

"Pull up a stool while you're waiting. You want a drink?"

"A Coke." As long as there weren't customers around, I spread the lists out on the bar.

"What're those?" Muskrat asked.

"The lists Dawson asked for, detailing who was in here the night Jason Hawley was killed. I don't know everyone, so I'm trying to figure out who was who."

"Why?"

"Because Dawson isn't doing dick on this case."

"So as the new candidate for sheriff you trying to solve the case and show him up?"

"The news already spread out here?" Another thought occurred to me. "Or did John-John have a vision about it?"

"No, he was here when the campaign committee asked you to fill in, remember?"

"Yeah, but I intended to say no."

"But you didn't say no. You said yes." Muskrat pointed to the lists. "Mind if I take a look?"

"Please." I cross-referenced and jotted down observations, Muskrat's mostly, which proved enlightening.

"What about Vinnie? Or any of his buddies? You've known them longer than I have. Vinnie and Jason did get into it that night."

"Vinnie is on parole. His parole officer shows up in here from time to time to keep an eye on him. And if I'm right"—he pointed to another name I hadn't recognized—"this Brad dude is Vinnie's voice of reason."

"I'll bet that's the guy who kept Vinnie from jumping in."

"Probably. If Vinnie gets another violent offense on his record, they'll throw Big Bertha at him."

"Big Bertha" was slang in law enforcement for the three-strikes rule. A fourth felony conviction in the state meant you'd be a permanent guest at the penitentiary in Sioux Falls.

Muskrat tapped a finger on Trey's name. "I'm surprised he ain't at the top of your list."

"Asshole. I wish I could just shoot him and be done with it. Part of me believes Trey could've had a hand in Jason's murder. But a larger part of me can't find the motive."

"You really are taking this investigative angle seriously."

"I have to since Dawson isn't." I scratched at Trey's name, as if it would erase him from existence. "See, Trey is lazy. Shooting and stabbing someone takes effort. There'd have to be monetary

gain for him. Although Trey works for Kit, I don't see Kit order-
ing the hit." I also knew Trey couldn't keep his mouth shut. He'd
need to brag to someone that he'd offed Jason.

Winona joined us, and we batted possible suspects back and
forth. Muskrat tapped the last question marks on my list. "These
guys are bad news, Mercy."

"You know them?"

"By the description of their jackets. Lone eagle feather dipped
in blood? That's Sarohutu's bunch."

I frowned. "Eagle feather? That mean they're from the Eagle
River rez?"

"Based out of there, but yeah, they're on all the reservations."

"But he sounds Japanese."

"He is. Half. Sarohutu's mother was Lakota. A Japanese doctor
on an exchange program on the rez knocked her up and left the
country before Barry was born."

"Barry Sarohutu?"

"He goes by Saro."

"Does his group have a name?"

"Nothin' official like the Banditos, or the Hombres. They're
into the same illegal shit as those other clubs. Biggest cash enter-
prise is drugs; they run every bit of the drug trade around here.
They're also in the sex trade. Buying and selling stolen stuff—
everything from cars and government commodities to artifacts.
But they're also security for several Indian casinos, and they
employ Indians to rip off tourists for authentic Indian experiences, like sweat lodges and spirituality quests." He shook his
head. "I ain't happy they've started coming in here."

From behind me, Winona said, "Luckily for us they've only
been in four or five times in the last couple weeks."

"They must've come in on my days off." Except for the night
J-Hawk was killed.

"If we tell them they ain't welcome, they'll retaliate."

I compared the lists again. "Is that why John-John didn't write
that group down?"

"Probably."

"Those are the guys you didn't want to wait on," I said to
Winona. "The finger snappers."

"I'd rather spit on 'em than wait on them. My cousins on Rosebud said even the tribal cops have a hard time dealing with them."

Was that why Dawson hadn't run an investigation? But without looking at the lists, Dawson wouldn't have known who'd been in the bar that night. Scratch that excuse.

Muskrat's eyes, body, voice turned menacing. "Steer clear of them, Miz Mercy."

Fat chance. "That's weird. I know there was a woman along, but I don't see her name listed."

Winona opened her mouth. Closed it. Slightly shook her head. She knew which woman I meant. She'd tell me—just not in front of Muskrat.

I changed tactics. "What about Rocky and Mike? Think they could've lain in wait for Jason outside and finished what he'd started inside?"

"No. If they'd been gunning for anyone, Mercy, it woulda been you. You showed 'em both up in front of the entire bar."

Somebody in the bar had to have seen something. It was just figuring out who, by process of elimination.

Now I had the perfect excuse to canvass the entire county and its residents to find answers. I drained my Coke. "Thanks for the help."

"Where you goin'?" Muskrat asked.

"To hit the campaign trail."

ELEVEN

Five of the guys on the list in Rocky's group lived around Flat Bluffs, ten miles up the road from Clementine's. Few locals kept their address and phone numbers unlisted, so matching names with addresses was easy.

Rocky Blount lived in a 1970s split level next to the lone ball field in Flat Bluffs. One big Dodge Cummins diesel was parked on the concrete slab next to a Dodge minivan.

I smoothed my hair and climbed out of my truck, practicing my campaign spiel. Then I knocked on the door.

"Mercy?" Rocky squinted at me. "What the devil are you doing here?"

"Campaigning. I'm running as the replacement candidate for Bill O'Neil for Eagle River County sheriff."

His bushy black eyebrows lifted. "You don't say."

"So I thought I'd come by and see if I can count on your support."

"I thought maybe you'd come by to apologize."

"Yeah, things did get a little out of hand that night, but you weren't exactly blameless, Rocky. You punched me in the head."

"It happens. But you can be damn sure I ain't gonna tear it up when you're on shift, again. Man, you've got a mean jab."

"Don't know if I oughta take that as a compliment." I acted hesitant, hoping it'd convince him to talk. "You know I found Jason Hawley later that night, right? It freaked me the hell out." I paused again, glancing around. "I've gotta ask. Were you freaked out that only a few hours after your tussle with him he wound up dead?"

Rocky nodded. "Guy was an asshole. But killed like that? Just ain't right."

"I don't suppose you paid attention to who he talked to in the back room before the fight?"

"Nah. I was pretty drunk, which is probably why I opened my mouth. And started swinging. Roger drove us home, maybe ten minutes after the fight. But Mike might remember." Rocky realized I'd led him away from my supposed campaign visit. His gaze turned sharp. "What's with all the questions?"

"Between us? I'm doing a little investigating on my own on this case. I wanna prove I have the chops, know what I mean?"

"Absolutely."

"Whoever did this needs to be behind bars. I'll be damn tough on crime if I'm elected." *Oh gag.*

"You've got my vote."

I thrust out my hand. "Thanks, Rocky. I appreciate it. If you remember anything else from that night, call me."

To keep up the campaigning pretense, I walked to his neighbor's house. The little white-haired lady next door was mean as an old mule. She told me to leave men's work to men and slammed the door in my face. I took the high road and didn't kick over her stupid garden gnome.

I visited the last two houses on the block, to lukewarm responses. Next time, I was bringing candy.

But I wasn't disheartened enough to skip Mike Aker's house. By the time I'd reached the end of his long driveway, he stood on the front steps.

I climbed out and smiled at him. "Mike."

"Mercy. Already hitting the campaign trail?"

"Yep. I have to make up some serious ground. I assume Sheriff Dawson has been out here?"

"Not as far as I know."

There was my opening. "See, that's why I'm making the effort to reach out to all voters, not just the ones within the city limits. Anyway, during my stop in Flat Bluffs, I ended up talking to Rocky about the night Jason Hawley died. Rocky said Jason was in the back room before the fight went down. Did you see who he was talking to?"

Mike scratched his chin. "Yeah, now that you mention it, I did see him talking to George Johnson and a couple of them construction guys. They didn't look none too happy with him."

"Why?"

"Don't know. But George would tell ya. He didn't like that oil guy neither."

The screen door opened. A stout woman half Mike's age emerged. "I thought I heard you talking to someone."

I offered my hand. "Mercy Gunderson."

"Nonie Jo Aker, Mike's *wife*."

She'd emphasized *wife*, as if I'd been planning to steal her man right off her front porch steps. Right. I'd easily kicked Mike's ass, so his attractiveness dropped to the near zero range for me.

"What're you doing here?"

"I'm running as a replacement candidate for Bill O'Neil in the upcoming sheriff's election."

Her critical, birdlike eyes darted over me. "What makes you think you can do a better job than Sheriff Dawson?"

"No need to be rude, Nonie Jo," Mike warned.

I plastered on a perky smile. "Dawson and I have different ideas on running the county, so it's not about being better, but offering the voters another choice."

"He's definitely better looking than you, so he's got my vote." Nonie Jo spun on her pink flip-flop and vanished into the house. Mike slunk in after her.

Campaigning had been well worth the effort. I'd gotten more info on the investigation in two hours than Dawson had in a week.

During the first official meeting with the campaign committee early the next morning, I'd asserted myself more than they'd expected. And I'd done it without a gun in my hand.

I said no to wearing my military uniform.

I said no to playing up the Indian angle.

I agreed to campaign door to door.

I agreed to Q&As at the senior center, the elementary school, and the high school.

I agreed to hold an informal coffee klatch at the Blackbird

Diner after they nixed my idea of a whiskey throwdown at Clementine's.

After an hour, the reality of what I'd agreed to do started to sink in. I stared out the library window to the neatly mowed grass spread out like a manicured golf green. I'd spent so many years in monochromatic landscapes that the verdant hue didn't seem real. None of this seemed real. Beyond the vivid swath was a single row of tulips, crimson exclamation points set against the blacktop.

"You haven't said much," Geneva said.

"I've been listening. Trying to take it all in."

"I sense you're having second thoughts, but we wouldn't have asked if we didn't believe you're up to the challenge."

I nodded. Voicing my concerns wouldn't matter. Geneva would offer reassurances, and if I didn't act like her pep talk was working, she'd get bent out of shape and accuse me of being a pessimist. Which was true, but beside the point.

"What are your plans for the rest of the day?"

"Ranch stuff," I said vaguely, because I couldn't share with her how I planned to spend my afternoon.

"See you tomorrow. If you need anything, call."

I practiced my fake politician's smile. "Will do."

I tracked Jake down behind the old barn.

He leaned against a shovel handle, studying me curiously. "I wondered if you'd show up, bein's your daily schedule has changed."

Nice dig. I gazed across the pasture. Tufts of green poked through the spots that weren't trampled into goop and covered in cow patties. Hoofprints were scattered every which way. A single path trailed from the stock tank and up over the hill. "What's on the agenda today?"

"Gotta spread a little hay around for the cattle." He hoisted the shovel over his shoulder and headed toward his truck.

"With all the rain there isn't enough new grass to graze?"

"It helps, but it also makes mud," Jake said, after we climbed in the cab. "Nursing mothers require a lot of feed to keep up their milk production, so we have to supplement."

"How many bales do you usually feed them?"

"Four. I'll probably dump five today so I don't have to come back out here tonight. Do you have gloves?"

"At the cabin."

"Ain't doin' you much good there." Jake stripped off his gloves. "Here."

"Thanks." Since I rode shotgun I had to open gates. Jake seemed surprised I didn't complain.

By noon the cattle were fed and we'd finished fieldwork.

"I need to check something at the Newsome house. You can just drop me off at the shelterbelt along the east side."

Jake didn't seem too keen on the idea, but he didn't argue.

I rummaged in the box on the floor, pocketing a wrench, a pair of wire cutters, a pair of pliers, and a flashlight before I slipped from the truck.

Sneaking around the Newsome house looked suspicious, especially since I owned the property. But I didn't want anyone to remember seeing me, so I hunkered down, keeping low to the ground until I reached the propane tank. This older model still had the outside gauge, and it read half full. The sticker indicated the tank inspection deadline had passed four months back.

Since the back door faced away from the road, I entered there. I hadn't been in Iris's house more than half a dozen times in my entire life, which was bizarre, considering she'd been our closest neighbor for four decades.

After buying the property, I'd toured the house with the auction company. Throughout the house I saw signs of a person who'd left briefly, expecting to return and finish household chores. Iris's dishes were moldering in the kitchen sink. Mail and newspapers were strewn across the dining room table. A half cup of coffee had turned into a science experiment in the living room. In the entryway, the vacuum was plugged in. The auction company agreed to clean up and haul everything away in exchange for 70 percent of the auction proceeds. I considered it a bargain.

I'd believed that once the Newsomes' personal belongings were purged from the space, it'd feel less menacing.

Not so. Now it seemed worse. The emptiness emphasized the

finality of an entire family. A sudden, inexplicable chill traveled up my spine. I whirled around, expecting to see . . . what? A ghost?

Get ahold of yourself.

I inhaled an *uji* breath and let it out slowly. Better.

Upstairs, I made sure the register vents were open in the bedrooms and the hallway. Ditto for the main floor. The seal around the front door appeared solid.

I ventured into the basement, basically a root cellar without an outside escape hatch. The narrow stairs were steeply pitched. With limited depth perception, I kept my hand on the bumpy wall to stop myself from falling forward. As I hit the last step, a dank odor filled my nostrils. Hello, gag reflex. Definitely a dead critter down here.

Or maybe the propane connection had already been compromised. Propane companies added scent to the odorless gas so that customers could tell if there was a leak in the line. The scent varied from the smell of rotten eggs to the distinctive odor of skunk perfume to the stench of rotting meat. Since I couldn't see, I couldn't determine if I smelled dead mice.

My grip tightened on the flashlight. If propane was seeping inside the house from a faulty connection, even the tiniest spark of metal on metal could ignite the vapors. It was sheer dumb luck I hadn't impatiently shoved the basement door open, causing the aluminum weather stripping to strike sparks against the carpet. Static electricity was as deadly as a match.

As much as I wanted to skip testing the flashlight as an explosive device test, I had to turn it on. Holding my breath, I painstakingly slid the plastic button on the flashlight up until it clicked and light bounced off the cement wall. Whew. I moved the beam of light across the floor until it reached the corner where the ancient heater and water heater were located.

Mice scurried from the light, little feet scratching on the cement floor.

A shiver of revulsion beaded my skin into goose bumps. Better mice than snakes.

I bent down and saw the on/off valve for the heater in the back where the tubing entered from outside. This heating system was beyond antiquated. Holding the flashlight in my left hand, I thrust my gloved hand through the world's biggest spiderweb, hoping I hadn't interrupted some big-ass black widow's nap. The valve squeaked on the first turn, and I stopped.

Remember, no metal sparks, dumb ass.

I turned it again. Slower. I kept turning a little at a time until it was fully open. When I removed my hand, sections of the heavy, sticky spiderweb clung to my forearm. Eww. Gross. But it could've been worse. What if I'd broken a hidden egg sac, freeing hundreds of baby spiders to crawl into my clothes, my hair, my ears, my nose, and my mouth? I shuddered.

The valve for the water heater was on the other side of the heater. Again, in a difficult spot to reach and dangerous as hell compared to modern-day systems. I crouched down and pressed my left side against the cold, dank wall.

The skittering noises increased, driving my pulse rate up.

Jesus. How goddamn many mice were there?

Do you really want to know?

No. What if it's not mice? What if it's ghosts? Or what if those scratching noises are just a figment of your imagination?

My head started to pound, and I focused on getting the valve opened. Either it'd gotten easier or I'd gotten better because this one didn't take long. Once I finished, I stood and brushed the dirt and webs—cob and spider—from my clothes and proceeded upstairs.

In the kitchen, I couldn't detect the rotten-animal-flesh odor, but I'd been in the house long enough that my sense of smell had adapted. I crouched in the space where the stove had been and thoroughly inspected the piping. The connecting end to the propane had been capped off, the valve shut off. Despite the difficulty in removing the cap while wearing gloves, I managed. Then I gradually cranked the valve on.

I did one last sweep of the house.

By the time I finished, sweat oozed from my pores. My head throbbed. I exited the back door, tools in hand. I debated on checking the propane tank gauge again, but I couldn't wait to get the hell out of there.

I ran all five miles back to the ranch, stopping only to toss

Jake's gloves and tools in his truck. As I wandered across the yard, light-headedness overtook me. I bent forward, bracing my hands on my knees to keep from passing out.

Vaguely, through the ringing in my ears and the blood pulsing through my body, I heard the screen door slam.

A shadow appeared. Then Hope said, "Mercy? You okay?"

"No. Shit. I-I—"

"What's wrong with you?"

I breathed in too many propane fumes. "I'm, ah . . . gonna be sick." I fell to all fours in the mud. The acid in my stomach churned, sending up my two cups of coffee. Half the liquid spewed out my mouth; the other half burned up my nasal passage and out my nose.

I retched until I hit the dry-heave stage.

Through it all, Hope stayed beside me, rubbing circles on my shoulders, murmuring to me. When I pushed back to rest on my haunches, she handed me a towel-like thing covered with tiny smiling ducks. I wiped my mouth, looked at the towel and then at her.

Hope shrugged at my confusion. "I always have a burp cloth on me these days."

"Handy. Thank you."

"You're welcome." She paused. "I don't know if I've ever seen you sick."

"Don't worry, it's not contagious, just self-inflicted."

She raised an eyebrow. "Really?"

"Not from too much liquid fun. I had meetings in town early. I helped Jake and then I decided to run back here. Not a good combination."

"You're always bitching at me about not taking care of myself. When was the last time you ate anything?"

"I had coffee this morning."

"Coffee ain't food," she scoffed. "Try again."

I thought back. "I don't remember."

"No wonder." Hope circled her fingers around my bicep and hauled me to my feet. "Come on."

When had my sister gotten so bossy? I tried not to lean on her too much as we hobbled toward the house, but she came to a full stop and got right in my face. "Dammit, Mercy, would the world end if you let me help you?"

"Umm. No."

"Then stop acting so damn tough and trust that I won't let you fall on your face."

"Fine." She easily bore my weight on her left side. "You're stronger than you look."

"Glad someone finally recognized that."

By the time we reached the porch steps I was woozy again.

Sophie held open the screen door, clucking at both of us. "Mercy, you look awful."

"Thanks." Puke alert. I dangled over the freshly planted flower bed. The colors swirled together like I'd taken an acid trip, and the sickly sweet floral scent lined my nose, making my stomach rebel.

"Don't you be barfing on my flowers, hey," Sophie warned. "Get her to her room."

"Bring a bucket," Hope said, and herded me inside.

I think she enjoyed manhandling me a little too much.

In my room, Hope studied me. "Feel like hurling again?"

I managed a scowl. "No."

"Good." She maneuvered the eyelet coverlet around where I sat on the mattress and jerked the sheet back. "Then you can crawl right in bed."

"In the middle of the damn day? I don't think so."

Sophie shambled in, setting a plastic bowl and a glass of water on the nightstand. She placed her hand on my forehead.

Ooh. That felt nice. "What's the prognosis, Doc Red Leaf?"

"Clammy. Not feverish. It'll pass."

"Like I told Hope, I just ran too hard, and I didn't sleep well last night."

"No matter. Your sister is right. You need to rest. All this sheriff, ranch, and bar stuff is starting to catch up with you."

I shook my head. "But I have to—"

"The only thing you have to do is put your head on the pillow." Hope stood in front of me, hands on hips. "You've always taken care of me. How about letting me return the favor for a change?"

Tired of arguing, and touched by Hope's concern, I muttered, "Fine." I toed off my shoes. I started to strip off my shirt when I realized Dawson might've gifted me with love bites the last time we slept together. Damn man delighted in marking me for some reason.

Sophie and Hope mistook my hesitation for shyness and booked it out the door.

I slipped on a long T-shirt and swallowed four Excedrin. The cool sheets beckoned, and I eased beneath them with a drawn-out sigh. My eyes drooped. My body relaxed. I'd begun to doze when the door opened.

Hope, with Joy perched on her hip, crossed to my nightstand and placed a package of saltine crackers next to the water glass. "Need anything else?"

"No." Impulsively, I reached up and curled my hand around Joy's bare foot. Such perfectly formed itty-bitty toes. Joy had spindly legs and arms, but her feet were little plumped sausages. "Damn, Poopy, you are one cute papoose."

Hope froze. "You must be sicker than I thought."

"Why?"

"Because you're paying attention to your niece."

I couldn't meet Hope's eyes. "You know I'm crazy about her."

"No, actually, I didn't. You tend to ignore her."

"It's hard to lavish her with attention when she's always in her mama's arms."

Rather than get snippy, Hope sighed. "True. I just can't not hold her. All the time. Even when she's sleeping. Sophie thinks I go overboard. Jake does, too. I know I'm being overprotective . . . but I can't help it."

"No one blames you, least of all me."

"That's good to know. But I was beginning to think you didn't like her."

"I like her just fine for a screaming, pooping thing who lives to projectile vomit."

Hope didn't crack a smile.

"What? I was joking."

"I know. But I've also wondered if you were . . . I dunno . . . jealous of her or something because you'll never have a baby."

My fingers strummed the backside of Joy's foot until she grunted and wiggled her toes away. "If you haven't noticed, I'm not exactly the maternal type."

"Oh, pooh. You're more maternal than you give yourself credit for." Hope wiped a long strand of drool dangling from Joy's mouth. Joy's spider legs kicked, and she made a soft *goo* sound. "You've always watched out for me."

"You've always needed it."

She smiled. "Or maybe I didn't try to stop you because I liked that you fussed over me when you never fussed over anyone else."

Once again, Hope surprised me with her insight. "Looking out for you is a hard habit to break. I'll probably still be deciding what's best for you when we're both little blue-haired ladies."

"I hope so."

I wondered if she'd still feel the same way after I blew up the Newsome house tonight. But this chat reinforced my resolve to protect her at all costs. Especially when she didn't understand that she needed protection.

She stopped at the door and faced me. "And sis, one other thing?"

"What?"

"Stop calling her Poopy." The door shut behind them.

"Poopy it is," I said sleepily, to the empty room.

The instant my eyes closed, I conked out.

I slept like the dead. No bad dreams. Sophie had left me a plate of biscuits and a bottle of 7Up—comfort foods from my childhood—on the dresser while I slumbered. Once I regained my bearings, I left my room.

The TV was on in the living room. I intended to walk straight to the bathroom, but something made me peek in.

Jake and Hope were on the floor, Joy on a puffy pink blanket between them. When Joy churned her chicken legs, Jake and Hope laughed, which only encouraged her to ham it up more. Jake spoke low enough I couldn't hear. Hope looked at him, happiness shining in her eyes. Jake reached over to tuck a loose hair behind her ear, and Hope angled her head into his touch.

I would've felt less like a peeping Tom if I'd caught them having sex.

Most days it didn't bother me I'd never have what Hope had—a baby and a good man who'd loved her for years. But I wouldn't know what to do with that kind of devotion.

Would I?

After I tiptoed back to my room, I nibbled on the biscuits. But the flaky goodness tasted like sawdust, and weighed heavily in my stomach as if I'd swallowed a stone.

Hope checked on me around eleven o'clock. With fake grogginess, I feigned exhaustion and promised I'd stay the night. As soon as she was gone, I locked the door. I ran over every aspect of the plan one last time.

Stealth, lies, and sacrifices for the greater good—my modus operandi never seemed to change. Except this time my solution wouldn't be carried out with Uncle Sam's blessing. Dawson could arrest me for real and make it stick if I got caught.

So I just couldn't get caught.

Around one a.m. I dug out my black leggings, black long-sleeved T-shirt, black balaclava, and black athletic shoes. From the top shelf in my closet I grabbed the case containing my H-S Precision takedown rifle, double-checking that it contained my night-vision scope. I put a bullet in each pocket, although I'd only need one.

My heart rate stayed normal until I entered the barn. I focused on the tack room where the ATV keys were kept and bypassed the empty horse stalls as quickly as possible. Any fears I thought I'd conquered when I wasn't standing in the barn reasserted themselves full force the instant that wooden door slammed shut behind me.

I palmed the key for the oldest, crappiest ATV, with one working headlight. As long as I didn't run the ATV at a high rate of speed, my nocturnal four-wheeling adventure shouldn't be loud enough to tip off any neighbors. I just hoped I didn't tip the damn thing over on myself because of my compromised depth perception.

Sneaking into position on foot had been my first choice, but for timing issues, I might be cutting it close, even on a machine that traveled twenty miles an hour. If the fire was spotted immediately, as the property owners we'd get called right away. I had to be home, tucked in bed, and surprised as hell when that happened.

With my rifle case strapped to the back, I pushed the ATV through the fence, trying to avoid mudholes. By the time I'd gotten far enough from the barn to start the machine, sweat poured down my body.

Took three tries for the engine to catch, and it released a puff of smoke. Yeah, this was some stealthy fucking machine.

On the earlier run from the Newsome house, I'd mapped out the path. Not the most direct route, or the fastest route, but the flattest route.

Clouds covered the moon. I relished the solitude and the stillness. Night air feels different after midnight. Colder. Fresher. Sweeter. It was exhilarating, traversing the great outdoors while the world around me slept.

My machine scared a raccoon family from the underbrush. The glowing eyes were accusatory and then gone. The back end of the ATV bogged down on a sharp rise. I revved the engine to max power. Anyone who heard the distinctive whining noise would assume the members of the LifeLite Church group were sending out ATV patrols, which they did all hours of the night.

I studied the ground, bumping over chunks of shale and whole yuccas. I became so mesmerized by the variances in the vegetation that I nearly smacked into a squat pine tree. I swerved at the last nanosecond and almost pitched myself ass over teakettle.

Pay attention.

I slowed when the shelterbelt came into view. This section veered off the path and the terrain was trickier. Standing gave me a better view of the sinkholes and big rocks randomly scattered about. I traversed nature's obstacle course and reached the fence. From there, I'd be on foot.

Since the ATV redefined piece of junk, I couldn't chance it not starting, so I kept it running. I jammed rocks beneath all four tires.

I cracked open the rifle case. Assembly, even under the cover of darkness, was quick. Once I snapped on the scope, I held the rifle by my side and jogged up to the hole in the fence line.

As I dashed across the field, my internal focus was absolute. I was one with the night—my breathing, my gun, my mission. This was my own personal nirvana.

I crouched by the flat rock with a bird's-eye view of the front of the house. I loaded the blue-tipped bullet, a .338 Lapua incendiary round I'd been saving for a special occasion. I dinked with the night-vision scope, gauging the target with my left eye. I tweaked the viewfinder again until I had the perfect angle for the front window.

Aim.

Breathe.

Fire.

Mental prep done, I was ready for the real deal.

One shot. Four hundred yards out. Piece of cake. I could do this with one arm tied behind my back. I could do this even with my left eye.

Finger on the trigger.

Eye on the target.

Breathe in.

Breathe out.

I fired.

Click.

The *whomp, whomp, whomp* as the fiery gas expanded from room to room echoed back to me was followed by . . . *BOOM. BOOM. BOOM.*

A blast of heat rushed across me as the house disgorged a ball of fire. Beautiful and grotesque. A red-orange orb, laced with roiling black clouds. I hadn't heard glass breaking, although I could see jagged pieces littering the ground like dirty ice. The windows were gaping holes, eerie open mouths, screaming in shock. The entire front of the house had blown outward. Pieces of lumber scattered the yard like a giant's game of pickup sticks. Chunks of plaster smoked, and tufts of insulation fell.

I grinned. "Thar she blows, matey."

Flames licked the walls with hungry red tongues.

The roof? Poof.

This house was completely uninhabitable.

No guilt or pride surfaced as I ejected the spent shell casing and shoved it in my pocket. Time to retreat, not gloat. I ran low to the ground, to the break in the fence. I ducked through the barbed wire and heard the sputtering engine of the ATV beneath the cacophony of crackling wood. After breaking my rifle down and fitting the pieces back in the case, I checked my watch.

Mission accomplished in under thirty-four minutes.

Now the real race began.

TWELVE

Nervous sweat plastered my hair to my face, my neck, and coated my scalp. In my room I shoved the gun case back in the closet. I ditched the ninja clothes at the bottom of the laundry basket and slipped back into my pajamas. I brought the covers under my chin, too wired to sleep.

I was half surprised I'd made it back to the house before the phone rang. Best-case scenario? No one reported the fire until it'd burned the house to the ground. The neighboring property belonged to the LifeLite religious group, and they hadn't volunteered to help when we'd had a fire on our ranch last summer, so I expected they'd turn a blind eye now.

My main concern was the volunteer firemen called to the scene to risk life and limb to save the structure I'd torched.

Ten minutes passed. Fifteen. Twenty. Just when I believed the fire would burn unattended, a knock sounded on my bedroom door.

Talk about jumping like a scalded cat. I didn't answer, just waited for the next knock.

"Mercy?" Jake said, a little louder. "Phone."

I opened the door. "Who is it?"

"Wouldn't say."

Snatching the cordless from his hand, I entered the living room. "This is Mercy Gunderson. Who's calling me at three o'clock in the goddamn morning?"

"Clayton Black with the Eagle River Volunteer Fire Department. There's been an explosion at the old Newsome house."

"An explosion?" I repeated.

"Where? What's going on?" Hope demanded behind me.

"Something at the Newsome house," I said, turning my back on her. "What happened?"

"We're not sure. Looks like a gas leak. We wanted to let you know we're doing all we can to save the house—"

"Forget about saving the house. There's nothing in it. Keep the firefighters safe."

"But the structure—"

"Might as well collapse, if it's as bad as you say." I looked at Hope; her face was as pasty white as her frilly nightgown. "Can you hold off on doing anything for the next ten minutes until my sister and I get there?"

"I guess."

I hung up and said to Hope, "Go throw on some clothes, and I'll meet you out front."

"But I can't leave Joy—"

"With her father? Come on. You'll have your cell if Jake needs something." I put my hand on the wall. "I might need you to drive since I've been sick."

"Then Jake can drive you. I'll stay here."

"Jake is a manager, not an owner. You will be a full participant in whatever decision we make, Hope. So get changed and meet me by my truck."

She raced upstairs, Jake behind her. I threw on sweatpants, slipped my feet into a pair of flip-flops, and grabbed my keys.

We reached the truck at the same time, and Hope climbed in the passenger's side. "What do you think happened?"

"They said some kind of gas explosion."

She was quiet, not the good kind of quiet. I felt her studying me, but I kept my eyes firmly on the road.

"Don't you think it's . . . convenient that after I tell you I want to move into the Newsome place, something like this happens?"

I looked at her. Hard. "Don't you think it's a goddamn good thing something convenient like this happened *before* you moved in with Joy and Jake?"

A comprehending look of horror crossed her face, and she shut up.

We saw the flames from a half mile away. They'd died down since the initial blast. I dodged parked vehicles lining the drive and rolled down my window upon reaching the Eagle River County Sheriff's Department blazer blocking access.

Shit. I hoped it wasn't Dawson. I so did not want to deal with him right now.

Deputy Jazinski leaned in the window. "Gonna have to leave it parked here, Miz Gunderson. Clayton's waiting for you around the left side of the pumper truck."

"Thanks." I was sorry I'd worn flip-flops as Hope and I picked our way through smoking piles of debris.

Once we had a clear view of the burned-out shell, Hope reached for my hand and gasped. "Oh my God."

From far away, I'd experienced the detachment I'd honed after taking out a target. Aim. Fire. Verify. Move on. Even now, faced with the destruction I'd set in motion and my sister's emotional reaction to it, I didn't feel a single ounce of remorse.

But I did have to fake it. "It's just . . . gone." The catch in my voice was a nice touch.

A man in a full firefighting suit approached and removed his headpiece. "Mercy. Clayton Black. We've never officially met, but I responded to the fire at your place last summer, and I was on scene at Clementine's."

"I imagine the next time you hear my name you'll head the other direction."

He smiled, making him look far younger than he'd sounded on the phone. "No. I've always been the type to run headlong into danger rather than away from it." He turned toward the house. "As you can see, there ain't much left." He pointed to the roof, which had broken into three pieces upon impact with the ground. "At this point we're treating this as a propone explosion. None of the outbuildings were affected. And we've had enough moisture that the flames scorched the ground in places but didn't start a full-blown fire."

"That's something, I guess."

"Since we spoke, we've been keeping an eye on it, and I gotta say, it's . . . unnatural for a bunch of firefighters to stand around and watch something burn."

"I imagine it is. But I'd rather see them safe on the sidelines than risk their lives on a building that ain't worth saving."

"And that's the question of the night, isn't it?"

The reddish glow from the flames backlit the man, emphasizing the fact that he wore street clothes, not a fireproof suit. His face was shadowed, but I knew who he was.

His gaze flicked between us. "Mercy. Hope. Thanks for getting here so quickly."

"No problem, Chief." Dave Klapperich had headed up the volunteer fire department for as long as my dad had been sheriff. During the week Dave ran a successful trucking company and was a shrewd businessman, so I wasn't surprised by the suspicion in his eyes. He suspected arson. I'm sure everyone did. But there was one glitch in their theory.

Klapperich cut to the chase. "So I'm curious as to why you told Clayton to let it burn."

The moment of truth. "Because it's not insured."

A collective pause.

Klapperich leaned forward. "Did you say this place wasn't insured?"

I shook my head. "When we learned of the first-right-of-refusal option in the Newsome will, we felt . . . obligated to buy it. Money was tight. Took all our extra cash just to put a down payment on the land. Then medical bills starting coming in, and we had to choose what took priority. Adding liability insurance on this structure wasn't on the list. I'd planned to do it next month."

Stunned silence.

"That's why I didn't want the firefighters taking chances. Damn place might as well burn to cinders, as much good as it'll do us now."

Hope cried softly.

I put my arm around her, and we watched the east wall cave in. Not a single wall was left standing. A sense of relief washed over me, but I kept my face somber.

Klapperich and Clayton Black seemed embarrassed by my confession of Gunderson money woes. I hadn't embellished that part. Now with my retirement pay rolling in and a great calving season behind us, things were looking up.

"We'll stick around and put out any embers until the last of it's burned away."

"I—we—appreciate it."

Hope shook herself out of her stupor. "If you don't need us, I have a baby to tend, and Mercy needs to get back in bed. She's been sick all day."

I ducked my face from view. The last thing I needed was Klapperich to ferret out my "sickness" being from breathing propane fumes while rigging this place to blow.

"No problem," Clayton said. "Feel better, Mercy. And good luck in the election."

"Thanks." I noticed he hadn't offered his support.

We walked back to the truck in silence. I didn't argue that I was perfectly capable of driving when Hope snatched my keys.

Halfway home, she stomped on the brakes. My body jerked forward as we skidded sideways to a dead stop in the middle of the road. Before I could snap, "Jesus. A little warning next time?" she whirled on me.

"You didn't think I deserved to know there wasn't insurance on the Newsome property? Did you forget I own just as much of the goddamned Gunderson Ranch as you do? I should've been in on that decision." She beat her fists on the steering wheel. "Dammit, Mercy, I felt like such an idiot standing there, not knowing any of this stuff."

"Good."

Hope's mouth dropped open. "*Good*? That's your response?"

"Yes. It's about time. Since Joy came home from the hospital, you've shown an interest only in her. I understand babies need full-time care, and without doubt you are a great mother."

"But?"

"But whenever I tried to talk to you about anything besides your baby, you tuned me out."

Her hands opened and closed on the steering wheel.

"So yeah, since I was saddled with the books, I made some decisions."

"You made them? Or you and Jake made them?"

"Just me."

"Good, because Jake is a manager, not an owner," she tossed back at me.

I didn't know whether to laugh or scream. But I preferred feisty Hope to fickle Hope. "What would you have done?"

"I would've put insurance on the Newsome property no matter what."

"Something had to give, sis. I looked at the books and went eeny, meeny, miny, moe and picked the one we could do without at the time."

"That's no way to do the books," Hope scoffed.

"If you think you can do a better job, you're more than welcome to take over."

"Seriously? You'd let me handle the book work for the ranch?"

The word *no* hovered on my tongue, but in truth, I couldn't do it all. I didn't want to do it all. Pretending I could handle every fucking thing thrown my way was beginning to feel more like a martyr complex than extreme efficiency. Everything would just get more complicated if I won the election. I sighed and rubbed my temples. Damn headache was back with a vengeance. "Yes. I'd gladly hand the books over to you if you're serious enough to stick with it."

The engine ticked, and her angry breaths slowed.

Her change in demeanor got my back up. I prepared myself for an epic fight. So I was completely stunned by Hope's squeal of delight. Then she hugged me.

What the fuck? I was used to her abrupt mood changes, but this bordered on manic. From sadness to anger to delight in mere minutes? I squinted at her, wondering if she'd accidentally breathed in toxic smoke fumes.

Her laughter bubbled out. "Don't look at me like I've lost my marbles. Doing the books is a rite of passage for the women in our family, and I've always wanted to do my part since I can't do nothin' else around the ranch. But Daddy claimed I didn't have a head for numbers and refused to discuss it."

Heat rose in my cheeks on her behalf. For all Dad's good points, sometimes he could be downright mean. "To be honest, I think you'll probably do a better job than me."

"Really?"

"Really. It's not my thing. So schedule an appointment with Carol. She'll give you the lowdown on weekly stuff. I want to keep her on to file payroll taxes and all the rest of that junk. As far as day-to-day expenses? You're in charge. You'll be dealing with Jake. Will that cause problems in your relationship?"

"Nope. He's already used to me calling the shots."

That did make me laugh.

She hit the gas, and we were lost in our own thoughts on the way home. She parked and shut the truck off. Before I hopped out, she said, "Mercy, wait."

"Look, Hope, before you say anything, I know you had your heart and mind set on living in the Newsome house. And I do understand that you want a home of your own for your family." My grip tightened on the door handle. "I promise we'll find you something. Even if we have to take out a loan and build you a new house, okay?"

"Okay. Jake don't say much, but I know he's not comfortable living in the house where his grandmother works as a house-keeper."

"I know."

"Are you mad?"

"No. But the deal is, no matter where you end up, Shoonga stays with me."

She smiled crookedly. "You and that dog. You spoil him as much as Levi did."

Levi. Just saying his name brought sadness that filled the air between us.

Hope whispered, "I miss him."

"I know." I swallowed hard. "I do, too."

"Joy is . . . well, the joy of my life. But she's not a replace-ment for my son. I think that's why I don't go out much. People in the community think I should be happy that I have another child. But having Joy hasn't erased the pain of losing Levi. He's still in my heart, and I wish to God he was still . . ." She sniffled. "Maybe that sounds stupid, but do you know what I mean?"

"Yeah, I think I do."

Hope wiped her tears. "Sorry. Anyway, I keep forgetting to thank you for the frog. Joy loves it."

I squirmed. I wasn't a good gift giver. Whenever I bought something new for my niece, I'd sneak into Hope's bedroom and place the stuffed animals in Joy's crib, or I'd set the clothes on Hope's dresser. "Um. You're welcome."

"She needs you, too, you know. Beyond the cute outfits and toys you buy her. As she's growing up she'll need a strong woman to look up to."

I was beginning to think my little sister was much stronger than I'd given her credit for. I reached for Hope's hand and squeezed, then bailed out of the truck before either of us said something that would ruin the moment.

THIRTEEN

In my sleep-deprived state the next morning, I listened to proposed county budget cuts.

The proposed reallocation of state funds for the county school district.

The proposed budgetary restrictions on fire and ambulance services.

The proposed increases in county vehicle maintenance costs.

My head pounded. I knew nothing about any of this.

"Neither did he, Mercy. You'll figure it out."

I looked up at Kiki, startled I'd mumbled the words aloud.

"Didn't you have to fill out requisition forms and stuff like that in the army?"

"No. The CO did it all, or I blackmailed someone into doing my portion." I sorted through the sheaf of papers. "I can't imagine my dad reading all this."

"He did. Oh, he grumbled, but it was just for show. Wyatt loved scrutinizing yearly budgets and questioning the county commissioners on where they'd allocated the taxpayer's money." Kiki put her hand on my forearm. "We only gave you this so you'd have an overview before you debate Dawson. He's been studying this budget for over a month, so you need to get up to speed."

My stomach lurched. "Whoa. A debate? No one said anything about me having to debate him."

"Part of the election process. The format is simple. You state your platform, he states his, and there's a dance afterward."

Overwhelmed by the responsibilities, I pushed away from the conference table and walked to the coffeepot. I was in way over my head.

I'd hoped running for sheriff would give me more insight into my father. But these meetings drove home the point that I didn't know Sheriff Gunderson as well as I'd believed. His employees—hell, even Dawson—had known him better than me. The campaign workers planned to play on my heritage—bogus as it was. The only thing Wyatt Gunderson and I shared was the same last name. And I'd reluctantly approved the campaign slogan: "Gunderson, the name in law enforcement you can trust."

How would the voters feel if they found out you'd torched your own building and lied about it? Or that you'd covered up a murder and lied about it?

Yeah, I was one trustworthy motherfucker.

"Mercy?"

I faced Geneva and watched everyone file out of the room. "Sorry. My head was spinning."

"I imagine, especially after what happened last night. Has Klapperich contacted you with any additional news about what caused the fire at the Newsome house?"

"No."

Geneva's bright blue eyes pierced me. "Why aren't you more upset?"

I shrugged. "I'd rather the damn thing blew up when no one lived there. And don't think I haven't heard whispers of the Gunderson curse surfacing again."

"Well, it's too bad you didn't have insurance on it."

"Live and learn." I scooped the stack of papers rivaling Stephen King's latest novel from her hands and jammed it into my messenger bag. I met Geneva's skeptical gaze. "I'll read it. I promise."

"No more the-dog-ate-my-homework excuses, okay?"

"It's better than the truth that I spilled whiskey on it."

After I ditched my bag in my truck, I stood on Main Street debating my next move. Then I noticed George Johnson's construction van sitting in front of Pete's Pawnshop.

Pete Parnell should've named his store Useless Crap No One Wants, because it wasn't as much a pawnshop as a place for Pete to shitpile the junk he scavenged from auctions. Or to take advantage of people low on cash by letting them hock every-thing from heirloom star quilts to wedding rings.

The place had a musty machine smell that hadn't improved since my childhood. My dad loved a bargain, and I'd spent what seemed like hours listening to Dad and Pete haggle. But beneath the familiar scent was another. New construction. The tangy pine of freshly cut lumber, the chalky smell of Sheetrock mud, and the sourness of paint primer.

Holy hell, the entire left side of the room was walled off.

"Looks good, don't it?"

I glanced at Pete, twirling on his bar stool behind the glass display cases. He wore too-small striped engineer overalls with a red hankie hanging out of the front pocket. His seen-better-days ball cap was emblazoned with PROUD TO BE AN AMERICAN across the front. Pete was bald as a pool ball beneath that hat—or so I'd been told. I'd never seen him without a cap of some sort cover-ing his head.

"What are you building, Pete?" I dodged plastic milk crates overflowing with mysterious machine parts and stacks of old *National Geographic*.

"A coffee shop."

That stopped me. "In here?" Eww. Who wanted dust and metal flakes in their coffee?

"Yep. Re-Pete's wife Sabrina has been going on and on about how popular them fancy coffee places are. We thought we'd get a jump on putting the first one in Eagle Ridge."

Pete's son, Re-Pete, had actually been born Pete Parnell Junior, but everyone—mostly his father—thought calling him Re-Pete would be the height of hilarity. I didn't envy Re-Pete the nick-name during our school years, and certainly not now.

"'Course, I promised Sabrina I'd spiff up the pawnshop a bit."

He'd have to spiff it up a lot before I'd patronize the place.

"Did you get a taste for them fancy coffees when you was traveling the world, Mercy?"

"Anything is better than the sludge the army served."

"I hear ya. So you're running for your daddy's old job?"

"Yep. Can I count on your vote?"

Pete folded his arms over his beer belly. "Seein's I ain't got a beef with the way Dawson's been doin' things . . ."

At least it wasn't a *hell no*. Tired of small talk, I said, "I'm look-ing for George. He around?"

"In the back. Be careful of the wet paint."

George gripped a paint roller in one hand and a cell phone in the other. Soon as he saw me, he cut his conversation short. "Well, if it isn't the woman who can stop a bar fight and run for sheriff."

"I can whistle while I juggle, too." I smiled. "Speaking of bar fights, I'm trying to track down some information about what went down the night Jason Hawley was killed, and I was hoping you could help me."

"Sure. Whatcha need?"

"I heard you were talking to him in the back room at Clemen-tine's before the fight."

"Yeah, so?"

"What did you talk about?"

He measured me, then shrugged. "Ain't a big secret he was trying to get local construction workers on board with sup-porting the pipeline. He pulled the usual 'great-paying jobs for skilled workers' line of bullshit."

"Did you believe him?' "'

"Some of the guys did. And they were pissed when they found out Hawley had forgotten to tell them they'd have to join the Pipelayers' Union in order to get hired. We don't need to pay a fucking *union* to get us jobs."

South Dakota. Not such a big union state. "Were any of your guys mad enough—"

"To kill him over it? Hell no. I can vouch for every guy there that night. They may get a little crazy, drink too much, mix it up with their fists when provoked, but no way would they kill for kicks."

"Did Hawley talk to anyone else after you?"

"Some Indian chick."

That was new. "Know her name?"

"Cherelle something. But she was trying to talk to him, and he was blowing her off."

"What'd she look like? Younger? Older?"

"Younger. Pretty until you noticed the scar running down the right side of her face. I felt sorry for her, but at the same time, she had this incredibly mean look about her." George squinted at me suspiciously. "Why you asking me this?"

"Has Dawson been around asking you?"

"No."

"Then there's your answer. I'm following a few lines of investigation he hasn't." I pointed to his roller. "Thanks for your help. I'll let you get back to work."

Outside, the fresh air alone wasn't clearing my head. I took off down the sidewalk at a brisk pace. Since Main Street was only three blocks long I'd run out of pavement before my mind really kicked into gear.

So far my one lead was that J-Hawk had talked to an Indian woman named Cherelle. I would've remembered a scarred woman.

I leaned against the brick building housing the Wipf Law Office. How long had J-Hawk been in the bank room before he came up to the main part of the bar and ordered a drink from me? Had he stuck around in the parking lot afterward because he'd been waiting for someone specific?

The reflection of a passing car flashed in my face, and I averted my eyes. My gaze caught on an SUV parked in the bank's parking lot between a boat and a pair of Sea-Doo Jet Skis. It was angled so I couldn't read the license plate. But I recognized it.

What was Jason's SUV still doing here?

I crossed the street and walked around the vehicle. Then I tried the doors. Locked. No surprise. I cupped my hands to block the light and peeked in the windows. The inside was clean as a whistle.

"I could arrest you for attempted breaking and entering," he drawled.

My heart raced a bit when I faced him. "I was just looking, Sheriff."

"Uh-huh. I saw you pulling on the door handles."

Busted. "Go ahead and slap the cuffs on me."

"Being's you're running against me, if I arrested you, some people might see it as an abuse of power on my part, so I'm gonna let it slide." He paused. "What're you doing here?"

"My truck is on its last legs. I'm considering an upgrade.

Thought I'd check the repo lot first. See if the bank's prices were better than at Stevenson's car lot in Viewfield."

Dawson grinned, but I couldn't read his eyes beneath his sunglasses. "You always have an excuse handy?"

"Only when I need one."

"So what's your excuse for not telling me you'd agreed to run in Bill O'Neil's place? You know, the night I spent in your bed?"

Mature of me, not to look around to see if anyone was listening to our conversation. "I hadn't decided."

"Bullshit."

"It's the truth. They asked me, and I told them I needed time to think it over. Then some stuff happened and . . ." *Stop talking, Mercy. You owe him nothing.*

"You running to spite me?"

"No, I'm running in spite of you, Dawson."

That startled him. "Good to know. But you're not going to win."

I offered him a bold smile. "Cocky much?"

He shrugged. "You wanna bet on it?"

"If I do win, will you stay on as a deputy?"

No answer.

"Don't want to work under a woman?" I taunted.

"Oh, if you'll recall, darlin', I do my best work when I'm under a woman."

I blushed. Damn him.

"I heard about the fire. Glad no one was hurt."

"Me, too. I was surprised you weren't there."

"Why?"

"You seem to be everywhere."

"You mean I'm present at all your catastrophes?"

"Not nice, Sheriff."

"Gotta admit, Sergeant Major, you've had more adventures in this county in the last nine months as a civilian than most residents have in their entire lives."

"Is this where you bring up the Gunderson curse?"

Dawson peered at me over the top of his sunglasses. "Is this where you tell me why you're somehow involved in every suspect thing that goes on around here?"

I opened my mouth to shoot back a retort, but approaching footsteps caught our attention.

Bob Schofield, bank president, hustled between us. "Should I be worried you two are coming to blows?"

"Ask the sheriff. I'm unarmed." I smiled with my teeth.

"That's a first." Dawson smiled with his teeth right back at me. Hey, he was enjoying this.

So are you.

"Everything is all right?" Bob prompted.

"Me 'n' Miz Gunderson were just having a friendly discussion."

"A friendly wager, you mean."

Dawson's eyebrow winged up.

Bob said, "Really? What's the bet?"

"I told the sheriff if he wins the election, I'll kiss a pig. In public."

"And Sheriff? What about you?"

When Dawson gave me that lethally sexy cowboy grin, I knew I was totally hosed.

"If she wins? I'll play the part of the pig and *let* her kiss me in public."

That pigheaded jerk.

Dawson eased away from the MasterCraft boat he'd leaned against. "Bob. Nice seeing you." He shook the banker's hand. Then he took a step toward me and offered his hand.

I had no choice but to take it. I expected he'd stroke his thumb on the underside of my wrist, or squeeze a bit harder than necessary. He did neither. He simply shook it and said, "See you around, Mercy."

The retort "Not if I see you first" automatically jumped from my mouth, and both men laughed.

Mature, Gunderson.

Tongues would be wagging about our exchange, and I wouldn't put it past Bob Schofield to start a betting pool. Bankers. Opportunistic bastards.

I walked to the Blackbird Diner and selected a table close to the front door. Starved, I ordered the noon special, a patty melt with potato dumpling soup.

My mind kept replaying every word of my exchange with Dawson, like some teen crush. Maybe I was a little shocked he wasn't more pissed off about my running for sheriff, just that

I hadn't told him sooner. That was the kicker; Dawson wasn't aware he *had* been the first person I'd told.

I looked up when the door chime jangled. Deputy Moore ordered a cup of coffee to go. She meandered over.

"Mercy. How you doing?" she asked, like she hadn't spent an hour with me, strategizing a campaign to overthrow her boss.

"Hungry. Got a minute to join me?"

"Only about that. I'm on a coffee run for the sheriff." She tossed her bag on the chair across from me. "Mitzi, bless her heart, always brews Sheriff Dawson a fresh pot, since he's so damn picky about his coffee."

How well I knew that about Mr. Coffee Connoisseur. "So have you heard about Pete's new venture? Enticing the masses in Eagle Ridge to buy four-dollar cups of coffee?"

"I imagine that we, in the sheriff's department, won't have a choice but to patronize it. Can't be accused of showing favoritism." She kept her eyes on mine. "I have a package for you. When the coast is clear, I'll slide it under the table."

"Okay." I watched Mitzi duck down beneath the hostess stand. "All clear."

With stealth I admired, Kiki passed it to me, while nonchalantly sipping her coffee. My fingers briefly grazed the edges of a manila envelope before I secured it in my trusty wonder bag. "What is it?"

"Is Mitzi hovering anywhere nearby?"

"No. She's wiping tables."

"She's got hawklike hearing. I swear she's Dawson's best source in this town. I debated coming in here or bringing it to you later."

"How'd you know where I was?"

Kiki quirked a brow. "Dawson's web of spies. How do you think he tracked you to the bank parking lot so fast after you left Pete's?"

Damn.

"Besides, I thought you'd want to see this right away. It's the coroner's report on Jason Hawley." Kiki leaned forward. "And the list of Jason's personal effects."

"How'd you manage that?"

"Wasn't easy. It came yesterday, and the boss immediately locked it in his desk."

I frowned. "Is that standard procedure?"

"No. Which is why I know something is up. He didn't show it to Jazinski or me. And neither of us was allowed to catalog the contents of the victim's vehicle or the motel room."

A small sheriff's department meant all employees, from the deputies to the office support staff, knew damn near everything that went on in the county office. So why wasn't Dawson sharing with his coworkers?

Maybe because he suspects those coworkers are leaking information about an open case to his competition.

"Why are you telling me this?"

Kiki removed her hat and raked a hand through her hair. "As a candidate for sheriff, you should be in the loop on current cases. Plus, I think you actually care about catching whoever killed Jason Hawley. Dawson doesn't seem to have the level of dedication you do. Which bugs the crap out of me and is also why I'm backing you."

"I appreciate it, but does Dawson know you're supporting me?"

"No. He never would've left me alone at the station today." Her nose wrinkled. "At least Jolene was working and not Jilly."

"Jilly?"

"The receptionist who fancies herself a supermodel?"

Ah. Robo-Barbie. "Who hired jiggly Jilly?"

"Who do you think?"

Dawson. Typical he'd chosen a hot chickie to play fetch and carry for him. "How'd you find out about the report?"

"Claire Montague dropped it off personally." Kiki scowled. "Stupid woman was all puffed up like a peahen, bragging that her instructions were to give it only to Dawson. That's not all she wanted to give him, if you get my drift."

A burst of jealousy flared inside me. "Is he interested in her?"

"Not in the slightest. When Dawson left to go home for lunch, I snuck into his office and copied the file."

"Did you have a chance to look at it?"

"Only to see a bunch of medical gibberish. You'll have to do some research to decipher it, which is why I wanted to give it to you as soon as possible."

"Thank you."

Mitzi delivered my food. The mix of fried onions, melted cheese, tangy horseradish sauce, and toasted bread smelled heavenly, but I'd lost my appetite. All I wanted was to hole up in my office at the ranch and dissect the reports.

Kiki stood. "I'll let you enjoy your lunch."

I didn't linger after the plates were cleared.

FOURTEEN

As I zipped toward home, I tried to stop obsessing about what information the reports held and took a moment to enjoy the drive. Even my dirty windshield couldn't mask the sky's brilliance. Cloudless. Vast. An intense shade of blue that straddled the color spectrum between turquoise and sapphire.

Few artists had captured the magnificence of a spring sky. Plenty of talented hands showcased the bleak winter sky. Or the hazy, hot, dry hues of a stormy summer sky. Or the color-leached tones of an autumn sky. Spring was so transitory in western South Dakota it almost wasn't a season. Which is why it'd always been my favorite time of year.

Shoonga bounded across the yard to greet me. Nothing like a dog's slobbering, barking, yipping as the ultimate welcome home.

Jake's head was buried in the engine compartment of the farmhand. Inside, Sophie sat at the kitchen table doing word searches as she hardboiled eggs. Hope watched TV, Joy asleep at her breast. Just a typical day at the ranch.

I locked myself in Dad's office. While I waited for the computer to boot up, I rifled through the stack of bills, intending to divide them in the order they needed to be paid, when I remembered book work was no longer my domain. I did a quick tally:

Not doing ranch books.

Not helping with the cattle.

Not doing domestic chores.

Wow. I was getting to be as useless as teats on a bull around here.

Not entirely useless. You cough up cash out of your retirement pay every month for operating expenses.

That thought was even more depressing. Had I really become the type of hobby rancher I loathed? And would I feel guiltier if I was elected sheriff?

Did your dad feel guilty?

Good question.

I opened the manila envelope and slid the papers out, shuffling until I found Jason's personal effects. The lists were separated into three categories: body, vehicle, and motel room.

Items listed found on and around the victim's body:

Clothing:

> *Brown leather jacket*
> *Jeans*
> *Long-sleeved dress shirt*
> *T-shirt*
> *Briefs*
> *Socks*
> *White athletic shoes*
> *Black leather belt*
> *Loose change in front right pocket*
> *Noticeably absent: any type of wallet or identification.*

I checked off the items, one by one. Another item was noticeably absent. J-Hawk's knife, which he claimed he never was without. He'd had it in Clementine's because he'd been waving it around like a madman. Maybe it was on another list. I kept looking.

Items listed found in victim's vehicle:

> *Vehicle registration*
> *Proof of insurance*
> *Manufacturer's manual*
> *South Dakota map*
> *Cell phone and charger*

Two boxes of folders filled with Titan Oil information
Four empty cans Red Bull energy drink
Twelve protein bar wrappers
Two pairs sunglasses
Three ball caps
Winter jacket
Windshield scraper
Leather gloves
Rubber boots

Duffel bag contents:

Athletic shorts
Sweatpants
Two T-shirts
Socks
Athletic shoes
Deodorant
iPod
Three water bottles
Four protein bars
Forty (40) unopened pill containers of prescription-brand
  OxyContin.

Holy crap. Forty? No wonder Dawson had spelled it out and listed it numerically. Be easy to assume a mistake had been made in the cataloguing.

My question? Why did Jason have that much OxyContin in his possession? Was working for Titan Oil that stressful?

I went back over the list. No mention of the knife. Anywhere. Something was wrong here. I scanned the next header.

Items listed found in victim's motel room:

Three pairs jeans
Four pairs suit pants
Four dress shirts
Two suit jackets

Two ties
Two pairs dress shoes
Five long-sleeved casual shirts
Three T-shirts
Seven pairs underwear
Nine pairs socks
Belt

Toiletry bag contents:

Toothbrush
Toothpaste
Condoms
Dental floss
Electric razor
Aftershave
Mouthwash
Nail clipper
Four (4) pill containers of prescription-brand Nexavar

What the hell was Nexavar? I'd never heard of it. My stomach flipped when I looked at the first item under the next heading.

Suitcase contents:

One hundred (100) unopened pill containers of prescription-brand OxyContin.

I stared at the paper, as if the meaning of the words would change.

The J-Hawk I'd known, the man who'd saved my life, had been a regimented career military man who walked the straight and narrow.

This Jason Hawley was either a drug addict or a drug dealer or both.

I scoured the paperwork again. I didn't discover anything new, but I realized there'd been no personal effects. No pictures of his family. No wedding ring.

No knife.

If the knife wasn't at the crime scene, in his SUV, on his person, or in his hotel room . . . where was it?

As much as I questioned Dawson's investigative progress, I doubted he would've missed such an important piece of evidence—given the fact Jason Hawley had been stabbed as well as shot.

Had Jason waved the knife at his attacker, like he'd done in the bar? Had the killer grabbed the knife and used it on Jason? What kind of sick fucker did that?

One smart enough not to leave evidence behind.

Frustrated and sickened, I flipped back to the first page. The coroner's report.

No autopsy had been performed, the coroner examined the body basically as it'd come to her. The first page was a diagram of the body. Each wound was listed with precise measurements. Each bruise, each scratch. The diameter of the bullet holes. The sizes of the exit wounds. The length of the knife gashes. The depth of the knife gashes. But no gashes on his forearms.

I found it interesting that the knife wounds had been inflicted after the gunshot wounds. Had the killer been afraid Jason would survive? So slicing and dicing him after riddling his body with bullets was extra insurance?

If Jason had been bleeding out, no defensive cut wounds on his forearms made sense; he'd had no need to protect himself.

The coroner's conclusion stated the victim had died between eleven p.m. and two a.m. There was no scientific way to know how long it'd taken him to die. If I'd gotten off shift early at Clementine's that night, would it have mattered?

Had Jason lain there dying, hoping I'd swoop in and save him from the grim reaper just like he'd saved me?

Sick to my stomach, I had to close the file and let that guilty thought soak in. I took a deep breath and flipped the page.

Blood work information. A list of the standard tests, which I didn't understand the necessity for. J-Hawk had obviously been murdered. What difference would it make if drugs were found in his body after the fact? Drugs hadn't killed him.

I scanned the list, because like Kiki had warned me, it

contained a whole lot of medical gibberish. A couple of details caught my eye. High levels of OxyContin. The second number was abnormally high—a drug I'd never heard of: Nexavar. But it was the same one found in his motel room. I typed the name in the search engine.

Immediately 275,000 references popped up. Clinical trials. Testimonials. Research papers. FDA approval.

Nexavar was a drug for the treatment of cancer.

Cancer.

J-Hawk had cancer?

No. Fucking. Way. Had to be a mistake. Maybe a misspelling of the common pharmaceutical name. I spelled it differently.

Same results.

Stunned, I sank back in my chair and stared at the screen, thoughts racing around my head like escaped lab rats.

If Jason had cancer, why hadn't he stayed close to North Dakota so his physicians could monitor his vitals?

My mouth dried. After what he'd told me, I knew he'd rather deal with a cancer diagnosis on his own, on the road, away from his family, instead of allowing his attention-monger wife to care for him.

Didn't cancer treatment make you tired? Wear you down?

Yes, but cancer treatment could be painful, so that explained the large amount of OxyContin in his system.

But it didn't explain the massive amounts of OxyContin in his possession.

So Major Jason Hawley, who'd hated taking even a simple aspirin during his army years, had started popping pills to erase the pain and side effects from the cancer meds? Or had he become addicted to drugs because they helped him cope with how much he'd hated his life?

What a vicious circle. I wished he'd confided in me earlier. Not that I could've done a damn thing about his cancer or his drug dependency, but it might've offered him some comfort that he did have friends he could talk to.

I wondered who'd known about his use of painkillers.

His wife? Not likely.

His employer? Not likely.

I wondered who'd known about his cancer.

His wife? Likely.

His employer? Likely.

Anna? No.

J-Hawk couldn't risk telling Anna he was dying. She would've said *fuck it* and stayed by his side until his life ended.

I couldn't tell her. I couldn't tell anyone, because technically, I wasn't even supposed to have this information. But really, what did one more secret matter? I'd just pile it on the 10 billion others I was keeping.

As enlightening and disheartening as this information was, it didn't get me any closer to finding out who'd killed him.

Might be a long shot, but I had to find out more about the woman he'd talked to that night.

I called Winona's cell. "It's Mercy. I'm still trying to put faces together with names on the lists. George Johnson mentioned a woman Jason talked to."

"What's her name?"

"Cherelle. She's young. Indian. Got a nasty scar on her face. I guess she's been in Clementine's a couple times, but I don't remember seeing her. Do you know her?"

"Yeah. Cherelle Dupris. She's bad news."

Damn static. "Could you repeat that?"

"I said she's with Victor Bad Wound."

I frowned. Another name I vaguely recognized. "Who is Victor Bad Wound?"

"Victor Bad Wound is Barry Sarohutu's younger brother."

"If Cherelle comes into Clementine's, no matter what time, will you call me right away? Please?"

"I guess. But I'm being honest when I say I hope she never comes in again." She hung up.

I tapped my fingers on the desk and stared into space. I needed more information on this Cherelle person. Who'd have access to that kind of information?

Bingo.

One person knew everyone and everything that went on around the Eagle River Reservation.

I called Rollie.

FIFTEEN

Given Rollie's reputation for maintaining a low profile when it came to his business dealings, I agreed to meet him out in the middle of nowhere. I understood his need for privacy and discretion, because it matched mine.

Besides, I was armed.

The dust rooster behind his truck clued me to his impending arrival a half mile before he skidded to a stop in front of me.

Rollie leaned across the seat and yelled through the open passenger's-side window. "Hey. Get in."

"Can't we talk here?" I'd already waited overnight for this chat, and Geneva had a million things for me to do today.

"Nope. I've got a meeting at elk crossing."

After three tries, the passenger's-side door on his truck finally shut, and we were tooling down County Road 2A, headed toward the reservation.

"I almost didn't come," he offered conversationally.

"Why?"

"Mebbe because you don't call me to meet just so we can shoot the breeze. You only call when you want something."

Was that a note of . . . hurt in Rollie's tone? Nah. And I refused to be put on the defensive. "The phone line runs both ways, old man. You can call me, too."

"I hate talking on the damn phone."

"I know. But I'm rusty on using smoke signals to get your attention."

"Smarty."

I smiled.

"So what's on your mind, Mercy girl?"

"First, if I want to ask you a couple of questions, will I owe you another favor?"

Rollie grabbed a smashed pack of smokes from the bench seat. He punched the lighter knob and shook out a crumpled cigarette. Cancer ritual complete, he faced me. "It depends."

Cryptic. "On what?"

"Coupla things. But they'll keep until the proper time."

Was Rollie waiting to call in those "favors" if I became sheriff? I'd blindly agreed to do whatever he asked me the first time I'd needed his help. Evidently I hadn't learned my lesson, because I was about to do it again.

"Ask away," he said.

"What do you know about Barry Sarohutu, his brother Victor Bad Wound, and the group they run?"

"Run is exactly the right word, hey. You oughta run as far away from them as you can."

Rollie? Scared of someone on the rez? That was new. "Do you run from them?"

"Wish I could. I know enough about 'em to make sure I stay on their good side." He blew a smoke ring. "Why you askin'?"

"Their group has been coming into Clementine's. Everyone's freaked out about it."

"They should be. No one wants Sarohutu and his guys around, but telling them to take their business elsewhere ain't smart."

"Why not?"

"Fear of their unique ways of retaliation. People call them the Lakota Yakuza."

I laughed.

"Ain't no laughing matter. Them guys'll carve you up if you so much as look at them wrong."

My smile dried. "Is that what happened to Cherelle Dupris?"

His gaze turned sharp. "You've seen her around Clementine's?"

"Not personally. But I've heard she was in, and I want to talk to her."

"She ain't gonna talk to you without Victor Bad Wound's permission."

"You sure?"

Rollie ground out his smoke. "Lemme tell you a story about Cherelle. About six years ago, Sarohutu returned to the rez to 'establish' himself after he'd run away to L.A. fifteen years before. He noticed Cherelle—hard not to, she was a beautiful girl. She competed in Junior Indian Princess pageants, and everyone believed she'd be Miss Indian South Dakota, maybe even Miss Indian America."

This was not going to be a happy Indian parable.

"She fell under Saro's spell. But Victor had his eye on Cherelle long before his half brother returned to the rez. His jealousy became an obsession, and he snatched her. Victor knew Saro would dump Cherelle if she wasn't the hottest chick on the rez, so Victor marred her. Rumor is her face isn't the only place he sliced her. Another rumor is Victor kept her tied up for three weeks, allowing the slice on her face to become infected so it wouldn't heal right. Victor thought he was being clever, giving her a 'bad wound' so everyone knew she belonged to him, not Saro."

What a sick fucking bastard.

"When Victor released Cherelle, she ran to Saro and told him what'd happened. She believed Saro would want her no matter how she looked, and she demanded Saro punish Victor for what he'd done." Rollie paused. "Saro beat her severely. When she recovered, he swore to keep her ugly face around as a reminder to everyone on the rez never to come between him and his brother. Saro announced the mark on her face meant she was Victor's property. Then Saro warned if she ever tried to leave Victor, he'd kill off her family members. One by one."

Sounded like an idle threat, yet I knew it wasn't. It reminded me of J-Hawk's wife. God, lots of psychopaths walked free, in every culture and in every walk of life.

"Cherelle didn't believe him. She went to Rapid City to stay with her cousin. Two days later, her *unci* was the victim of a hit and run. After the funeral, Cherelle moved in with Victor and cut herself off from her family. She's their errand girl, their go-between, their whore for hire. She's whatever they want her to be."

I was sickened by the story. I didn't doubt the truth of it, but I wanted to know how Rollie had come across the information. Or if it was common knowledge on the Eagle River Reservation.

Took him a long time to answer. "The basics are common knowledge. But Cherelle is Verline's cousin. Verline was thirteen when that happened." He fingered his necklace. "Verline begged me to do something about Saro and Victor. No doubt what they done ain't right. Mebbe if I'da been twenty years younger I'da taken them on. But I'm an old man. Ain't proud of using that as an excuse, but it is what it is."

No point in building up Rollie's ego; he'd see through my insincerity and take offense. I changed the subject. "How is Verline?"

"Mean." He sighed. "She's pregnant again."

Holy Viagra. Verline, Rollie's live-in, was barely nineteen and younger than any of his six kids from his various relationships. I suspected Verline was younger than Rollie's oldest grandkid. She'd given birth to their son seven months ago.

"You'd think by your age you'da figured out what causes that situation."

"Smarty." Rollie slowed behind a Lexus parked at elk crossing, which was a sign by a gravel pullout that warned of wildlife at large. He threw it into Park. "Be right back."

In the side mirror, I watched Rollie approach the vehicle and pass a small box through the window opening. The driver handed over folded cash. Rollie unfolded it and counted it. He nodded, tucked it in his shirt pocket, and sauntered back to the truck as the Lexus roared away.

Don't ask, Mercy.

But I had to poke Rollie a little, to see if he'd share the information I wanted. He'd do it to avoid answering my question about what he was selling on the side. "So if I had drugs to unload in this area, who would I get in touch with from Saro's group to see if they were interested in buying?"

Rollie's face remained placid as he whipped a U-turn. "Don't think our sheriff candidate oughta be dealin' drugs for extra cash."

"Not me personally, but hypothetically speaking."

"And you're askin' me, hypothetically speaking, about illegal shit like this because . . . ?"

"You da man on the rez, Rollie. Nothin' gets past you."

"You use that damn sugar mouth on a man just like your mama did," he grumbled.

But I saw his half smile through his half-assed protest. "For instance, say someone has prescription drugs. Say you're traveling through, new in the area with no plans to stay long term. You've got top-quality product. How do you know who to contact to unload it?"

Rollie grunted. "First off, you gotta expect if you're unloading drugs that you've already been in contact with someone who directed you through the proper channels. Ain't no one gonna show up here and walk up to Victor or Saro, especially not on the rez, and say, 'Hey, man, I've heard you own this territory, and I'm hauling some premium product.' Other associates along the supply chain would've already vouched for you, understand?"

I nodded. "So if I pass the 'she's legit' test, then what?"

"If they're looking to buy what you're peddling, the next step is an in-person meet with Saro's rep."

"Who's that?"

No answer.

"Come on, Rollie."

"Cherelle."

Dammit. J-Hawk had been talking to Cherelle, which confirmed every fear I had.

"She's always first contact. That way if a federal agency is setting up a sting, she's implicated."

"Wouldn't Cherelle turn on Saro and Victor and blab for immunity?"

Rollie shook his head. "They'll go after her family. She'd be better off keeping her mouth shut and doin' time."

"If Cherelle clears me and my product, who do I end up dealing with?"

"Victor. He sets the meeting times. The meeting places. He makes the payments. Saro is the brains; Victor is the muscle. They're like yin and yang. And trust me, they play up that angle like crazy. Because, *kola*, they are crazy. Make no mistake about that."

I let that all soak in. I looked up, and Rollie was pulling in behind my truck.

"I'm gonna give you some advice, Mercy girl. Let it go. People who get involved with Saro wind up dead . . . I don't gotta spell it out for you."

"Meaning Saro's untouchable?"

"Perhaps."

My spine snapped straight with indignation. "No one is above the law. That's the whole reason I'm running for sheriff, Rollie."

He lit another cigarette, giving me the one-eyed squint through the smoke. "Is that really the reason?"

I counted to twenty before I answered. "If Saro's drug, torture, and sex-for-trade business has been going on as long as you claim, then my dad was just as guilty as Dawson is for letting it slide. I won't look the other way. I won't let it go."

"Your funeral."

"Yep. I'd rather die trying than live in fear and not try at all."

He grinned. "Can we use that as your new campaign slogan, hey?"

"Smarty-pants," I volleyed back.

"What else is on your mind, Mercy girl?"

Intuitive old man. "Did you ever meet up with any of the guys you fought with in Vietnam? You know, a few years after you came home?"

"The surviving guys from my platoon have a reunion every year."

"Do you ever go?"

The beads at the ends of his braids clicked together when he shook his head. "I ain't the type to reminisce about stuff that still gives me nightmares." He flicked ashes out the window. "You been havin' them dreams?"

No need to explain what "them dreams" meant. I shrugged. "Some. Mostly the booze lets me sleep in peace."

He snorted. "*Shee*. You mean booze lets you pass out with a false sense of security."

"It's a moot point now, since I'm not drinking nearly as much as I was."

"Which is a good thing, girlie. So why you askin' me about my marine pals, hey?"

"I just wondered if . . . you ever . . . felt you owed them or something."

His hand curled over my fingers, which were picking at a hole in his dashboard. "I can't help you when you're talkin' in riddles."

I shared a condensed version of my past with J-Hawk and my frustration with Dawson's apathy about finding out who'd killed him. I hadn't told anyone my reason for accepting the bid for sheriff. So when I said it out loud? For the first time it seemed childish, petty, and impulsive.

Rollie eased back and fingered the necklace of bone. He looked at me. "People change, Mercy. This J-Hawk guy don't sound like the man you used to know. Mebbe if you go digging, you'll find things you'd've been better off leaving be."

"Too late. And he saved my life. I literally would not be sitting here right now if it weren't for him. So I'm supposed to chalk up his murder to bad luck or bad timing?"

"What if Dawson's right and that's all it is?"

"Then it shouldn't be that goddamn hard to investigate, should it? Even I should be able to crack the case."

Rollie smiled. Not his sneaky smile, but his genuine smile of pride. "You have a warrior heart, Mercy. Do you want me to tell you if you find justice for your friend it'll even the score of what you feel you owe him?"

"Yes."

"I can't do that, 'cause life don't work that way. But you'll do what you have to and won't rest until you've got an answer, whether or not it's the answer you wanted."

I rolled my eyes. "Thanks for just repeating my question back to me in another form."

"Anytime you need token advice from the wise old Indian, you know where to find me."

The door on his truck wouldn't budge, so I bailed out the window. I'd rounded the back end when he called out, "Be careful."

• • •

The ranch was the last place I wanted to go but the only place I wanted to be. I missed my dog, but really, even Shoonga would ditch me and my crap attitude today.

Having the truck windows rolled down and feeling dusty air blowing across my face helped. As did singing along loudly to the Dierks Bentley tune on the radio. By the time I reached the cabin, I wasn't about to waste such a splendorous day reading snooze-worthy paperwork.

When in doubt, pull the handguns out.

I grabbed ammo for my .22 "plinker," a Smith and Wesson model 41 semiauto, which was the most accurate .22 I'd ever used, and .45 ammo for my grandfather's Colt 1911, which I'd gotten accurized, a new slide lapped to the existing frame, a new barrel and barrel bushing, and a new competition hammer and trigger. I tossed in a whole bag of tin cans. I'd rather shoot a moving target than a static one. Next time I hit Scheels in Rapid City, I'd buy an automatic clay pigeon thrower so I could mix up my shooting practices and use my shotguns. I'd inherited an antique, handheld variety of pigeon thrower from my dad, but it didn't work for solo shooters.

I set up in a flat section of prairie, along an old section of fencing a little ways from the cabin, where the fence posts were old pieces of wood, not metal poles. I lined up the cans, donned my earplugs, and commenced to blasting holes in the tin, keeping the distance around fifty yards. The days of my needing to practice to maintain accuracy in hitting a target at five hundred plus yards were history. Short range with just the naked eye was enough challenge.

Plus, I'd proved I still had the mettle the night I'd blown up Newsome's house. That thought boosted my spirits.

Some shooters always used a scope, even for target practice. Maybe especially for target practice. Snipers by and large couldn't function without scopes. I understood it and more often than not used one. But when faced with a situation where I had to rely on my instincts, I eyeballed it. It hadn't affected my accuracy rating at all. Until the eye injury.

I shot ten clips from the Smith and Wesson and then ten clips from the 1911. I'd reloaded and replaced the cans, exhilarating in the familiar. Aiming. Firing. For the most part, I put the bullets exactly where I'd intended to put them. Even with my left eye.

I missed this feeling of confidence. This was what I was good at. This was what I wanted to do. This was what I was meant to do. Meant to do and *allowed* to do were two different animals. I paused, setting my gun on the ground. After removing my earplugs, I closed my eyes, waiting for the snarky little voice inside my head to appear and remind me of my failings.

"You're still pulling to the left a hair."

The voice was right behind me, not inside my head.

I whirled around.

"I thought it'd be best not to surprise you while you had a full clip." The petite Mexican woman, wearing her customary all-black outfit, flipped her waist-length braid over her shoulder and smiled at me. "Surprised?"

"Anna. You sneaky bitch." I tackled her. As soon as I had her on the ground, she pulled a reversal. I rolled my hips, throwing her sideways. Then we were back on our feet facing each other, arms up to block, keeping a wide stance with our legs, just like we'd been taught.

I let my hands fall to my side. "Jesus Christ, A-Rod, you couldn't have warned me you'd planned a trip to South Dakota?"

She shrugged. "It was close, so I figured what the hell. I'd see firsthand what the big draw this no-man's-land was for you."

"Close to where?"

"North Dakota." Anna held up her hand, stopping my protest. "And before you lecture me, I had a choice in saying good-bye to Jason this time and I took it."

I should've known nothing would keep her from J-Hawk's funeral. If she asked why I hadn't attended, I'd give her the bullshit excuse that I'd had to work at the bar. Easier than admitting I'd said my private good-bye the day the hearse rolled out of town. I grabbed her and hugged her, which probably shocked her more than my tackling her.

Anna was a tiny thing, five feet one, and she weighed less than a hundred pounds, but she held her own in hand-to-hand fighting with just about any man. Having grown up bilingual in

California, she'd been tapped as our language specialist. But like the rest of our team, she was above average with firearms.

"You okay?"

"Not really." She pushed away from me and wrapped her arms around herself. "I'm pretty fucked up about the Jason thing to show my Mexican face in the white-bread Midwest. Jesus. Is there any racial diversity here? Or are you all some freaky blond hair, blue-eyed Aryan children of the corn?"

"Hello? Part Indian standing in front of you."

"Sorry." Anna glanced at the handguns on the ground and then at me. "You done with practice?"

"Yep, unless you want to fire off a few rounds."

"Maybe later. Right now I need a drink."

I did, too. I jogged to the cans and tossed them in the garbage bag. Another rule I still followed. Always pick up your targets and never let anyone know how well you can shoot. Then I started picking up spent shells.

"You reload?" she asked.

"Yeah. Waste not, want not. Besides, the bigger cals are expensive as hell to replace." I'd stashed my guns and unused ammo in my sports bag and slung the strap over my shoulder. Anna didn't offer to carry my guns. She knew better. "So how'd you get here?"

"Drove. I parked at the main house and some Indian guy directed me over the river and through the woods."

"You sticking around?"

"If you don't mind."

"*Mi casa es su casa.*"

Anna groaned. "Is that all the Spanish you remember?"

"*Si.*" I slid her a sly glance. "*Bésame el culo.*"

"Redneck."

"Wetback."

"Damn, Gunny, it is good to see you."

"You, too, A-Rod."

A bottle of Wild Turkey and a bottle of Jose Cuervo sat on the plastic table between us. Upon returning to the cabin, we'd stretched out on lawn chairs to soak up the fading rays of sunlight.

When I finished telling her about my recent foray into the law enforcement race, she said, "No. Fucking. Way."

I swigged whiskey straight from the bottle. "You mean no way am I going to win? Or no way because you're shocked I'm actually doing it?"

"Both."

"Harsh."

"Just calling it like I see it. Maybe this Dawson is a douche and can't find his ass with both hands, but people will vote for him because he's a dude. You might be the former sheriff's daughter, but that ain't gonna make any difference." She tucked a loose strand of hair behind her ear. "Besides, you've been away, Mercy. Women who've been at war . . . well, I'll bet you feel more like an outsider now than you ever did."

Her response stung. Another slug of Wild Turkey didn't soften the blow or cool the heat in my cheeks. So I turned it back on her. "Did J-Hawk's wife know who you were?"

"Hell no. It wasn't like I gave her my condolences. But if looks could kill?" Anna aimed the half-empty bottle of tequila at me like a gun. "She'd be dead."

I waited. And drank.

"It's more than me just hating her because she had him and I didn't. I hated that she didn't understand him, and she sure as hell didn't deserve him."

What was I supposed to say? That J-Hawk fucked up by staying with his psycho wife in order to protect his children? He'd willingly made that choice, but even with his death, Anna wouldn't see that. And I couldn't tell her the truth.

"His youngest daughter looks just like him."

"Anna. Don't do this to yourself."

"Too late. A part of me wanted to stand up and scream during the service, scream at his perfect little blond wifey-poo, scream that she'd killed Jason a long time ago. It was her fault Jason was dead now. If he hadn't been trying so goddamn hard to get away from her, he wouldn't have ended up on this path, murdered by some stupid redneck and left in a field to die."

The gruesome vision of J-Hawk's blood-soaked body appeared.

I closed my eyes, but the image stayed burned in my mind. And the damn whiskey wasn't scrubbing it away.

"When I sat in the back of the church, I saw the type of monster she is, Mercy. Sometimes Jason would tell me some of the passive/aggressive, just plain nutso stuff she did or said." She laughed bitterly. "And I wondered if he wasn't making her out to be way worse than she was to alleviate his guilt about being with me. I mean, come on, isn't that whole married-guy bullshit about his wife not understanding him clichéd? Isn't that what you tried to get me to understand?"

"Yes." But I didn't have the whole story back then, like I did now. Confirming her theory that he'd ended up with a miserable life served no purpose for anyone. Especially Anna, who was mourning him hard.

Anna kept talking. Needed to get it out, I supposed, and I should've applauded her effort. But I preferred to keep this life-altering emotional shit bottled up inside and parcel it out in small doses.

One thing was clear. As much as I thought I'd known J-Hawk, I hadn't. After Anna's rant, I looked at her and felt that same sense of discord. Did I really know her?

Do you ever really know anyone?

"You're looking at me like you've seen a ghost, Gunny."

A shiver did ripple down my spine when I remembered J-Hawk had said the exact same thing to me. "No. I'm just wondering . . . Why are you here?"

"I missed you?"

I couldn't even crack a smile.

"We both know I wouldn't be here if Jason wasn't dead." She tilted her head back and closed her eyes. "I hate even saying the words *he's dead*. I should accept that Jason's death was as ugly as his life. But when I stood in the church with my hand on his coffin? I felt nothing. No closure. Nothing but anger. It's not fucking fair."

"I know."

Tears dripped down her face and dotted the slate beneath her chair. "I loved him, Mercy. Loved him like I've never loved anyone else. It's made me aware of my own mortality. Made me wonder if Jason's soul is finally at peace."

I gulped whiskey as I considered my answer. "What about your soul?"

"I have no soul." She stood and wiped her face. "I gotta take a leak. Or what was that funny thing you and Jason always used to say?"

"Gotta see a man about a horse," I said absently.

"That, too. And when I get back? We're getting shitfaced and playing poker."

Just like old times.

SIXTEEN

Someone was trying to beat down my door.

"Jesus Christ. Grow a little patience. I'm coming."

I flipped the dead bolt and jerked the door open.

Ow. When had the morning sun gotten so bright?

"It's about damn time." Geneva bulled her way inside. Her eyes took in my camo tank top, boxing shorts, and extreme bedhead. "Why aren't you dressed? We have a meeting in half an hour."

"Shit."

"Is your bleary-eyed state due to the empty Wild Turkey bottle and the empty Cuervo bottle on the table outside?"

"The Cuervo bottle was mine." Anna sat up on the couch and threw off the afghan. "Man. I'm never drinking again."

I snorted. "Right. I've heard that a time or twenty."

"Fuck off."

Geneva lifted both eyebrows at the exchange.

"Geneva, meet my army buddy, Anna Rodriguez. Anna, meet my oldest friend, Geneva Illingsworth."

They mumbled at each other.

"Are you staying long?" Geneva asked Anna.

"Haven't decided."

"So you're not in the army?"

"No, ma'am. In fact, I got out two years before Gunny."

Geneva looked perplexed at Anna's use of my nickname, but she recovered fast. "Well, I'm afraid I'll have to cut your visit short for a bit this morning. Mercy has a meeting scheduled."

"No sweat. I'll tag along." Anna stretched. "Won't take me long to get ready."

Anna was less sociable than me, and I couldn't deal with both her and Geneva first thing this morning. "Tell you what—hang out here, and I'll be back before you know it."

"Huh-uh. I'm going." She shook her finger at me. "Pissing me off when I'm hungover is a bad choice. You know that."

Anna's threat wouldn't fly with me. Once her superior; always her superior. "Back off, A-Rod. I'm dealing with campaign stuff and don't need your help. Work on losing your bitchy attitude while I'm gone."

Anna whizzed a decorative pillow at my head. I caught it and flung it back at her Frisbee-style. She grinned. "Just testing your reflexes, Gunny. Hate to think you were getting soft."

"Soft my ass."

She hip-checked me as she walked by. "The couch sucks. I'm sleeping it off in your bed."

I managed to grab my clothes before she slammed the bedroom door in my face. I showered, braided my hair, and slathered on makeup. Dressed in my newest Cruel Girl jeans, a sleeveless blue-plaid shirt, and my sparkly red rhinestone belt, I epitomized the red, white, and blue hometown cowgirl.

Geneva gave me a once-over as I slipped on my Ariat Fatbaby boots with the ostrich skin toes. Wouldn't be prudent to wear a gun, although I felt half naked without one.

"Do I pass your inspection, campaign boss?"

"Part of me says no, because it's too casual. Part of me says yes, you look amazing, and I don't think my ego can handle seeing you in dress clothes."

My head snapped up. A compliment? From Geneva?

She smirked. "Shocked I have a civil side to my tongue?"

"Uh-huh. That and the fact no one's called me amazing in a long damn time."

Except Dawson had a few nights ago. He'd murmured, "You are amazing, Mercy," as he'd kissed every inch of my skin. Dammit. I didn't want to think about Dawson and what my active campaigning for his job would do to our relationship.

What relationship? It's just sex, right?

"Mercy? You okay?"

I looked at her, guiltily, I'm sure. "Sorry. Just thinking about something else."

"Let's go."

Geneva drove a minivan, which didn't bother me. She drove like Mad Max on meth, which did bother me. It occurred to me, as I white-knuckled the dash, that if I was elected sheriff, I'd have to cite her for speeding.

Too bad I didn't have the damn badge and ticket book right now. But I gritted my teeth, trying not to look at the speedometer. Or the road whizzing past. Or how she fiddled with the climate-control buttons instead of keeping both hands on the wheel.

"Mercy, I need to ask you something."

"If it's about my military service, there are some things I can't discuss."

"It's not that."

"Then what?"

She blurted, "Are you a lesbian? I don't care if you are, I mean, I'll still love you . . . but not in that way. It's just . . . well, you've never been married, you've never talked about any kind of long-term relationship. Then you're into guns and all that macho military stuff, and you haven't dated anyone since you've been home. Now Anna shows up and your relationship with her seems really . . . close."

Maybe keeping my encounters with Dawson a secret hadn't been a smart move. If I'd piqued Geneva's curiosity about my sexual orientation, did the rest of the county question it, too? My petulant side wondered if Dawson's marital status would be called into question. Would Dawson admit he was in a relation-ship?

What relationship? It's just sex, right?

Seemed my brain, pissed off by the alcohol-induced pounding headache, had decided on that theme today.

"Sorry if I made you uncomfortable. It's none of my busi-ness—"

"Of course it's your business. But don't worry that a former female lover will step forward during the campaign and out me, because I'm not gay."

Geneva turned her head and looked at me. "You're not?"

"No." She'd drifted completely into the other lane. "For Christsake, Gen, keep your eyes on the road."

"Oh, shit. Sorry." When she swerved back into the proper lane, I swear the wheels left the pavement.

Jesus. I could not watch the woman drive. "Out of pure nosiness, we've been friends forever. You've known me longer than anyone. Did you really think all of a sudden I might be batting for the other team?"

She rolled her eyes. "You pointed out to me last summer how much I didn't know about you, and that I never knew you as well as I thought I did, so it's a legit question, Mercy."

"True."

"Besides, you never talk about this kind of girly shit with me. So I don't have any idea if you've been in any serious relationships."

"A few. My inability to have kids is a big issue. If things became more than a fling, I'd 'fess up and most guys walked away. No big loss. I focused on the career I loved and kept all relationships casual. Men have come and gone. Some stayed longer than others, but they've all moved on."

"I didn't ask to be nosy."

"Yes, you did."

Geneva laughed. "Also true."

"But know what's funny? I have been seeing someone since I moved back here."

Dumb move, Gunderson.

What had possessed me to share that secret? It didn't feel like I was trying to give Geneva back the trust she'd lost with me; it felt like I was offering her proof that I wasn't a lesbian.

"Really? Who?"

I didn't answer.

Geneva mulled over the possibilities.

When she hit the brakes and we skidded to a stop on the shoulder, I knew she'd figured it out. Damn good thing my seat belt worked.

"Please tell me it's not Dawson."

"I can't."

"Can't what?"

"Can't tell you it's not Dawson, when it is him."

Geneva flat-out gaped at me. "Jesus, Mary, and Joseph. Mercy, you've been screwing around with the sheriff?"

"Uh, yeah."

"How long?"

"Off and on since last summer."

"Even after he arrested you?"

"The irony is we'd been together before he arrested me." Even I knew how freaky that sounded.

"Who else knows?" she demanded.

"John-John, only because he overheard something he shouldn't have. I doubt Dawson's told anyone. We've kept it private, for obvious reasons." I felt her gaze burning into me, and I found the guts to look at her. She wasn't mad; she wore a look of pity. That got my hackles up. "What?"

"Why are you doing this?"

"Running against him? Because you asked me to."

"Mercy, you know that's not what I meant."

"I don't know, okay? When we're alone and everything is good—great actually—I can forget who he is. But when it comes to him doing his job, I compare him to what my dad did as sheriff. Then I wonder what the hell I'm doing with a man who doesn't measure up."

Geneva was quiet, which drove me batshit crazy.

"Jesus, Gen, what?"

"Hate to burst your bubble, but Wyatt Gunderson wasn't a saint. However, Dawson did measure up, or else your dad wouldn't have given him his endorsement for sheriff."

"Don't remind me."

"I've known you a long time, Mercy, and you're damn good at self-sabotage."

I faced her. "Are you talking about what happened with Jake?"

She poked me in the arm. "See? More'n twenty years have passed by and you still haven't gotten over it. Stop using your one bad long-term relationship as an excuse. And for God sake, stop comparing all men to your dad. It's really kind of twisted."

I hated that she had a point.

"So why did you come out of the closet to me about your relationship with Dawson, Mercy?"

"Your job as my campaign manager is to keep me focused

on the issues. Make certain that I keep whatever weird fucking thing I feel for Dawson out of my decision-making process. I'm doing what's right for the county, not for myself."

Geneva eased the car back on the road. Her silence bothered me more than her constant chattering. When I couldn't stand the silence any longer, I snapped, "Spit it out before you choke on it."

"Speaking as your campaign manager? I'll do everything to help you get the win you deserve. But speaking as your friend? My heart is breaking for you and the decision you've made to put duty ahead of your personal life again." She careened into the library parking lot and screeched to a stop. "I accused you of being selfish last summer. Christ. You can't know how that eats at me, Mercy, because I see how wrong I was. You've given everything for everyone else. You deserve something good for yourself."

How was I supposed to respond to that?

Luckily, I didn't have to. Kiki knocked on the window and tapped her watch.

"We're late. Come on, candidate Gunderson, your committee awaits you," Geneva said, and the matter was closed.

For now. But she'd given me a lot to think about, none of it campaign related.

Anna and I were lounging on the sofa, drinking beer, watching the first season of *Lost* on the TV/DVD combo she'd haggled for at Pete's Pawnshop, when my cell phone rang. "Hello?"

"Mercy? It's Winona. Look, I don't have much time, but I wanted you to know that Cherelle just walked in."

"She alone?"

"For now."

"Good. I'll be there in fifteen. Keep her there—give her free drinks, whatever."

"I'll try." Winona hung up.

I vaulted to my feet and shimmied out of my loungewear, dressing in the ensemble I'd worn earlier. Except I added my favorite accessory in my back pocket: my Kahr Arms P380. I sat on the bed and tugged on my blue-camo Old Gringo boots.

Anna leaned in the door frame. "Where's the fire?"

"Clementine's. It's not on fire, but someone I've been wanting to talk to just showed up, so I've got to go."

"Is this more campaign crap?"

"No."

A gleam appeared in her eyes. "This has to do with Jason?"

She'd see through a lie, so I didn't bother. "Yes."

"I knew you wouldn't let this just fade away. You still feel like you owe him, don't you?"

"I *do* owe him, Anna."

"So do I. I'm coming with you."

I didn't have time to argue with her. "Get a move on then."

Surprisingly, Anna didn't pester me for more details on the drive to Clementine's.

My candidacy was the perfect excuse to wander through various clusters of bar patrons. Anna hit the bar, and I presented a big ol' smile to George Johnson's group. "Hey, guys. How's it going?"

"Good. You out on official business?" George asked.

"Yep. Pressing flesh. I figured I deserved a little liquid fortification beforehand."

Mike lifted a plastic cup off a stack in the center of the table and poured me a beer. "The first one's on us."

"Thanks."

"How about a toast?" Rocky raised his cup, and the guys at the table followed his lead. "To Mercy Gunderson, the next sheriff of Eagle River County."

I smiled and drank up. For the next few minutes, I made banal chitchat with my supporters as I closed in on my real target in the back room.

After I talked to members of the dart league, I waltzed right up to Cherelle's table and thrust out my hand. "Mercy Gunderson. I'm running for Eagle River County sheriff."

She ignored my hand. But she didn't duck her scarred face from view as I'd expected. A sneer settled on her misshapen mouth. "I don't give a flying fuck who you are. Not interested. Get lost."

"Now, Cherelle, is that any way to start a conversation? When I just want to talk about the issues that affect you personally?"

Her eyes flashed annoyance. "If you know my name, then you also know you don't wanna be around when my friends get here."

"Speaking of friends . . . we have a mutual friend."

"I doubt it."

I paused. "But you did know Jason Hawley, Cherelle."

"Never heard of him." Cherelle slid to the end of the booth, intending to leave.

"No need to run off. My buddy Anna just got here. And look. She brought refreshments."

Anna set three cups and a pitcher of beer in the middle of the table. She slid in. I turned and bent forward to snag a chair from an empty table, making sure Cherelle got a good look at the bulge in my back pocket.

When I turned back around, Cherelle demanded, "Since when are *you* allowed to carry in here?"

"Since always." I straddled the chair, allowing easy access to my gun and blocking her in. "So, Cherelle, here's what we know. You talked to Jason several times, even on the night he was murdered. We have a few more questions about that topic of conversation."

"I ain't telling you shit, cop," she spat.

"Although I hope to win the election, I'm not a cop yet, which means anything you tell me is off the record."

"Right."

Anna shoved a cup of beer at her. "So who fucked up your face?"

The bluntness caught Cherelle off guard.

"I'm betting it was some asshole guy who wanted to mark his territory." Anna swallowed half her glass of beer. "I hope you castrated the son of a bitch."

Cherelle's gaze darted between us. "You are both pathetic. You think you can flash a piece at me and I'll piss my pants because I'm scared? Of you two old bags? Don't make me laugh." She focused on Anna. "You think acting all fake, like we're sisters under the skin, united against asshole men, is gonna make me break down because I've finally met a woman who understands what I've been through? Fuck off. You don't know nothin'."

"Yeah?" Anna jerked her T-shirt down, pointing to the long

gash that ran from the right corner of her collarbone to her sternum. "I know exactly what it's like to have some sadistic fucker cut you up." She lifted her shirt, exposing the five knife wounds scattered at random intervals across her lower abdomen. "Ever been stabbed? Clear through your body so the knife comes out your back? You ever had to wait, knowing the insane motherfucker was going to stab you again? So don't you sit there all fucking smug and tell me I don't know nothin'."

Cherelle stared at Anna with unabashed interest.

Some of Anna's story was exaggerated. The gash on her chest was from scaffolding slicing her that night in Bali. But the stab-wound story was real. At age sixteen, Anna's ex-boyfriend cornered her at a public park in California and attempted to kill her. An army medic saw it happening, called the cops, and stabilized her until the ambulance arrived. Surgeons repaired her liver, but Anna lost a kidney, her appendix, and her uterus, and gained a new appreciation for the army.

"Looks like you win this round. But tell me, *Anna*," Cherelle repeated her name sarcastically, "do you ever see the guy who used you as a whetstone?"

Anna shook her head. "He's in jail."

"See, that's where we're different. I have to live with the guy who did this to me every day of my life."

Tempting, to chug the whole pitcher and quit bitching about my lot in life.

"Why do either of you give a damn about that Jason Hawley guy? If the dude was trouble, I think you'd"—Cherelle pointed at me—"be happy he wasn't around anymore."

I started to answer, but Anna beat me to it. "Maybe she is happy, but I'm not. Jason may've been a scummy guy to her, but to me he was . . . mine. Know what I mean?"

Cherelle's forehead puckered with total skepticism.

Anna pounded her beer and poured another. "Look, I'm not good with words, and I won't bore you with the star-crossed-lovers bullshit, although it was true for me 'n' Jason. He was . . ." Anna closed her eyes. "Dammit. He was great. He was everything. We had the real deal. Had it, and now it's gone."

The confession appeared to be working. Cherelle wasn't looking defiant, just . . . interested. Concerned maybe, but not totally convinced.

"When Mercy called me after she'd found his body, I had to come here. I don't know, probably sounds stupid, but I thought maybe I could . . . sense him or something."

Ooh. Anna was good.

Cherelle broke the silence. "I do know what you mean. I had that real thing once, too."

"Got it taken away from you?" Anna asked.

"Yeah. Just like you did. It sucked. Still eats at me."

"So it doesn't get better?"

Cherelle shook her head.

Anna confided, "I'm going crazy. I'd be grateful for anything you can tell me about what he said or did the last time you talked to him."

Cherelle's voice was so low I strained to hear it. "I met with him a couple of times. The last night we couldn't come to terms and . . . that was the end of it."

Bullshit. I waited, but I suspected that's all we'd get from her. We'd probably gotten more than most. Definitely more than Dawson.

"Who are your new friends?"

Cherelle glanced up, eyes wide with panic, and she shrank into the booth.

It appeared her paramour had arrived.

I stood. "Hey, there. I'm Mercy Gunderson, running for sheriff."

He glowered at Cherelle. His body vibrated with menace.

"Anyway, hope you don't mind I bent Chantal's ear. Whenever I come across a voter who's undecided, I get a little carried away." I forced a laugh. "So poor Chantal has been a captive audience." Was intentionally bungling her name too over the top?

Victor said, "Do I look like I care who you are? Get your ass to our table, Cherelle. Now. I need a beer."

I moved aside so Cherelle could escape.

She scooted past me without a word, Victor hot on her heels. Naturally, I followed.

As did Anna.

Victor shoved Cherelle in a chair and sat next to her. When he realized we'd followed him, his reptilian eyes slitted further. "Did you hear me invite you over?"

I smiled. "I warned you I was relentless in my pursuit of potential votes." I faced the Japanese/Indian man, the infamous Barry Sarohutu, who looked bored with the scene. "I'm Mercy Gunderson. I'm running for sheriff."

Saro crossed his arms over his chest. "So?"

"So I wondered who you were voting for?"

His eyes bored into me. I allowed myself to stare back, if only briefly. Up close, Saro wasn't bad looking. I guessed his age to be between thirty-five and forty-five. He'd slicked his jet-black hair into a ponytail. His dark eyes held the slant of his Japanese ancestry; however, his prominent nose was all Sioux. He radiated real danger, not the false cockiness I frequently ran into. This guy was ruthless and probably a total psychopath.

I hated him on sight. I hated that I had to continue this charade and couldn't put my .380 between his eyes and blow his brains out across his brother's smug face. But I especially hated I had to drop my eyes first and look away.

But my cowed behavior loosened his tongue. "You related to the former Sheriff Gunderson?"

"He was my father."

Laughter from the other five guys at the table echoed around us. "Weren't you just bartending in here last week?"

I lifted my chin. "Yep. I know firsthand how hard it is to make a living in this county."

"No, you just gotta be on the top of the food chain."

More laughter.

Cherelle sat with her head bowed.

I couldn't hold my composure much longer. "So can I count on your vote?"

Saro cocked his head, studying me like a piece of meat. Or a piece of ass. "I'll vote for you. But you gotta do something for me."

Don't ask. Just walk away.

"What's that?" I managed.

"Get on your knees." Saro's gaze whipped between Anna and me. "But maybe you don't know what that phrase means?"

Seething, I blinked, acting confused.

"Yeah, bro, you might be right. Maybe Cherelle should demonstrate. Since you're *friends* and all. She could give you a few pointers." Victor grabbed Cherelle by the hair, bringing them acne-pocked cheek to scarred cheek. "Get on your knees. Show them how *you* make a living."

I couldn't stand by and watch forced humiliation. "That's not necessary," I said, backing away. "Nice talking to you but I, ah, see some other people I need to touch base with." I purposely staggered back and raced into the back room.

Self-satisfied male laughter burned my ears.

I braced my hand on the wall and sucked in several deep breaths. Once I'd calmed down, I glanced at Anna.

"Well, that was fun. *Not.* Can we go now?"

"No. As soon as they're gone, we'll go."

Meeting Sarohutu and Victor convinced me they'd been involved in J-Hawk's murder. I just couldn't fit all the pieces together. Not yet. But I would.

If my performance tonight was believable, Saro and his hyenas wouldn't see me as a threat. They'd see me as a girl trying on daddy's shoes for size. Which is exactly what I wanted them to see.

We stuck around ten minutes after Saro's group took off. With my tendency to shoot first, I didn't want to run into them in the parking area.

Anna grilled me the instant we entered the cabin. "What the fuck was that about? What aren't you telling me about Jason?"

"Calm down."

"The hell I will. I want to know what's going on, and I want to know right fucking now."

"Fine." I snagged two beers from the fridge. No need to beat around the bush. "What do you know about the prescription drug OxyContin?"

"What does that have to do—?"

"Just answer the question."

Anna snatched the beer from my hand. "OxyContin is as addicting as meth or cocaine. Some people call it hillbilly heroin." She looked at me. "Are you saying that Jason was taking it?"

I nodded. "I got a peek at the coroner's blood-test results, and J-Hawk had extremely high levels of OxyContin in his system."

"So? That isn't what killed him."

"There was also a large amount of OxyContin in his motel room and in his vehicle."

"How much?"

"A hundred and forty bottles."

She drank as she paced. "Maybe he'd been stockpiling prescriptions. During your discharge, didn't the army shrinks try to load you up on medicine to help you 'adjust' to civilian life? I remember I had my choice of Ambien or Lunesta to help me sleep. Abilify to fight long-term anxiety. Xanax to fight situational anxiety. If I'd mentioned suffering from chronic pain, they would've prescribed the all-purpose OxyContin like candy."

"How do you know all this?"

"I've been out of the service longer than you. At this one VA I visited in California? Looked like the damn stock exchange when the nurses turned their backs. Guys were trading OxyContin for Vicodin. Or Xanax for Adderal. High-dosage pain pills of any kind were big-ticket items. That's how some vets made their living. They'd go to the doc, get the prescriptions, and sell them for cash. I can name at least a dozen straight-arrow soldiers, like Jason, who craved that combat high. They couldn't handle normal. The only way to achieve the high was through artificial means. So they made up aches and pains to get that rush."

I studied her. "Do you miss it? That rush of adrenaline?"

"Like you wouldn't believe."

"Is that why you hired on as a merc? To feed that need?"

"Yes." Anna gave me the unflinching stare that'd made several Iraqi interpreters start praying.

"Do you think Jason needed that rush?"

"Meaning, do I think he needed a way to escape his shitty life in North Dakota? Yes. So it's no wonder he loaded up on as many bottles as the doctors would prescribe for him."

"That's the thing. There were no pharmacy prescriptions on the bottles. Just the manufacturer's labels."

Anna froze. "He stole them?"

"It appears so."

She began pacing again. "Why would he take that risk? His income as a retired army officer is a helluva lot more than mine as enlisted. I'm sure his job with Titan Oil came with a pile of cash. Did stealing give him that high? Or did he have a death wish?"

I was beginning to wonder that myself. "That's what I'm asking you, Anna. You said you knew him down to the bone."

"I do."

"You mean you *did*."

Lightning fast, Anna was in my face. "What about you, Sergeant Major? Do you miss that rush? Knowing you're at the top of your game? Confident few women in the world can best you at what you do best?"

"I was an excellent sniper. But I never aspired to be an excellent killer."

She backed off as quickly as she'd invaded my space, but I didn't relax. Couldn't. Unhinged Anna scared me.

"Same thing. I'm just doing what the army taught me. Be the best I can be. Putting the killing skills I learned to the test in the real world. You know all that *Rah, rah! Go, Army!* shit that lured us into enlisting in the first place. Now I'm supposed to pretend that's not who I am?"

"People change, A-Rod."

Her cell phone rang, and she looked at the caller ID. Then she smiled haughtily. Meanly. "Speaking of . . . putting my skills to the test in the real world, I do believe this is about a job." She whirled away from me and took the call outside.

This conversation hadn't gone well—not that I'd expected less. I'd told her some of the truth about J-Hawk, but if her reaction was any indication, I couldn't tell her all of it. Especially not about the cancer.

But it bugged me, how had toe-the-line Major Hawley started selling prescription drugs? Just to feed his adrenaline-junkie side? Had it started when he was unemployed? Had he decided no one would notice small-scale stuff? But once he'd tasted easy money, had he moved on to bigger stuff? What if he'd unknowingly muscled into another group's territory?

Cross the wrong people, like Saro's group, who laugh at obeying the law, and bye-bye.

They'd kill him. Without hesitation.

So if I suspected J-Hawk's death was a drug-related incident, when I wasn't a professional investigator . . . why hadn't Dawson come to the same conclusion? And if he had, why hadn't he done anything about it?

Once again, someone beating on my door roused me out of slumber. Pity Anna hadn't shot the idiot for disturbing her R&R. I squinted at the couch as I shuffled past. Huh. No Anna. That explained the lack of bullet holes in the door.

I flipped the locks and opened the door. My belly did a little flip.

"I see you took my advice and started locking up."

"You doing door-lock checks across the county this morning, Sheriff? Or am I special?"

"Smart-ass."

"What're you doing here?"

"We need to talk." Dawson brushed past me, stopping in front of the empty coffeepot. "You haven't made coffee yet?"

"I was still in bed."

Grumbling, he filled the grinder with beans. Poured the water in the machine. Dumped the old grounds and nestled a fresh filter in the basket before refilling it with freshly ground beans. It didn't bother me that he knew his way around my tiny kitchen. In fact, it was sort of . . . sweet.

After he hit Start, he turned, resting his backside against the counter. Arms crossed over his chest. Chin set in a hard line. No shades masked the steely glint in his eyes.

Yeah, Dawson was pissed. I prepped myself for an ass-chewing session and mentally took back my "sweet" remark.

"Is there a reason you didn't tell me you knew Jason Hawley prior to his employment with Titan Oil?"

"Yes."

"What would that reason be?"

"Because you didn't ask me."

"Goddammit, Mercy, that's not—"

"The response you were looking for?" I supplied. "Tough. Maybe if you hadn't been such a dickhead to me the night I found my friend murdered, I would've given you specifics. But when you're tossing around threats, taking away my gun, accusing *me*, for Christsake, of murder, I ain't about to offer anything up that wasn't specifically asked."

"And what about the next day? When you and John-John came into the office? I asked you specific questions then. You had ample opportunities to come clean about your previous relationship with him."

"No. You gave me some bullshit theory about how my friend, a man I respected, a man I entrusted my life to, a man who'd literally brought me back from the dead, had somehow gotten himself robbed—and oops, too bad, so sad, accidents happen. He's not from around here anyway, so who cares? Move on and forget about it. Well, guess what? I couldn't."

Dawson was by my side—in my face—in an instant. "What do you mean he brought you back from the dead?"

The damn man was a bulldog when it came to digging things out of me and the hell of it was I didn't always mind. Didn't mean I always told the gospel truth, however.

"Mercy?"

Hearing the softness in his tone, I tabled my intent to lie. Or hedge, anyway. "When Jason found me, under rubble and bodies, I was . . . dead. No pulse. Not breathing. He wouldn't give up, even long after he should have."

"Tell me everything. In detail. Right now."

I retreated from his menacing stance and maintained a clinical detachment in the retelling. I left nothing out, including J-Hawk's relationship with Anna. Needing something to do with my hands, I poured us each a cup of coffee, automatically handing Dawson his favorite Smokey the Bear mug.

"Does Jason Hawley's murder have anything to do with you deciding to run for sheriff?"

"Yes."

An exasperated noise rumbled in his chest at my curt response. *"And?"*

"And you want to know why I said yes? Not because of all

the people claiming my father would be proud if I followed in his footsteps. Not because I have a burning desire to wear the snappy uniform and get paid to carry a gun again." I locked my eyes to his. "What kicked me over was when I saw the customer lists you'd demanded, sitting unopened on your desk, *days* after Jason's murder. I knew you wouldn't give the case the time it deserved."

The displeased muscle ticked in his jaw. "You don't know why . . . you don't know what the hell you're talking about."

"No? Are you denying you put a murder case on the bottom of your priority pile?"

"I'm damn tired of your accusations about my lack of dedication and direction as sheriff. Didn't we go through this last year? With the cases involving Albert Yellow Boy, Levi, and Sue Anne White Plume? Didn't you accuse me of apathy and ineptness then, too? Didn't it come out in the end that I did my job?"

The jury was out on Dawson's effectiveness as an investigator. True, Albert Yellow Boy's death had been ruled an accident like he'd postulated. Theo Murphy had confessed to me about killing Sue Anne, not to Dawson. And my nephew Levi . . . well, I'd figured out who'd murdered him and lied to Dawson to cover for the person who'd killed the real killer.

"Yes, you got to the bottom of them eventually. But your focus has been elsewhere because of the election. I knew if you wouldn't investigate Jason's murder, I had to. No matter what. Even if it pissed you off."

Even if it costs you something you're only beginning to understand the value of?

Where had that thought come from?

And Dawson was as angry as I'd ever seen him. "Why are you jumping headfirst into the deep end of the pool when you don't have the first clue about what's underwater?"

My bitchy rejoinder, "I oughta leave the investigating to a crackshot professional like you?" dried on my tongue when I recognized the frustration in his eyes.

"I understand how a shared military history with life-and-death situations creates a strong bond. I did my time. There are guys I would've died for."

"Then you understand why I owe Jason. He saved me."

"Is that what this is about? You think you could've saved him?"

I notched my chin higher. "Maybe."

"Trust me, Jason Hawley was beyond saving the second he showed up in my county."

"You didn't know him."

He shot back, "Neither did you."

I started to argue, but Dawson jumped back in first and came out swinging.

"Has it ever occurred to you that you wouldn't have died if Jason and Anna hadn't coerced you into going into the club? If you'd said no instead of feeling pressure to help them maintain a lie, you would've been safe in the hotel where you belonged. Jason Hawley should've gone out of his way to bring you back to life because it was his goddamn fault you died."

Talk about a slap in the face. I staggered back from the force of his harsh words.

"You never thought of it that way, did you?" he prodded.

No. Stunned, I snapped, "You're still missing the point."

"So are you."

"Which is?"

"Sometimes you lose sight of the main objective when your emotions conflict with the hard truth."

Was he talking about us? Or J-Hawk's case?

"Sometimes you don't have a fucking choice but to do what's expected of you. Remember that if you win this election."

"Dawson—"

"Bureaucracy sucks. It can crush you. Ruin you. Destroy trust. Damage something promising, something good, something real. For what? Who does it benefit? Who does it hurt? Ask yourself that when this is all over, Mercy."

Dawson set his cup on the kitchen table and stormed out, leaving me as confused as ever.

SEVENTEEN

The inside of Anna's Land Rover resembled a traveling rummage sale.

"Where to?" she asked, poking the buttons on her GPS.

"The elementary school. Don't know how long this will last, so you can drop me off and go back to the cabin if you want. I can catch a ride home with someone else."

"Nah. I'll see what new goodies Pete has today. Nothing to do at the cabin anyway. I can't believe you don't have cable TV."

"I can't believe you care. Hell, A-Rod, you used to be happy if we got to sleep in an actual tent. Next you'll be expecting chocolates on your pillow."

"Fuck off. I've been living in my car for a month."

I wasn't surprised, given the state of her car and her nomadic tendencies. "I thought you were on assignment."

"I was. The job ended earlier than I'd planned and I had no other place to live, so this became Casa Anna."

"Why not chill with your mom in California?"

She shrugged. "Didn't wanna deal with family drama. You know how that goes."

The drama in my life owed nothing to my family for a change.

Anna double-parked in the fire-and-ambulance zone in front of the one-story sandstone building. "What are you doing at an elementary school anyway? Judging a paste-eating contest? Because, dude, these ankle biters can't vote."

"Ask my campaign manager. I think she's filling my hours with busy work so I don't get discouraged."

"Having second thoughts about running for sheriff, Gunny?"

"And third thoughts. And fourth." The earlier conversation with Dawson bothered me on a level I couldn't explain.

"Nice to see you have a human side."

I turned in my seat to face her. "What do you mean, a human side?"

"Sergeant Major Gunderson, the ideal American soldier. Honorable. Noble. Dedicated. Always accepts the call to duty. An inspiration to us all."

"You want to come into the school with me and wave the flag while I hum the national anthem?"

Anna grinned at me. "No, it's just different hanging out with you as a true civilian, Mercy. In uniform you never showed insecurity. Rarely questioned our orders or our part in the war machine. It was as intimidating as hell. Well, that, coupled with the fact no one could outshoot you, made you one scary mo-fo."

"You're boosting my confidence already. I'll call you when I'm done."

The main entrance to the building still had the welded-steel handrail that we'd used as monkey bars. I'd skinned my knees, bruised my elbows, and fallen flat on my face on the sidewalk more times than I could count.

Hopefully, history wasn't about to repeat itself.

Anna and I hung out at the cabin the rest of the afternoon.

She took off the same time I headed to my next campaign gig.

By the time I finished the second event at the county high school, it was close to nine o'clock. I was starved and needed a beer.

Stillwell's in Viewfield was a throwback to the small-town taverns that served cholesterol-laden comfort food and cheap booze. The interior hadn't been updated in forty years. Cheap paneling covered the walls. Neon beer signs were tacked up for "atmosphere" and burnt-orange Naugahyde bar stools were tucked around the shellacked bar. No karaoke machine. No digital big-screen TVs. No fancy brands of whiskey or tequila. No buffalo wings or nachos on the menu.

Stillwell's had one TV. One pool table. One dartboard. One electronic trap-shooting game. One bartender. One cocktail waitress. One short-order cook.

But lots of customers. It'd been my dad's favorite hangout.

Steve Stillwell, a fiftysomething bachelor who'd inherited the business from his father, gazed at me curiously as I straddled a bar stool. His resemblance to an owl was striking, given his round face, black eyes, and beard layered in colors from white to gray that looked like feathers. His head nearly spun around when a customer called his name, reinforcing the owl comparison. "Steve, you haven't aged a day in twenty years."

He flapped the bar rag at me. "Charmer. You needing to absorb a little class away from your other watering hole, Miz Gunderson? Or out campaigning?"

I wondered if Steve would poke me about working at Clementine's. "Neither. I'm looking for a beer and a break. What's on tap?"

"The usual domestics."

"Bud Light. Small one." I admired his pour technique and said so. He slid the mug across the counter. "Is the kitchen still open?"

"You wanna look at a menu?"

"Nope. Hook me up with a hot beef sandwich. Extra gravy."

"That was your dad's favorite, too." He yelled, "Order up!" and spun the ticket on the metal wheel. Then he rested his elbows on the bar top, settling in for a chat. "So I hear you found that oil fella who got himself killed."

I nodded and swallowed a mouthful of beer.

"I ain't surprised someone offed him. Nobody liked that guy."

"You knew him?"

He shrugged. "He came in here a couple times. Always acted a little . . . twitchy. Like he was on drugs."

My mug stopped halfway to my mouth. "Really?"

"Uh-huh. Met with some guys from the rez." Steve scowled at someone over my shoulder. "I don't like them types showing up in my place, spooking my regular customers. You have any problems with undesirables showing up at Clementine's?"

"'Undesirables' describes our entire clientele," I reminded him.

His crooked smile appeared. "Guess that's true. How'd the event go at the school tonight?"

"As well as can be expected. Harold McCoy, who emceed, cut me off when I listed points on why we should all fight the pipeline."

"I imagine Harold did shut you down. He's another one of them who's gung ho about the pipeline going through. Lemme ask you something."

"Shoot."

"If this Titan Oil Company wanted us to believe the pipeline is good for everyone in the county, why didn't they hire a local to convince us?"

"That's easy. Any local person willing to lie to the landowners and the business owners about the supposed benefits of the pipeline is screwed because they have to live in the community afterward. Some guy from out of state doesn't have to stick around and deal with the fallout."

"Good point. But most of the business owners in Eagle Ridge are on board." Steve pushed back and polished a spot on the bar top. "Ain't you running into that mind-set while you're campaigning in town?"

"I'm focused on campaigning door-to-door in the country. I figure Dawson has the town vote sewn up."

"Probably." Steve squinted at me as he lit a Pall Mall. "Why'd you decide to run for sheriff anyhow?"

"Bill O'Neil's campaign committee asked me to fill in."

"That the only reason?"

I smiled coyly. "What do you think?"

"I think your military service taught you to evade like a pro." He shot a look at the guy two seats over and lowered his voice. "Here's something you might not know about your competition. Nancy Greenbush, over at the feedlot, said Dawson promised them a closed-door meeting with the county commissioners about their right-of-way issues. What do you know about it?"

"Geneva filled me in. That issue has been going on a long time. But Nancy realizes a meeting with the commissioners is no guarantee the county will allow them to reconfigure their access road, right?"

"Nancy said it sounded promising for a change. Lots of folks are willing to vote for him if there's something in it for them."

Dawson's platform was murky, mostly because he didn't need one. "What else has Dawson been pledging?"

Steve flicked a column of ash off his cigarette. "Nothin' major. Talking about adding more patrols. Harsher penalties for underage drinkers and the businesses selling liquor to minors."

"Do you have problems with minors?"

"Owning an off-sale liquor license means there's always kids who try to buy beer and booze. Usually the same ones. Chaps my ass they think I'm so damn stupid. But we've had two teenage drunk-driving deaths in the last year, so it is a problem."

"Why isn't Dawson already focused on that?"

"Exactly my point."

The waitress dropped off my meal, and I tucked in. Thinly sliced roast beef piled on top of four squishy pieces of white bread, surrounded by homemade mashed potatoes, covered in thick, salty brown gravy. My near orgasmic moans of bliss sent Steve scurrying toward other customers.

More people wandered in, and the booths filled. Busy place. The panel of mirrors behind the glass shelves reflected the bar happenings. I recognized about half the customers. Two hotshot cowboys showed off their pool skills, attempting to catch the eye of the chippies rocking low-cut blouses, big smiles, and even bigger hair. Singles and couples socialized. Some couples even played bridge. Definitely a different clientele than Clementine's.

Belly full, I focused on the TV screen above the bar, featuring ESPN Classic. I wondered why anyone would watch a sporting event for which the winning outcome had been determined years ago. Then I realized it wasn't any different than watching a repeat episode of a favorite TV show or a movie. ESPN was running an encore presentation of the 2002 National Finals Rodeo in Las Vegas.

South Dakota cowboys were well represented in the bareback and saddle-bronc categories. I groaned along with the two older Indian guys at the bar, when the heelers in the team-roping division had a devil of a time catching a single hind leg on the calf, let alone two. Trevor Brazile wore the sponsorship colors and insignia of the U.S. Army, which made him my favorite for the coveted all-around title.

The bulldogging section started. I liked watching buff

cowboys launching off a galloping horse and throwing a steer into the dirt as much as the next woman, but nature called. And I did not want to miss my favorite event: bull riding.

A crowd in the bar meant a long line for the ladies' room. Five minutes later I couldn't cut through the mob to get back to my seat. No surprise a fight had broken out. I looked around for the bouncer and remembered Stillwell's didn't employ one.

About then the group shifted, and I saw a jock pummeling a cowboy half his size.

Money exchanged hands among the spectators. Betting on a fair fight was one thing. The scared-rabbit look in the cowboy's blood-caked eye indicated he was way out of his league.

I looked at the bully—an Indian male in his late teens. A fatheaded, ham-fisted, mean-faced bully. When he smacked the cowboy in the jaw and his teeth clacked together, I'd seen enough.

Snagging a pool cue, I wound through the crowd of voyeurs and moved in behind the jock. I whacked him on the back of the thighs, dropping him to his knees. Then I pulled the pool cue across his windpipe and jerked him against my body, trapping his calves between my boots.

All this took about ten seconds.

His hands clawed at the stick that was cutting off his air supply.

"What the hell is wrong with you?" I demanded, directing my question to the bully as much as the worthless ghouls watching the scene unfold without stopping it.

Infuriated and humiliated, the cowboy regained his composure. He roared and charged, his pointed boot connected with the jock's groin. Hard.

Male groans filled the air, and a few even cupped their nuts in sympathy.

Although I had zero compassion for the bully, I released the pool cue, allowing him to clutch his crotch and curl into a fetal position on the floor. Before I could enjoy hearing him gasp in pain, I was blindsided by a fist to the head.

Dots wavered in front of my eyes. Motherfucking son of a bitch, that hurt. On autopilot, I turned, blocked other blows with the pool cue, and swept the guy's feet out from under him. Once he was flat on his back, with my foot pressed into his throat, I placed the chalked end of the pool cue on his forehead. "Consider yourself lucky I didn't crack your skull open for that sucker punch, asshole."

Red-faced jock number 2 glared at me as he gasped for breath.

I hadn't even broken a sweat. Fights lasted an eternity on TV and the movies, but in real life? Sometimes it just took one punch. I twirled the chalked tip of the cue across his brow, leaving a blue smear. "Get the hell out of here. Both of you." I released him, gripping the pool stick like a baseball bat until they scampered away like cockroaches.

Murmurs started. The buzz danced up my spine like burrowing insects. People avoided me, including one stoop-shouldered man I recognized as my dad's buddy, Denver Jordan, who gave me the stink eye.

I braced myself for his recriminations. Putting myself on display. My utter lack of femininity. Shaming my sweet-as-pie dead mother and smearing my dead father's reputation—yeah, I'd heard it before.

"Folks, this is your candidate for sheriff. Mercy Gunderson." He raised his mug. "Vote for her. Tell everyone what you seen here tonight, and tell them to vote for her, too."

In addition to the relief Denver hadn't lambasted me, I felt an honest-to-God blush rising up my neck when some people clapped. A bar fight probably wasn't the type of PR Geneva hoped for, but, hey, word of mouth got my name out there.

As the crowd dispersed, Denver clumsily patted my shoulder and trudged outside.

I squinted over the lump swelling on my cheekbone and plopped back on my bar stool.

Steve passed me an ice pack and a fresh draft. "If you don't win the sheriff's race, maybe we oughta hire you away from Clementine's as a bouncer."

"With all due respect, Steve, I ain't looking to stay in the bar business permanently. I'm too damn old."

"You're too ornery."

"That, too." I swigged my beer, holding the ice pack to my face, and focused on the TV. Good. Barrel racing had just started. Bull riding was up next.

I was so engrossed in watching the final ride I didn't notice them until the hair on the back of my neck stood up. My gaze tracked their approach in the mirror.

Of all the nights not to be carrying.

Victor Bad Wound and Barry Sarohutu eased onto the bar stools on either side of me. I nonchalantly sipped my beer and watched the credits roll for the next program on ESPN Classic. Boxing.

Steve stopped in front of Victor. "Getcha guys something?"

"Two double shots of Chivas."

"Don't got Chivas. Crown's the closest."

Victor leaned in front of me to address Saro. "This is why we don't come in here, bro."

I made a mental note to tell John-John to stop carrying high-end whiskey. Might solve his "undesirables" problem.

Victor angled his head to speak to Steve, but kept me blocked in. "Two double shots of Crown." As soon as Steve hustled down the bar to fill the order, Victor addressed me. "So we hear you like mixing it up?"

Since I hadn't the foggiest idea what he was talking about, I didn't respond. I suspected a nonresponse would piss him off, and gee, I was in the mood to tangle with him.

Saro laughed. "Ain't talking to us?"

I shrugged.

"Maybe you oughta give her an incentive to talk, Vic."

That comment earned Saro a cool once-over. "Try it and see what happens."

"You think you're a tough chick?"

"Nah. She's just stupid," Victor said.

Come on, assholes, keep it up.

"Since you're slow, and we ain't got all night, I'll spell it out. We don't appreciate that you jumped into a fight that didn't have nothin' to do with you. Our nephew, Benji, ain't none too happy you held him back, while you let a loser white cowboy kick him in the balls."

Now this visit made sense. I finally looked at Victor. "That Indian kid is related to you guys?"

"Surprised?"

I laughed. "No. But I don't know which makes your nephew more of a pussy. That a woman twice his age got the drop on him, or that he whined to his uncles and sent them to fight his battles. What a douche bag. Here's my advice. Tell Benji if he ain't got the fists to back up his big mouth, he'd be better off keeping it shut."

Stunned silence. I doubted anyone spoke to them like that.

Victor got close enough to treat me to the booze on his breath and the stench of pot smoke clinging to his greasy hair. "Who the fuck you think you're talking to?"

"Is your macho posturing supposed to scare me? Guess what? It doesn't. So if you came here to get an apology from me for poor little Benji getting his feelings hurt? You might as well leave, 'cause it ain't happening." I jerked my thumb toward Saro. "Need me to spell it out for him, too? Since you ain't got all night?"

Steve set down the two shots and hightailed it away. Smart man. Out of the corner of my good eye, I saw Saro upend his shot.

When Victor realized he couldn't win our game of "don't blink," he quickly reached for his glass, expecting I'd flinch.

I didn't. I didn't break eye contact either.

He slammed the booze and backed off.

"Not smart to push us," Saro said conversationally.

"It's my nature."

"Wasn't your dad's nature. He laid down like a beaten dog whenever he had to deal with us."

"Which is hard to do when you're old, crippled, and stuck in a wheelchair," Victor added. "One time, the almighty sheriff even pissed his pants in front of us."

"Rumor on the rez? Toward the end, Daddy Dearest pissed and shit himself all the time." Saro's fetid breath fanned my ear. "But you wouldn't know about that, would you, tough girl? Since you weren't around when Daddy was dying. Too busy planning on how you'd look trying to fill his shoes? Or should I say . . . shoe?"

An inferno of fury spread through me. I inhaled slowly.

"Didn't think we did our homework on you? Think again."

Victor leaned in and taunted me. "Looky here, bro, I think she's gonna cry."

I pictured snapping Victor's neck. Seeing the last look of surprise on his ugly face before he crumpled to the floor like a bag of rotten meat.

"Why so quiet?" Saro mocked. "You burning brain cells thinking up a smart-ass response?"

"No. I'm just thinking about the differences between me and my dad, Barry."

He stiffened slightly. Ah. He didn't like being called Barry. Too bad.

"See, I've spent my life taking down bullies like you. And Barry, guess what? You're not special. Bullies are the same across the globe, whether you're wearing a towel on your head, a snappy suit, or braids in your hair. You prey on the weak. So fair warning. When I'm elected sheriff? Prepare yourself, because I will be preying on you. I am not weak. Not even fucking close."

"That so?"

"Uh-huh. I will enjoy taking down your organization piece by piece. Body by body, if I have to."

"Don't start something you can't win."

"Don't be too sure I haven't already laid the groundwork and you're the ones who'll lose everything."

Victor moved and grabbed me.

I let him keep his death grip on my forearm—it was hard as hell to do, but I had another point to make. I locked my gaze to Saro's. "Tell him to let go of my arm, or I will break his fucking nose."

A beat passed, and Saro inclined his head.

Victor released me.

I refocused on the TV, dismissing them.

They got the hint and vanished without speaking. And without paying for their damn drinks.

Again, the bar hummed with excitement. This type of confrontation was old hat to me and the customers at Clementine's, but here . . . not so much.

I didn't stick around long after that. My foray into reestablishing ties in the community, outside of Clementine's, hadn't turned out so well tonight—either at the high school or the local watering hole.

Probably everyone in the whole damn county was whispering about that crazy Gunderson woman.

Probably they were right.

EIGHTEEN

After a quick rundown of my daily duties the next morning at the Blackbird Diner, Geneva left me to brood in the far back booth, isolated from the restaurant activity.

A shadow blocked the patchwork of sunlight. I glanced up, expecting another nosy supporter, but Shay Turnbull slid into the high-backed bench seat across from me.

I folded the newspaper and slapped it on the table. "If you want this booth, you can have it."

The waitress appeared. "Can I getcha something?"

"Coffee. And bring candidate Gunderson a refill."

After she waddled off, I said, "I was leaving."

"*Was* being the operative word." Shay didn't speak again until the coffee arrived.

Screw this. I wasn't interested in whatever cryptic comment he'd make. I started to leave.

His hand shot out, and his fingers tightly circled my wrist. "I said you're staying."

"If you like that hand without broken bones, you'll let go of my arm right now."

"Threatening me will only cause more problems for you, Sergeant Major."

He knew my rank? "Who the hell are you?"

"I'm so happy you asked." Shay used his free hand to drag a wallet out of his front shirt pocket. Except it wasn't a wallet. It was a badge. He flipped it open and thrust it in my face.

My eyes focused on the tiny text.

Fuck me. Shay Turnbull was a fed. Specifically, an agent with the ICSCU—whatever the hell that was.

"It stands for the Indian Country Special Crimes Unit," he said as I continued to scrutinize the gold metal and black lettering.

"I still don't know what means, *Agent* Turnbull."

He released my wrist and pocketed the badge. "It means this division of the FBI works with everyone."

"So you're what . . . a super-duper double-secret agent? Able to leap from agency to agency with a single bound? Slice through bureaucratic red tape with your wit and charm? Allowed to skulk around wherever the hell you want with absolute impunity?"

"You asking if I have autonomy? Yes. And no. You asking if I answer to anyone? Don't we all?"

Smug jackass. "So you work with the BIA?"

He nodded.

"The DEA?"

"Yep."

"The Department of the Interior?"

"Them, too."

Agent Turnbull studied me with the air of detachment all government clones had perfected. How had I missed the signs? His sudden unexplained appearances. Disappearances. The ominous warnings. The snappy, hip clothing and brooding good looks had thrown me off.

He angled across the table; his eyes snapped fire. "Tell me, how is it that you can fuck up a multiagency investigation, one that's taken over five months, in a little over a week?"

"I have no idea what you're talking about." Which was not a lie . . . for a change.

"Don't try my patience, Sergeant Major, I'm not in the mood."

I hated that he'd used my military rank. Hell, I hated that he even knew my military rank. "You know about me, but I know nothing about you, and I don't mind saying . . . that seriously pisses me off. You've had occasions to tell me exactly who you were, Agent Turnbull, and you haven't. So I'm inclined not to cooperate with you."

No response.

"If I'd known what you were up to, maybe you wouldn't be pissy about me supposedly fucking up your op."

Stone-cold glare.

I kicked my antagonism up a notch. "But just like all the other spooks, you prefer to follow your own agenda and place blame after the fact, right?"

"You don't have a high opinion of the government after being in Uncle Sam's employ for so many years," he said dryly.

Inside I seethed, but I kept my tone even. "My opinion of the armed forces is just jim-dandy. My opinion of governmental agencies that showed up and tried to tell us how to do our jobs, while infringing upon our ability to do those jobs? That makes my blood boil. I've been down this road before, far too many times. Ask a question, and your ilk pulls the standard 'We can't discuss classified cases' line of bullshit. Jesus. Sometimes it was easier dealing with the Taliban than the inner workings of U.S. government agencies."

"Your past experiences with other agencies—good or bad—are not my concern."

"Then why are you here?"

That gave him pause. "Why do you *think* I'm in Eagle River County, Mercy?"

"Besides to annoy me? I'm guessing if all those federal agencies are involved, it's something big."

"That's vague." Agent Turnbull folded his arms over his chest. "Come on, you're a smart cookie, yet you're struggling to believe what's right in front of you."

I allowed the same cool stare he'd leveled on me.

"Indulge me," he prompted. "What conclusions have you drawn in your quest to find out who killed your buddy, Major Jason Hawley?"

Don't do it. Maybe he doesn't know diddly and he's trolling for information.

As much as civilians claimed the right hand didn't know what the left hand was doing, elite government agencies made it their business to know every goddamned thing.

My mouth engaged before my brain. "I'm betting you're here because Jason Hawley had more than a couple of bottles of Oxy-Contin in his possession. Since he crossed state lines, it becomes a federal matter, so the DEA is involved. But the group that runs the drug trade in these parts is based out of the Eagle River

Reservation, which means involving the BIA. Since the BIA deals with the FBI, they're also brought on board. So every agency knows the particulars, except local law enforcement. For some reason you've kept the Eagle River County Sheriff's Department in the dark." I mimicked his posture—arms crossed, head cocked pertly. "Am I close to getting a cookie, Agent Turnbull?"

"Not bad. With a couple of exceptions. One, the DEA turned the cases involving reservations over to us—the multigroup task force—early this year. We've maintained a low profile, even while we've been tracking the movements of the suspected key players on this specific case. Two, we haven't kept Eagle River County Sheriff's Department out of the loop. Sheriff Dawson is cooperating with us fully."

My jaw dropped. I must've misheard him. "What?"

"Sheriff Dawson is aware of our multiagency objective. He's not happy about us taking over all aspects of investigation of this case."

"*All* aspects of it?" I repeated inanely.

"Every bit. He's not allowed to discuss this case with his deputies or anyone else. He cannot proceed with any line of investigation he initially started. He cannot issue a statement of any type about this case without contacting me first."

The breath whooshed from my body. I'd jumped in the race for sheriff because I believed Dawson hadn't been doing his job clearing up J-Hawk's murder. When in reality, Dawson had no choice. He hadn't been slacking in his investigative duties at all. The feds had tied his hands and his tongue.

Fuck.

My thoughts raced back to Dawson chewing out Turnbull for showing up at the crime scene at Clementine's. It must've rankled Dawson, knowing he'd lose out on investigating the case before the victim's body had cooled. Knowing his investigative techniques would be questioned again. Knowing I'd be his harshest critic. Except this time, I'd taken my concerns public, setting out to prove to the community that I was better qualified to be sheriff than Mason Dawson.

Now I really felt like tossing my cookies.

The almighty Mercy Gunderson, who prided herself on her cool-headed, rational approach, had gone off half cocked. The thought of losing the election wasn't nearly as excruciating as the suspicion that I'd lost something even more important.

Agent Turnbull stared at me. "You all right?"

No. I wasn't in the mood to play nice. Or to reveal my insecurities on any level to a fucking fed. "As I'm a candidate for sheriff, you should've told me about this task force earlier."

"Why?"

"Because if I win the election, I'll be in Dawson's position, looking like an idiot when it appears I'm not doing my job, when I've sworn I'd handle things differently than he does specifically for that reason."

"I warned you not to make blanket statements." He rested his elbows on the table, the picture of earnestness. "Look, this caught you off guard. I'll tell you what I know, but I'll need your word it won't go farther than you."

"Fine."

"Early this year, across North and South Dakota, four Intertribal Co-op Health Hospital storage facilities were hit, and their inventory of OxyContin was stolen. The problem is, no one knew when the thefts occurred, outside of a general time frame."

"Why not?"

"The ICHH buys in bulk twice a year, based on the previous six months' sales, then distributes to the individual hospitals' storage facilities. The pay-in-advance business model has been standard practice for years."

"Why?"

Bitterness flickered in his eyes. "From the advent of the formation of the ICHH, none of the pharmaceutical companies trusted the tribes to pay their bills. They refused to offer them credit and required advance payment and advance orders. No exceptions."

"Even now?"

"Yes, except if an individual hospital needs additional prescriptions, it can reorder in small quantities. Cash up front."

"Is the bulk-ordering mandate common knowledge within the ICHH?"

Agent Turnbull shook his head. "Just among the key administrators, and they're subject to nondisclosure."

I held up my hand. "Interesting, but what does this have to

do with Jason Hawley? He's not Indian. Chances are slim he'd know about this arrangement."

"Major Hawley received the information about the separate storage facilities at ICHH and delivery of pharmaceuticals from his Titan Oil coworker, Ellis LeFleur. Near as we can figure, LeFleur was fired by the ICHH about two months before he started working for Titan Oil."

"Why was he fired?"

"Suspected sexual harassment. He claims a white female office worker falsely accused him, and the hospital administration didn't back him up. No charges were ever filed, but they fired him outright."

"What was his job at ICHH?"

Agent Turnbull looked chagrined. "District warehouse manager. Plus, LeFleur was a registered member of the Standing Rock Tribe. So Titan Oil hired him as their token Indian."

"Token Indian?" I repeated.

"Titan Oil needed the Indian landowners around the various reservations to get on board with the pipeline, and LeFleur was their Native American man to offer a convincing argument." Turnbull scowled. "Rumor had it LeFleur could charm the bees from the flowers. But he was young and inexperienced in sales, so the executives paired him with a more seasoned pitchman."

"Jason Hawley."

He nodded. "Information from here on out is speculation because we've got no official documentation. We assume LeFleur told Hawley about the warehouse setup. Whose idea it was to steal the product . . . again, pure supposition. Maybe LeFleur wanted revenge. Maybe it was strictly about the money. LeFleur and Hawley didn't have much planning time, roughly two months."

"But if LeFleur had that much insider knowledge, he didn't need much prep time."

"Precisely. LeFleur knew enough about the supply-and-demand cycle to leave five full boxes containing the real Oxy-Contin on top of two different stacks—"

"So how—"

"I'm getting to that." Turnbull held up a hand, waving the waitress over for a refill. "The original manufacturer's boxes were still in the individual locked storage areas at the facilities, but the prescription bottles inside the boxes had been replaced."

"Replaced with what?"

"Everything from bottles filled with Flintstones vitamins to bottles filled with Tic Tac breath mints to bottles filled with Hot Tamales candies."

"So if the inventory manager looked in the storage area, he or she would see the stacks of boxes of OxyContin and assume everything was A-okay?"

"Exactly. That's why the actual time frame is unclear. Nothing was discovered until one of the reservations in North Dakota cracked open a box at the bottom of the stack, at the end of January, and found the tampered products. But we're guessing they struck right after the shipments were delivered."

"No surveillance cameras?"

"We checked. They were disabled on two separate occasions, two weeks apart."

Disabling cameras would've been child's play for J-Hawk, whose military job required high-tech breaking and entering.

"LeFleur maintained ties with the other warehouses, in addition to relationships with the other warehouse managers."

The brotherhood vibe in the Native American community was strong, so LeFleur had an easy in, especially if he'd been hung out to dry by his white bosses on the sexual-harassment issue. "How long did it take the other hospitals to check their inventory?"

"A couple of weeks."

"Why wasn't it prioritized?"

"It was. It would've taken longer due to infighting between the hospitals and the tribes. We had to call in the DEA, and they ran the rest of the physical checks with permission from the individual tribal councils."

"How many bottles of OxyContin are we talking about?"

"Total? Four thousand."

My eyes nearly bugged out of my head. "That much OxyContin is prescribed on the reservations?"

"Apparently."

"What's the street value?"

His gaze slid away. Then back. "The average street-sale price is about a dollar a milligram. For easy math, let's say a bottle of one hundred eight-milligram pills sells for eight hundred bucks on the street. Multiply that by the number of missing bottles . . ."

I did a quick calculation. "That's over three million dollars."

"Not exactly chump change."

"Why haven't I heard about this on the news?" Seemed every media outlet loved to release stories about Indians that held a negative slant.

Agent Turnbull lifted a brow. "What part of covert ops is confusing, Sergeant Major?"

"What part of arresting Jason Hawley for interstate drug trafficking is confusing, Agent Turnbull? Especially if you knew he was involved?"

"The agencies didn't originally connect Major Hawley—who we're aware is a decorated war veteran—to the thefts."

"Why not?"

"Because like you said, Hawley wasn't Indian. He was only partnered with Ellis LeFleur for a short time. According to people who knew LeFleur, he vanished at the end of January. Hawley was a family man who stuck around the area. Initially, we focused on tracking LeFleur because we suspected an inside job."

"Did you find LeFleur?"

He nodded. "About two months ago in a mangled mass of metal after a high-speed chase in Kansas City that didn't end well."

"Did LeFleur point the finger at Hawley?"

"No, he died in the accident. But his girlfriend survived. We recovered seven hundred fifty bottles from their residence. There wasn't enough cash on hand to convince us LeFleur had taken the whole lot of four thousand. When we offered the girlfriend immunity from prosecution, she admitted LeFleur had a partner but swore she didn't know his name. So we backtracked. During the search, we learned Jason Hawley had been diagnosed with incurable cancer."

I kept my face neutral.

"Why was a dying man spending all his time on the road, away from medical treatment, away from his family? It sent up a red flag."

"And you'd been following him for the last month, waiting for him to . . . what? Make a mistake? Make a sale?" Die? I could not wrap my head around that devious, thieving side of my friend.

The maroon fake leather had no give when Turnbull sank back. "We'd been waiting for him to make a sale."

"You know who the buyer was?"

"Again, suspected. And it was confirmed when Hawley contacted Cherelle Dupris. He had contact with Cherelle on three separate occasions, that we know of. Which indicated to us that Saro and Victor were playing hardball with him."

"Why?"

"Who knows what goes through drug dealers' minds? Probably Victor and Saro demanded a reduced price and it pissed Hawley off because he knew exactly what his product was worth. We're ninety percent sure Hawley decided not to sell to them the last time he met with Cherelle."

The night he was killed at Clementine's. No need for either of us to point that out, but the picture for motive was becoming clearer. "Had Hawley sold much out on the open market?"

"Near as we can figure he was down to eight hundred bottles. So assuming he and LeFleur made an even split, he'd managed to dump twelve hundred bottles over the last five months."

"Where?"

Agent Turnbull's face shuttered. "I'm not at liberty to say."

"So it's pointless to ask if you've tracked down the other six hundred sixty bottles that weren't in Jason's hotel room or in his vehicle?"

"Where did you get the information about Hawley's personal effects?"

"I'm not at liberty to say." My neener-neener response made him mad, although he tried to hide it. "Where's the money? If J-Hawk was hocking drugs, he'd have a lot of cash. The omnipotent feds haven't been able to track it down?"

"No." His eyes turned hostile. "Thanks to you, we're right back where we started."

"How can you blame any of this on me?"

"We know you discovered that Cherelle was Saro and Victor's screen and approached Cherelle at Clementine's. Instead of walking away when Victor and Saro showed up, you followed them and kept up the pretense of campaigning for sheriff. Any law enforcement sniffing around spooks them."

"Ah ah ah. Wrong, bucko. No pretense. I *am* campaigning for sheriff. Anything I said to Victor and Saro dealt with my campaign. Since I assume you or one of your G-men were in the vicinity, you also know I never wavered from keeping the conversation about getting their votes. So try again."

"Then explain last night at Stillwell's? What the fuck were you doing going after Benji Bad Wound? Showing him up in front of an entire bar full of witnesses?"

"I had no freakin' clue who he was. But it doesn't matter, because I'm not the type to sit around and let a bully have free rein to beat the shit out of someone. No one else stepped in, so I did."

"Why do you think no one else got involved?"

It occurred to me, for the first time, that everyone in the bar probably knew Benji was Saro and Victor's nephew. The reason no one—including Steve Stillwell—had stepped in? Nobody wanted to incur the wrath or attention of the reservation bad boys. But I'd heard that blasted "Underdog" theme song inside my head and jumped in, fists flying.

Great plan, Mercy. Maybe the logic center of your brain has been rattled by too many IEDs.

But Agent Turnbull wasn't done railing on me. "And to make matters worse, you threatened Saro and Victor when they showed up at Stillwell's to talk to you about humiliating Benji."

"They threatened me, Agent. I told them the truth—I'd derive great pleasure in taking them down if I was elected sheriff. Oh, and that was after they'd dropped hints about what a tool my father was."

"Now, thanks to your macho behavior and the chip on your

shoulder about your dearly departed dad, Saro and Victor have closed ranks and holed up on the reservation where we can't get to them."

"Get to them for what?"

No response.

My jaw popped I clenched my teeth so hard. "You have proof one of them killed Jason Hawley?"

Agent Turnbull stared at me blankly.

"Goddammit. Tell me."

He offered me a snakebite smile. "I don't have to tell you a thing, Sergeant Major."

"Is he bothering you?"

Startled, I glanced up to see Sheriff Dawson. His face was pure business, his posture pure agitation as he braced a hand on the back of the booth above my head and loomed over Agent Turnbull.

Yikes.

"Or am I interrupting something?"

"No. Agent Turnbull and I were finished."

At my use of his title, Turnbull scowled.

"Would you like to join us?" I asked Dawson politely.

"I'll pass."

But Dawson didn't move. Agent Turnbull didn't move. I didn't move. A machete couldn't have hacked the thick air.

Agent Turnbull's curious gaze winged between Dawson's impassive face and mine. A knowing smile upturned the corners of his lips. "I'm not interested in muscling in on your territory, Dawson."

"You've been on my territory since the second you stepped foot in this county. I'll cooperate with the feds because I've got no choice, Agent Turnbull, but I don't gotta like it."

Dawson was purposely being obtuse. Again, I was reminded of his fierceness. Of his sweetness. He'd rather take an insult than allow one to be directed at me.

You're such a sucker, Mercy. Maybe you oughta pucker up, bat your eyelashes, and squeeze his big biceps, too.

Turnbull, being a nosy asshole fed, didn't let it slide. "Tell me, Sheriff. Does knowing what she's capable of make it hard to fall asleep next to her some nights?"

I ground my teeth at hearing Turnbull voice the question I'd asked myself.

Dawson flashed his teeth. "Have a nice day, Agent." He looked at me, no differently than usual, and said, "You, too, Miz Gunderson."

After Dawson swaggered off, Turnbull asked, "How many people know about you and Dawson?"

I pretended to give the question serious thought. "Probably everyone, with the exception of the folks in the Restful Acres Nursing Home. Most of them have limited recall, and I doubt they even know who's in the sheriff's race. But everyone else knows I'm running against him."

He rolled his eyes. "That's not what I meant."

I know. "Excuse me." I ducked out of the booth. I didn't run, but with his long-legged stride I didn't catch Dawson until we were in front of Pete's Pawnshop. "Dawson. Wait."

He seemed surprised to see me. Surprised and wary. He glanced over his shoulder. "If you're gonna chew me out, I'd prefer you did it in private."

"I didn't chase you down to rip into you."

"Then why *did* you chase me down?"

Because I'm just as much a tool and a fool as I feared. "To ask why you didn't tell me."

"Tell you what?"

"About Shay Turnbull. Who he is, who he works for."

The angry muscle ticked in Dawson's jaw. "Why does it matter now?"

"It just does."

"That's a bullshit answer, and I don't have time for this." Dawson spun and started to walk away from me.

Frustrated by his dismissal, I grabbed the back of his shirt to stop him.

Within two seconds he'd snagged my wrist and strong-armed me into the alley. "What the hell is wrong with you?"

"I'm pissed off."

Dawson snorted. "Like that's news."

"Why didn't you tell me Turnbull was a fed? God, Dawson, if I'd known the feds had taken over the investigation, and you had no choice but to let the Hawley case drop, I never would've agreed—"

"To run against me for sheriff?" he supplied. "It's a little late for that now, doncha think?"

The full brunt of my mistake knocked the breath from my lungs.

"Answer me, Mercy."

I could barely work up enough spit to swallow, let alone speak.

He crowded me against the brick building. "Do you know what's the worst part of this situation?"

Too many awful reasons surfaced. It was hard to shake my head in response, when it was so damn hard to hold it up.

"Realizing how little you think of my professional abilities."

Direct hit. "Dawson—"

"Let. Me. Finish. Last summer I chalked up your distrust of me to your replacement issues about your father. I chalked up your skepticism of my investigative skills to the personal stakes when your nephew was murdered. But when you automatically accused me of not doing my job *again*? That jab hurt worse than a knee to the balls. Or so I thought, until I started to wonder if you'd kept our personal involvement your dirty little secret because professionally you consider me no better than Barney Fife."

The haunted look in his eyes made me want to hide my face in shame. But he was wrong about how I'd treated him . . . wasn't he?

"I thought I could count on you to understand. *You*, of all people, Mercy, know what it's like when the government forces you to keep your mouth shut, forces you to turn a blind eye, forces your compliance at any cost. You've lived that life. Hell, as far as I can tell, you still embody that unquestioning code of military ethics—personally and professionally. Yet here you are, judging me as lacking, for sticking to that exact same set of standards."

A hot wash of shame burned as the words *hypocrite, hypocrite, hypocrite* sliced through me as sharp and painful as barbed wire.

My God. Talk about being sanctimonious. How many years

had I been forced to follow protocol without question? Why had I questioned Dawson's methodology? Because I was accustomed to being highest on the pecking order? Because *my* timetable, *my* way of doing things, and the answers *I* demanded should always be priority number one?

Delusions of importance much, Sergeant Major?

I squeezed my eyes shut.

Why hadn't I considered that as sheriff, Dawson would be held to rigid rules and legal standards? Why hadn't I realized my father hadn't talked about his duties as sheriff, not because he didn't want to but because he couldn't?

I hoped for Dawson's warm, rough fingers to nudge my chin up even as I steeled myself against his recriminations.

But his footsteps faded as he walked away from me and I was left with nothing but regret.

NINETEEN

I hated slapping on a happy face, and hitting the happy trail, after the shitty start to my day. What was the point? I should just withdraw from the race.

And become a quitter? No.

Cowgirl up, Mercy.

I preferred solitude to socializing, so it was ironic that the door-to-door aspect of my campaign duties had become my favorite part. Even when folks told me to my face they planned on voting for Dawson, I couldn't hold it against them because it was rarely said with malice.

Older community residents, who'd known my family for generations, delighted in revealing my parents in a different light. The stories they shared were new to me, even if the tales were forty years old.

At the first stop, Maxine Crenshaw plied me with homemade doughnuts and recalled the night my father pulled over her husband for erratic driving. Milt Crenshaw, in the early stages of Alzheimer's, had left the house without his eyeglasses or his pants. He'd also forgotten the state had revoked his driver's license. Rather than toss Milt in jail, my father escorted Milt home and advised Maxine to hide the car keys.

Simple. Direct. I could visualize the scene, the amused set to my father's mouth upon finding Milt in his boxers. Would I ever overcome the need for more time with Dad to hear his stories of life behind the badge?

Over sweet tea and pecan cookies, Esther Beecham told me about my parents getting tossed out of Barb and Joe Jorgen's wedding dance. Apparently my mother instigated a hair-pulling

fight with another bridesmaid. When the man who tried to separate the drunken women got a little too friendly with Mom, Dad
beat the crap out of him. The aggressive side of my dad didn't
surprise me—cowboys liked to express opinions with their fists.
But the ever-proper Sunny Gunderson, in a knock-down, drag-
out, girl fight? In public? That'd shocked me.

Maybe I was as much a chip off Mom's block as I was Dad's.

I only made those two stops. In my gut I knew I was done
actively campaigning. I couldn't shake the feeling I'd become a
poseur of the worst sort and continuing this charade would dis-
honor my father's memory.

The drive to the ranch was a blur. I ignored the ranch hands
as I marched through the barn. ATV keys in hand, I climbed
aboard my escape vehicle and took off like the hounds of hell
were chasing me.

Shoonga loped by my side as I navigated the muddy grooves
forming a path across the field. Damn dog loved getting sloppy.
His antics lightened my load as he tried to hurry me along, as if
he knew where we were going. By the time I reached my destination, the tightness in my chest had loosened somewhat.

Years had passed since I'd last traversed this rough terrain in
the spring. An abundance of rain meant mud, mud, and more
mud. I abandoned the ATV and hiked the incline, my boots
weighted with wet earth, which made skirting the delicate ferns
and clumps of grasses near impossible. A decade of drought
forced plants into dormancy. But months of spring rain coaxed
them out, including four species I'd never seen.

At the top of the plateau, the damp wind lifted my hair, whip-
ping strands back across my face with stinging force. I tipped
my head to the gloomy sky. Billows of white and gray skittered
across the endless horizon. Patches of pale blue appeared fleet-
ingly, punch holes of sanity beneath the roiling storm clouds.

I know how the sky feels.

I spun a slow circle so I could take in the vista. From here I
spotted deciduous trees lining the river's gouge across the land.
The differences a little moisture brought to the color palette in
the valley were astounding, representing every green hue from
jade to mint.

From here I could locate the weather-beaten mounds of desiccated earth known as the Badlands. Hauntingly beautiful in its barrenness. Its isolation. Its monochromatic fortitude.

I closed my eyes and listened to the music of the wind. The dissonant changes in pitch. The harmonic whistling tones. The melodic ferocity of the gusts. The wind ebbed and flowed like the tides, but wind wasn't tied to the moon. Its power was absolute. And wind raced and raged across the prairie as if it were its due.

Through the mournful squalls, I heard the rumble of an ATV in the distance. Then closer. Then it stopped.

Shoonga rose from his resting spot, tail wagging, chippy little barks telling me who'd disturbed me.

I kept my face to the wind, zeroing in on the musky scent of wet mud, the pungent sage, the occasional hint of sweet floral, and now the whiff of gas and machine oil.

The dog settled, content with the attention from two masters.

Once he'd leveled his ragged breathing, Jake spoke. "Pretty spot. One of my faves."

"Mine, too."

Wind blew. Time passed.

Finally, Jake said, "You okay?"

"Not really."

"You left the ranch in an awful damn hurry."

He waited for me to speak. To confess.

I'll admit it took me a while to admit, "I've done a dumb thing, Jake."

"I doubt that."

A fresh gust of air, laden with moisture, churned around us. I wanted to scream my frustration to the sky to see if the wind would carry the sound away. But the scream remained lodged in my throat, burning me. Choking me. Unvoiced. Unwanted.

"Storm's coming," he said.

"It'll pass." How I knew that, I don't know. I just did.

I wished for thunder, lightning, howling wind, and driving rain. When I focused on angry external elements, I could keep angry ones raging inside me at bay.

As the wind gentled, three things became clear.

One: the J-Hawk I'd known, the man I'd been so determined to find justice for, had been long gone before I'd found him dead.

Two: I'd made the wrong choice, running against Dawson instead of running to him.

Three: out here, on top of this bluff, was the only place I didn't feel like I was drowning in the enormity of my mistakes.

"You'll find it, Mercy."

"Find what?"

"Whatever it is you're looking for."

Jake squeezed my shoulder and left me to my demons.

I dreamed of Levi.

We were sitting side by side on the bank of the Cheyenne River. The water was low; the sun was high. Big black clouds of gnats zigzagged above the water in an oddly beautiful insect ballet. The heat-baked scent of clay lingered beneath the stagnant stench of the river. The late-summer levels of the Cheyenne had turned the water into reddish-brown sludge. The mud spatters on the stones resembled blood.

"Why are we here?" Levi asked, skipping a piece of shale across the murky surface. "There's nothin' to do. Can't swim. Can't fish."

I slapped a mosquito on my thigh and a bloody bump welled. "Can't we just hang out? Enjoy spending the day together? It seems like I never get to see you anymore."

Surly, he stared across the unchanging landscape, keeping his face in shadow. "All we ever do is sit around the stupid ranch."

"I'd think you'd act happier since we're not there right now."

Splash. Plunk. More stones met the river bottom. "How come you never take me anyplace cool? Like to the waterslides or to the lake?"

Heat fried my scalp. Insects swarmed me, biting my sweat-slicked skin, angrily buzzing in my ears. "Because your mom won't let me. She worries about you. She wants to keep you safe."

Levi leaped to his feet, graceful as a young antelope. He walked into the river.

"Levi, come back here."

"Why? The water is ankle deep. You think I'm gonna drown? Or maybe a mud hole will open up and swallow me?"

Fear lanced me, sharp as a spear. "Don't say that."

He took two more steps in, water sloshing into his ratty-assed athletic shoes. His head whipped around, his hair glinting in the sun like a piece of dark amber. Levi grinned at me. That cocky, boyish grin that buoyed my spirits and broke my heart.

"Please. I'll take you to the damn waterslide. I'll take you anywhere you want to go. Just come back . . . okay?"

His smile faded. "I can't come back, Aunt Mercy. You know that."

Then Levi shimmered away like a heat mirage and receded into nothingness.

And the scream I'd been holding inside me all day finally broke free.

TWENTY

I tossed and turned for two hours after the freakish dream about my nephew. Finally, I got out of bed, rolled out my yoga mat, and worked through four repetitions each of asanas A, B, C, and D. When I stretched out for *savasana*, my muscles were pliant, my thoughts calmer. I closed my eyes.

Synchronicity between my mind and body vanished when my cell phone shattered the solitude. Geneva had insisted on giving out my number to everyone to prove my accessibility as a candidate, so I felt compelled to answer. "Hello?"

"Is this Mercy Gunderson?"

"Yes. Who's this?"

"Cherelle Dupris. I don't know if you remember me."

"I remember you. We met in the back room at Clementine's. You're the one—"

"With the scar. Yeah, I know, I should change my name to Scarface."

Not that I blamed her, but being snippy with me wasn't a good way to start the conversation. "So you calling to volunteer for my campaign?"

"No. I'm, ah . . ." A beat passed. "You'll think this is really weird."

"Probably, but it fits with my life. What's on your mind?"

She blurted, "Victor is missing."

I bit back my immediate response of *So what?* "Victor Bad Wound? As in your . . . ?" *Tormentor* came to mind, but again, I kept the smart-ass answer to myself.

"Yes."

"If Victor is missing on the reservation, the tribal police have jurisdiction. Did you call them?"

"What for? They ain't exactly gonna break out a search party for him."

No kidding. I could give a rip about a missing criminal who'd carved Cherelle up, beat her up, and dealt in thugs and drugs on a daily basis. But if I was elected sheriff, I'd have to put aside my prejudice about lowlifes like Victor and remain neutral. No time like the present to put it into practice. "Where'd you get the idea to call me?"

Pause.

Every second I waited for her to answer, the relaxing benefits of my yoga practice diminished.

"Estelle Yellow Boy. After I met you at Clementine's, I remembered last year she said you'd helped her with Albert. I thought you might help me find him."

Estelle and I hadn't parted on the best terms. I doubted she was handing out recommendations. "Why didn't you go to Saro? Victor is his brother, right?"

"That's how I know Victor is gone. Saro called me, pissed because Victor missed a meeting. Saro ain't seen Victor for a day, and Victor ain't answering his cell."

"You haven't talked to him?"

"Nope. He don't answer to me. He'll be the first to tell you that."

"So maybe Victor took off on his own. Just to get away?"

"Huh-uh. Any time he goes off the rez, he's got one of Saro's guys with him."

Was Victor so vital to the organization that he required a bodyguard? Or didn't Saro trust his brother as much as he claimed? "When was the last time you saw Victor?"

"Night before last. He came to bed around one and was gone in the morning when I got up. He didn't call, which ain't unusual. He didn't show up last night."

"Didn't that worry you?"

"I didn't think nothin' of it because Victor spends a couple nights a week at Saro's place."

"Where is Saro's place?"

"Here on the rez in the middle of the housing development across from the park."

"When did Saro contact you?"

"First thing this morning. He sent some of his guys out to see if they could find Victor or his truck, but they got a big fat nothin'. Which means Victor ain't around here."

"Had you gone out looking for Victor on your own at any point?"

"Nope. No need to. Now I can't go track him down even if I wanted to. Saro has a guy sitting outside my house. He told me to stay put. When Saro says stay put, I do it."

Weirder and weirder. "You sure Victor and Saro didn't have a falling-out?"

"Are you kidding? Saro and Victor never disagree on nothin'."

Even my mild-mannered sister and I traded verbal blows on occasion, so it stretched the limits of credibility that two volatile personalities such as Saro and Victor would be unicorns and butterflies all the time. "Never?"

"Never. Saro tells Victor what to do, and Victor does it."

"Without question?"

"Uh-huh. Saro is the brains; Victor is the muscle. But Saro would be lost if not for Victor."

Was that a hint of . . . pride in her voice about Victor's station in the organization? I shuddered and thought of Stockholm syndrome. "No one would try to come between them on purpose? Play one against the other?"

"It'd never happen. Not with the guys in the group who owe their allegiance, and no one outside the group wants to cross either of them."

That much jibed with what I'd heard. "Did Saro ask where you thought Victor had gone?"

"I told him I thought Victor was with him, which ain't a lie. Sometimes, Victor bangs that whore Jessalynne, a runner who lives out east of town, but Saro checked and Jessalynne ain't seen Victor for a few weeks."

"So everything was hunky-dory between you and Victor the last time you saw him?"

She snorted. "Same shit sandwich. Different day."

A disturbing thought occurred. Was she calling me as a cover? Acting the part of the concerned girlfriend when she already knew what'd happened to Victor? That was a stretch, but no more of a stretch than a stranger asking for my help finding her criminal and abusive boyfriend.

"I know you don't understand why I care. I mean, you're probably thinkin' good riddance, eh?"

"Maybe."

"See, that's why I called you. No bullshit. That night in Clementine's when you were talking about being a different type of sheriff? The thing is . . . I believed you."

Cherelle was all pro at using a flattering hard sell—and sadly, I wasn't immune to it. "I'm headed into town in a little bit. What does Victor drive?"

"A white pickup. Might be a Ford."

Off the top of my head I knew thirty people who drove white pickups. "Does it have reservation plates?"

"Nope."

"Any distinctive markings?"

Pause. "It's got a Bambi basher on the front and no tailgate. He's only had it a couple of weeks. He's in love with the stupid thing, so he ain't gonna be far away from it."

"I'll keep my eyes open."

I finished my bank business and avoided Geneva. Seemed pointless to try to charm my constituents in my bad mood. I'd look for Victor's truck—probably another futile endeavor.

I cruised down Main Street. Plenty of white trucks, but none fit the description of Victor's. I made a slow pass through the residential areas, thinking he might have a new chick on the side. Nothing. Same for the parking lots of the school, the bank, the churches, and the funeral home.

As I drove the road leading toward the reservation, past broken-down trailers, I considered the possibilities. Had Victor really gone missing? Given the way Saro's men were supposedly watching Cherelle, they suspected her. Hell, I suspected her.

Had Saro's goons canvassed the whole reservation? Or just the town of Eagle River? I assumed the latter.

The sunlight vanished as dirty white storm clouds tumbled in, covering the azure sky. I preferred snow to the bursts of spring rain. Rain always seemed an omen of impending doom because it was a rarity in western South Dakota.

As the dilapidated plywood sign for the Diamond T trailer court came into view, I ignored the impulse to stop at Rollie's place to pick his brain about why Cherelle had called me. I suspected Verline had given Cherelle my number, not Estelle. Arguing with a pregnant teen wasn't my idea of fun.

A mile down the road from the Diamond T was Mulligan's. The unofficial Eagle River County junkyard was a fallow field featuring abandoned vehicles, broken farm equipment, and old appliances. It'd been in existence as long as I could remember, and I'd never understood why the property owners didn't mind strangers dumping on their land. Some things were left there because they could be parted out. Others were useless hunks of metal decaying in the elements, reduced to rust and peeling paint. Oddly enough, no one tossed bags of plain old trash on the premises, nor did teens from the surrounding communities use it as a party spot—too close to a frequently patrolled road.

Yet, Mulligan's was almost always deserted. It was a perfect secluded meeting place between the rez and Viewfield.

Perfect place for a drug dealer to set up a meeting.

Nah. It couldn't be that easy. If I pulled in there, I'd find nothing.

To prove myself right, I slowed at the entrance and crossed the corroded cattle guard, bumping across the potholes masquerading as a road. About a hundred yards in, a pile of tires blocked the way to the other side. I parked, shut off the truck, jammed my Taurus in my back pocket, and climbed out.

It was as damned spooky in a car graveyard as in a real graveyard. Visions of Stephen King's killer car Christine danced in the periphery of my thoughts. The ghostlike clouds added to the creepy atmosphere. All the scene needed was a rusted hinge screeching and swaying in a nonexistent breeze.

I quickened my step.

I picked my way around mud puddles and car parts strewn on the ground. How vandals hadn't destroyed this place amazed me. Sweet-faced Johnny-jump-ups poked their cheery purple-and-yellow heads from the scant patches of soil. One flower had even taken root in a rusted-out tractor rim. The phrase "bloom where you're planted" popped into my head. I bypassed cars, hoods gone, revealing bare cavities where the engines should've been. Seeing those gaping holes, the mechanical guts ripped away, leaving an empty shell, bothered me like I'd witnessed the gruesome aftermath of a ritual killing.

Knock it off. This isn't helping.

The traversable area narrowed considerably. Unless I wanted to duck-walk or limbo through the equipment to get to the other side, I needed to return to my truck.

Screw it. This was a stupid idea. I'd proven myself right, and now it was time to trot on home.

As I spun in the opposite direction, I caught a glimpse of the top of a white truck cab.

Far too pristine a white for this car jungle.

Goddammit. When I wanted my eyesight to fail me, it never did.

In my haste to get closer, I stepped on a hubcap, losing my balance when my boot slid into a shadowed oil slick. As I righted myself, I whacked my knee into the jagged grille of a 1970s gas-guzzler.

Knee smarting, I limped past my truck toward the vehicle parked in the clearing. Not camouflaged, but sticking out like a white thumb. Someone wanted this truck found. Lucky me to once again draw the short straw.

I approached the vehicle with my weapon drawn. "Victor?" I felt stupid saying it, but I repeated his name anyway. "Victor? You in there?"

No reply. No surprise. Didn't stop my heart from thudding erratically or perspiration from geysering out of my pores. I flashed back to the times early in the war, when we checked abandoned vehicles in Iraq when the bomb squad specialists were shorthanded. I had the same sense of panic. Of dread. Of the certainty of my own mortality.

Breathe.

But the instant I inhaled, the odor of decay assaulted me.

I'd been around the putrid scent of decomposing flesh enough times to recognize it—nothing else smelled like death.

My gaze swept the vehicle, and I noticed the blood spatters on the inside windows of the cab.

On the driver's side, I used my shirt to hold on to the handle with one hand while I stepped up onto the running board and peered in.

Victor was sprawled across the bench seat. Half his head blown across the tweed seat covers, the windshield, the back window, the side window, even the slate-blue console. In addition to the blood sprayed everywhere, his body was puffed like a toad's. I didn't know enough about time of death and all that medical/CSI jargon to discern how long he'd been a corpse. All I knew was he was dead, bloated, and stinking to high heaven.

The window hadn't been shattered to make the kill shot. This hadn't been a robbery attempt because the keys still dangled from the ignition. So Victor had opened the door to whoever had killed him. But the killer hadn't been satisfied with almost taking Victor's head off; he or she had also sliced Victor's abdomen from side to side, practically cutting him in half.

Another whiff of rotting meat set off my gag reflex. I barely made it to the fence before the contents of my breakfast spewed out my mouth and hung on the dried stems of the bromegrass. Even Poopy would've been impressed with my projectile vomiting. Wiping my mouth on my sleeve, I tried to maintain my composure as everything inside me urged me to flee. I couldn't just "discover" another body. I might as well change my name to Jessica Fletcher in this county.

Yet, as much of a piece of shit as Victor Bad Wound was, I couldn't leave him moldering in his vehicle. I held my ground against the wind, the spitting rain, and my own nausea as I dug for my cell phone and dialed.

"This is Deputy Moore."

"Kiki? It's Mercy."

"Hey, Mercy. If this is about the campaign, it'll have to wait until I'm off duty."

"It's not. Can you talk without anyone overhearing you?"

"I'm alone in my patrol car. Why?"

"How far are you from Mulligan's?"

"Twenty minutes. Why, what's going on?"

I looked over at the pickup, my mind flashing to the grisly sight of what remained of Victor Bad Wound's face. And the deep gash across his lower belly where his blood had dried his jeans and shirt to his bloated form. "I found a dead body."

Silence. Then a terse, "At Mulligan's?"

"Yeah."

"Do you know who it is?"

"Victor Bad Wound."

"Jesus, Mercy. How the hell did you—"

"Look, he's been missing. Cherelle Dupris asked me to keep an eye out for his truck. While I was out campaigning, I found it, and him in it—dead."

Deputy Moore swore again. "How long ago did you find him?"

"Just now. You're the first person I've called. Before you ask, I don't know if Cherelle is involved. I just know *I* can't be involved. Understand?"

I almost heard the gears turning in her head.

"Kiki, you have to find the body. You're on patrol, right? Just swing by Mulligan's like you were doing a routine check. Victor's white pickup is parked in the back by itself."

"What about you? Who's next on your call list?"

"No one. I won't contact Cherelle because I found nothing— *you* did. By the time you get here, I'll be long gone."

"But Dawson—"

"Will think you've done a bang-up job as an investigator. That's what really matters, right? That justice is served no matter who does it?"

She sighed. "I ain't comfortable taking credit when everyone in the county should know you're the one who did the 'bang-up' investigative work. It'd help your campaign."

"The election is the last thing on my mind, Kiki. Maybe I'm not as qualified for the sheriff's job as you all seem to think I am."

"Why's that?"

"Because things will be a whole lot better for everyone now

that Victor Bad Wound is dead. That's not exactly an unbiased opinion."

"But it's not any different than mine or anyone else's in the county." She sighed. "Fine. I'm on my way."

"Thank you." I hung up and sprinted back to my truck.

I needed a drink. I deserved one.

Hello, Clementine's.

The parking lot held more cars than the usual weekday-afternoon crowd.

John-John sat on a bar stool behind the bar. He poured a shot of Wild Turkey in a lowball glass and slid it in front of me.

"That obvious, huh?"

"Only to me, doll."

I could've sipped the whiskey, but I guzzled it.

"Another?" John-John asked.

"No. I'll take a Coke." I looked around. Place was damn near empty. "Where is everyone? There had to be ten cars out there."

"In the back. Tootsie is teaching her fellow retirees how to shoot darts."

Tootsie, a sassy, spry "woman of age" was one of my favorite customers, not only because she'd palled around with my mother. "Why?"

"Guess at a bridge game the gals' husbands commented about them being too old to learn new tricks. Tootsie took offense and plans to teach 'them duffers' a thing or two."

I rolled the cold soda glass between my sticky palms. Had Kiki reached Mulligan's yet? With her iron stomach I doubted she'd be puking her guts out over the fence line.

"Mercy?"

"Hmm?"

"You wanna tell me what's goin' on that you didn't even chuckle at Tootsie's antics?"

"Sorry. Just thinking."

"Wanna share with the class?"

"It's about some of that woo-woo stuff."

John-John dropped two maraschino cherries in my Coke. "Is the woo-woo stuff happening to you?"

"Yeah. Something that another Indian guy said to me."

He gasped like an offended spinster. "You been seeing another *winkte* behind my back?"

That brought a half smile. "No worries, *kola*. You're the only two-spirited person in my life."

"I worry you're carrying too many burdens, doll."

"I am."

"So tell me."

I studied him. Warned him. "Okay. Just don't get pissy that I haven't told you before. A few years ago, I died. I was literally dead to the world for . . . several minutes, at least. It's stayed classified in my medical and military records. The day after I found Jason's body, I ran into this Indian guy. He told me because I'd been brought back to life, dead spirits are drawn to me. That I have some sort of dead man's ESP, which is just fucking awesome."

John-John studied me. "Are you asking me if this is true in the Sioux spiritual world?"

"I guess. I don't know. Hell, I don't know anything except I'm sick and tired of being a divining rod for the newly departed."

John-John leaned across the bar until I looked up at him. "Have you found another dead body recently? Since Jason Hawley?"

"Uh-huh."

"When?"

"About thirty minutes ago."

He poured another shot and nudged it at me.

I knocked it back. "Jesus Christ on a pogo stick, John-John. Why me? Don't you think I've dealt with enough death? Don't you think it's cosmically unfair that now I have to spend the rest of my life worried I don't stumble over rotting corpses?"

"Where did you run into this Indian guy?"

"The first time? He came in here. Remember that good-looking Indian dude you were flirting with?"

"Ah." John-John smiled. "He is a hard one to forget. What's his name?"

"Shay Turnbull."

"That name don't sound Sioux, not that it matters. I talked to him but didn't get a sense of . . . well, anything."

My eyes widened. "You can sense others with enhanced senses?"

"Yep. And I've got great gaydar, too. Pity this Shay guy ain't batting for our team. But back to your question. He's right. It's kind of a cosmic lottery how often this sensibility will appear or how it'll affect you for the long term."

"And to think I wanted to win the lottery." Sweet juice burst in my mouth as I bit down on a fat cherry. "So if I know the person, even in passing, my odds are . . . ?"

"Even higher."

Mercy Gunderson, bloodhound of the dead. I wondered if it was too late to get that as my campaign slogan.

"Who'd you find?"

I looked over my shoulder, then at him. "Victor Bad Wound."

John-John blanched.

"Cherelle called me because he's been missing and Saro's on her ass. I went looking. And lucky me, I found him on my first try."

"Did you just leave him there?"

"No. But I couldn't face Dawson and his suspicion about me finding yet another body, especially when he already thinks I'm a walking catastrophe, so I called Kiki. She's taking credit for my accidental police work." I drained my Coke. "I need to go home. Thanks for the ear."

"Anytime, doll."

Anna wasn't around when I returned to the cabin. Chances were she was at Pete's Pawnshop, pawing through junk and jawing with Pete. I didn't get her fascination with the place, but I was secretly happy she wasn't underfoot.

So far, Anna's purchases, besides the TV/DVD player, consisted of a crusty milk can, a rainbow crocheted tissue box, and a pair of spurs. When I asked her about the spurs, since she'd never ridden a horse, she handed them to me as a gift and explained the spurs were a daily reminder for me to face my fears.

Maybe it was snarky, demanding to see what she'd bought for herself. She showed me a tiny plain tin box. I opened it, expecting to find a treasure, but there was nothing within.

Anna explained the box represented her: small, unadorned, tough on the outside, but inside . . . empty.

I'd stopped asking about her purchases after that.

With no campaign events scheduled, and no job demanding my time, I looked forward to a night at home. But I needed something to take my mind off finding Victor's body. Or from wondering if Cherelle had played me. Or from wishing I'd never agreed to run for sheriff.

I wasn't in the mood to target shoot, but I could quiet my mind and keep my hands busy by catching up on reloading.

Catch up. Right. I had bins of shell casings. Not only because I'd spent a lot of time shooting, but in my boredom, I'd stumbled across my dad's storage cache of casings. His "storage" method consisted of throwing spent shell casings in Sheetrock buckets in the barn. It'd taken me a solid week to sort, throw out, clean, and organize the shells.

Not all shooters reload their ammunition. I did it in a limited capacity. Shells were damn expensive and harder to come by for larger calibers. Since my dad taught me to shoot, he'd also taught me to reload. The tangy scent of brass reminded me of him, and today I had the overwhelming urge to connect with some part of him.

A clement breeze, overloaded with the scent of the chokecherry blossoms, eddied around me as I headed to the storage shed. I grabbed the reloading bench and carried it into the cabin. Most people didn't reload in the house, but the shed was too small, too dark, and just plain uncomfortable. Any activity with firearms, including bullets, made Hope nervous, so I'd hauled everything—the bench, the tools, the die sets, the scale, the tumblers, and the cans of gunpowder—from the barn to the cabin. If I wanted to set up my reloading bench in the damn kitchen, I could. My house, my rules.

I'd already "cleaned" the cases by tossing them in the tumbler with ground walnut shells. Then I sealed them in plastic bags so they were ready to reload when I had time.

I chose the die I needed for pressing out the spent primers and resizing the cases, screwing it into the top of the loading press. Getting the first case properly sized took the most time.

My mind was blessedly blank as I focused on each step. I'd managed to finish half the lot in blissful silence when I heard a car in the drive. Anna had returned.

She wandered in and tossed her ball cap on the couch. "Hey, you're doing something useful, imagine that."

"Fuck off."

"Do you ever just sit around and do . . . nothing?"

"Not if I can help it."

"Sad. You want a beer?"

"Nah." Mixing alcohol and gunpowder? Not a good idea.

Anna plopped down next to me after helping herself to a Corona. "So. Reloading, huh?"

I tapped powder into the scale and adjusted the weights. "Yep."

"I've never reloaded."

"You've never had to buy your own ammo," I pointed out.

"True. And usually I don't have time to hang around and pick up brass. I'm too busy hauling ass away from the scene."

We drifted into companionable silence as she sipped her beer and watched me work.

"How many empty casings do you have?" she asked.

"Depends on the caliber. I've got bins in the tool shed if you wanna take a peek. I must have a thousand of this type for my dad's Remington 722 bolt-action varmint rifle. Because it's an off caliber, .222, it's hard to find casings."

Anna whistled. "Man. I guess it's true what they say about rednecks having a secret arsenal."

"Ain't a lot to do out here besides shoot, A-Rod." I tipped the powder into the shell.

"No kidding. Don't mind telling you, I never thought I could miss the millions of people in California, but I do." She picked up a casing. "So what was the last varmint you shot with your dad's rifle?"

"Prairie dogs."

"I don't know if I could kill a prairie dog. They're so cute."

My mouth stayed firmly shut. Anna had no issue shooting a person? But she balked at shooting a rat with a brain the size of a dime? I ignored the dichotomy and said, "I should've smoked the damn mountain lion that crossed my path, but I didn't."

"I'm actually really happy you didn't kill it."

I bristled. "Whatever pity that kept me from shooting her that morning came back to bite me in the ass. A couple days later she got into the herd and attacked a calf. The mama cow stomped the hell out of her and eventually killed her, but the calf died anyway." That'd been a fun conversation with Jake.

"You people have such a different life out here. It's like you're from another planet.

"Says the woman who grew up in L.A." I changed the subject. "What'd you do today?"

"This and that. Hung out with Pete and Re-Pete."

"What'd you buy?"

"A funky old cane. You should check out Pete's place, Mercy. He brings in all kinds of new stuff every day."

"After he buys it for pennies on the dollar and jacks up the price," I muttered. *Not nice, Mercy.* "How's their coffee shop biz?"

"Opening next week. Since I'm 'citified,' they wanted my opinion on their new pumpkin-spice coffee."

"And?"

"And I told them they didn't have to put actual chunks of pumpkin in for it to be authentic."

I stopped measuring powder and looked at her. "Are you serious?"

"No." She laughed. "You never used to be so gullible, Gunny."

"Seems to be a theme today."

"Trouble on the campaign trail?"

I shrugged. I couldn't tell her about Victor. Doubtful she'd shed tears for him anyway. "I'm just having trouble processing a couple of things."

"Like?" she prompted.

Like are Shay Turnbull and John-John's claims true? Am I predisposed to a connection with the newly dead?

"Like making a decision and not knowing whether it is the right one."

Anna drained her beer. "Be specific. We talking life-and-death decisions? Or dealing with those murky gray areas?"

"Murky gray," I admitted.

"You've always had trouble with them, Gunny."

I bristled again. "No, I haven't."

"Yes, you have."

"Name one time."

"The time we were on convoy detail and you couldn't take out that old man."

Goddammit. I hated that I'd goaded her into bringing it up because I'd tried like hell to forget it'd ever happened.

During our stint at the start of the Iraq War, while we were awaiting new transfer orders to St. Mere, aka Camp Fallujah, we were stationed at Camp Ramadi and tasked to provide escort "services" along with the marines as part of their Tactical Movement Team. Our job was to protect the supply convoys traveling between Camp Ramadi to Combat Outpost to Camp Corregidor and back.

At the time, that area was the most dangerous stretch of road in all of Iraq, nicknamed "the Gauntlet." Our convoys were consistently subjected to IEDs, sniper fire, mortar rounds, grenades, RPGs, Molotov cocktails. Basically, anything they could throw at us—or shoot at us—they did. "They" meaning rebel kids as young as five and old arthritic men. The insurgents used every dirty, inhumane trick in the book, and the hell of it was, it worked . . . at first. Our side sustained plenty of casualties.

Those of us unfortunate enough to be in the forefront of the first wave of "protection" passed the intel back to the powers that be, who revised the ROE (Rules of Engagement), which details the level of force authorized, in addition to the EOF (Escalation of Force), which provides criteria for reaching that deadly force threshold. The rules were in place for a reason, but it was frustrating when we were subjected to restricted ROE—usually at the behest of whoever was in command.

Normally on the convoys, we were assigned to the gun trucks. None of the marines or our fellow army soldiers blinked at having a woman manning the machine guns. The most qualified person was selected for the job. Gender was a nonissue, and what defined "combat" was a murky area at best. Getting hit with mortar rounds every damn day at base camp meant we were all in combat situations, regardless of whether we were officially deemed in the field or not.

With limited manpower, each vehicle averaged four soldiers.

One of our sniper team members was on each truck, usually running the M240B or the M2, along with a marine driver and the TC (Truck Commander) who operates the radios, monitors in-vehicle chatter, and is linked to the main battle command system BFT (Blue Force Tracker). The third person was a spare gunner in case something happened to the first gunner—sadly, that was a frequent occurrence.

Corporal McGuigan, a young marine, was behind the wheel. As the highest-ranking officer, Captain Thrasher took the passenger seat as the TC. In this particular procession, I was relegated to the backseat of the Humvee, the designated spare, while my team member A-Rod manned the turret.

Since it was a convoy situation, if we took sniper fire, we weren't allowed to stop, pinpoint the source, and remove the threat, which was usually our job on the sniper teams. Instead, we had to duck and cover, wearing full battle rattle, and keep the convoy moving. That always chapped my ass, but like a good soldier, I did my job, shut my mouth, and snapped off a "Yes, sir."

We rolled out at 2200, so by the time we saw the sun come up hours later, we'd almost be at our destination. The "no unscheduled stops" had been drilled into our heads from day one.

About four hours into the slow-going desert trek, we were advised to take a tactical pause—army speak for a piss break. Answering the call of nature was no big deal for the guys. Although most female soldiers balked at any kind of special treatment because of our gender, the darkness was a godsend for quick, private relief. The women I served with had incorporated unique tricks to emptying full bladders while in the midst of several hundred men and when confined in a vehicle. Consequently, I didn't need to relieve myself and opted to remain inside the Humvee.

Turned out to be a smart move on my part, because we immediately came under attack from small-arms fire.

Chaos ensued. I heard shouts outside the vehicle, shouts in my headphones as everyone was ordered to cease fire. When I saw two of the other drivers dragging McGuigan behind our vehicle, I immediately scrambled out to check his injuries before Captain Thrasher barked at me to get my CLS (Combat Life Saver) bag.

McGuigan was dazed. The Kevlar vest had kept the sniper bullet from piercing the kid's chest. A bullet had grazed the inside of his right thigh, just missing the femoral artery. It bled like a son of a bitch. I managed to get him patched up enough until we reached camp with medical facilities. McGuigan also sustained an enormous bruise on the back of his skull after smacking his head into the vehicle when he'd gone down. I made him as comfortable in the backseat of our Humvee as quickly as I could.

Without making eye contact with me, Captain Thrasher snapped, "You're driving. Let's go."

I hated to drive. I tended to pass the buck to a subordinate whenever possible, but this time I didn't argue. Thrasher out-ranked me, and every TC I'd ever dealt with would only give up his command post if he took direct fire and died.

Hours on the road without further engagement or incidents lulled me into a false sense of security. Around sunrise, when the shadows lengthened and played tricks on weary eyes, I saw something in the road two hundred yards ahead. I'd glanced at Thrasher, but he was fiddling with the headset. I briefly closed my eyes, reopened them, expecting a mirage, but I realized it *was* a person in the middle of the damn road. An old man drag-ging a goat tethered with a rope. At one hundred yards out I took my foot off the gas.

Thrasher looked up and said, "Why are you slowing down?"

"Civilian in the road, sir."

Thrasher swore and then spoke to A-Rod through his headset. "Sergeant Rodriguez. Eliminate the obstacle in the road."

"Roger, sir."

The vehicle started to shake; A-Rod had fired up the M240B. The gunfire started and stopped abruptly. Over the headset I heard A-Rod say, "Sir, the gun jammed, and I missed the target. Give me a sec."

"No time." Thrasher faced me. "Run that fucker over, Master Sergeant."

My grip increased on the steering wheel. "I'm just supposed to hit him head-on and watch him splat like a bug on the windshield?"

"Yes. And that's an order."

When I was behind my gun scope, I saw targets, not people. Procedure is simple: Aim. Verify. Shoot. I rarely remembered the faces of the targets I'd been ordered to eliminate, but this was different, this was an old man, probably someone's grandfather. Wearing tattered *dishdashas*. Tethered to a goat. Probably the only livestock he owned. I saw the man's face and his haunted, desperate eyes.

Which was probably why I swerved to miss him at the last second and set off the IED buried on the side of the road.

Dirt exploded across the windshield. I heard pieces of shrapnel chinking against the side of the vehicle. The Humvee rocked on its wheels, and we bounced hard before coming to an abrupt stop.

My ears rang, my head pounded, my body ached. The smell of burning rubber and oil was thick in the confines of the Humvee. And the taste of salt and dirt coated my lips and tongue.

Completely rattled, I squinted out the window, trying to take stock of the situation. Another man, not the old decrepit man who'd willingly sacrificed himself in hopes of taking a few of us out with him, was racing across the desert like a world-class sprinter.

Son of a bitch. The triggerman. We would've been fucked either way. I reached for my gun the same time the man's head burst into scarlet mist and chunks of his body flew up like he'd been tossed into a meat grinder gone haywire.

As activity burst around me, I didn't budge. I couldn't believe I'd felt an ounce of sympathy. My hesitation, or dare I say my show of . . . humanity . . . disturbed me. The tip-off would've been obvious even to a wet-behind-the-ears private. No one stands by the road, alone, in a desert, in the wee small hours, defiantly facing down a U.S. military convoy.

And if they did? They certainly didn't live to tell about it.

The IED didn't significantly damage the Humvee, nor did A-Rod sustain anything but superficial injuries. She didn't say a word when Thrasher and his commanding officer chewed my ass up one side and down the other.

I'd convinced myself I was doing A-Rod a favor by letting her drive, but the truth was, I needed to feel the stinging sand and scorching rays on my face to burn away my shame.

For years after that incident, I never faltered in my responsibilities. I pulled the trigger—literally and figuratively—every single time.

Until I'd run across that lioness.

I'd never let sentimentality affect my judgment again. Never.

"Mercy? You still with me?" Anna said.

"Yeah." I put a bullet on top of the casing and pushed the ram down, seating the bullet to the proper depth. "Just reliving that fun time when I realized I'd fucked up and nearly got us all blown up." I looked at Anna. "Has it ever happened to you?"

"What? Freezing up to the point that I didn't take out my target?"

I nodded.

She took a drink of beer as she measured me. "Nope. Not ever. Not when I was enlisted, not now that I'm a private contractor. Then again, we're different, Gunny."

"How so?"

"You follow orders. I follow my gut instinct. Sometimes, doing what's wrong is the only thing that feels right."

A chill ran down my spine that didn't have a damn thing to do with the cool breeze blowing in.

Three raps sounded, and Sheriff Dawson appeared in the open doorway.

Why hadn't I heard him drive up?

"Mind if I come in?"

I said, "Sure. You here on official business?"

His face took on a guarded expression, as if he couldn't believe my antagonism right off the bat.

Quickly, I amended, "I only asked if you were off duty because if you are, I'll offer you a beer."

Dawson relaxed into the door frame. "I'll pass. But thanks."

"So you just out making the rounds?"

"Yes and no. I'm here to give you a heads-up."

"What's going on?"

"A homicide."

I played dumb. "Another one? You're kidding me. Who?"

"Deputy Moore found Victor Bad Wound's body this afternoon at Mulligan's."

"Holy shit. Really? How long had he been missing?"

"No one knows because it wasn't officially reported."

I frowned. "Huh. How'd he die?"

"Multiple gunshot wounds. We're tentatively placing time of death between twenty-four and forty-eight hours ago."

"So you came by to . . . warn me a shooter is on the loose or something?"

"Not exactly." He shifted his stance. "You crossed paths with Victor a couple of times."

"Unavoidable when Saro's group started coming into Clementine's. I broke up a fight involving his nephew at Stillwell's, and Victor and Saro cornered me. But that was the extent of my contact with him."

"Did you threaten him at Stillwell's that night?"

Not a casual question. "Am I a suspect or something?"

Dawson just stared at me.

"I don't fucking believe this. Am I suspect?" I held my hands out. "If you've come to do a gunpowder residue test on me, I'm telling you right now, I'll fail it."

He smiled benignly. "Thanks for the tip. But I'm here strictly on a fact-finding mission. Of course, if you want to tell me your whereabouts for the last two nights . . ."

As I composed a tart reply, Anna jumped in. "I can answer that. Me 'n' Gunny have both been here, drinking beer, shooting the shit, and watching DVDs of *Lost*. Debating the hotness factor of Sawyer and Jack versus Sayid and Jin."

"Which brings me to the second reason I'm here." Dawson looked at Anna. "I've heard from a couple of people that you're friends with Victor's live-in, Cherelle Dupris?"

Anna rolled her eyes. "Out here in the boondocks if you talk to a person a couple of times you're best buddies? Give me a break. Me 'n' Gunny talked to her one night about campaign stuff. I played one game of pool with her. I talked to her one other time while I sat at the counter at Clementine's and she picked up a bottle to go. So yeah, I guess I can see where you'd think me 'n' her are now BFFs."

I ignored Anna's sarcasm. "Why does it matter?"

"We're looking for anyone who might know Cherelle's whereabouts."

Dread curled in my stomach. "Is she a suspect?"

For a second it appeared Dawson would hedge, but he nodded. "According to our sources on the rez, she hasn't been at the house she shares with Victor since yesterday. We want to talk to her."

If Cherelle hadn't been at the house, then where had she called me from this morning? And why had she lied?

"*Talk* to her?" I asked.

"Better to talk to us than what'll happen if Saro gets ahold of her first."

I fiddled with the ram on the reloader. "Where is Saro?"

"Holed up in his house. Again, according to our source, Cherelle isn't with him. Just his drug-running gophers."

"So you're thinking this could be a drug-related hit?"

"Possibly. Miz Dupris isn't the only suspect we've got, but right now she's the most important."

Too bad if Dawson thought I was poking at him, but I had to ask. "Is Turnbull involved?"

Dawson's mouth twisted with disdain. "Big fucking surprise. It's only been a few hours since the body was found and we're already being cut out of everything."

"Not everything, if you've got inside info."

"True. Wherever Cherelle has gone, she didn't drive her car."

"Do you think Cherelle ran?"

"I hope so. Going off the reservation is the only chance we'll have of talking to her. Even if she didn't kill Victor, we're guessing she has an idea who did."

Anna got up and grabbed another beer.

Dawson and I stared at each other in silence.

Had Kiki told Dawson I'd discovered Victor's body? Was he waiting for me to be honest with him? If I didn't, would he arrest me for obstruction of justice? How could I confess that if

I hadn't been running for his job I would've phoned everything in like a dutiful citizen?

Running for sheriff should make you more responsible to the truth, not less.

"Mercy?"

Lost in self-recriminations, I hadn't realized Dawson had spoken to me. "I'm sorry. Could you repeat that?"

"Turnbull doesn't know I'm here. In fact, he'd blow a gasket if he found out. So if he happens to swing by . . ."

"He won't. But I'll keep my mouth shut." It irked me Anna was here. Be nice to have one honest goddamn conversation with Dawson for a change. "But why are you telling me all this?" *When you wouldn't before* went unsaid.

"Because as a candidate for public office, you should be informed on what's going on in this county. I understand that now."

That almost sounded like . . . a partial apology.

"Besides, I wouldn't want you to make a rash decision on faulty intel." He smiled and pointed at my reloading press. "I'll let you get back to it."

"Thanks. I'll see you tomorrow night at the debate."

Dawson pushed off the door frame and rammed his hand through his hair. "About that. Are we keeping it civilized? Or are we going for the jugular?"

"Civilized. I wish this whole damn thing was over."

"Me, too." His gaze sought Anna's. "Miz Rodriguez."

She lifted her bottle in mock-salute. "Sheriff."

As soon as the sound of tires on gravel faded, Anna said, "I hope you win the election, because that man is an idiot."

No, he's not.

I couldn't defend him without raising Anna's suspicions.

Why are you defending him anyway? Would your defense be on a professional level? Or on a personal one?

Although she'd been preoccupied since her arrival, and off doing her own thing 90 percent of the time, it seemed strange Anna hadn't asked if I was involved with anyone. Then again, knowing Anna, she'd assume if I'd hooked up with a guy, I would've mentioned it to her.

"Well, it ain't looking good for the home team, A-Rod."

"No matter. You'll bounce back, Gunny. You always do." Anna tossed her beer bottle in the trash. "Is there any food?"

"Peanut butter and fruit."

"You still eat like your choices are MREs," she complained. "I'm hungry for real food. Like pizza."

"No pizza joints around here. You can get pizzas at the bar or buy frozen ones at the grocery store."

"Think I'll head into town and pick one up. You need anything else while I'm there?"

"Nope."

She spun her keys around her index finger. "Be back in a bit."

I lined up the next ten cases and squirted lube on the pad. "No rush. I've got plenty to keep me occupied."

"One of these days, Gunny, you're going to stop trying so damn hard to do it all."

I smiled at her. "Don't bet the farm on that."

TWENTY-ONE

The table-and-chair configuration at the community center resembled a wedding dance, not a hall for a political debate. Red, white, and blue streamers floated overhead in an elaborate twist that originated at the stage.

The stage.

My belly jumped as I lingered by the main door. Did I really have the guts to stand up in front of all these people and make a spectacle of myself? Especially after I'd spent the last two decades striving to stay inconspicuous?

The Parker Brothers Band were tuning guitars, checking mics, repositioning amps and speakers for when they took the stage after the debate. If I listened closely, I could hear the impatient tapping of cowboy boots and the palpable anticipation of the crowd.

I didn't delude myself that attendees were here to listen to Dawson and me argue the issues. The people running my campaign refused to accept that swaying voters was moot at this point. I bet 99.9 percent of voters had made up their minds before I'd filled Bill O'Neil's slot on the ballot. This debate was an excuse to party, as it was the first large-scale community event after the long winter, calving season, and branding.

Andrew Parker spotted me. He grinned, and all six feet five inches, three hundred pounds barreled toward me.

I braced myself for Andrew's standard greeting. He'd bind me in his massive arms, swing me in a circle, whooping and hollering as if we were still eight-year-old kids on the school playground.

"Lord have mercy, I feel my temperature rising," he sang as he grabbed me and—yep—spun me around. Twice.

I closed my eyes and let him.

Once Andrew set me on my feet, he pushed his straw hat back on his bald head. "You'll save me a dance? For old time's sake? Please?" He waggled his eyebrows. "A slow one?"

"No way. Marcie will kick my ass." I peered around him and looked for his petite wife. Marcie, a world-class barrel racer with the awards and belt buckles to prove it, was still the tough cowgirl who loved a good catfight. "Where is she?"

"Home. Her ankles puffed up like marshmallows. She didn't feel like kickin' up her heels with the baby kickin' her bladder every five minutes."

Hard to fathom my classmates were still having babies. Even harder to believe? Some of them were already grandparents. "When is she due?"

"Next month."

As I debated on whether to ask more nosy questions, Andrew's curious gaze burned into me. "What?"

"Just wondering if my favorite candidate is still singing?"

"Only in the shower and in the truck."

He bumped me with his shoulder. "Come on, 'fess up, Mercy. You were too damn good to've given it up completely."

"I did. Not a lot of singing gigs in the army."

"Bet you still know all the words to every Patsy Cline song."

"So?"

"So . . . get up on stage with us tonight and sing a couple."

"No."

"Not even for old time's sake?"

"No."

"Just one?"

"No."

"Please?"

"No."

"Bet it would get you more votes," he said slyly.

"What part of *no* is confusing you, Andrew? You get hit on the head with a concrete boom or something?" Andrew had followed in his father's footsteps and taken over the family business.

Which made me wonder . . . Had I been predestined to run

for sheriff? Following parental footsteps like so many of my friends?

"Your dad would've loved to hear you sing. He was so proud of you in everything you did. Singing. Soldiering. Now running for sheriff. It'd be a great way to remember him."

I hissed, "You suck, playing the dead-father card."

His brown eyes softened. "I didn't mean it that way. Wyatt was a great man, Mercy. We all miss him."

That soothed my flash of temper. "Thanks."

He paused for all of fifteen seconds before he started badgering me again. "So? What do you say?"

I looked around. No one was nearby. I belted out the first stanza of "There's Your Trouble" by the Dixie Chicks and felt smug when his jaw dropped.

"Don't sing no more, my ass," he groused. "You oughta be ashamed, lyin' to a gullible country boy like me."

"That's what you get for making me feel guilty."

"So you'll do it?"

"Not a chance in hell."

Still grumbling, Andrew disappeared onto the stage behind the slide steel guitar.

People streamed in and filled up the seating area.

Dawson had his crowd. Jazinski. Robo-Barbie. My dad's best buddy, Dean Whittaker. A couple of the guards from the jail. Business owners like Pete. Mitzi. Larry Manx, who owned the Q-Mart. Chet, from the propane company. All locals I'd have to deal with regardless if I won or lost the election. Would that be awkward? How had my dad handled knowing the names and faces of the individuals who'd opposed him?

A crush of people surrounded me. I smiled. I chatted. I anxiously shifted from foot to foot, glad I'd worn my dressiest pair of Old Gringo heeled boots instead of Geneva's suggestion of "strappy" high heels.

Geneva dragged me aside. "Okay. This is set to start in two minutes. Need anything?"

A full flask. "Nope."

"Good. You've got a lot of supporters here, Mercy."

I looked at the crowd. No division of factions, like the separate bride's side and groom's side at a wedding. Good thing—it'd be mortifying if half the seats on my side were empty. Hope, Joy, Jake, and Sophie were in the audience supporting me, which actually made me more nervous.

I readjusted the belt on my newly purchased gray wool dress slacks—I loved online shopping—and snapped out the fancy French cuffs on my new white blouse. I finger-combed my hair for the tenth time, hating I'd been coerced into letting it hang loose around my shoulders instead of slicking it back into a ponytail. I didn't feel like me. I didn't look like me—duded up in tailored clothes, coiffed hair, and no gun.

"You ready? You're on first."

"Let's do it." I walked up to the speaker's platform. I inhaled an *uji* breath and released it. "Welcome, everyone. My name is Mercy Gunderson, and I'm running for Eagle River County sheriff."

Everything blurred after that. What I said. What Dawson said. Thank God it only lasted around thirty minutes.

Dawson and I shook hands and exited the stage to our separate camps. Geneva assured me I'd done great. Even Kit gave me a thumbs-up. I resisted the urge to flip him off.

Distortion from the speaker system made me cringe as Andrew Parker took the microphone. "Now rumor has it . . . that these two candidates have a secret . . ."

My heart raced. *Don't do it. Don't even say it, Andrew.*

". . . bet going about what the loser has to do for their opponent after the election." Andrew zeroed in on Dawson first. "Sheriff? Care to elaborate on that side bet? Something about kissing a . . . pig?"

Dawson laughed. "Sorry, I'm pleading the fifth."

Andrew's attention zoomed to me. "Mercy? How about you?"

"I'll follow the sheriff's lead and stay pigheaded."

Laughter.

"How many of you would like to see a show of goodwill between these two fine candidates as they lead us in the first dance?"

Oh, hell no. I glared at that rat bastard Andrew, but the crowd didn't notice. They were on board with the idea. They clapped, whistled, stomped their feet.

Geneva snapped, "For Christsake, what is *wrong* with these people?"

"No booze. If they were getting loaded right now, they wouldn't care."

"You have to refuse to dance with him, Mercy."

"Now how petty would that make me look?"

"Think of how it'll look if you and Dawson start grinding on each other," Geneva hissed.

"Puh-lease. We are adults. We'll behave accordingly."

I met Dawson halfway and took his outstretched hand. He bowed and kissed my knuckles.

I pretended to punch him in the stomach.

It played well with the crowd.

The band started a cover of George Strait's "Check Yes or No," a tune not too fast, nor too slow. Dawson clasped my left hand in his right. He placed his palm in the middle of my back and brought me in close to his body.

I set my hand on his shoulder in proper two-step position. No harm, no foul, no sweat. I could do this. Then I looked up to see his annoying Cheshire cat–like grin. "What?"

"I've wanted to dance with you for months."

"Too bad my dancing skills will probably disappoint you."

"The only disappointment is acting as if dancing with you is a chore for me, Mercy."

Shoot. That was really sweet. "Dawson—"

"Just keep smiling. And let me lead, will ya?"

Let him lead? Damn man always took the lead.

Wrong. You always take point and expect him to follow.

So yeah, I let him lead . . . but just this one time.

Dawson knew his way around the dance floor. Every muscle in my body was rigid as curious couples joined us. His nearness caused a disjointed sensation inside me. I felt like one of those magnets—both repelled and attracted.

"Relax," he muttered.

"I *am* relaxed."

"Right. You're strung tight as a new barbed-wire fence." He pulled me closer. "You look great tonight."

"Hey. You're not supposed to say stuff like that."

"Why not?"

"Because this Fred-and-Ginger routine is all for show."

"Not for me it isn't."

My face heated. "Dammit, Dawson, knock it off. This is not the time or the place—"

"Tough shit. I'll say whatever the hell I want, and you'll suck it up and smile."

"Channeling your inner caveman?"

"You bring out the best in me, Sergeant Major."

"I think you mean *beast*."

Dawson chuckled. "That, too. So you'll damn well listen to what I have to say while I have your undivided attention."

"Or what?"

"Don't push me, darlin'. If you'll recall, I push back. In fact, I almost said screw it and snuck back to your cabin last night. Hell, I'm such a masochist, I looked forward to you pulling a gun on me as foreplay."

That comment shouldn't have made me smile, but it did.

Encouraged, he traced the ball of my thumb joint up from the inside of my wrist. The move was lazy, teasing, and seductive as hell. My heart and my feet stumbled simultaneously. I caught myself and hissed, "Stop it."

"Not a chance."

When he switched directions on the dance floor, his mouth grazed my ear, and he murmured, "I miss you."

I stumbled again. My cheek brushed the smoothly shaven section of his throat between his jawline and his collar. I fought the temptation to lean into him and bury my lips in that vulnerable fragment of skin just to see him shiver.

"I'm winning you over with my caveman tactics."

A statement. Cocky man. I laughed softly.

"I miss hearing you laugh as much as I miss touching you."

About two seconds before my hormones took control, I snapped back to reality. Tactics. This was all a stupid political ploy, and I was falling for it. "If you're spewing this lovey-dovey crap because you think it'll show the voters your softer side with the competition—"

Dawson stopped in the center of the dance floor.

"What the hell are you doing?"

"What I said to you doesn't have a fucking thing to do with the election, and you goddamn well know it."

Geneva had been right; this'd been a bad idea. "Will you please stop screwing around? People are staring."

"Let 'em stare. I don't care."

I did. "What do you want?"

"For you to admit that you're deliberately misunderstanding me."

"Fine. You're right, I have no freakin' clue how to handle this, okay?"

"This . . . meaning . . . what?"

"You know. This." I gestured at the scant space separating us. "Personal stuff."

"At least you're acknowledging there is personal stuff between us."

"You know there is, dumbass." I tugged on him until he started to move again. "But the only reason we're here, dancing cheek to cheek, is because of the damn election. So can we please keep focused on that?"

"For now."

I broke eye contact with him. "I hate that people are gawking at us like we're a circus act, dissecting our every move."

"Get used to life in the public eye."

Great.

As we spun and glided, I swore they'd chosen the longest song in the history of the world. Maybe if I stumbled, I could fake an injury and escape.

Dawson would just pick you up and cart you off like the last time he found you lying in the middle of the road with a twisted ankle.

Like I needed that reminder of another instance of his caveman tactics.

"How long is your buddy Anna staying?" he asked, breaking the silence.

"I don't know. As long as she wants. Why?"

He shrugged.

I recognized the evasion. "Why do you care?"

"Because she's bad news."

That got my back up. "You don't know fuck all about Anna."

"Wrong. I know she's dangerous."

"Hazard of our training, Dawson. We're all like that."

"Wrong again. She's nothing like you." Dawson locked his gaze to mine. "Nothing. Maybe once you two were alike, but not anymore. She'll drag you down to her level rather than you bringing her up to yours."

"Why don't you come right out and say what you mean?"

His teeth flashed. "I tried to when we first started dancing, but you didn't want to hear it."

Dammit, he was twisting my words. "You drive me crazy."

He whispered, "It's part of my charm."

The song ended, and I attempted to leap back, but Dawson wouldn't release my hand until Andrew acknowledged us.

"How about another round of applause for our candidates?"

The clapping had waned. People were as raring to dance as I was to put distance between Dawson and me.

Dawson's campaign manager herded him away. I turned and smacked into Shay Turnbull.

He grasped my upper arms. "Whoa there, candidate Gunderson. What's the rush?"

"Sorry. Just trying to escape the dance floor."

"And here I fought the crowd so I could claim your next dance."

A drop-dead gorgeous man like him wouldn't be short dance partners. "Why in the hell would you want to dance with me anyway? I suck."

He smiled. "It's refreshing that you are as unaware of your own allure as you are brutally honest. Come on. One dance."

"They're your broken toes," I mumbled.

Shay held me more formally than Dawson had. "Thousand Miles from Nowhere" by Dwight Yoakam began. I'd hoped for a fast one like Alan Jackson's "Chattahoochee," but this medium-slow tune would allow for conversation.

"You and Dawson put aside your differences."

"For one dance. It wasn't like either of us had a choice."

"Despite the political tension, it looked like you and the sheriff had danced together before tonight."

Nosy bastard. "Nope. First time."

"Really? You moved well together."

He didn't know the half of it.

"I expected more fireworks during the debate. I thought you'd give him hell. Pinpoint why you think he's doing such a lousy job as sheriff."

Why was he baiting me? "You angling to join my campaign committee, Agent Turnbull? So you can teach me how to take a man to task?"

"No." Turnbull laughed. "You don't need help from anyone on the most efficient way to execute a task."

Inside, I froze.

"See, that's what doesn't fit. You didn't detail Dawson's investigative mistakes. He didn't point out your lack of experience. Neither of you went for the jugular during the debate. It was all very . . . boring and civilized."

"Maybe. But believe it or not, Dawson and I aren't here to publicly nitpick each other's qualifications. We're here as an excuse for the county residents to have a dance and call it a debate."

He had no response for that observation.

We danced. He wasn't as smooth on the dance floor as Dawson—not that I was comparing.

"You heard about Victor Bad Wound?" he asked.

"Hard not to in a community this size. Any leads?"

He didn't answer beyond a grunt.

I couldn't resist poking him. "Did the feds off him?"

"I wish. But no. We're looking at Cherelle Dupris as the main suspect."

I bit back asking if they'd tracked down Cherelle yet. "Does ICSCU have her locked up someplace nice with lots of mirrors as you try to get her to turn on Saro?"

Agent Turnbull gave me a measured look. "What do you know about it?"

"Nothing. No one is mourning Victor's death except his brother. If the feds suspect Cherelle killed Victor, she'll need protection from Saro. What better way for her to seek immunity from a murder charge than to give the lowdown on Saro's organization?"

"You are a smart cookie, Sergeant Major. And that'd be an ideal situation . . . if we knew where Cherelle was."

I faked surprise. "Think Saro already got to her?"

"We don't know. That's why I'm here."

"You're looking for her . . . at a community dance?"

"Yeah, I'm hitting all the hot spots," he said dryly.

"I feel so used. You didn't really want to dance with me?"

"Believe it or not, this is part of my job, so it could be worse. I'll cut to the chase. Have you seen Cherelle?"

"Cherelle and I aren't friends. We're not even passing acquaintances."

"Just checking. If you do happen to run across her, call me."

I snorted. The only way I'd "run across her" was if she were dead. "No offense, Agent Turnbull, but I've got more important things on my mind. A little thing like the county election."

"Yeah, good luck with that. You'll have plenty of time on your hands after tomorrow night."

"In other words, you're assuming I'll lose."

Turnbull's smile bordered on placating.

I ignored him for the last thirty seconds of the dance and whirled away the instant it ended.

Geneva gave me her final pep talk and bailed. The remaining campaign-committee members were out on the dance floor cutting a rug. I wandered through the crowd, declining dance requests, specifically Kit McIntyre's.

I noticed Dawson had left after he'd danced with Claire Montague—not that I was keeping tabs on him or anything. Hope, Joy, Jake, and Sophie were gone. Anna, too. It surprised me she'd hung around as long as she had. Heck, it really surprised me she'd even shown up.

I desperately needed to decompress, preferably with a beer, preferably away from people. I weighed my options. If I returned to the cabin, I'd have to make nice with Anna. If I showed up at Clementine's, I'd have to rehash the debate with those who hadn't bothered to attend. If I headed to the ranch, Hope, Joy, and Jake would all be tucked in bed for the night.

The ranch it was.

Bluish-gray images from the TV flickered across the living

room windows as I passed the front of the house. I parked in my usual spot, noting the absence of the light burning on the porch. In the past few months, I'd been here so infrequently, Hope had stopped leaving the light on. Sadness tightened my gut, and I felt ridiculous for the melancholy. Would I burst into tears if Shoonga didn't race out to greet me, too?

The old truck continued to clatter after I'd clicked off the ignition—a victim of engine run-on. Damn thing was on its last legs, and I'd have to at least consider putting Dad's beloved pickup out to pasture. I hopped out and scanned the yard . . . out of habit, I supposed. My gaze stopped at the lump next to the machine shed. Squinting, I couldn't tell what it was. A furry lump?

Shit. Not Shoonga. I'd become so attached to Levi's dog that losing him might just break me.

I ran even while my brain screamed, *Caution!* And images of dead animals appeared, animals propped in the middle of roads in Iraq, loaded with explosives, animals used as a lure.

But this was Shoonga. Not the same thing. This was my goddamn dog.

As I neared the lump, I didn't catch the usual stench of death. I skidded to a stop. It wasn't an animal, but a bag of garbage with a hide thrown over it.

An old Indian trick. I reached for my gun, only to come up empty-handed.

My head was jerked back as a hand twisted in my hair. A knife flashed in front of my face, then pressed against my throat.

Saro.

"Don't fight me."

"What do you want?"

"Where's Cherelle?"

"You're the third person to ask me today. She's a popular girl."

He slid the knife across my skin, cutting me. "Smart answers don't amuse me. Where is she?"

"I haven't seen her."

Saro sliced me again. "Try again. Where's Cherelle?"

Damn, that burned. "The last time I saw her was that night I was campaigning at Clementine's."

"I don't believe you."

"I have no reason to lie."

"Did you help her plan to kill my brother? Because she ain't smart enough to figure it out on her own."

"No."

"Keep lying, and I'll keep cutting."

My skin had heated the metal so the blade at my throat was no longer cool. A breeze swept over the cuts. Shallow, of course, so they bled a lot. "I don't know where you've gotten the impression that Cherelle and I are pals, Saro, but we're not. I've met her once."

Another slice. Deeper.

I hissed in pain.

"Then why did her cell phone record show she called you the same day the cops found my brother murdered?"

If he'd tracked my cell number, he'd also known how long we talked. "Yes, Cherelle called me. She babbled about the campaign. Then she asked me if I could recommend her for my old bartending job at Clementine's. It was so random I thought she was either drunk or high."

"I. Don't. Believe. You." With each enunciated word, Saro wiggled the knife in the cuts he'd already made.

I gritted my teeth against the ribbons of pain. "I've got no reason to lie. Maybe Cherelle was smarter than you gave her credit for."

"Wrong. She was stupid, lazy, and useless."

"If she killed Victor, she knew you'd back-trace her every move." I paused. "How many other dead ends have you found?"

Silence.

"I don't know where she is. Trust me, if I did, I'd already have her ass in jail."

"Why?"

"Because Dawson is looking for her, too. Do you know how sweet it'd be if I one-upped him in Victor's murder investigation? I'd win the election for sure."

"I don't give a rat's ass about the election. I don't want Cherelle in jail. I want her dead."

"But you have to find her first."

Slice.

Blood flowed down my skin, and I sucked in a breath at the fire exploding across my neck. He knew precisely where to cut to make it hurt.

"Oh, I'll find her."

Then Saro was in my face with the chisel-like tip of the tanto blade under my chin. One wrong move, and I'd be tasting that steel on the bottom of my tongue.

"You know something else. Tell me. Now."

Through clenched teeth, I said, "You want me to talk? Move that fucking blade."

Saro pressed the tip against my heart, leaving a hole in my new blouse, causing more blood to ooze out of me. "Talk."

"If I talk, you talk."

"This isn't a negotiation."

I didn't budge. Didn't speak.

He watched my face as he twisted the blade into my breast. When I finally winced with pain, he said, "Okay. Ask your question."

"Did you kill Jason Hawley?"

"You ain't gonna let this go, are you?"

"Nope."

Saro angled forward. "I didn't kill him."

"Did you tell someone else to kill Jason? Someone like your brother?"

Anguish filled his eyes and then disappeared. "No matter. Victor is dead."

"Exactly. If Victor didn't do it and you didn't do it, someone else did. Cherelle?"

"Cherelle was with us all night. Victor wouldn't even let her take a piss by herself. But I will let you in on a secret. We saw Hawley's body that night after he'd been gunned down."

"And you did nothing?"

"Why should we? He was already dead. Me, Vic, and Cherelle weren't the only ones who came across it." He stared at me. "Fortunately, we used the situation to our advantage as a business maneuver. Besides, no one cared he was dead."

"I cared."

"So the fuck what? All I care about is finding the bitch who murdered my brother."

"I told you. I don't know where she is."

Another empty stare. Then he smiled, and it was cold enough to chill me right to my soul. "You know, I believe you. But here's some advice: if you're unlucky enough to get elected sheriff tomorrow, be smart. Look the other way when you come across Cherelle's body."

"And if I don't?"

An even crazier smile distorted his face. He reached inside his leather jacket and pulled out a stuffed pink teddy bear. From Joy's room. From Joy's crib. The pink bear's head hung from the plush body by a one white thread. White stuffing burst out from the gaping neck hole.

Panic clawed at my insides. This crazy son of a bitch had been in my house, messing with my family. "If you've touched a single hair on her head—"

"You'll what? For all you know, I might've already slit her soft little throat and left her to die in her crib with the bunny rabbit mobile spinning above her head."

I jerked toward him, and the knife tip gouged my skin.

"Or maybe . . . your sister with her pretty strawberry-blond hair and that ferocious Sioux warrior are bleeding out on the gray carpet after I gutted them. He should've done a better job at protecting them. Or trying to protect them."

I made a break for it. Saro knocked me to the ground. He yanked my arms behind my back and kicked me in the side hard enough that I couldn't breathe.

I was suffocating.

He placed the blade at the base of my neck. "One wrong move, and you're paralyzed from the shoulders down. Understand?"

Sadistic fucking bastard. Maiming me for life would be worse than killing me.

"Don't cross me. Any restraint I had died with my brother."

"What do you want from me?"

"If you find Cherelle alive, turn her over to me. If you find Cherelle dead, let it go."

Spots danced in front of my eyes. I felt a pinch between my shoulder blades, and I lost consciousness.

When I came around after Saro's Vulcan death grip, I booked it to the house. I tripped and skidded on my hands and knees on the gravel. Cursing, I scrambled to my feet and scaled the porch steps with one leap. The door wouldn't budge. I twisted the handle. It was locked?

I fumbled with my keys.

Come on, come on, come on.

The door gave way. I didn't bull my way in, in case nothing was wrong.

Please, Saro. Be a complete and total fucking liar.

I checked the living room first. Jake was stretched out on the couch, mouth open as he snored, with the TV projecting shadows across the room. I vaulted up the stairs, *please, please, please* pounding in my skull.

My sister was curled in the middle of the bed she shared with Jake. Her hair spread across the pillow. No blood soaking the sheets. No blood on her anywhere. I watched the rise and fall of her chest.

Thank God.

I tiptoed to the crib against the wall and peered inside.

A small sliver of moonlight shone in. Big hazel eyes blinked at me. Arms and legs flailed with excitement. She smiled, pleased as punch to have someone awake to entertain her.

My breath caught on a sob.

Joy was all right. Hope was all right. Jake was all right.

My relief was short-lived when Joy fussed at me for not picking her up. I shot a look at Hope. She hadn't moved.

I wasn't sure I even remembered how to pick up a baby. Had I ever known? I started to slide one hand under her head when I noticed my hands were filthy. And bleeding. Too sullied to touch such innocence. I grabbed a burp cloth and draped it over my hands, then slid one beneath Joy's head and the other beneath her butt. I slowly lifted her from the crib, holding her in front of me, afraid I'd ruin her fluffy-soft pale yellow sleeper if it brushed against my dirty clothes.

Her warmth flowed through me. Surrounded by sweet baby scents—shampoo, powder, and lotion—I had the overwhelming urge to weep. For once, I gave in to it. I whispered, "Hey, Poopy. Lookit you."

Baby girl remained somber, her body still, probably deciding whether this crazy lady who was crying and bleeding was going to drop her on her head.

That's your fear, not hers. She just wants someone to see to her needs.

Don't we all.

Joy blinked, fighting sleep. Her long, dark lashes swept her plump pink cheeks. I watched her, held her, until her eyes stayed closed and her mouth went slack. I carefully returned her to the crib the way I'd found her, lying on her back, a rainbow butterfly fleece blanket covering her from chest to feet.

Hope was in the same position, sleeping peacefully. I tugged the covers under her chin and smoothed her hair back from her cheek.

I didn't allow myself to break down until I stood in the shower. The horror of what could've happened knocked me to my knees. My blood and tears mixed with the water and swirled down the drain.

TWENTY-TWO

Election day.

I didn't bounce out of bed, bursting with enthusiasm. Rather, I shut off my cell phone and yanked the covers over my head. Maybe nobody would miss me.

At eight, Sophie beat on the door. "Mercy, Geneva's called for you three times. You need to get up and call her back, hey."

At nine, Hope knocked. "Are you sick again?"

If heartsick counted, then yes.

I'd bitten off way more than I could chew with this running-for-sheriff business. I didn't want to win. I didn't deserve to win.

The knife slices in my neck burned. I'd coated them with arnica gel, trying to speed up the healing process. Bruises dotted my body from Saro tackling me. Bruises lined my shin from smacking into machinery at Mulligan's before finding Victor's body. And then there were the bruises to my ego.

Two weeks had passed, and I hadn't figured out who'd killed J-Hawk. Until last night, I'd wondered if instead of choosing the death-by-cop form of suicide, J-Hawk had chosen the death-by-drug-lord type of suicide. Murder beat waiting for cancer to consume him. It beat dealing with the fake sympathy he'd get from family. Double-crossing violent drug dealers assured that he exited this world in a sensational manner, not wasting away riddled with cancer like an average joe. It would've been a mercy kill.

But I didn't buy that hypothesis any longer. Sure, Saro could've been lying to me when he'd said they weren't responsible. But I suspected he'd told the truth that they'd used the circumstances of J-Hawk's murder for gain.

Another angle I hadn't considered. Had J-Hawk's wife ordered the hit? Hired someone to kill him while he was on the road, working for Titan Oil? Maybe she'd discovered her husband was selling drugs and decided to save herself the humiliation of his getting busted. It'd be a win-win situation for her. The husband she loathed would be dead, and the potential for lawsuits against Titan Oil and Clementine's would be very much alive.

I'd lain in the dark for hours last night. Berating myself. Saro. Victor. Cherelle. Turnbull. Anna. J-Hawk. Geneva. Rollie. Kit. Kiki.

But strangely enough, not Dawson.

More persistent knocking. I'd geared up to scream "go away" when the lock tumbled and the door opened.

What the hell? Who was breaking into my room and invading my privacy? I threw back the quilt, brushed my hair from my eyes, and saw John-John shooing both Sophie and Hope away before he slammed the door in their faces.

"What are you doing here?"

"*Unci* asked me to come by."

"Damn meddling old woman. Why'd she call you?"

"Because you've freaked her out, as well as your sister; you've locked yourself in your room, and they know you're heavily armed."

I fell back into the pillows. "Were they worried I'd backslid into my drunken ways?"

"Not even close."

"That's something. Look. It's no big deal. I just wanted alone time to mentally prep for the election stuff today. Tell them everything is fine. Tell them I'm not armed and dangerous."

"For a change." He sat on the bed. "So this alone time? That includes avoiding Geneva, your campaign manager, and lying in bed?"

"Can't get nothin' past you."

"Can't get nothin' past your sister either." John-John dangled a burp cloth in front of my face. The one I'd used last night to pick up Joy. "Now do you understand why they're worried about you?"

Seeing the dirt and blood smears sullying the cloth, dotted

with happy little pastel teddy bears, brought my fears from last night racing back. "I had to make sure she was all right."

"Why wouldn't Joy be all right?"

Because of me.

John-John leaned in when I didn't answer. "No one here but us, doll. Talk to me." His gaze roved over my face, down my neck, and stopped. "What the fuck . . . are those . . . *knife* cuts?"

I turned my head toward the window in total shame.

But he was having none of it. He grabbed my chin, forcing me to look at him. "What happened last night? Who did this to you?"

"Saro."

"Did you call the sheriff after it happened?"

"No."

"Goddammit, Mercy. What is wrong with you? Whatever is going on personally between you and Dawson doesn't change the fact he needs to know that a citizen was brutally attacked in his jurisdiction." Still muttering, he reached in his front shirt pocket for his cell phone.

I batted it out of his hand. "It's way more complicated than that. Saro attacked me last night here, after I came home from the forum. That was after he'd already been in the house, John-John."

The blood drained from his face.

"After Saro finished trying to extract information from me with his tanto blade, he hinted he'd already taken care of Hope and Jake. Then he showed me Joy's teddy bear with its head sliced off . . ." My voice caught. "Bastard used a pressure point trick on me and knocked me out cold. When I came to . . . I ran into the house, not knowing what I'd find. Joy was in her crib, and I had to pick her up, just to make sure she wasn't . . ." I swallowed the lump of fear still clogged my throat. "The baby was fine. Hope and Jake were fine. But me? Not so fine."

John-John threaded his fingers through mine and squeezed.

"That's exactly the type of terror Saro evokes. He wanted to prove that he could get to any member of my family any time he wanted."

"Did he warn you not to contact the cops before he knocked you out?"

I shook my head. "That's where it gets complicated. Saro counted on me not calling the sheriff's department last night, because how would it look? The other candidate for sheriff can't handle her own issues? She has to summon help from Sheriff Dawson on the eve of the election? The very night I'd touted my qualifications to the entire community? He knew just where to strike and strike hard.

"And it doesn't help it'd be my word against Saro's. He's supposedly holed up on the reservation, grieving Victor. I'm already on the feds' shit list because they believe I screwed up their investigation by having direct contact with Victor and Saro. So even calling Agent Turnbull wasn't an option."

John-John's brow wrinkled. "Agent Turnbull? The hot guy is a fed?"

"Yeah. Ain't that a kick in the ass? Of course, no one told me anything about J-Hawk's murder being a federal investigation, and I went ahead and jumped headfirst into the sheriff's race, fucking up any chance of a relationship with Dawson, because in my wisdom I've repeatedly questioned his method of investigating on every fucking homicide case that's crossed his desk since I've been home. But the 'look who's an idiot' tag is taped to my back because I'm no closer to knowing who killed Jason Hawley than I was the night I found his body.

"That was my sole reason for getting involved in any of this. I owed him. Except now, in trying to pay back a debt I only imagined, I've garnered the interest of the biggest psychopath I've ever met. He's looking at retaliating against my family because somebody retaliated against his."

His jaw practically hung to the mattress when I finished.

"So see? Complicated."

"Okay, I get it. But I really think the case solved itself."

"What do you mean?"

"Rumor has it that Saro's group is taking credit for killing Jason Hawley. They're claiming he double-crossed them. The rumor has legs, since details on the murder are vague. Hawley is used as an example of what happens when people change the details of deals with Saro."

My breath stalled. Saro had mentioned seeing a "business opportunity."

"Where'd you hear this?"

"At Clementine's. I'm surprised you didn't know, but you haven't been in much." He cocked his head. "Didn't Anna tell you?"

"No. We've each been doing our own thing. But how could she've forgotten to mention that?"

"I dunno. I thought it was kinda . . . strange that Cherelle called you to look for Victor, especially when she and Anna were chummy."

Anna and Cherelle were chummy? I remembered Dawson questioning Anna about her friendship with Cherelle, and she'd blown him off. "When did that start?"

"Right after Anna got into town. She'd come into Clementine's and hang out. I figured you had campaign stuff to do and she was bored. She and Cherelle played pool. Drank in the back room. But then Victor and Saro musta jerked a knot in Cherelle's leash because she stopped coming in. Then Anna did, too." John-John frowned. "Huh. Anna didn't tell you none of this?"

I shook my head because I couldn't speak. Shock expanded in my chest and cut off my air supply.

I knew who'd killed Victor. Beyond a shadow of a doubt.

Anna.

John-John squeezed my hand. "You all right?"

No. But I couldn't get the word past my tight lips. I feared it'd come out as a scream.

"Doll, you're scaring me."

I managed to swallow. I even offered John-John a wan smile. "Sorry. Delayed reaction to remembering how scared I really was last night."

"You sure? You're pale as snow."

"I do feel light-headed."

John-John stood. "You oughta lie back down. Didn't mean to push you, Mercy, but I'm glad you told me."

"Don't tell Sophie and Hope anything about this. Please."

"I won't."

"Just tell them I'm nervous about the election and I had a restless night. I'll be fine if I can crash for a bit longer."

"No problem." After he tucked the star quilt around my shoulders, he kissed my forehead and left me alone.

As soon as he was gone, I tossed back the covers. My body felt like it was on fire, and the quilt only increased my feeling of suffocation. I walked to the window and pulled the shade.

Bright, beautiful sunlight streamed in. Another glorious spring day. The trees lining the driveway were leafing out. In my mother's flower garden, little red spikes of peonies poked through the dirt. Colors exploded like an artist had created them from a special palette. Emerald leaves. Cerulean sky. Shades of pewter on the tree bark. I opened the window, needing the familiar scents of home to ground me. Dust, manure, hay. Instead, the scent of lilacs wafted in. Even my favorite scent in the world couldn't offer me respite from the awful truth bouncing around in my brain like a possessed Ping-Pong ball.

Anna had killed Victor. Anna had killed Victor.

Why are you surprised? Anna is a killer.

So am I.

Not anymore.

Yes, Anna was still a merc. She got paid to kill bad guys.

Had Anna told Cherelle how she made her living? Had Cherelle offered to pay Anna to eliminate the man who'd tormented her for years?

No, I didn't see Cherelle acting so blatantly, taking the chance her offer would somehow get back to Saro. The better option, the smarter move, would be for Cherelle to let it "slip" that Victor had killed J-Hawk. If Cherelle was as shrewd a judge of character as I suspected, she'd know immediately that Anna was out for revenge, and Victor would wind up dead.

Problem solved, right? Cherelle is freed from Victor's control. Anna avenges her lover.

So why would Cherelle call me? To throw suspicion away from herself? Extra insurance? She expected I'd call the cops. I'd have to go on record as saying Cherelle had called me . . . as a concerned girlfriend because Saro scared her to death.

I realized that Anna had alibied herself when Dawson stopped by the cabin the other night, asking where I'd been. She'd told him we were at home, watching TV, for two nights. So in alibiing me, she'd alibied herself.

But Anna hadn't been around. She'd been conspicuously

absent in the mornings, and some nights she hadn't come home at all.

Now that the pieces were clicking into place, one detail bothered me. Anna Rodriguez wasn't easily played. If she'd been hanging out in Clementine's, listening to the rumors fly, she'd arrived at her own conclusion about who'd killed J-Hawk. She'd used Cherelle's ramblings to get information on Victor, so she'd strike the right chord in setting up a meeting with him.

I wondered how she'd lured Victor out to Mulligan's. Sex? Money? Drugs? Teasing him that she had information on the OxyContin that J-Hawk had been peddling? Once she'd gotten him out there, had she scared a confession out of him?

Or was that when she realized she had the wrong guy? Had Victor told her the same story that Saro had told me? None of them could've killed J-Hawk, but they'd all seen him dead and done nothing about it.

That would send her into a killing rage.

More raps sounded on the door. What the hell was with my bedroom turning into Grand Central Station today? Cursing, I dove under the covers, intending to continue my exhaustion charade.

"Mercy?" Sophie called out. "You have a visitor."

Before I could ask who, Anna walked in.

"Hey, Gunny."

Speak of the devil. "A-Rod. What's up?"

"You didn't come back to the cabin after the debate last night." Anna smiled and propped a hip next to mine. "You still in bed this time of day when you're not hungover means something's up."

"Just exhausted." I let my gaze roam over her face. Anna wasn't traditionally pretty, but there was something compelling about her. Compelling and deadly.

"Can't blame me for worrying with all this craziness going on."

Craziness that you caused by killing Victor Bad Wound?

"Anyway, I know it's a big day for you, but I wanted to touch base and let you know I'm taking off tomorrow morning."

"Places to go, people to kill?" I said only half jokingly.

"Yeah, some stuff's come up. And I think I might've overstayed my welcome."

I didn't deny it.

Her gaze winged around the room. "I can see why you'd rather sleep here. Does Sophie serve you breakfast in bed, too?"

"Screw you. Sophie would whap me upside the head if I even suggested it."

Anna smiled. "I know, Gunny, I was just trying to lighten things up."

When she reached over to squeeze my arm, I flinched.

She froze.

Smooth, Mercy. "Sorry. Habit when I'm nervous."

"Understood. I'll see you tonight."

Anna's body language changed, as did her expression. I backtracked and became contrite—hard as it was. "You're coming tonight?"

"Wouldn't miss it for the world," she said brightly.

"I'm glad." I sighed. "Look, Anna, I'm sorry. I know this wasn't the type of visit you had in mind, with me being busy with election stuff. It sucks we didn't get to hang out more . . . especially with what you're going through. But I'd like to make it up to you. Yes, I'll be busy tonight, but we should plan on breakfast tomorrow morning before you leave."

She relaxed. "Great, meet you at the diner? Ten o'clock?"

"It's a date."

I hauled my ass out of bed and faced the day.

TWENTY-THREE

Election night in Eagle River County was as laid-back as any other night. No ringing banks of phones. No media demanding real-time interviews. No one obsessing about exit-poll numbers. The polls were closed. The county election workers were tallying votes in the courthouse basement. We'd know the outcome of the election the same time as the Rapid City TV stations announced the winners.

The Gunderson campaign committee was headquartered in the basement of Leo Harvey's Coast-to-Coast hardware store. I'd suggested Clementine's. No one had taken me seriously. Or maybe they had, and that's why we were here.

I looked at the people who'd shown up to support me. Hope with Joy. Jake. Sophie. John-John. Geneva and her brood. Kit. Rollie. Anna. My neighbors. Community members I'd known my entire life. A few people were absent. Muskrat was holding down the fort at Clementine's with Winona. Kiki was on duty tonight since Dawson and his campaign crew were at the Blackbird Diner, just a block down the street from us. Tempting, to sneak out and peek in the diner windows to see Dawson's supporters.

Anna had wedged a folding chair into a corner and rested her head against the wall. She appeared to be sleeping, and several people sent disapproving looks her way.

The same disturbing thoughts I'd shoved aside earlier resurfaced. I knew Anna was a killer. It'd never bothered me. Not when I watched her snuff a terrorist. Not when she'd become a private soldier. But it bothered me now.

If I was elected sheriff, could I arrest Anna for killing Victor? Or would I keep my mouth shut and let her go? Really, what purpose would throwing Anna in jail serve? Victor Bad Wound had been a horrible man. Who cared if he was dead?

But no one had cared when Jason Hawley turned up dead either, so I couldn't help but draw the parallels.

And if I really wanted to throw a monkey wrench into my decision, I had allowed a murderer to go free before. In fact, it'd been my bright idea to cover up the murder. How could I possibly justify letting Jake off the hook for killing Iris, and not do the same for my grieving friend who just wanted to avenge the man she'd loved?

Despite my claims that no one was above the law, I'd taken the law into my own hands several times. Everyone, including law enforcement, already believed Cherelle was guilty of murdering Victor. Seemed logical to say nothing and see how it played out.

"Mercy. How you holding up?"

I faced Leo Harvey. I'd snap like a chained pit bull if one more person asked me that question. I pasted on a smile. "Doing great, Leo. Thanks again for letting us use your store tonight."

"My pleasure. Anything you need?"

A shot of Wild Turkey. "No, I'm good. Your wife laid out quite a spread for us. I can't thank her enough."

"Barbara lives for this kinda stuff."

Hope waved at me frantically from across the room. "Leo, if you'll excuse me." I wove through the crowd until I reached my sister. "What's wrong?"

"Oh, nothing. Good news for a change. I've been talking to Kit. He has a line on a new double-wide trailer outside of Rapid that was in mortgage default. He said me 'n' Jake can look at it tomorrow. Isn't that exciting?"

"Very. Where would you put it?"

Hope switched Joy to her left hip. "Where my old trailer was. Like Jake said, all the hookups are already in place, so it'd be a quick move in."

"But you'll be okay living there?"

"It wasn't the location I hated, Mercy. It was the trailer. I hated the reminder that Levi wouldn't ever slam that crappy door again. Or leave his pop cans all over the living room." Her eyes welled with tears, and she hugged Joy closer. "There was just too much of him in such a small space. I felt like I was suffocating in the silence of him not being there."

"Hope—"

"I'm okay. I miss him. Not an hour goes by that I don't think of him."

Instead of witnessing the pain in my sister's eyes, I poked Joy's jelly belly. "You deserve a place of your own. But the house will be empty and quiet with you guys gone. I'll miss you all."

"Prove it." Hope thrust Joy between us.

"Whoa. What are you doing?"

"Making you hold your niece. She's five months old. Don't you think it's time?"

"I just can't—"

"Yes, you can. You did last night. I watched you."

"You did?"

"Yes. I still don't know why you were bleeding, but I figure if you'd wanted me to know, you'd tell me." She stepped closer. "Now. Go on. Take her."

I panicked and started to back up. "But—"

"No buts." Hope softened her tone. "Mercy. You won't drop her. I promise. I'll be right here."

Shame heated my cheeks. "How did you know—"

"Sophie told me. I trust you with her. But, that said, I wasn't gonna let you hold her when you were drinkin' all the damn time." Her eyes narrowed on mine. "You haven't been sneaking shots of whiskey tonight?"

I shook my head. Then I looked at Joy's perfect little face, her tiny little body. I had guns that weighed more than she did. The next thing I knew, Hope was pressing Joy against my chest. My heart galloped. "Wait a sec."

"You're fine. Just hold her with your left arm, like this"—she pulled my forearm across Joy's rounded belly—"and slide your right arm under her butt. Perfect. She likes to face the front so she can see what's going on."

Joy made a funny noise, then turned her head to stare at me. Were her eyes scared? Did she sense my fear? Would she take advantage of my inexperience and squirm out of my arms?

Something else caught her interest, and she looked away.

Whew. I didn't bounce her or adjust my position. At all. I was statue aunt.

Hope beamed. "See? Is that so bad?"

"Umm. No."

"So, after me 'n' Joy and Jake move out of the main house, are you gonna come clean about the guy you've been seein' on the sly?"

"What guy?"

She smirked. "Nice try, but I even know who it is."

I ignored the spike in my pulse. "Do tell, little sis."

Hope whispered, "Bobby Sprague."

"Eww. That's gross." Bobby Sprague was the fat, mean, stupid kid that everyone had hated. As an adult he was still fat, mean, and stupid, and I avoided him like Sophie's bran-pumpkin muffins.

Joy grunted and wiggled. My pulse spiked again. "Umm, Hope? I think Poopy's trying to escape."

"C'mere, baby girl. We've taken up enough of Aunt Mercy's time." Hope plucked Joy from my arms. "And stop calling her Poopy."

For the next hour, I paced, although it appeared I was mingling. My cheeks ached from smiling. Geneva and the election crew were falsely upbeat, so I suspected either Rollie or Kit had an inside source for the preliminary election results.

Things weren't looking good for team Gunderson.

The ten o'clock news came on. Few elections were taking place in West River, so it wouldn't take long to learn the results.

The room went still as the information scrolled across the bottom of the screen.

Winner, Eagle River County sheriff race: *Mason Dawson def. Mercy Gunderson.*

I lost?

The screen didn't change.

Yes, I lost. In the county I was born in. In the county my father had served for two and a half decades.

Dawson won with a margin of 70 percent to 30 percent of the votes.

Disappointment floated around me so thick I could've choked

on it. Any semblance of a smile was long gone—on my face and everyone else's.

Don't be a sore loser, girlie; he won fair and square.

Thanks for that pep talk, now, Dad.

I knew I'd have to call Dawson and concede, but why in the hell did I have to make the call in front of everyone? In the name of good sportsmanship?

Screw that.

I turned my back on the room—I didn't care if they thought I was hiding my teary face—and flipped open my cell phone to text Dawson.

Congrats. You won. Don't be a smug prick about it. Official phone call to follow.

My unofficial concession made me feel better, if nothing else.

His immediate answering text read: *So noted, and so gracious.*

I faced the campaign workers—my family, friends, and locals who'd pinned their hopes on me. I almost wished they'd berate me; it couldn't be worse than the guilt I was heaping on myself.

Geneva approached me. "You all right?"

"What do you think?"

She leaned forward and whispered, "I think you did better than Bill O'Neil would've done."

I stared at her. Hard. Then it hit me. "You didn't expect me to win."

"Of course not."

"Then why did you—"

"Because the county needed a choice, Mercy. If Dawson had run unopposed, no one in the county would've respected him, or his authority, or thought he'd 'earned' the right to be sheriff for the next four years." She squeezed my hand. "Don't get me wrong. I would've loved it if you'd won. But I was looking at the bigger picture."

"You sure you've never been an army war strategist?"

Geneva smiled. "I have six children. Knowing the right strategy is a necessity. Now that your guilt commitment is over, here's some advice. Allow yourself to have something that doesn't owe a damn thing to your father's legacy, the Gunderson

Ranch, or your military history. Dawson's really not a bad guy. And now that I think about it, he is your type."

"What type?"

"A cowboy in uniform." She whistled to get everyone's attention. "Listen up, Mercy is making the call."

I started to call him but realized people might be suspicious if I had Dawson on speed dial. "Who has the number?"

Only I saw Geneva roll her eyes.

Kit handed me a piece of paper. "Here."

I hesitated. "Look, I appreciate that you all put your trust and faith in me. I'm disappointed that I lost. But the voters of the county have spoken. Dawson won. So I'd appreciate it if you give Sheriff Dawson your full support so we can keep the county united and move on. I know I will be behind him one hundred percent."

The clapping following my impromptu speech actually sounded genuine and not perfunctory.

I punched in the numbers and hit Dial.

Dawson answered on the third ring. "Hello?"

"Sheriff Dawson. Candidate Mercy Gunderson officially conceding this election and wishing you the best of luck in the next four years serving the community and Eagle River County as sheriff."

"Thank you, Miz Gunderson. Your father would've been proud that you stepped up and filled in as a replacement candidate for Deputy O'Neil on such short notice."

"Thank you."

The conversation ended quickly.

My family and friends left without saying good-bye. Even the campaign workers were scared off by my don't-fuck-with-me vibe, and I found myself alone with Leo as he locked up.

I trudged to the parking lot behind the building, feeling more melancholy than I imagined.

He won. You lost. Get over it.

Yeah, but I deserved to wallow for more than thirty lousy minutes, didn't I?

I heard a noise and looked up from staring at my feet.

One sodium light flickered above where Dawson leaned against the driver's-side door of my pickup.

He didn't look thrilled for a man who'd just handed me my ass in my own damn county.

I stopped about ten feet from him.

"You didn't pull a gun on me," he said dryly. "I think that's a first."

"Geneva wouldn't let me carry on election night."

"She's such a spoilsport."

Silence.

"What are you doing here?"

He didn't blink, or move; he just watched me.

"Shouldn't you be whooping it up with your committee?"

Dawson kept his hands shoved in the front pockets of his jeans. He looked every inch the cowboy—new Wranglers, a gray pearl-snap shirt, a black leather vest, scuffed black cowboy boots. He wasn't wearing a cowboy hat or championship belt buckle.

Shame, really.

"Dawson?"

"Yeah, I probably should be popping a top with the crew."

"Then why aren't you?"

A heavy sigh followed another pause. "Here's the thing. I'm damn happy that I won." His eyes searched mine. "But the truth is, you're the only one I want to celebrate with, which sucks, since I suspect I'm the last person you want to see right about now."

I studied him. A sharp ache—a combination of guilt and need—moved through me. Dawson could be anywhere, with anyone, and yet here he was. With me. Waiting on me. I shoved my hands in my pockets, mimicking his stance, unsure what to do.

"Do you want me to go?"

I shook my head, expecting he wouldn't accept my silence. He'd verbally push me until my words erupted like a geyser. But Dawson just watched me patiently. That unnerved me even worse.

"You know what bugs me about this situation? Here it is, not even an hour after I lost, and I'm not all that upset that you beat me. I'm . . . relieved. And that pisses me off. It pisses me off that I'm not spitting nails at you for winning."

"Why?"

"Because . . . fuck, I don't know. Maybe it was all about the competition. Maybe I was trying to live up to expectations that aren't mine."

"Sounds like an excuse, and you ain't the type to Monday-morning quarterback, Mercy, so try again."

"Fine. The truth? My dad picked you because he trusted you."

"And?"

I struggled, trapped by the weight of my pride. "Despite claims to the contrary, if my dad was alive, I believe he'd still consider you the better candidate. He'd back you for sheriff, even against me, his own daughter." I laughed. "Took me a while to realize this, and even longer to admit it, but the crazy thing is? I do trust you, Dawson. You are qualified, immensely so, and the comparisons I've made between you and my father aren't justified and aren't fair."

He lifted a quizzical brow. "Meaning?"

"I was wrong."

"So you don't think I'm a complete and total fuckup?"

I shook my head. The glint in his eyes kept me from elaborating.

"You're withholding something."

Jesus, Mercy, just fucking say it.

"And . . . I-I'm sorry. Okay? I'm just . . . sorry."

"You sure your tongue ain't bleeding after choking those words out?"

"Ha-ha. Don't be a jerk, Sheriff."

His answering smile was a little slow, a little smug, but he'd earned it. "Apology accepted, Sergeant Major."

"So now what?"

"You tell me."

I threw my hands up. "I don't know. Do we kiss and make up? Do we just go on as we were before?"

Dawson shook his head. "That's not enough for me."

My face heated. "You saying I'm not enough for you?"

"No, I'm saying it's all or nothing."

The part of me that didn't like ultimatums bristled. But it wasn't strong enough to make me walk away. "I don't know how to do this."

"Do what?"

I gestured at the space between us. "Be in a relationship."

"You think I don't know that this is uncharted territory for you? You think I don't know you've been fighting me every god-damn step of the way?" Irritated, but attempting to stay calm, Dawson shifted his stance. "Hate to break it to you, sweetheart, but we already have a relationship. It's as dysfunctional as I've ever seen, but it's there."

Relief swept through me that I hadn't completely screwed this up. "I know that now."

"Do you?"

"Stop bouncing everything back to me as a question," I snapped. "This is hard."

Dawson shrugged. "It doesn't have to be."

"See, that's why we need to establish some . . . ground rules. I relate better when I have rules."

"Fine. I'll make the rules if you'll follow them."

"Blindly?"

"Yep."

Shit.

Could I do this?

Time to fish or cut bait, girlie.

"I'll try," I offered.

"Yes. Or no."

"Fine. Yes."

Dawson's hands came out of his pockets. He pushed away from my pickup with deliberate ease, ambling toward me.

Damn if my heart didn't beat faster, but I didn't move.

He didn't ask for permission to touch me, as he sometimes did. He curled one hand around the back of my neck and brought his mouth down on mine with purpose and intent. And heat. God. The heat between us always caught me by surprise.

One kiss shouldn't make the world fall away, but it did. I clung to him with my body, my hands, my mouth, until I realized how needy I must seem. I tried to pull away, but Dawson wouldn't let me go.

His lips slid to my ear. "Come home with me. Now."

"If that's a rule, I like it."

He chuckled. "That's not the first rule."

"Umm. What is the first rule?"

"When I say get in the truck, you get in the truck."

"That's it?"

"Huh-uh. Second rule: don't question the first rule."

I smiled against his chest. "It can't be that simple."

"Oh, sugar, nothin' with you is ever gonna be simple. I accepted that the first time I clapped eyes on you."

"And yet, you don't sound like that's a bad thing."

"It's not. I like who you are, Mercy. I wouldn't have snuck around in secret with you the last few months if I didn't believe there was something worth sneaking around for."

Relieved—and yet terrified—I pressed my face into his neck and breathed him in, this man who was tough enough to stand firm . . . against the craziness that was me. "Dawson, we should—"

"Ah ah ah. What's the first rule?"

"Get in the truck."

"So why are you still standing here?"

I got in the truck.

No. No. No.

Stop. Please.

I bolted upright, gasping, heart slamming in my chest, body sheened with sweat. Where was I? Why didn't I recognize anything in my room?

Because I wasn't in my room.

This was why I rarely spent the night at Dawson's place. In addition to dealing with the nightmare, I had to find my sanity in an unfamiliar place.

Dawson didn't stir as I pushed the covers back and escaped.

The moonlight glinted off the white countertop in his kitchen. My hand shook so hard that I spilled half the glass of water on myself. Gripping the glass, I stared out the window facing the field behind his trailer.

Part of me knew the nightmare stemmed from wrestling with my conscience on whether I should tell Dawson my suspicions about Anna.

Hadn't you already decided?

No. Turn her in; let her go. Either decision seemed wrong. But I wasn't sure what I could ever do to make it right.

"Mercy?"

I jumped. "Dammit, Dawson. Don't sneak up on me."

"Sorry. I've been standing here awhile."

Now I felt the need to apologize. "I didn't mean to wake you."

"I know. How bad was it?"

I wasn't surprised he knew. Maybe the gasps of terror tipped him off. "Bad enough."

Dawson didn't push, which I appreciated. Even if I wanted to talk about it, I wouldn't know where to start.

But he did. "About six months after I got out of the marines, I had a flashback on a commercial plane. One second I'd dozed off, the next my hands were wrapped around the throat of the guy in the seat next to me."

"What happened afterward?"

"I apologized to the guy. The flight attendants moved me to the back of the plane. After I checked in to my hotel, I proceeded to get very, very drunk."

"I've found that therapy doesn't work long term."

"Me either."

I took another sip of water. If Dawson saw my hand shake, he didn't mention it.

He moved in behind me. "Mercy, come back to bed."

"But—"

"Your choice. We stay up and you can explain if the combat nightmares are somehow related to the fresh knife wounds on your throat and the puncture wound on your chest. Or you can come back to bed, and I'll find some . . . inventive ways to distract you from thinking about any of it."

My pulse quickened, in a good way for a change. "Promise?"

"I promise."

TWENTY-FOUR

Anna was a no-show.

Since Dawson had to be in the office early, I'd stayed in his bed until right before my scheduled breakfast with Anna. My laziness was only half from exhaustion. The other half was from avoidance.

When I'd tried to talk to Dawson last night, he'd made a new rule on the spot. No talking about cases or campaigns. He wanted one night with me where it was just us. Mercy and Mason. I even called him Mason a couple of times, just to prove to him—and maybe to myself—that I saw him playing a different role in my life.

On a whim after I left the diner, I entered Pete's Pawnshop. Anna had spent enough time in here that maybe Pete was privy to plans she hadn't shared with me.

Pete came from the back room, a gooey doughnut clutched in his hand, frosting coating his beard. "Morning, Mercy. Sorry to hear you lost the election."

Liar. "Thanks."

"You don't look as upset as I'd imagined."

Did he expect I'd be bawling my eyes out? In public? Like that'd ever happen. "Naturally, I'm disappointed, but Dawson knows his stuff, so the county will stay in good hands for another four years."

Pete's smile showed the chocolate glazing his teeth. "That's a mighty good attitude to have. Your buddy Anna could learn a lot from you."

"Speaking of Anna"—I glanced around the dusty space—"we were supposed to meet at the diner for breakfast. Have you seen her today?"

"Sure. She was in here earlier, checking out the display cases."

I frowned. "You mean the gun cases?"

"No. The cases up there." He pointed to the semicircle of glass cases ringing the cash register.

I walked to the case he'd indicated. Trays of Black Hills gold jewelry lined the top and bottom shelves. Next were trays of watches. Beside that display were diamond rings and earrings. Boggled my mind that some women remembered to put that crap on every day. And people gave me grief about always wearing my gun? At least a gun was useful, not ornamental. "Anna isn't exactly the jewelry type."

"I know. Which is why she's been looking at the knives."

"Anna bought a knife?"

"Shoot. I sure hope it wasn't a gift for you or nothin'. Forget it."

"Can't put the cat back in the bag, Pete. Tell me about the knife."

His gray eyebrows squished together. "You ain't gonna go tattling on me?"

"Nope."

"She was interested in one that came in right before closing time yesterday. A stainless-steel Kershaw. Sweet piece. Told her I could buff off the engraving if she wanted, but she swore it was fine the way it was."

The hair on the back of my neck raised up. My mouth opened, but no sound came out.

"Mercy? You okay?"

Be cool. "Actually, no, I'm a little stunned. Anna's been searching for a replacement knife like that since she lost mine in Afghanistan a few years ago. Do you remember what the engraving said?"

Pete began to pick dried chunks of frosting from his beard. "I dunno. Something sappy about forever."

Son. Of. A. Bitch. J-Hawk's missing knife had surfaced. Had she suspected it'd show up here? Is that why she'd been hanging around? Why hadn't I seen that angle?

Because you're not exactly a hotshot detective.

"Who'd you buy the knife from?"

"You two are peas in a pod and a nosy lot. Anna asked the same question."

"Did you tell her?" *Please say no.*

"I almost didn't, client confidentiality and all that. But Anna's been a good customer, and I didn't see the harm. It really don't matter, because them yahoos who sold it to me just wanted fast money for booze or drugs or whatever they're doin'."

"What yahoos?"

"Tweedle-Dee and Tweedle-Dum."

I resisted grabbing Pete by his overalls and shaking him until his dentures rattled. "Be specific, Pete. Those names fit lots of folks around here."

"Oh, you know, Cliff Garber and Tyler Lewdonsky? Cliff's blond. Tyler's a redhead. They're always getting in scrapes 'cause they're mouthy little shits. Them boys are practically joined at the hip. Don't go nowhere or do nothing without the other. Kinda makes you wonder if they're really just 'friends.'" Pete emphasized the last part with air quotes.

My hands tightened on the edge of the glass counter. I remembered they'd come into Clementine's the night J-Hawk had been murdered, and I'd kicked them out for no IDs. "Now I know who you mean. They claimed to live with their dad."

"Damn liars. They live in that old Brubaaken trailer. Place is for sale, but no one is gonna pay that kinda money for it."

"Where's the Brubaaken place?"

"Quarter mile past Red Gulch Canyon turnoff on County Road Seven."

"Did you tell Anna where they lived?"

"Uh-huh. Why?"

"How long ago did she leave?"

"An hour or so. Why?"

I didn't answer, as I was too busy running out the door to my truck. As soon as I cleared the city limits, I pressed the pedal to the floor. Piece of crap truck topped out at 65 mph.

I ran through several scenarios, but the truth was Anna wouldn't let either of those guys live. She'd shoot me if I got in her way of dispensing justice for J-Hawk. So going in alone half cocked was full-out crazy. I'd had enough crazy to last me a lifetime. No way could I let Anna get away with this, and I felt damn guilty for not sharing my suspicions last night. Maybe this could've been prevented. I snagged my cell phone and dialed.

"Anna figured out that Cliff Garber and Tyler Lewdonsky killed Jason Hawley. Because they pawned his knife. The knife she gave him. Yes, I knew it wasn't listed in his personal effects, but I never thought it'd show up. She's probably already at the Brubaaken trailer on County Road Seven. I'm on my way out there now." I listened. "No, I'm going in because she won't hesitate to kill them both, and if they die it's on my conscience."

My brain filtered through the images of Anna in full soldier mode. Picking our way through the chaotic streets of Baghdad. Keeping our heads bowed, finding the targets, killing up close and personal under the cover of darkness and the flowing fabric of our burkas. No wasted effort. No wasted time. Get in, complete the mission, get out.

But I knew that wouldn't be Anna's way this time. This time, it was personal. This time she'd make a point to make it hurt. She'd draw out the torture until the punks detailed everything they'd done to J-Hawk. Everything J-Hawk had said in return. Then she'd return the pain tenfold.

I feared her. But I also feared my reaction to this vengeful Anna. Could I pull the trigger if it came down to choosing her life or the lives of the scumbags who murdered the man who'd brought me back from the dead?

Lost in thought, I accidentally drove past the turnoff. I whipped a U-turn and backtracked, slowing as I approached the McIntyre Real Estate sign by the road.

Stealth entry was probably pointless, but it was the only advantage I had. I parked in the ditch and grabbed my Taurus.

No rush of adrenaline. Just coldness in the pit of my stomach. I crouched in the yellow sweet clover lining the ditch leading to the driveway. My gaze swept the broken-down barn, a caved-in chicken coop, and the rickety wooden pallet serving as stairs to the trailer's door.

A puke-green, rusted-out International Harvester truck sat sideways next to the trailer. Sections of metal skirting wound through the weed-choked yard like steel ribbon. Anna's Land

Rover was parked halfway between the truck and the barn. The back end was open. Sunlight glinted off the metallic cardboard suitcase of Coors Light.

She'd lured them out with booze. Not her usual strategy. If she'd stormed the trailer, she could've killed them while they slept.

But she'd want them awake. Alert. Afraid.

A far easier way for Anna to get them outside: pretend to be a buyer who asks for a tour of the property. Offer them beer. Act like their friend. Wander to the backside of the barn. The side that wasn't visible from the road. That's where I would've taken them. Lined 'em up against the wood barn siding and emptied the clip. Reloaded and done it again.

A pain-filled shriek echoed from behind the barn. My gut tightened. I ran across the patches of gray dirt dotted with clumps of dead grass. Color appeared. Random splatters of red on the path became a discernible blood trail.

Shit, shit, shit. Mouth dry, heart racing, I sidled to the edge of the barn and peeked around the corner.

A scene from a horror movie played out in front of me.

Anna's .45 H&K combat pistol dangled by her right side, J-Hawk's knife in her left. The redheaded guy was lying on the ground. Hands tied behind his back. A bloody hole where his belly used to be. A chunk of his left thigh was gone. Exit wounds, which meant she'd shot him from behind.

An ear-shattering screech sounded. Not coming from the guy she'd just stabbed in the gut, but from the blond, who was being forced to watch as Anna thrust the knife into his friend.

Then Anna loomed over him. "Is this how you did it? Did you laugh as you stabbed him with his own fucking knife?"

The redheaded guy wheezed, and blood bubbled over his lips.

She smacked the blond in the ear with her gun. "Answer me."

"Leave him alone."

She buried the knife in the redhead's right leg and said to the blond, "Start talking, or I'll make you watch as I make him a Columbian necktie."

"No! I told you. We were high!"

"High on what?" Anna demanded.

"Tweakers. We wanted to come down. Then that bitch in Clementine's wouldn't sell beer to us—"

"Be careful who you're calling a bitch," she warned. "Why him?"

The kid said something that froze me in place. "It wasn't personal. It wasn't because it was him! It could've been anyone!"

That outburst caught Anna off guard. "What?"

"That oil guy had bought us beer before. A couple of times. After that b—chick wouldn't sell to us, and no one else would even fucking talk to us, we saw him leaning against his car at the back of the parking lot, so we asked him to buy for us. He just laughed and said no.

"Then he turned his back on us. Like we were nothing. Like we were just loser punks. Me 'n' Tyler knocked him down and he still laughed at us. Tyler shot him. But instead of shutting up, the guy kept going on. Said if we were gonna do the job, not to do it half assed like a bunch of fuckin' pussies. To do it all the way. Said he was as good as dead anyway. Said he'd rather go out with a bang than a whimper. It was like . . . he was daring us to kill him. So we did."

I briefly closed my eyes and leaned against the barn.

Goddamn you, J-Hawk. You made a bad situation worse.

"I think we went a little crazy after that. We shot him a couple more times. Picked up his knife and stabbed him with it. Then we grabbed the stuff and took off.

"When I woke up, I thought it was some crazy crank dream. Until I saw the blood all over my hands and my clothes. Tyler's hands were worse than mine. I found the dude's wallet and his knife in my pocket. I had to get rid of it. It was like a bad luck charm."

"A lucky charm for me, because you ditching it for cash led me straight to you."

The kid sobbed.

Nothing drove Anna to the trigger faster than false remorse. The kid never said he was sorry. He justified taking a man's life by being drugged up.

Anna laughed and kicked the redhead's prone body. "Well, looky here. Your buddy gave up the ghost."

"What? What does that mean?"

"Means he's dead."

"Tyler?" He scooted closer on his ass in the dirt.

She eased the knife out of his body, and it made a horrible wet sucking sound. After Anna wiped the blood from the blade on her pant leg, she clicked the thumb release and pocketed it.

"Ty? Ty?" Each repeat of the name got louder and more hysterical.

Anna cuffed him in the mouth. "Shut the fuck up. Jesus. Show some dignity."

Enough. When I moved closer the back of my shirt got hung up on a nail, releasing a loud *riiiiip*.

"Show yourself, whoever you are," Anna said.

Shit. I tried to press myself deeper into the wood.

"I know you're there, and if you don't come out, I'll use the shrieker here for target practice."

I rounded the corner, weapon drawn.

"Mercy. Guess I'm not surprised to see you."

My gaze dropped to the mutilated body at her feet. Guilt punched me in the gut. If I'd turned her in to Dawson last night, that kid would still be alive. "Put down your gun, Anna."

She aimed at me. "No can do. This little shit-ass loser will be begging for me to kill him before I'm even close to done with payback."

"Enough." Two more steps. "Anna. Let it go. It's done."

"I can't. I have to finish this."

"You did finish it. You found the knife. You found out who killed Jason. He wouldn't want you to go to jail."

"Too late. I doubt the cops will believe I shot this punk because he tried to escape my custody after a citizen's arrest."

"Don't make it worse for yourself."

"How could it get worse, Mercy? The man I loved is dead. We'll never be together now."

Jesus, I was sick of hearing her whine about lost love. Probably wrong to taunt her, but I did it anyway. "How is that different than not being together for the last five years?"

"You know we had no choice. But we both believed we'd be together someday the way we were meant to be."

"Don't bet on it. There were things you didn't know about J-Hawk, Anna. Things he told me the day before he died."

"Nice stalling technique. But I know all your tricks, remember?"

"Not stalling. No tricks. Go ahead. Ask me about it."

Her demeanor changed. "Tell me, or I'll give him a new set of H&K piercings."

The kid whimpered.

I knew she didn't bluff. "Jason had cancer."

"Bullshit."

"It's true."

"How do you know? He was here, what, two weeks? He just confessed that to you?"

"No, I read the coroner's report. The tox screen came back with high levels of a cancer-treatment drug called Nexavar. Several bottles were found in his motel room."

Anna's resolve didn't waver. "What kind of cancer?"

"Liver or stomach or esophageal, all incurable. Then I knew why he looked so bad. He probably only had a few months left."

"Why didn't you tell me?"

"You were already grieving, and it wouldn't have changed anything."

"So regardless if Jason had been murdered, he'd still be a dead man." She laughed. "So why did you continue investigating his death, Mercy?"

"J-Hawk deserved better than to be left to die in a field in the middle of fucking nowhere by a bunch of drunk rednecks."

"Which is why this guy has to pay."

"You already made Victor pay."

"Victor was a fucking prick. After he convinced me that he hadn't killed Jason, it was too late. I was already pissed off."

"So you shot him."

"Uh-huh."

If Anna knew Cherelle had lied to her to serve her own means, and a man was dead by Anna's hand because of it? Anna would waste Cherelle without a moment's hesitation. "Did you kill Cherelle?"

"I would've if I'd found her. But that weasel's gone to ground. No matter. Saro will kill her."

I took a step closer. "Put down the gun. Let me help you."

Anna fired by my right foot, and dust puffed over my boot. "Stay there, Gunny. Don't move again or I'll shoot you." She grabbed the kid by his hair and jerked him upright.

The kid shrieked. He probably couldn't stand with the hole in his leg. Anna jerked hard enough the second time she ripped hair from his scalp.

"If you wanna live, you'll get up."

While the kid struggled to his feet, I tried to focus, but I constantly adjusted my hand position on the gun. "Stop."

"You don't sound very convincing, Mercy."

"Let him go."

"I will. Just as soon as I'm in my Land Rover." She had one hand in his hair; the other held the gun under his chin as they slowly moved sideways.

What are you waiting for? Shoot her.

Every muscle in my body cramped. My breathing was erratic. *Take her out.*

Images of our past floated through my mind, blurring my vision and my purpose. I gritted my teeth and forced the words out. "Stop or I'll shoot."

"This punk's life is worth more to you than mine?"

Don't listen. Don't negotiate. Don't hesitate.

Before I could repeat "Drop the gun," I heard movement through the grass. Which meant Anna heard it, too.

"I can't believe you called the cops."

"What you're doing, this vigilante justice, is wrong."

"Then why didn't you turn me in when you figured out I'd killed Victor?" Anna demanded.

"Shut up."

"You knew. I sensed the change in you yesterday. You realized I'd done it. So why the sudden bout of conscience?"

"Shut. The. Hell. Up."

"The Gunny I've known for years, the soldier I fought side by side with for a decade, never would've done this. We protect our own first. Remember that?"

My hands were dripping sweat. I tightened my grip, and the gun wobbled. "I'm not the same person I was, Anna. Neither are you. So put down the goddamn gun."

"No way. If any of these country bumpkins shoot at me, chances are good they'll hit the civilian. And it's all about protecting this lowlife scum, isn't it?"

I fought the shame and panic that I'd fail my training. That I couldn't pull the trigger. She knew it. She used my fear against me.

"You're the one person here who could make the shot, Mercy. One click."

"Give it up, Anna."

"You could kill me. Even with compromised vision you could take me out. Even though we're friends you could do it."

I ground down on my molars so hard I swore that chips of my teeth sliced my tongue.

"Take the shot."

"Stop talking. Stop moving."

"Why won't you shoot me? Afraid to show everyone your true self? Mercy, the merciless killer?"

"I'm warning you. Stand down."

Anna kept blabbering. "Show them how a sniper snuffs out a life without a second thought."

"Last warning."

"Really? But you *are* having second thoughts, aren't you?"

Yes. Make her shut up. Make this stop.

"You can't kill me, can you?"

Yes, yes, I can.

"I remember a time when your cold-blooded efficiency scared even me, Mercy."

You can put an end to this.

"Those days are long gone. You won't do it."

"You sure?" The fog of indecision lifted. My purpose clicked.

Site.

Adjust.

Aim.

Breathe.

Fire.

"Yep. You've lost your edge. You've gone soft. Sentimental. Useless."

I fired. Twice. One in the chest. One in the face.

Chunks of blood, bone, and brains splattered across the

hostage's face. He screamed as he and Anna crumpled to the ground.

I didn't bother to check to see if I'd made the kill shot.

Law enforcement shouts of "Move in. Go, go, go!" filled my ears.

How many times had I heard those orders after I'd cleared the obstacle in my crosshairs?

Too many.

But I was glad I'd called the sheriff's department.

I let my chin fall to my chest; my gun sagged by my side. I backed up. Ten, twenty, thirty steps. I didn't care if I fell on my ass. I needed distance. In mind and body.

Numbness spread. I welcomed it. But it wouldn't last. It never did. My subconscious would play this scene over and over, mixing it into the soup of combat nightmares for a little spice and variety.

You fell right into her trap. You could've wounded her. Instead, you took the shot and killed her.

I did my job.

More shouts, more footsteps. Tan uniforms blew past.

But one uniform stopped directly in front of me.

Dawson.

Rough fingers nudged my chin up. I didn't want to look in his eyes, afraid of what I'd see, so I squeezed mine shut. Tears leaked past my defenses anyway.

"Mercy."

"Don't say it."

"What?"

"Anything," I whispered.

Silence.

My knees buckled, spots swirled behind my lids, and my gun hit the ground.

Dawson clamped his fingers around my biceps and held me upright. Not speaking. Not really touching me. Just keeping me from collapsing.

When the light-headedness didn't dissipate, I breathed slowly. Steadily. Trying to level the adrenaline in my system. Trying to keep it together.

"Sheriff?" someone shouted.

Duty called. Dawson had more important things to do than babysit me. "Thank you. I'm fine now." I attempted to retreat, but he held fast.

"You're far from fine. Let me take you home."

"That's okay. You've got work to do."

"I'll delegate."

"Dawson—"

"Look at me."

"I can't."

"Goddammit. That was not a request."

I opened my eyes.

Something dark and fierce stared back at me. "I am *not* leaving you alone."

My gaze flickered to the action by the barn.

But Dawson's right hand slid up and curled around my jaw, holding my damp face in place, keeping my physical focus on him. "Nothin' you need to see over there."

"But—"

"Listen to me. There's nothin' you need to see. I'm getting you out of here right now."

"Last time I shot someone you threw me in jail. Is that where you're taking me?"

"You'll never let me forget that, will you?" he murmured.

"Probably not."

"No. I'm not taking you to jail."

"But what about taking my statement?"

"I'll get it later."

Why was Dawson being so goddamn nice to me? I'd just killed a woman. Not any woman. A friend. A good friend. A friend who'd pulled my ass out of the fire more times than I could count. And I shot her. I just pulled the trigger and ended her life.

How many more pieces of your soul can you lose before it's gone completely?

"Hey, Sergeant Major. Come back to me."

I looked in Dawson's eyes since he was about an inch away from me. I flinched. Shuddered. The coldness was overtaking me.

His thumbs skated over my cheekbones. "Let me help you, Mercy. Please."

"How?"

The determination in his eyes didn't waver. "I don't know, but we'll figure it out."

At least he hadn't lied and given me platitudes about everything being all right. We both knew it wouldn't be.

Someone approached from behind, but Dawson never looked away from me. "What is it, Deputy Moore?"

"The ambulance is en route for the hostage."

"Good."

"What do you want me to do next?"

"Secure the scene. We're leaving, and you're in charge, Deputy."

"Ah. Sure, boss. But I've never—"

"Then it's past time you learned. Besides, this is linked to the FBI's case, specifically Agent Turnbull's case, and he'll be here any second to take over. Defer to him."

"This is the feds' case?"

"Yes. And I've never been so glad to say that in my life."

Dawson's hand fell from my face. He came alongside me, blocking my view, draping his arm over my shoulder. I leaned on him. At another time in my life I would've been resentful, prideful, mindful of appearing weak. Right now I didn't care. I just wanted to curl up in a ball and hide.

TWENTY-FIVE

Three weeks later . . .

Being cooped up in the house made me antsy. Six guns and six hundred rounds of ammunition should've been enough to blow my blues away. But it wasn't.

The first week following Anna's death had been a blur. Dawson dealt with Agent Turnbull. He dealt with the county prosecutor. He dealt with media and speculation. Then he dealt with me.

Dawson hadn't let me retreat to the cabin, which would've been my preference. He hadn't let me crawl into a bottle, which had been my intention. I appreciated that he didn't push me to talk. He didn't hover, but he didn't leave. Dawson was just there for me in a way no man had ever been. Not even my father.

I was tired of keeping him at arm's length. Denying us both a chance for something real. Something permanent. Something good.

In typical Dawson fashion, once he'd sensed the change in me, he'd gone on the offensive. He moved in. Completely. Bringing his dog, his horse, his guns. The fact I let him share my gun vault and my bed was a good indication I had strong feelings for him.

And he fit in with my family, too. He asked Hope for advice on the best way to connect with his son. Sophie baked his favorite cookies and set a place for him at the dinner table. Jake asked for his help setting up their new trailer. Even Poopy charmed him with gummy grins and cute baby antics.

I didn't ask if everyone in Eagle Ridge was aware of the change in our relationship. To be honest, I didn't care.

So while everything was going swimmingly on a personal level, on the professional front, I was back to square one. I realized, like Dad, I needed more than ranch work to fulfill me. Jake and I had a long talk, an honest talk, and we were both pleased with the result.

Dawson asked me if I'd consider applying for the deputy position left vacant after Bill O'Neil's resignation. I declined. I'd finally drawn a line between Dawson the sheriff and Dawson the man, and I intended to keep it that way.

While I contemplated my place in the universe, I lined up my shots. It wasn't pointless to keep up with a skill that'd defined who I was—and who I still am. I practiced because I liked it. Because it soothed me. Chances were slim I'd ever use my sharpshooter skills in another occupation. While that was bittersweet, I'd finally accepted it.

I'd also accepted that I needed professional help coping. Not only with killing Anna, but also with the aftermath of my military retirement.

During my outprocessing, the army shrinks detailed the stages of the loss I faced in the transition from soldier to civilian. Loss of purpose, loss of power, loss of camaraderie, loss of skills, loss of structure . . . blah blah blah. Yeah, whatever. I'd convinced myself I was truck tough. Rock solid. Good to go.

I'd been so insistent that past combat and deployment issues would never affect me that I hadn't recognized it *had* affected me. Isolation. Physical exhaustion. Insomnia. Irritability. All of which culminated in excessive drinking, rigorous training, violent thoughts, and depression.

And nightmares.

So I called the VA and self-identified. In the past I'd secretly sneered at those combat soldiers who admitted needing professional help with combat-related stress issues. But when I took a good hard look at myself, I picked up the phone. Dawson volunteered to drive me, but I declined. I wasn't afraid that he'd see me as weak or in a bad light, but Rollie was a better choice, and he'd been happy to take me.

Shoonga started to bark at something beyond the tree line.

Not his squirrel-chasing bark but the one that warned me an animal was nearby—of the human variety. I flipped the safety off the Sig and waited.

Agent Shay Turnbull appeared.

Great.

He whistled, and Shoonga quieted down. Damn dog even wagged his tail. Neat trick. I'd ask him how he did it. If I didn't shoot him first.

"Sergeant Major."

"Agent Turnbull. How'd you find me?"

"Followed the sound of gunfire."

"Wrong. Try again."

"Okay. Jake gave me directions."

Jake, that traitorous jerk. "Did you come to say good-bye?"

Turnbull laughed. "Don't sound so hopeful."

"A girl can dream."

He stared at my gun, then at me, mirth gone. "Mind putting the safety back on?"

"Afraid I'll accidentally shoot you?" I flashed my teeth at him. "Sorry. If I shoot you, it'll be on purpose."

"You have a warped sense of humor."

"I have a warped sense of everything, Agent Turnbull."

He studied me intently. Too intently. It set my teeth on edge. "What?"

"How are you holding up?"

Placating bastard. "How would you be holding up if you'd killed one of your fellow agents after they'd gone rogue?"

"Who says I haven't been in the same situation?"

Not what I'd expected. "You wanna compare stories?"

"I'll pass on reliving that ugliness, thanks. I just wanted to say I've been there. It sucks ass. You did what you had to, Mercy. You probably can't see it now. But you will eventually."

My flip response stuck on the roof of my mouth.

A minute or so passed. While he looked at the bluffs in the distance, the rise of the rolling hills, the rickety fences, the twisted trees and oceans of mud, I looked at him.

Finally, he said, "Beautiful piece of dirt you have. Can't say as I blame you for not wanting a pipeline running through here."

"It'd be a few years before it's a done deal, but I'm holding out hope that it's not inevitable." I set the gun on the tailgate. "You didn't just happen by to talk about scenery and local political issues, Agent Turnbull."

"Astute one, aren't you?"

"All that woo-woo, psychic, seeing-dead-bodies part of my Indian heritage," I said dryly.

He snorted. "You know what it means to be Indian like I know how to run a whaling ship."

"Meaning . . . nothing."

"I call it like I see it." Turnbull shifted his position. "Look, I'm sure you have questions, and believe it or not, I'm here to give you some answers. But what I'm about to tell you stays off the record. If you ever repeat it? Full denial."

Did I really want to hear this?

Yes.

"Understood. Now spill it."

"We knew Anna killed Victor."

"We . . . as in the FBI?"

He nodded.

"How?"

No answer.

Then it hit me. Had the FBI been following Victor? Had they watched Anna kill him and done nothing to stop it?"

"To answer your question, no. We didn't stand by and do nothing when Anna killed him."

The man was too goddamn spooky reading me.

"When Saro spread rumors they'd killed Major Hawley, we knew she'd be gunning for Victor and Saro, and we knew Cherelle encouraged Anna to believe Victor was responsible."

I stared at him. "The FBI condones murder?"

"No." He scrubbed his hands over his face. "There are certain things we know, Mercy. Things we have to stand by and watch happen. We know Saro and Victor run the drugs in Eagle River and other reservations. We know they've killed and buried the bodies on the rez or fed them to the wild dogs. They've done all sorts of bad things they should be locked up for. But because of the laws and lines we can't cross, we can't do a damn thing but watch it happen over and over.

"I'm not bothered in the slightest that Anna took out Victor. Saro is off the rails with grief and anger. It's put Saro's organization into pure chaos. They'll make mistakes, and when they do, we'll finally have our chance to bust them."

"And if Anna would've killed Saro, too?"

"I would've thrown her a freakin' parade."

"Contradictory much?"

Turnbull smiled. "Make no mistake, I woulda tossed her ass in jail right after the confetti fell."

"What about Cherelle?"

"We're pretty sure in those extra meetings, she figured out a way to cut Saro out of the drug deal and Hawley told her where he stashed the rest of the OxyContin. After he died she took it. And being Saro's screen, she'd know exactly who to contact to get rid of it fast."

"So she's just vanished?"

"With that face? She's not exactly inconspicuous. We'll find her. Eventually."

"If you knew Anna killed Victor, did you also know those two punks killed J-Hawk?"

"No. Dawson suspected a robbery from the start. But after we took over the case, we forced him to drop that line of investigation so it wouldn't interfere with our objective."

Still made me feel like a douche bag for assuming Dawson was an idiot, who didn't know the first thing about investigating, who only cared about his own agenda, when he'd had no choice but to drop the case.

"I hear you and the sheriff have mended your fences."

My relationship with Dawson wasn't up for discussion with Agent Turnbull. Ever.

"He's a good man."

I didn't need Turnbull to tell me that. "Okay, you've filled in the blanks for me. But I've gotta ask . . . why?"

Shay Turnbull studied me. "Because we want you to come to work for us."

Talk about blindsided. "Excuse me? You mean the FBI?"

"ICSCU could use you, Mercy."

"No. Way."

"Hear me out. Five minutes."

"Nope. Have a nice trip back to wherever you're from." I cocked my head. "What corner of hell *are* you from, anyway?"

"Hilarious. I live in Rapid."

"No, I mean originally. What reservation?" I sensed his irritation, but he'd answer if he wanted to keep me talking.

"Flandreau."

"So you're a member of the . . ."

"Santee tribe."

"I knew you didn't look Lakota Sioux."

Turnbull wasn't sure if that was a compliment. "So back to business at hand. You interested?"

"For the third time, no."

"You're making the decision without giving us a chance to state our case?"

"Yep."

"Typical. Don't know why they freakin' bothered when I tried to tell them it was pointless."

"Why'd they send you?"

"As a test of my neutrality. To see if I could convince you to meet with ADA Shenker, despite my reservations about you."

I lifted my eyebrows. "Your personal reservations about me? Oh, Agent Turnbull, now you've piqued my interest. Do tell."

"You've had an exemplary military career, which means you can follow orders. You've had covert-ops training, which means you can blend. You're extremely proficient with firearms. Since you ran for sheriff, it shows you have a sense of community and a desire for a broader sense of justice. You've recently enrolled in the tribe, so you're finally embracing part of your heritage."

"But?" I prompted.

"But, you don't take help when you need it. You slide into drinking binges. You lie. You like to intimidate people who cross you with your firearms. You have an unnatural attachment to said firearms. Bottom line? You're a wild card. I don't like wild cards."

"So this 'come to work for the feds' wasn't your idea?"

He shook his head. "I argued against it. Pretty hard, actually. And I would've won too, except you self-identified. We both know how much the higher-ups dig shit like that."

"So because I admitted I needed mental help, now I'm a perfect candidate for a job . . . as a fed?" I laughed. Hard. I laughed until my stomach hurt.

"Laugh it up. But we both know you're going to say hell no, then you'll order me off your land, probably while peppering my ass with buckshot. So why don't you tell me to shove it one more time so I can head on home."

That stung. The contrary part of me itched to blow their (mis)perception of me and say yes. But Turnbull was shrewd. I wouldn't put it past him to use reverse psychology.

"Tell you what. I'll make you a deal. If you can outshoot me, I'll show up at the meeting."

And yeah, maybe it was petty, but I felt smug when Turnbull's smile slipped. If he knew as much about me as he'd claimed? He also knew I'd placed first in every official and unofficial military sharpshooting event in the last fifteen years.

Turnbull pushed away from the pickup. "Deal."

Sucker. "Pick your poison. I've got six guns."

"I'll use my own gun, if it's all the same to you."

"Suit yourself. What's the caliber?"

"Nine mil."

"Same as mine. We'll gauge by the ring of three."

"That'll work."

The ring of three was a standard marksmanship test. Distance marked at thirty feet. Eight bullets in the outer ring. Eight bullets in the middle ring. Two each at twelve o'clock, three o'clock, six o'clock and nine o'clock. Five bullets in the center in the shape of a plus sign. Closest mark to the line in each section wins.

I released the clip on the Sig and reloaded. I had two other clips, each held ten bullets, so I reloaded those, too. I looked over at Turnbull. "I don't suppose you've got extra clips."

"No. Didn't know we were gonna have a shoot-out at the Gunderson corral."

I smiled and slammed the clip in. I jogged to the hay bale and switched out the paper target. I marked off thirty feet and drew a line in the mud with the heel of my boot.

Turnbull inclined his head. "Ladies first."

I stepped up to the line. My focus sharpened. I lifted the gun and solidified my stance. After flicking the safety off, I sited in my first two target shots in the outer ring.

Bang bang.

Then I fired rapidly, until I emptied the clip at the top of the inner circle. I ejected the clip and shoved in a fresh one. Although I still had bullets left after I finished the middle ring, I changed clips for the five shots in the center so I could squeeze them off without interruption.

Bang bang bang bang bang.

We walked to the target. My shots were damn close to perfect. Symmetrical. Precise. "Okay, hotshot, show me what you've got."

Pause. "You know, I've changed my mind."

I smirked. "Really?"

"Yeah. I believe I will use your gun."

Damn. And here I'd hoped he'd decided to back out. I ejected the clip and handed him the Sig. I yanked down my target and tacked up a fresh one. We walked back to the truck in silence. As I watched him speed-load the clips, my first sense of unease surfaced.

Agent Turnbull aimed and fired. He emptied and replaced his clips almost without pause.

Bluish gray smoke eddied around us, and the ground was littered with hot brass.

He handed back my gun. The wet earth squished under our boots as we returned to the hay bale. Shoonga trotted happily along beside us, oblivious to the tension, panting from chasing his tail.

I stared at the target in complete disbelief.

His shots weren't side by side in the inner and outer circles. No, Agent Turnbull had put *both* the bullets through the same hole. Not once, as a fluke, but in both rings. So instead of having sixteen holes . . . he'd made eight. Eight big, ragged holes, so I knew he hadn't fired off to the side to trick me. His bull's-eye shot was clean, meticulous, and perfect.

I'd been had. Big time. I gaped at him. Because I'd never met anyone who could shoot like that. Never.

Agent Turnbull pulled a pen out of his pocket and scrawled

across the top of his target. He ripped it off the hay bale and handed it to me with a grin that rivaled the devil's. "See you next Tuesday, Sergeant Major."

Son. Of. A. Bitch. I poked my finger through each jagged hole. I'd known some amazing shooters, but this? This was damn near art.

When I looked up to ask him where he'd learned to shoot like that, he was gone.

Typical.

I memorized the address and phone number before I folded the target and shoved it in my back pocket. It wouldn't hurt to just *listen* to what they had to say, would it?

Shoonga yipped agreement.

I loaded up. With my dog by my side and the truck windows open to savor the temperate spring breeze, we drove down the dusty gravel road leading home.

ACKNOWLEDGMENTS

I'd like to thank the following people for their assistance in helping this book come together. I'm lucky to have experts who are willing to share their knowledge with me:

A big *Hooah!* to George Reynolds, Col., U.S. Army (Ret.), not only for his fast, invaluable assistance in reading and fact-checking certain combat scenes, and for his good humor and patience while gently steering me in the right direction, and for giving me the best compliment an author could ever hope to receive, but he also gets my heartfelt thanks as an appreciative American for the thirty years he served this great country in the U.S. Army.

To my "baby cousin" Shannon Gutzmer, Pharm.D., and to Melvin "Mick" Harris, B.S., R.Ph., for the wealth of information on prescription drugs and pharmacy protocol.

To Ev Murphy, for her speed and expertise in phonetically translating the Lakota words and phrases for the audiobook version and for the Lakota pronunciation guide on my website.

To Mark Sanders, whose vast knowledge of everything under the sun, especially about critters like mountain lions, is invaluable. I'm proud and lucky to call Mark a friend.

To Mary LaHood, for her willingness to critique my work at the drop of a hat and to give it to me straight.

To Karen Hall, for the insight and information into the permit process and environmental impact for proposed oil pipelines, and her amazing ability to boil the language down so a non-engineer can get a tiny grasp on what it means.

To my husband Erin, not only for tracking down all the gun info for me, even after he's been working in the gun business all day, and trying to ensure I don't somehow royally screw up said info in translation, but for the love and support in all aspects of my life.

To my daughters; I'm proud and humbled by these amazing young women every day, especially when they don't complain when I'm under deadline again.

Thanks to my awesome editor, Stacy Creamer.

Thanks to my agent, Scott Miller.

Any content errors in the book are mine alone.

TOUCHSTONE READING GROUP GUIDE

MERCY KILL

FOR DISCUSSION

1. In the first scene of the book, Mercy is faced with a decision of whether or not to kill a sick female mountain lion that she spots during target practice. Ultimately she chooses not to kill the animal. What does this decision tell you about Mercy? Why do you think the author decided to open the book with this scene?

2. Early on in the story, when Mercy is discussing with Rollie her drinking, Mercy refers to herself as "just another drunk Indian." Were you surprised that Mercy thinks of herself in this way? What does Mercy's comment indicate to the reader about her personality and the way that she views herself?

3. Mercy does not like Kit McIntyre, but admits that since he spends so much money at Clementine's, she can find a way to disregard her personal issues and make nice with him. Does this decision seem out of character for Mercy? Why or why not?

4. Given how close they were and the fact that he had saved her life in the past, were you surprised by Mercy's reaction upon finding J-Hawk's body? Do you think that the way she reacts is a reflection of tough character and/or the influence of her army background, or do you think that she is still in shock at this point in the novel?

5. When Mercy is talking to John-John about her relationship with Dawson, she comments that she has a hard time "separating the man he is from the job he does." Could the same thing be said about Mercy and how she views herself and her profession? Do you think that Mercy recognizes her similarities with Dawson or not?

6. Do you think that Mercy compares herself to Anna? Does she compete with her or embrace the similarities between them?

7. Despite the fact that she is the former sheriff's daughter and her background in the army, Mercy is not flattered when Kiki and Geneva approach her to run for sheriff. Why do you think that Mercy is reluctant to run when she is such a strong and qualified candidate for the job?

8. Is Mercy's disappointment with Dawson's police investigation into J-Hawk's murder a reflection of her trust issues or a reflection of his capability as sheriff? Why doesn't Mercy trust him to do his job even though she trusts him in other aspects of their relationship?

9. Cherelle is a very interesting character in that her "flaws" allow the reader to discover a great deal about the surrounding characters, namely Mercy and Anna. How do Mercy and Anna relate to Cherelle? Can you relate to Cherelle at all and if so, how?

10. Since Mercy is a strong woman who would not tolerate abuse like the kind that Cherelle suffers at the hands of Victor and Saro, what do you think explains Mercy's reaction to Cherelle's situation? Does Mercy have sympathy for her and her abusive home life?

11. During Mercy's interaction with Saro and Victor in Stillwell's, it seems imperative to Mercy that she not be intimidated or back down from the situation. Do you think that this was more important to her personally, or do you think that she just didn't want to look weak in front of friends, acquaintances, and voters?

12. Why do you think the author chose to have Mercy actually take the final shots and kill Anna? What does Anna's death symbolize? Do you see symmetry between this climactic

scene and the opening scene when Mercy declines to shoot an injured mountain lion?

13. By the end of the book, do you think that Mercy has changed, or do you think that she remains essentially the same person as she was at the beginning of the book?

A CONVERSATION WITH LORI ARMSTRONG

This is your second time writing about Mercy Gunderson. Now that you've spent more time with Mercy, in what ways do you relate to her?
It's always a challenge writing the second book in a series, because I know more about Mercy now than when I started, but in most cases her actions on the page surprise even me. I relate to her in that we both have a low tolerance for BS, and she and I have the same taste in music.

In what ways do you not relate to her?
Mercy's tendency to drown her troubles in alcohol is something I don't relate to at all. Nor do I understand her inability to ask for help. But those types of characters fascinate me just for that reason, because we are so different.

Are any of the characters in the book based on people that you know?
No. I'm a self-admitted people watcher, so I'm constantly observing interactions and mannerisms and physical characteristics. And I will use pieces of what I've seen, be it hair or eye color, or a funky mannerism, or a certain way a person speaks or walks or interacts with others. I've leaned a lot about human nature just by watching and listening. But I've never based any fictional character on anyone I know personally.

You address many social and racial issues surrounding Native American culture in America in this book. Why did you choose to incorporate such themes in your writing?
Because it's such a huge part of our life in western South Dakota, and to gloss over it would be a disservice not only to all the people of my state, but to people who've never been to South Dakota, who only know about historical Indian "issues"

from what they've read in textbooks, detailing things that happened more than a hundred years ago. I get asked a lot on book tours if I know any "real, live" Indians, and I honestly have to stop and think about what that means, because I think some people still think of western South Dakota as the untamed Wild West, where Indians ride horses, wear elaborate headdresses, live in tepees, and hunt buffalo. Although many Native Americans never stopped celebrating their culture, religion, and traditions after being relegated to reservations, many hid their practice or denied their heritage, in some cases—like Mercy; she knows little of her Indian heritage because her mother didn't deem it important.

You live in South Dakota and have expressed in various interviews that you really wanted the setting of South Dakota to come through in your writing. Why did you choose to set Mercy's story in South Dakota?
I never considered setting the book anyplace else, and that's not just because the research is easy, since it's right outside my door. I'm a South Dakota girl and even if readers don't see the beauty in the area the same way I do, I think it's obvious I love where I live, and hopefully that's what gives the books the authenticity I'm striving for.

Many of the male characters in Mercy's life are kind, thoughtful, and gentle (John-John, Jake, and Rollie) turning typical gender roles on their heads. Did you intend for these characters to serve as foils for Mercy?
Yes and no. Mercy is a tough-as-nails character, and it's been a challenge to keep her from becoming a caricature. The loner who doesn't need anyone, which always seems sadder, somehow, when it's a female character. I didn't intentionally set out to ground her with men who might be seen as soft, but I wanted her to interact with men she'd had history with—the best friend, the former lover, the father figure—all men who knew her and loved her in some form, before she became so hard and tough. All these men remind her of who she's been—as well as who she can become.

What's next for Mercy Gunderson?
I'm working on the third book, titled *Dark Mercy*, which will send Mercy in a new direction.

If *Mercy Kill* was made into a movie, who would play Mercy?
I get this question frequently, so you'd think I'd have an answer . . . but I really don't. I can tell you physically what Mercy looks like, but I hear her more than see her. On a purely gratuitous note, I'd love to see North Dakota native Josh Duhamel play Dawson.

Who are your favorite authors to read, mystery or otherwise?
I read widely across many genres, but my must-have mystery/thriller authors are J. D. Robb, Robert Crais, and C. J. Box.

Whose writing, if anyone's, would you say has had an influence on your own style?
Sue Grafton, Stephen King, Carolyn Keene, and Laura Ingalls Wilder are the biggest influences, which is a pretty eclectic list! But whenever I think of books that've had the biggest long-term impact, it's always the first book I read from those authors that have stuck with me.

ENHANCE YOUR BOOK CLUB

1. Prior to the book discussion, read a brief article or essay about the history of the Native American reservations in the Dakotas. Several of the main characters are from the Lakota tribe, and reading about their culture in particular will provide better insight into the story. Here are some suggested articles and websites:

    • http://memory.loc.gov/ammem/award97/ndfahtml/ngp_nd_native.html

    • http://www.crystalinks.com/sioux.html

    • http://www.accessgenealogy.com/native/tribes/reservations/sdreservations.htm

2. Discuss whether or not you have ever known any family or friends who have been part of elite branches of the military (Special Forces, Green Berets, Navy SEALs, etc.). If so, and if you're comfortable talking about it, please explain what that experience was like for you and for your friends and/or family.

3. Since much of the book revolves around nature and the outdoor elements, hold one of your discussions in a local park or, if possible, a nature reserve. This will give you unique insight as to how nature affects Lori Armstrong and her main character, Mercy. Consider your relationship with nature and how it affects your day-to-day life.

4. Learn about the author, Lori Armstrong, by visiting her website www.loriarmstrong.com and on the Simon & Schuster author page authors.simonandschuster.com/LoriArmstrong/47550782.

FROM THE SHAMUS AWARD–WINNING AUTHOR OF *SNOW BLIND*

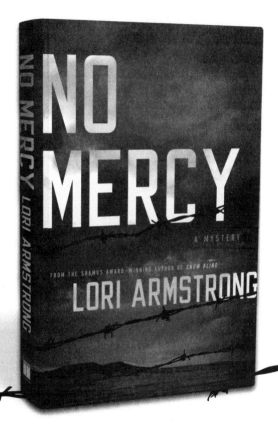

When the body of a Native American boy is found on Mercy Gunderson's land, the tough-as-nails former Army sniper is determined to bring the killer to justice. As she investigates, dangerous secrets are unearthed and Mercy must race to stop the killer before everything she's fought for is destroyed.